The Dark Horse of Shanghai
Kent W. Sorensen

Published by
Tuesday Publishing
18677 Melody Lane, Sonoma, California 95476

First Edition
ASIN: 0985383216
ISBN-13: 978-0985383213

Praise for *The Dark Horse of Shanghai*

"Since the passing of James Clavell, we haven't had that much in the way of exciting "inside look" compelling cultural fiction set in modern Asia. Kent Sorensen's *The Dark Horse of Shanghai* unveils Chinese business practices in a fascinating way because the author has been there and done that in real life on a major scale. I'm looking forward to his take on Japan with *The Jutaku Affair* and then on to the next stop of his hero, Kip Duchene, because Sorensen's writing makes me feel like I'm visiting a fascinating Asian tour that I might never come close to experiencing in real life."

Skip Press -- Author and Screenwriter

"An accomplished writer and photographer, Kent Sorensen brings us his newest exciting work, *The Dark Horse of Shanghai.* The novel captures images of setting, characters and actions in a cross-cultural tale of intrigue, mayhem and romance. With a sharply drawn plot, the book rests on one man's terror reign and another's skill and determination to defeat him. Mr. Sorensen knows what it is like to do business in another, unfamiliar country, culture and language and brings the reader along. Not only is this story an adventurous read, but it allows us a rare peek into the world of international business in China. The first in a promising series, *The Dark Horse of Shanghai* is a page turner."

Arletta Dawdy – Author of the Huachuca Trilogy

"Kent W. Sorensen draws the reader into the world of Kip Duchene with compassion and intrigue as Kip navigates the streets and customs of Shanghai, sometimes with finesse, sometimes with unpredictable results. Opening the pages to *The Dark Horse of Shanghai* reveals a fascinating world about cultural differences, friendship, loyalty, diplomacy, success and second chances."

Marlene Cullen – Editor and Writing Facilitator

Notes to the Reader

In writing *The Dark Horse of Shanghai*, I referred to my journal notes and personal experiences in China from 1989 to 2007 as the primary source of ideas for the story. The Chinese customs, business practices and places cited in the novel are based on personal observation. The stories about Uganda are true. Shanghai Shores and the basic plot are imaginary, along with the characters described. Any resemblance to real persons is coincidental.

It is a fact that the United States deliberately bombed the Chinese Embassy in Belgrade, but the underlying reason for doing so remains a mystery today.

In Memory of

Margaret O'Connor Sorensen

Acknowledgements

My appreciation of John Donne's poem, *No Man is an Island,* became abundantly clear to me during the process of writing *The Dark Horse of Shanghai.* I couldn't have written it without the generous help of many friends, business colleagues, and family members.

The original idea of the novel came when I managed a golf course and expat housing community in Shanghai. The managers reporting to me were the finest, and every one of them helped me understand the Chinese way of doing business in China—not an easy task. Those who distinguished themselves far beyond my greatest expectations were Sherry Wu, Martin Ajobe, Chris Brooke, Paul Haviland, Denise Zhang, Sabrina Yu, Annie Sat, Paul Wang, Zhou Yuan, and Mr. Zhuang *(my loyal driver).*

As I began to first envision the storyline for the novel, help came from an unlikely source, a Hollywood screenwriter, Skip Press. After reading his *The Complete Idiot's Guide to Screenwriting*, I made contact with Skip and revealed my intentions to write a novel about China. Without hesitation, he offered sage advice of immeasurable value and a friendship that continues today.

Once I completed a draft of the novel, a group of courageous people offered to proof read it and provide initial feedback to the basic question: Do I have a novel worth publishing? To my great relief, they all said yes. My deep gratitude goes to Joy Reis, Thor Rayward, Xifan Rao, Lesley Sorensen, Tichelle Sorensen, and Helen Nackos Sorensen.

Many rewrites later, I reached a point with the novel when professional editing was needed. Fortunately, I found the best in Marlene Cullen and Jordan Rosenfeld. The painstaking job of proof reading was aptly done by Bonnie Pierce and Rosemary Jackson. Every page and scene benefitted greatly from their combined efforts.

Along the way, I periodically received thoughtful emails from Lisa See, the bestselling author of many outstanding novels about the soul of Chinese people and their deeply rooted culture. Her advice to me was simple, yet cogent—keep writing.

Lastly, I want to thank my writing critique group and adopted second family: Ron Davis, Arletta Dawdy, Sharon Hamilton, Shane McGarrett, and Robin Moore. With patience, love, and diverse literary skills, they helped me reach the last mile needed to publish my own story about China from the perspective of an American man.

Epigraph

"A dark horse which has never been thought of,
and which the careless St. James had never even observed
in the list,
rushed past the grandstand in sweeping triumph."

Benjamin Disraeli

Map of
Shanghai
Puxi   Pudong

Yangtze River

Huangpu River

Sal's House

East
China
Sea

Jin Mao Tower

Reggie's Penthouse

Abandoned Factory

Canal

Shanghai Shores

Chaoyang Village

Longdong Avenue

Chuansha

Bicycle Ride

Pudong International Airport

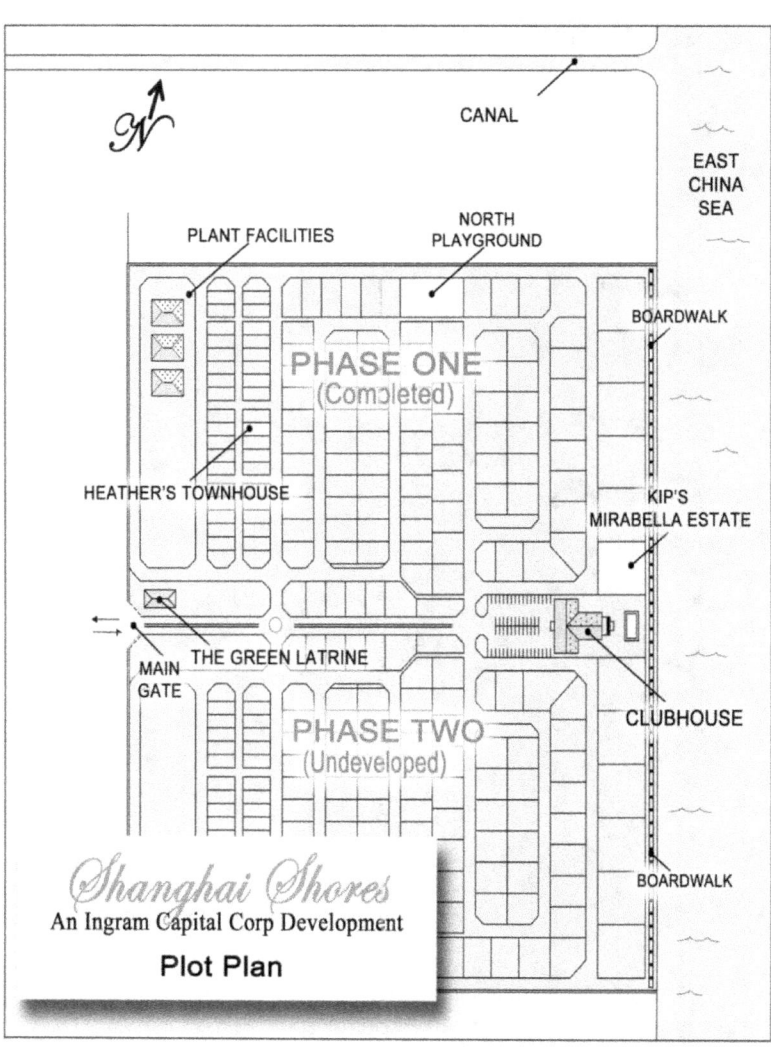

CANAL

EAST
CHINA
SEA

PLANT FACILITIES

NORTH
PLAYGROUND

BOARDWALK

PHASE ONE
(Completed)

HEATHER'S TOWNHOUSE

KIP'S
MIRABELLA ESTATE

THE GREEN LATRINE

MAIN
GATE

PHASE TWO
(Undeveloped)

CLUBHOUSE

Shanghai Shores
An Ingram Capital Corp Development

Plot Plan

BOARDWALK

THE DARK HORSE OF SHANGHAI

Kent W. Sorensen

Prologue
Hainan Island, China
May 8, 1999

Rico Niu snapped wide awake with a predawn telephone call from his uncle. Squinting at the bedside clock, Rico knew something was terribly wrong to hear from him at this hour. It was 4:47 a.m.

"Just a minute," Rico whispered and slipped out of bed without waking up his wife. He padded across the darkened bedroom of their luxury suite and stepped out through French doors onto a palatial balcony. Twenty-three floors below, the glow of streetlights surrounding Haikou Harbor penetrated the humid air. He quietly closed the doors behind him and brought the phone to his ear. "Yes, uncle, what is it?"

Thirteen hours later, Mr. Renhe Niu—known in China by his nickname, "Rico"—was the first passenger to disembark from the Hong Kong flight to Tunxi City in Anhui Province. His beloved mother, uncle, and several other family members still lived in Huangdun, a nearby farming village where he was born. A few years earlier, Rico surprised them by having their homes remodeled, the first in the small village to have indoor plumbing. He could afford it. Within ten years of establishing a gambling enterprise on the southern island of Hainan, he'd become a millionaire—and a ruthless gangster. The few who dared to go up against the man were quickly silenced with various degrees of violence. Others weren't so lucky.

Rico, with his ever-present bodyguard, knifed through the dense mass of people waiting just outside the arrival gate of the aging Huangshan Air Terminal. Locals who recognized Rico stepped respectfully back, leaving ample space for the two men to pass. Despite his unsavory reputation, the townspeople were proud that a local boy had fought his way out of poverty and grown up to become wealthy. He was a dashing man in his mid-thirties with jet black hair cropped close to his head. As usual, he was impeccably dressed in a Polo shirt with a designer sweater draped over his shoulders, gabardine pants, and hand-made Italian loafers.

In stark contrast to Rico, his bodyguard looked repulsive. Mr. Tao was grotesquely marred by several jagged scars on his face and a congenitally deformed left ear.

The unlikely pair quickly walked out of the terminal and into a black limousine parked at curbside. As it pulled away, Rico thought about his uncle's telephone call and mulled over the possible reasons his mother had him place the call so early in the morning. He concluded that something extraordinarily serious must have happened. She'd never asked him to rush home like this before.

Ten minutes later, the limo reached the downtown area of Tunxi where an unruly crowd was demonstrating. Rico pushed the intercom button. "What's the problem?"

"I don't know, boss," replied the driver as he started to slow down.

Many of the noisy demonstrators had spilled onto the street and were impeding traffic. The limousine was now close enough for Rico to read the crudely-painted placards that people were waving: AMERICAN DEVILS, NO MORE LIES, and MURDERERS AT BELGRADE.

Rico blurted out, "Shit! Now I understand."

Mr. Tao said, "What's happening, boss?"

"It's about the Americans. They bombed our Embassy in Belgrade yesterday and killed three of our countrymen. The White House said it was a regretful mistake, but that's complete bullshit. Our leaders rejected their stupid explanation and called it a dangerous provocation against Chinese sovereignty. People are taking to the streets all through China."

As the limo inched by, the angry faces of the people could be seen up close. Rico turned to Mr. Tao and said, "You can add this to the reasons I hate the fucking Americans."

The bodyguard just smiled, revealing badly-stained teeth.

On the other side of town they headed northeast on the Tunhuang Highway that followed the Xin'an River towards the family compound. Rico tried to relax by taking in the sights of the rural countryside he knew so well. Along the fields bordering the muddy-green river, an old man trudged behind a water buffalo as he plowed his plot of land. Bare-chested, the farmer wore a wide-brimmed straw hat and loose-fitting shorts cinched tightly around his waist. Chickens roamed freely between the simple homes of the local farmers. A peasant walking along the roadside saw the fast-approaching familiar limousine and waved blindly at the blackened windows in case Rico Niu was inside.

An hour from Tunxi, the limo turned off the main highway and slowly crunched along a gravel road for another mile before coming to a stop. Rico stepped out and stretched as a cloud of dust slowly drifted away in a light breeze. He saw several family members working in the far side of the rice fields. They stood upright with hands propped on their aching backs, shielded their eyes from the setting sun, and waved in Rico's direction.

His uncle was standing in front of the doorstep of the house to greet Rico. He motioned with his head. "Your mother's waiting for you upstairs . . . she's in bed."

Rico walked into the pungent incense-filled bedroom and quietly sat down on the bedside chair. His mother lifted her head from the pillow and began to sob, "Oh, son, I'm so sorry to tell you this." With a shaky hand, she wiped away the tears from her red, swollen eyes.

He gently held her hand. "What happened, dearest mother?"

With a trembling voice, she said, "I received a telephone call from a government official in Beijing at four o'clock this morning. They found a fourth body in Belgrade."

When she told him who it was, Rico felt like a sledgehammer slammed into his gut. Hardly able to breathe, he could no longer hear his mother speaking. He forced himself to look out the window and focus on the blood-red sun setting over the tops of a bamboo grove.

After several minutes, an eerie smile crept across his face. He turned back to face his weeping mother and patted her hand. "I know what to do."

Chapter 1
One year later

Kip Duchene would soon regret listening to anyone talk about doing business in China. But on the day he attended the 2000 Investment Forum in San Francisco, he understood as much about the Chinese way of doing business as most other Americans—hardly anything.

Sitting next to his best friend in the front row at the Moscone Convention Center, Kip enjoyed listening to Reginald Ingram's keynote address before a mesmerized audience. He leaned towards Sal Estrada and said, "*Yani*, I'm glad I came. Your boss is a hell of a damn good speaker."

Sal chuckled. "Yeah, the old man hasn't lost his touch. Just like I told you, *amigo*, every time he's the keynoter at one of these affairs, the crowd goes wild."

Kip had to admit that the man was more than just a good orator; he was a dynamic force at the podium. In his mid-sixties, the speaker had a tanned face and well-groomed hair, dark on top and silver on the sides. His perfectly trimmed mustache was also laced with silver. Despite immigrating to the United States more than twenty-five years earlier, he still spoke with a pronounced British accent. While the audience was applauding, Kip looked behind him and scanned the standing-room-only crowd of admirers. He turned back to Sal. "I can see that."

Sal jabbed Kip with his elbow. "I told you."

Kip and Sal had a lot in common. Both were six-foot three, thirty-one, alumni of the Stanford Graduate School of Business, and strikingly handsome.

Ingram Capital Corporation was a prestigious investment banking firm with offices in San Francisco, Shanghai, and Dubai. Internationally recognized as a global financier and a generous philanthropist, Reginald Ingram worked behind the scenes with cunning diplomacy. He was revered by the investment community for his ability to discover fledgling companies and mold them into leaders in their respective fields. Wherever he spoke, people flocked to hear about his latest ventures and his vision for the future.

As Mr. Ingram was holding up his hands to quiet the audience, Kip thought how proud he was that his buddy had been picked out of Stanford to join the Ingram organization. After turning down Sal's invitation to hear Ingram speak on three previous occasions, he was glad that he decided to attend the conference that day. Besides, the Moscone Convention Center was just a short drive from his bachelor apartment on Buena Vista Hill.

As the applause died down, the chairman deliberately looked around the audience and continued his speech, "As you know the relations between China and the United States reached a low point last year when we mistakenly bombed the Chinese Embassy in Belgrade. What you may not know is that the White House sent a delegation of senior government officials to Beijing in an attempt to sort it out. After three days of secret talks, the U.S. agreed to pay a large sum of money to the families who lost their loved ones. Not satisfied with the offer, the Chinese hinted about the idea of the U.S. transferring homebuilding technology to them. If you follow, homes built in China are bloody wretched. The Chinese use mostly red brick, a material is that structurally weak and susceptible to catastrophic failure, particularly from earthquakes."

Ingram abruptly stopped his speech and looked up at the massive ceiling trusses supporting the auditorium roof. As the people in the hall followed his gaze, he timed his next comment perfectly. "Let's see . . . we're in San Francisco. Ah, yes. Quite right."

The audience broke out in laughter.

Before Ingram resumed, Kip leaned over to Sal and said, "Your boss sure knows how to work the crowd, doesn't he?"

"*Si, como no,*" said Sal, with a big smile spreading across his face. Despite the ominous-looking scar tracing down his left cheek, he was known by his friends as a gentle "Teddy Bear." His humor and affable manner were infectious to those around him.

In contrast, Kip held his emotions in check, revealing little of inner feelings to others. A shy man who rarely talked about himself, Kip was nevertheless brilliant. The remarkable success of the Duchene Group made him a millionaire before his twenty-ninth birthday. Sitting next to his buddy, Kip Duchene looked the part, impeccably dressed in tailor-made pin-striped suit.

At the podium, Ingram was saying, "—eager to accommodate the Chinese, our government readily accepted their proposal. The ensuing bilateral agreement became known as the Sino-American Housing Initiative. As a gesture of goodwill to the Chinese, President Clinton personally signed the initiative."

The audience listened with rapt attention.

"By March of this year, Chinese representatives identified a bloody good piece of property on the Shanghai coast, perfect for building high-end homes to showcase the initiative. It will serve as a demonstration project of cooperation between the two countries. Homebuilding technology from the United States will be combined with Chinese labor. The Chinese government will apply what they learn from the project to build affordable homes for its people in the future. The two countries agreed to have the project funded and managed by the private sector instead of the government, inviting Chinese and American companies to submit proposals. Only two companies made the final cut: Ingram Capital and a Chinese company from Hainan Island."

Mr. Ingram looked up from his notes and broke out in a broad smile. "I thought you should be the first to know that we were awarded the contract."

The hall erupted in applause.

Ingram continued, "In naming the development 'Shanghai Shores,' we intend to create a community where east meets west, if you follow. Diplomatic goodwill between the United States and China will be enhanced if this project succeeds. So we want to assure ourselves that it ends up bloody perfect. We're very excited and look forward to breaking ground sometime in December . . . I dare say, anyone interested in moving to Shanghai?"

A ripple of laughter rolled through the audience.

"Adding Shanghai Shores to our projects in China will require us to ramp up our capabilities and recruit the best people we can find. It is my pleasure to introduce you to the newest member of our Shanghai office. A native of Shanghai, Miss Angie Li recently graduated with honors from University of California at Berkeley, receiving her MBA. She is extraordinarily bright, speaks five languages, and will help strengthen our position in China."

Turning his attention to the front row, he smiled and motioned with his hand, "Angie, my dear, would you please stand?"

About ten seats to over from where Kip sat with Sal, a remarkably beautiful Chinese woman rose, turned to the audience smiling, and gave a tentative nod to her new boss before sitting back down.

Someone sitting in the far left side of the hall let out a flirtatious whistle.

Pointing directly at the culprit, Mr. Ingram said, "Give it a rest, old boy!"

The audience openly laughed.

"Okay, *Yani*, you've been holding out on me," Kip said to Sal, clearly mesmerized by Angie Li. "Jesus, she's one gorgeous woman. How about introducing me?"

"Sure will, *Tuchi*," said Sal.

As people were filing out of the auditorium, no one paid any attention to a well-dressed Asian man still seated in the back row. His companion had grotesque facial scars and a deformed left ear. Neither man said anything. They just sat there and watched people shuffling up the aisles towards the exit.

Chapter 2
Five years later

As planned, Kip made the necessary arrangements for his reluctant trip to Shanghai. While laying out clothes on his bed, he thought about Marci. *Can you imagine, princess, I'm going to China of all places? You know that Sal's the only one who could have persuaded me to take the job.*

He leaned over to the bedside stand and finished off another can of beer. It was 5:05 p.m. The framed photo of Marci smiled up at him. He looked back at her. *I know, I know. I'm cutting down. I can control my drinking now. I really can.*

The Haight-Ashbury district spread out below from the seventh floor window of his Buena Vista Hill apartment. Looking north, he could see the brick-colored towers of the Golden Gate Bridge jutting above the incoming tendrils of fog. His line of sight caught the restaurant where he and Marci regularly ate. Tears trickled down his cheeks.

His thoughts were abruptly broken by the muted chirping of his cell phone. Groping toward the sound, he found it between a stack of trousers on the bed. "Hello?"

"*Que pasa, Tuchi?*"

"Don't worry, I'm packing."

"Shit, I'm not worried. Now that you're eating properly and cutting down on the booze, you'll be just fine."

"Easy to say, *Yani.*"

"Listen, once you clear customs in Shanghai, just head out the exit to the arrival area. I'll be waiting for your sorry ass."

"Got it. What's the weather like in June?"

"Hot and fucking humid."

"You know, the chill of the San Francisco fog sounds pretty good to me about now."

Sal chuckled. "See you tomorrow."

Duchene stood in the First Class line at the SFO ticket counter. The company booked his trip on United Airline's Flight 857 to Shanghai. Despite knowing he'd fly in relative comfort, he wasn't looking forward to being cooped up for twelve hours. He also wasn't pleased to discover that he'd be sitting in the middle section, the only area in First Class where two seats were side-by-side. He dreaded the idea of listening to a chatty passenger during the long flight.

After boarding and making his way toward the front of the aircraft, he saw a middle-aged woman up ahead sitting next to his assigned seat. After stowing his carry-on cases, he slipped into his seat. The woman wore a stylish Baume & Mercier wristwatch. She must be well off. Her nails were perfectly manicured. Duchene busied himself by slipping his laptop computer in the side compartment of the seat and connecting the headphones.

A smiling flight attendant leaned down to the two passengers. "Mrs. Wentworth, it's nice to see you again."

She smiled in return and said, "Thank you."

"You probably know the menu better than us, but here it is. Would you like a glass of cranberry juice as usual?"

"Yes, that'd be nice."

"And Mr. Duchene, what can I get for you?"

"I guess no beer yet?"

"I'll take care of you as soon as we're airborne and the seat belt signs are off. How about a glass of Champagne?"

Duchene smiled. "Perfect."

After the drinks were served, Mrs. Wentworth turned to Kip and said, "Hi, I'm Eleni."

"It's nice to meet you. I'm Kip." *Please don't be a talker.*

"Are you headed for Shanghai or connecting to a flight elsewhere?"

Ah, jeez, I really don't want to get into a conversation about what I'm doing. "Shanghai."

The woman said, "How nice." She opened a copy of the in-flight magazine and started to work on the crossword puzzle.

Kip asked for a refill of Champagne.

The big 747 shuddered as the tow tractor nudged it back from the gate. Once the tractor disconnected on the tarmac and motored away, the jumbo jet's engines spooled up and powered it along the taxiway. Kip was thinking – *I wonder if I was rather short with the lady. I just don't feel like talking.*

Fifteen minutes later the four Pratt and Whitney engines revved up to full takeoff power, propelling the jumbo jet down runway 28R and lifting it effortlessly above South San Francisco. As the California coastline slipped quietly away, Duchene felt the pain of sorrow wash over him. He was leaving Marci behind.

As soon as the seat-belt sign blinked off, he motioned to the flight attendant. "Miss, could I get that beer now?"

Kip and Eleni ate an enjoyable lunch together, both drinking the rich, black-cherry flavor of a 2003 Merlot. She had only one glass compared to his four. Mellowed by the wine and the idle chatter, Kip decided that he liked Eleni Wentworth after all. She had a distinct Mediterranean look with a smooth, olive complexion, dark eyes, and dark hair with reddish highlights. He picked up a subtle scent of her perfume. She was an elegant, attractive woman. When she smiled, prominent dimples added to her inviting charm. Her manner of dress was smart but not overdone. Kip guessed that she was in her late forties. After the dishes were cleared, he turned to her and said, "I hear a slight accent. Are you Italian?"

"No," she chuckled. "I was born on a small Greek island called Amorgos. When I was twelve, my parents moved to Oakland. Since then, I've mostly lived in the Bay Area."

She reached into her purse and pulled out a business card. "I have a real estate agency in Shanghai that specializes in finding rental housing for expatriates."

"Interesting." The card revealed that she was president of Discovery Shanghai. He thought that of all people to be assigned next to him, she owned a business coincidently related to Shanghai Shores. *With her experience, maybe she can give me some good tips.* "How's the business climate for expatriate housing over there?"

"It's doing quite well, particularly after China was admitted into the World Trade Organization. As a result, foreign executives began to increase their presence in China, many of whom brought their families with them. All need suitable housing to rent."

"I see."

"Does this happen to be your first visit to China?" she asked.

"How'd you guess?"

"After fifteen years of making this trip, I can usually tell if a person is a seasoned traveler to China. Sometimes I get it wrong though. Many of the passengers on this flight make the trip to Shanghai so many times they start to recognize each other. You know, the American community in Shanghai is very tight—we kind of stick together to battle the enormous difficulties of doing business in China. I'd be happy to introduce you around."

"Thank you, I'd like that."

"May I ask what brings you to Shanghai?"

"I recently retired from my consulting business in Menlo Park to take some time off. As a favor to a friend, I agreed to go to Shanghai for the next six months or so to figure out why an expatriate housing development is failing."

"Oh, really. What development's that?"

"Shanghai Shores – it's in Pudong."

"I know it. It's got quite a reputation.

"For what?"

"Well, I hate to say this, but everyone in town knows the property has been mismanaged from the start. It's gone from bad to worse and many people now think that it can't be saved. Sadly, Shanghai people are now referring to Shanghai Shores behind closed doors as '*hei ma*,' the Dark Horse of Shanghai."

Kip raked his fingers through his hair. "No kidding?"

Eleni nodded. "That's right. I'm frankly surprised to see these kinds of problems happening with an Ingram company. In the investment banking community in Shanghai, Reggie Ingram is king."

"Do you know him?"

"Oh yes. We've met at a number of social events over the years. We also belong to Amcham, the American Chamber of Commerce in Shanghai. The curious thing about Shanghai Shores is that it's failing at a time when the real estate market is booming."

"I hadn't known." He pulled out a notebook and gave Eleni his full attention.

"Yes, it's a sad story," she said. "When Ingram was awarded the right to develop Shanghai Shores rather than the Chinese company, I believed the project would become a smashing success. Ingram Capital Corporation was well known in China as an upstanding company. Reggie's photo is regularly seen in Shanghai newspapers for donating millions of dollars to charitable causes in China. Maybe more importantly, he quietly funds promising graduates from Chinese universities to get their post-graduate education in the United States. Otherwise they could never afford it."

"That's generous of him."

"Yes, but maybe there's a touch of the fox in the old henhouse."

"How's that?"

"Well, just think about it." Eleni's eyes lit up. "Reggie has funded some of the brightest Chinese students for an opportunity of their lifetime. What kind of loyalty do you think that brings back to him? Many of those students became founders of some of the best performing companies in China. And guess who owns stock in those companies?"

"I see. Earlier, you mentioned a Chinese company who lost the bid to develop Shanghai Shores. Do you know anything about them?"

"Yes. It's owned by a notorious racketeer from Hainan Island."

"What's his name?"

"Rico Niu."

Chapter 3

Kip said, "Rico sounds more Portuguese than Chinese."

"Many Chinese take on nicknames, mostly English like John or Eva. Why he chose Rico I couldn't guess."

"So what's the big deal with this Rico guy?"

Eleni looked around the cabin and leaned closer to Duchene. "He's a ruthless psychopath. Word is out that he's now making regular trips to Shanghai. Some say that his visits are in connection with Shanghai Shores, but I can't confirm that as fact."

"Sounds rather ominous if it's true."

"I agree. But let me go back and try to answer your question of why I believe Shores is failing. The company has too many internal problems. Even though Shores is out of the way for some people, the property itself is really quite lovely. In contrast to the noise and air pollution in the downtown area, Shanghai Shores is located on the coast with much to offer. It has fresh sea breezes, peace and quiet, natural wildlife, and close proximity to the airport."

Kip said, "Clearly Reggie has impeccable credentials as a brilliant thinker in the investment community. With him being so smart, why do you think Shanghai Shores had reached the point where I've been brought in to salvage it?"

"Ah, a good question. While I'm not in a position to know for sure, I have a good hunch."

"I'm listening."

"Well, first, real estate development is very different from the kinds of businesses that Ingram Capital had previously invested in, like biotechnology, pharmaceuticals, retail franchises and semiconductors. A place like Shores requires hands-on management, not oversight from a central office. I think that Reggie got too personally wrapped up in the glamour of Shores while underestimating the skill level that was needed for onsite management. As Ingram was growing in China at an unprecedented pace, Reggie had put too much trust in Ralph Maddox, the general manager of Shores."

Lowering her voice, Eleni said, "Between you and me, Ralph is a downright sleazy character who is regularly seen around town with young Chinese girls hanging all over him."

"How old is he?"

"I'd guess that he's in his early fifties. Anyway, he's a slick talker and a drunk, plain and simple. The word around town is that he kept feeding Reggie blatantly false but optimistic reports about Shores. On the positive side though, I've heard that Reggie belatedly discovered that he'd been misled by Ralph and has quietly put steps into motion to stop the hemorrhage. I understand he transferred one of his best performing executives from their San Francisco office to Shanghai a couple of months ago to focus entirely on their operations in China. I haven't met him yet but I understand he's outstanding and speaks fluent Mandarin."

"I'll introduce you to him sometime," said Kip. "His name is Sal Estrada. He and I are close personal friends. Actually, he's the guy who roped me into coming over to clean up the place. Be forewarned though, he's a colorful character."

"Not like Maddox, I hope."

"The opposite." Kip chuckled. "Despite his humorous and sometimes raunchy antics, he's truly a solid guy who's happily married and has three adorable children."

"How did you two get together in the first place?"

Feeling a little awkward about talking so openly, he simply said, "It's a long story."

She smiled and arched her eyebrows. "We've got time."

Feeling the loosening effect of the wine, Kip thought—
why not? Setting the notebook down, he said, "Well, we
met while attending the Stanford Graduate School of
Business. He had a warmth about him that I'd never
experienced in my own family. We got along so well that I
asked him if he'd like to move in with me in my two-
bedroom apartment."

"How'd that work out?"

Kip chuckled. "Well, I had a little scare while he was
unpacking. A menacing-looking stiletto knife with a
glistening pearl handle dropped out of one of his storage
boxes. With a flip of the wrist, Sal snap opened the knife.
Catching my surprised reaction, he said, 'Every once in a
while, I pull this old friend out from my days in Tehachapi
and I'm reminded how fortunate I am.' So I asked him if I
needed to be worried about that thing being around the
apartment."

"And?" asked Eleni.

"He looked directly into my eyes and said that if I ever
gave him any lip, he'd stick my white ass."

Eleni laughed at the image.

"Then out of the blue, he started to call me *Tuchi*. Since
he was teaching me how to get beyond textbook Spanish, I
tried to look up the word in my Spanish dictionary but
couldn't find it. Later, I asked him what it meant. I can't
repeat it to you, so let's just say that it's a shortened version
of a filthy greeting."

"Were you upset?"

"Not at all. Actually, it's an affectionate insult used
between male friends living in a certain area of Mexico. I
kind of liked it. So I found an equally disgusting name and
have called him that ever since."

"What is it?"

"*Yani*. The only time I find myself calling him 'Sal' is
when I'm either angry or deadly serious."

"You two sound as though you've forged a close
friendship."

"I regard Sal as the brother I always wished I had, and he feels the same way."

"What a wonderful story."

During the long flight, Duchene dozed on and off and tried to catch up on studying a compendium of reports on Shanghai Shores that Sal had sent him. He was pleased that Eleni understood when Kip wanted to talk and when he preferred to be left alone.

He was privately surprised that he'd shared his personal experiences about Sal. When the two men were at Stanford, Kip found out that Sal had to fight for everything he got, compared to his affluent lifestyle growing up in Santa Monica.

Sal was raised in the rural town of Tehachapi by poor parents who emigrated from Mexico. When Sal was a boy, they lived in a one-room house in a pear orchard on the outskirts of town. Sleeping areas were separated by blankets hanging on wires strung from opposite walls. He had five sisters. When any of the kids had to use the outhouse in the backyard, his mama would remind them to watch out for scorpions and Mojave Greens—rattlesnakes common to the area. By the time Sal entered Tehachapi High School, they'd moved into a simple three-bedroom house closer in town. While the entire family regarded it as a palace, Sal nevertheless believed that the white kids looked at him as being second-class.

Duchene woke up when an overhead speaker crackled to life with the captain announcing they were twenty minutes from landing at the Pudong International Airport. Kip was glad to hear they were near their destination. He had a splitting headache and his entire body was sore from the long flight.

As the plane's engines started to throttle back, Eleni turned to Kip and asked, "How you doing?"

"Sore, tired, but okay."

"Good. By the way, where are you staying?"

"The company's putting me up at the Ritz-Carlton for now. They maintain an apartment there year around."

"It's a marvelous hotel. They have all kinds of shops and restaurants in the complex. Expats call it the Shanghai Center. I'd be happy to drop you off."

"Thanks, but Sal's picking me up."

"Well, feel free to call me if you ever need help or have a question about doing business in China."

Kip said, "Thanks. Say, I'm curious what you do for entertainment in Shanghai?"

"Well, there's always a good selection of live stage shows in town. When my husband's in town, we usually enjoy going out for a nice quiet dinner at one of our favorite restaurants. For you, however, there are a number of more lively places to go."

"I have no interest in the lively stuff. I came over here to fix a problem and that's all I intend to do."

"Kip, if you don't mind me saying, it's obvious that you've gone through some difficult times. Don't ask me how I know—chalk it off to woman's intuition. But, I'd like to leave you with one piece of advice, if I may."

"What's that?"

"Some of the most beautiful women in the world can be found in Shanghai. Many young women in China desire to marry a foreign man and start a new life elsewhere, particularly in America. Life in China is still hard for the typical Chinese family. If a woman happens to be beautiful, she has good reason to use her looks to snag a foreigner and break away from a predictable, bleak life in China. Wherever expats hang out, you'll find a bevy of gorgeous young ladies. Most are smartly dressed and immaculately groomed. When they walk, they mimic the exaggerated swagger of runway models. It's almost comical. They have perfected the fine art of eye contact followed by a coquettish smile."

Kip laughed. "Sounds like Southern California to me."

She countered, "Ah, but there's a difference. Sorry to say, but American men can be incredibly stupid at times—

even the married ones. Many are not used to getting this kind of flirtatious attention from beautiful women and mistakenly believe that they must be something really special. Once you get settled, look around and you'll soon see older expatriate men walking hand-in-hand with beautiful Chinese women, some half their age."

Kip said, "Again, I see more and more of that in the States."

"Well, just tuck what I've said in the back of your mind. It may come in handy someday."

"Thanks." *I wonder where in the hell that came from?*

"Oh, and one more thing. You'll find most Chinese people absolutely wonderful. China as a whole is developing at a pace impossible to duplicate anywhere else in the world. Remember that everything in the Chinese culture revolves around 'good face' and family. They resolve conflict in this country completely opposite to the way we do it in the States. The idea of "win-win" over here is difficult for most Chinese to grasp. Throughout centuries of trading with the rest of the world, they have learned that someone wins and someone loses. They have no intentions of losing."

"I'd better pick up a good book on Chinese culture. There's no question that I've got a lot of catching up to do."

By the time the 747 gently touched down, Kip felt that his tailbone was about to drop off. Uncomfortable that his hand tremors were becoming more noticeable in the last hour, he hoped that the hotel was a short drive from the airport—he needed a drink.

In the baggage claim area, Kip stacked his luggage on a cart and headed for the exit.

Since Eleni's luggage arrived five minutes earlier, she had already disappeared through the exit gate. On her way to an awaiting car, her cell phone rang.

"How'd everything go, my dear?" the caller said.

"Perfectly. My gosh, Reggie, he's quite a charming and intelligent man. I think you've made a very good choice."

"Brilliant!"

Feeling exhausted, Kip pushed his luggage cart through exit doors after clearing customs and was startled by what he saw. A noisy throng of people were packed up against a stainless steel barrier separating the public from arriving passengers. The onlookers were craning their heads to recognize a family member, friend or business acquaintance. Some held up signs with names printed in English or in Chinese. There were a few foreigners scattered among the Chinese faces. Feeling claustrophobic, Kip scanned the crowd to find Sal, but he wasn't anywhere in sight. *Jesus, this is all I need.*

At six-three, Kip could easily look over the heads of people to the other side of the arrival area and spotted the terminal exit. Seeing that the crowd was not stepping aside for passengers to pass, Kip followed behind a group of Chinese pushing their way out. Nearing the exit, he heard a familiar voice.

"*Oye, baboso!*" called out Sal.

As the two friends embraced, Kip said, "Keep your slobbering cow remarks to yourself, *Yani.*"

"I just wanted to greet you Mexican style." Sal flashed a smile.

"Mexican style or not, I'm glad to see you. Get me out of here. This place's a zoo"

Sal said, "You should see it when it's busy."

Kip chuckled. "You're kidding."

"I swear." He made the sign of the cross and then grabbed the handle of Kip's luggage cart. "Here, let me take that."

Just in front of the exit, Kip stopped to read an overhead message board.

**FLT NO SC738 FROM JINAN
HAS BEEN DELAYED
DUE TO SOME REASON**

Sal turned around and looked at Kip. "What's wrong?"

Kip pointed to the sign. "Am I reading that right?"

With a broad smile spreading across his face, Sal said, "Welcome to China, *amigo!*"

Chapter 4

The air outside was warm and humid. At curbside, Sal's driver jumped out of a black Buick and opened the back door for them. As he loaded the luggage in the trunk, Sal nudged Kip. "How ya doing?"

"Okay."

Sitting in the back seat, Sal patted Kip's knee. "That's all I wanted to hear. How was the flight?"

"Too damn long."

Sal leaned forward in his seat and said something to his driver.

Kip broke out laughing.

Settling back in his seat, Sal said, "What the fuck's so funny?"

Kip was still chuckling. "I've never heard you say anything in Chinese before, that's all. It seems weird not to hear you say, *chingada*, every other word."

Sal slowly shook his head. "It must have been a long flight, *Tuchi*."

As the car pulled away from the curb, Kip said, "Speaking of the flight, I sat next to a fascinating woman. She owns Discovery Shanghai, a real estate agency in Shanghai. Have you heard of them? "

"Yeah. Eleni Wentworth, a very close friend of Reggie's. I haven't met her yet."

Kip arched one eyebrow. "Quite a coincidence that she was on the flight with me."

"Sounds like it. What'd she talk about?"

"She gave me some good tips about getting around, including advice on how beautiful Shanghai ladies troll for American men."

"So what was her advice?"

"Be careful."

"Damn good advice. Remember that when you see Angie again."

"Not the least bit interested."

"If you say so."

During the ride towards downtown Shanghai, Kip took in newly discovered sights while struggling to stay awake. China looked much different than he thought it would. "Why's it so dark out there?"

"Shit, man, it's nighttime!"

"No, I don't mean that. I see hardly any lights on. It's almost pitch black."

"Oh that. Well, people don't use any more electricity than they have to over here. Too expensive. The same holds true with office buildings. As soon as employees leave for the day, buildings are typically plunged into darkness. Except along the main boulevards, there are fewer streetlights compared to the States."

"Well, the effect is gloomy—almost foreboding."

"You'll get used of it."

Kip said, "Why so hazy?"

"Air pollution. The central government is finally addressing their fucked up environment. Believe me, they need to. Raw sewage freely flows into rivers and lakes, and factories belch out millions of tons of toxic pollutants into the air."

"So that explains the haziness?"

"Yeah. Air pollution blankets almost the entire eastern part of China. When I fly from city to city on the east coast and look down from my window, I rarely see the ground because of the thick layer of haze. You'll see what I mean tomorrow. Even though the weather forecast calls for a clear day, you'll notice that the sky will be a chalky-blue rather than the deep blue we see in the Bay Area. Unfortunately, Beijing's air quality is much, much worse."

"When's the next flight back to San Francisco?"

Sal laughed. "Just relax. Actually, the Chinese are really amazing people. They can do most things faster than the rest of the world when they set their minds to it."

"Like what?"

"Only twenty-five years ago, the Pudong area was an undeveloped wasteland of rural farms and small villages. Today, it is viewed as one of the most spectacular urban developments in the modern world. During my Asian studies in San Jose in 1989, I spent two weeks traveling around China on a studies-abroad trip. When we swung through Shanghai, I remember standing on the boardwalk of the Bund and—"

"Of the what?" interrupted Kip.

"It's a levee on the Huangpu River that snakes through the downtown area. Anyway, when I looked across the river to Pudong, there was almost nothing there to see except for a bunch of farms. Then when I returned to Shanghai after joining Ingram just five years later, I couldn't believe my eyes. It was like looking across the Hudson River to Manhattan – a panoramic view of modern skyscrapers. It was a remarkable sight."

Kip said, "I've seen the word 'Pudong' on a Shanghai map but don't really understand what it means."

Sal said, "You should be paying me for explaining all of this shit."

"Come on. I need to know."

"Well, Shanghai is split in two by the Huangpu River. The west side of the river is called Puxi. 'Pu' means river and 'xi' means west. Since 'dong' means east, you can then conclude that Pudong means east of the river."

Kip said, "Some of these Chinese words could make you laugh, couldn't they?"

"I thought you were tired?"

"My ass is dragging, believe me. How much longer until we get there?"

Pointing ahead, Sal said, "See the large glowing area in the haze up ahead?"

"Yeah."

"That's downtown Shanghai. As I told you, we've put you up in the Portman Ritz-Carlton hotel on the Puxi side. Since you'll be spending so much time in Pudong, I thought that you'd like getting acquainted with the area along the famous Nanjing Road. It's lined with never-ending shops and restaurants and has quite a story to tell in the colorful history of Shanghai."

"Sounds good."

As they crossed over the Lupu Bridge into the downtown area, Kip was awestruck by colorful lighting on the skyscrapers that jutted up all around them. "I had no idea that Shanghai would look anything like this." Kip was turning his head from side to side, looking out the windows to see everything possible.

Sal said, "Do you know what the official bird of Shanghai is?"

Kip said, "No idea."

"The crane!"

"The crane? I don't get it."

"It's said that twenty-five percent of all of the building cranes in the world are here in Shanghai."

"Got it."

While they were slowly snaking their way through congested traffic on an elevated freeway, a dilapidated-looking apartment building came into view on the right. It was wedged between two towering skyscrapers. The building was drab with a soot-stained exterior. Some of the apartment units inside were lit up brightly with overhead fluorescent lights. From the car, Kip got strobe-like flashes of the people living there. In the first window, an old man in a sleeveless T-shirt was hunched over his evening meal. In the next window, a middle-aged couple was practicing dance steps. In the next, someone was sitting in a darkened room in front of a TV, silhouetted by bluish light flickering on the back wall. From a wrought iron balcony, a woman was pulling her futon in from a clothesline. In the apartment next to her, men were sitting around a table and playing a board game. *I wonder what kind of story each of these people could tell.*

As the Buick took the turnoff for the Yan'an Elevated Road, Sal said, "Well, we're almost there. After you check in, we can have a light dinner together."

Two hours later, Kip slipped the magnetic door card through the slot of his room and stepped inside. It was beautifully designed with contemporary furniture in warm earth-tone colors. After setting his attaché case down, he unlocked the mini-bar and downed one of the little bottles of Scotch to settle his nerves. He then walked to the far side of the room and opened the curtains in front of bay windows. The view was spectacular. From the thirty-eighth floor, he looked down to Nanjing Road in front of the hotel and saw that it was jammed with cars, mostly taxis or luxury cars. It occurred to him that he'd seen more Mercedes-Benz, Lexus, and BMW's on the way in from the airport than he'd ever seen in the States. The Stalinist-designed building across the street was bathed in a warm glow of floodlights and resembled the tiered levels of a square wedding cake. It was topped off with a star mounted on a fifty-foot gold spire.

He headed for the bathroom to take a hot shower. Despite feeling sore and exhausted from the long flight, he felt invigorated by the stinging spray of water. After toweling off, he grabbed another Scotch.

The sight of the featherbed was welcoming. Lying there and looking up at the ceiling, he fidgeted with his wedding ring and was comforted by it. He rolled on his side and looked at the framed photograph he'd set on the bedside stand. He and Marci were posing along the seawall below the Golden Gate Bridge. Before flicking off the light, he smiled at her—*Princess, can you imagine? Here I am in Shanghai on the other side of the world. I would give anything if you could be here with me.*

Kip woke up feeling disoriented. He looked toward the bay window on the other side of the darkened room and saw red navigation lights blinking on and off on the top of nearby buildings. Gradually he remembered that he was at the Ritz-Carlton Hotel in Shanghai. The green glow of the bedside clock indicated that it was only 3:24 a.m.

Pulling the comforter up around his shoulders, he tried to go back to sleep. But it was no use. He thought about Marci. He struggled with a sinking feeling of being sucked into a vortex of smothering quicksand, of deep sadness, of lost hope. He tried to force his mind to think of something else, but it refused to release him. He heard the deafening sound of the crash and Marci's lifeless face staring straight ahead. He remembered the doors being jammed, the splintered glass, and the sound of sirens. With blood oozing down her face, he gave her mouth-to-mouth resuscitation in desperation, but was forcibly pried away by paramedics. Staring at the kaleidoscope of flashing red lights, he got a surreal snapshot of Marci being wheeled towards the ambulance. Someone called out, "Oh god, NOOOOOO." He didn't remember that the terrified voice came from *him*.

While the ambulance pulled away, Kip heard a distant sound: *beep-beep, beep-beep, beep-beep.*

The beeping sound continued as Kip's eyes blinked opened from his bed at the Ritz Carlton. He was soaked with sweat. Disoriented, he padded over to the window toward the direction of the sound and looked below. A garbage truck was backing out of a narrow alley across Nanjing Road where a man behind it was giving the driver arm signals.

Exhausted, he walked back to bed and sat—*My god, how will I ever be able to do this?*

Chapter 5

Kip looked over at the bedside clock. It was 6:07 a.m. *Let's see, Sal said he'd meet me in the lobby for breakfast at eight. I'll have time to walk around the block.*

He took a quick shower and slipped into a pair of khakis and a polo shirt. Before leaving the room, he walked over to the window to get a bird's eye view of the neighborhood from the 38th floor. Along the sidewalk directly below, he could make out clusters of Chinese doing exercise routines while others were dancing.

On his way through the lobby, Kip stopped at the concierge's desk.

An impeccably dressed Asian man looked up from the counter. "Good morning, sir. What can I do for you?"

"I'm curious about that ornate building across the street, the one with the gold cross on top."

Smiling, the man reached under the counter and handed Kip a pamphlet. "It's the Shanghai Exhibition Center."

"Is that Stalinist architecture?"

"Yes. The center was built during the 1950's to commemorate friendship between Russia and China." He motioned with his hand. "That brochure will explain the rest."

"Thanks." Kip picked up the brochure and headed for the exit. Before reaching the sidewalk, he felt the sticky Shanghai air closing in on him. He slipped his jacket off and draped it over his shoulder.

Nanjing Road was a wide boulevard that ran directly in front of the hotel. Kip headed east down the street, shielding his eyes from the red glow of the rising sun. A few doors from the hotel, a group of Chinese women were executing a form of synchronized movement with gleaming swords. As Kip walked by, he could hear the "swoosh-swoosh" of their swords slicing through the air. Near the end of the block, an elderly Chinese man walked past him going *backwards* at a brisk pace. He was wearing flannel pajamas and a flashy pair of new Nike shoes. Kip chuckled. *Now that's different.*

While he waited at the curb for the light to change, Chinese pedestrians paid no attention. One by one, they made their way to the other side of the crosswalk without regard to the red light. Feeling somewhat awkward, Kip nevertheless stood in place. When the light turned green, he stepped off the curb, but was forced to jump back to avoid getting hit by a taxi running a red light. *Okay, I get it—these lights don't mean shit.*

Curious about the people doing various routines in front of the exhibition center on the other side of the street, he sprinted over when he saw a break in the traffic. The first group he passed on the sidewalk was practicing the graceful movements of *T'ai chi*. Just beyond them, about twenty women were waving long, colorful scarves in unison with undulating motions.

Farther down, older couples were dancing to music blaring from a CD player, wrapped on one end with duct tape. The scene was so enchanting, Kip sat down on a nearby bench to watch. As soon as he did, one of the female dancers walked over to him with a big smile, held out her hand, and said something he couldn't understand. Embarrassed, he just shook his head. Still smiling, she turned back to join the other dancers.

Within the next fifteen minutes, the group danced the waltz, jitterbug, and tango, unfazed by the onlookers around them. Wanting to see more of the area before he had to get back to the hotel, Kip stood and brushed off the back of his pants.

Walking east, he was struck by the absence of homeless people. He remembered seeing derelicts sheltered in cardboard boxes in subway stations throughout Tokyo. He assumed that Shanghai would be the same—but it wasn't. He also imagined the streets of Shanghai would be littered with debris—but they weren't. The streetscape was well designed with an abundance of shady Sycamore trees, shrubs and colorful flowers bordering the sides of the road for as far as he could see in both directions. Several women wearing crisp blue uniforms, blue baseball caps, and white surgical masks were sweeping the sidewalk in front of him.

On the next block, three different men walked up to Kip trying to sell knock-off wristwatches. "Cheapa watchee ... Rolex watchee." One of them persisted in following Kip across the street, finally giving up after Kip angrily pointed to his own Rolex watch—and *it* wasn't a fake. Noticing that it was almost eight, Kip turned around and headed back to the hotel.

In the lobby, Sal was pacing in front of the elevators when he saw Kip walking in through the main entrance.

After the men embraced, Sal said, "You took a walk?"

"You should have warned me. I almost lost my ass out there trying to cross the street."

Sal laughed and draped his arm across Kip's shoulders. "I can't wait to hear all about your little venture, *amigo*."

As they approached the entrance to a restaurant called Element Fresh, a Chinese waitress opened the door for them. Sal turned to Kip and said, "Mind if we eat outside?"

"Sounds good to me."

The young woman escorted them through the restaurant and seated them at a picnic table in the patio area in back. There were about fifteen tables with green umbrellas. Nanjing Road ran past one story below.

Kip scanned the menu and said, "Hey, *Yani*, their breakfast menu looks great. Could you order a three-egg breakfast with bacon, country potatoes with a toasted bagel and cream cheese for me?"

"They all speak English here—you can go ahead and order for yourself."

Sal spread out a map across the table. "I've had the office draw up a location map for you showing a few landmarks for reference. This will help you understand the basic layout of Shanghai."

Kip said, "Thanks."

Pointing to the left side of the map, Sal said, "Here's where we are now. You can see that we're on the Puxi side of the river. Later, we'll go over the Nanpu Bridge to Pudong and head east on Longdong Avenue all the way to—"

Kip chuckled. "Sorry?"

"What?"

"*Longdong?*"

"I know, I know," said Sal. "The name has nothing to do with your *pelonga*. Getting back to our itinerary, Longdong Avenue will take us due east onto a frontage road that goes through a little village called Chaoyeng. Shanghai Shores is just on the other side of the village. You can see on the map that the development is about ten miles north of the Pudong International Airport."

Sal's explanation was interrupted by the waitress setting plates of food in front of them. He refolded the map and handed it to Kip.

Steam rose off the large platter of country potatoes and eggs that Kip had ordered. He said, "This looks great. I woke up this morning absolutely famished."

"I take that as a good sign." While they were digging into their breakfast, Sal said, "After we eat, I'll show you a few popular sites around downtown Shanghai. Then this afternoon, we'll head out for a quick visit to Shanghai Shores. On weekends, the place is quiet without a lot of hubbub. Most employees are off during weekends, except for the clubhouse receptionist and a few women from housekeeping. That'll give you a chance to take a good look around before you're introduced to the managers tomorrow."

As Sal talked about the plans for the day, Kip's mind drifted off to the sights and sounds surrounding them: the constant din of honking horns on the road below, muted conversations in Chinese, English, and German drifting over from the adjoining tables, overlapping circular stains on the wooden tabletops left behind from sweating glasses of ice water, two attractive Chinese girls sitting across from them, both wearing oversized dark glasses and talking non-stop on their cell phones, ultra-modern skyscrapers jutting up from all sides, and whispers of wind rustling through the Sycamores that lined both sides of Nanjing Road. Kip turned his attention back to Sal, hearing him say, ". . . and I think that all will go well when the staff meets you tomorrow. The managers meet every Monday at 10:00 a.m."

Quickly recovering, Kip said, "Good. What's the situation with the former general manager?"

"I met with Ralph Maddox on Friday evening and broke the news that we're making a change. Despite his dismal performance at Shanghai Shores, we gave him a generous severance package to avoid problems later. Ralph was fairly fluent in Mandarin when he came to China."

Kip took a sip of coffee. "What do you think went wrong with him?"

"He was an arrogant asshole. He looked at Chinese as being inferior and thought that he could straighten them out. He also spent more time drinking and screwing the lovelies in town than working. I learned from some of the staff that Ralph was showing up at work less and less in recent months. As a result, major decisions were left to staff management, some of which were good, but most weren't. So tomorrow morning at the managers meeting I'll surprise the staff by telling them that Ralph is gone and you're his replacement."

Kip laughed. "I can't wait to see their reaction. If I'm going to succeed in turning Shanghai Shores around, I'll need a lot of help from someone I can trust who speaks the language and understands the culture. Of the 1.3 billion people in China, I know exactly five – you, Maria and three kids."

"Oh, I forgot to tell you who's joining us for lunch today."

"Who?"

"Angie Li."

"No kidding?"

"I'm serious. She agreed to meet us for lunch. She's also one of the savviest Chinese that you'll meet."

Kip said, "If I remember right, isn't she tall for being Chinese?"

"Yeah, she is. People around here would guess that she's from Beijing by looking at her."

"Why's that?"

"As a rule, the tallest people in China come from the north and the shortest come from the south. At five-nine, Angie would be pegged as a northerner."

"But she's from Shanghai, right?"

"Right," said Sal. "Getting back to the point, Angie used to be Reggie's executive assistant in our Shanghai office. She was indispensable to him and kept the operation running efficiently. She's damn smart and knows how to make things happen. Her one-year marriage ended when her husband decided to knock her around a little in a fit of jealousy. The next day, she packed her bags and moved out while he was at work and quickly divorced his sorry ass. Despite being strong-minded, she was nevertheless badly shaken by the experience. Two weeks later, she confided to Reggie that she was having a hard time concentrating on the job and needed some time off. Reggie told her that she could take as much time off as she needed with full salary. That was two months ago, a little before I came over."

With the rising sun bathing the two men in warmth, Sal picked up a napkin off the table and wiped beads of sweat from his forehead. "After I told Reggie about your decision to come aboard, he immediately thought of Angie, believing that she would be an ideal person to assist you. Even though we have our share of corrupt officials in Washington, the problem is far more rampant in China. Without having someone savvy by your side, you'll be quickly overwhelmed by the frustration of dealing with the shit."

"What does Angie think about assisting me?"

Sal raised his hands and shrugged his shoulders. "Well, I've only talked to her on the phone. I reminded her that you were with me at the investment forum in San Francisco, the guy who was too fuckin' shy to say hello to her."

Kip reached across the table and whacked Sal on the shoulder. "The hell you say."

"Anyway," continued Sal, "I was surprised that she even remembered you. I also told her that you had a hell of a record for turning around troubled companies. While she wasn't completely sold on the idea, I could tell that she was at least intrigued. I also told her that you agreed to come to Shanghai as a personal favor to me."

"Did you tell her about Marci?"

"No, *hermano*. That's a private matter. Anyway, I made reservations at a seafood restaurant in San Jia Gang, a quaint little fishermen's village on the coastline not far from Shores. It'll be entirely up to you and Angie whether she works with you or not. Hopefully, she'll want to head over to Shores with us after lunch."

"Thanks."

"Well, unless you want to just sit here overdosing on caffeine, let's *vamanos*!"

Kip ran up to his room to retrieve his attaché case and camera. Five minutes later, the two men were picked up in front of the hotel.

"How do you like having your own driver taking you wherever you need to go?" asked Kip.

"Sometimes it's great—sometimes I miss the freedom of just jumping in a car and taking off. I have to admit, though, my driver knows how to drive safely through Shanghai traffic, a rare skill for Chinese drivers. As you may have noticed last night, people drive crazy here. For this reason, Reggie doesn't allow any of his American staff to drive—too much liability. You'll be assigned a driver and a car before the end of the week."

"Good. The walk this morning reminded me of the old arcade game, *Frogger*, where you try to get the frog across a road without getting squashed by a passing car."

Sal said, "My mistake. I should have warned you before you went out. Pedestrians walk across the street at their own peril in Shanghai. Here, there's no such thing as a pedestrian right-of-way. My best advice to you when you're walking around is to stay in the middle of a pack of Chinese when crossing the street. They have the timing down to a tee. Most pedestrians ignore traffic lights unless there's a traffic cop around."

"I noticed," said Kip.

"One more piece of advice before we head out."

"Go ahead."

"Because of the political involvement in establishing Shanghai Shores, some Chinese and American diplomats have let us know in no uncertain terms that they're unhappy about the problems we're having. The worse of the lot is Milt Avery, an officer with the U.S. and Foreign Commercial Service in Shanghai. He's what I would categorize as an authentic asshole. Shit, the man calls our Shanghai office almost every week, demanding a status report on what we're doing to solve the problems at Shores. The man shows he's an unprofessional moron as soon as he starts yelling in the phone. Anyway, *Tuchi*, I suspect he'll hone in on you the moment he learns you're here."

"Thanks for the warning. A few of the venture capitalists I've dealt with in Silicon Valley proved to be amazingly uncivil. I'll know how to handle Avery."

Just as Sal had predicted coming in from the airport, the hazy air was pronounced, causing the sky to appear powder-blue rather than deep blue.

After Sal gave his driver directions, they visited a fabric market near the Bund and then took an hour to meander through the Xiangyang Market, open-air shops that occupied an entire city block.

Sal said, "Okay, partner, we'd better start to head for the restaurant to meet with Angie. We don't want to be late."

Kip felt beads of sweat forming on his forehead. "I could use a drink."

Chapter 6

As the car turned into the parking lot in front of the seaside restaurant, a cadre of attendants snapped to attention. One of the men waved Sal's driver towards a parking stall, but he ignored the directions and headed directly to the restaurant's entrance where he let Sal and Kip out. Just inside the foyer, young ladies clad in traditional red dresses were chanting a Chinese greeting to arriving patrons.

A nice touch—thought Kip.

Sal pointed to the noisy dining hall. "I reserved a private room for us instead of sitting in there."

"Why's that?"

"Well, take a look."

Kip peered in. "Jesus, the place is already packed."

"Exactly. Chinese live for only two things: to eat and to eat. That's when they conduct most of their business or socialize with family or friends. You'll also quickly learn that Chinese diners are incredibly curious when sitting next to Americans."

"So we eat out of earshot of them."

"Yes, unless you want the entire population of China to know what we talk about before we have a chance to pay the bill."

Kip shook his head.

A smiling hostess led Kip and Sal down a zigzag narrow hallway and into a nicely-furnished private room. A round dining table with a glass Lazy Susan on top sat on one side of the room. On the other side, two sofas faced each other separated by an ornate Chinese coffee table. Sal pointed to one of the sofas. "Let's relax until Angie gets here."

As soon as the two men sat down, a waitress poured tea for them and stepped back, standing obediently across the room waiting to serve them.

Kip said, "*Yani*, how about that beer?"

"What kind?"

"Tooheys Extra Dry would be perfect."

Sal laughed. "Coming right up." He motioned to the waitress and ordered a beer. After she skittered out of the room, Sal turned back to Kip and asked, "How are you doing with cutting back?"

Kip said, "Great. I've got it under control. Listen, how do we want to play this with Angie?"

"Let's not worry about it. She's either ready to get back to work or not. Besides, you may not feel right about her once you've had a chance to get acquainted."

"Maybe."

Moments later, there was a light rap on the door and Angie walked in. She wore black slacks, a black safari shirt, and a long tan silk scarf which hung down from her shoulders. Her silky black hair was pulled back in a tight bun. Her eyes were dark and glistening.

Kip and Sal stood. Sal said, "*Hay carumba!* You're so beau-ti-ful." He walked up and gave her a hug.

Angie smiled. "Thank you, Sal." She turned toward Kip to shake his hand. "Mr. Duchene, I'm pleased to meet you."

"The pleasure's mine. Please call me Kip."

"Kip it is."

Sal said to Angie, "Let's sit down. I've ordered tea for us and a beer for Kip."

The two men sat on the couch opposite of Angie. She said to Kip, "Sal claims that you're a genius for solving corporate problems."

Kip said, "Ah, you didn't know?"

"Know what?"

"He lies."

The surprised look on her face dissolved into a smile. "Okay, you're kidding."

Sal said, "Angie, he's still jet-lagged."

"Don't pay any attention to him," said Kip. "Let's hope that my experience in the United States will rub off on Shanghai Shores."

She raised her eyebrows. "You'll find out soon enough, won't you?"

Confused by what she really meant, Kip said, "Yes . . . I guess I will."

After an awkward silence, Angie said to Sal, "Should I go ahead and order for us?"

"Have at it."

She scanned the menu and rattled off directions to a nervous waitress.

Kip thought—*I have a feeling that Angie doesn't take shit from anyone.*

Angie turned back to Kip. "I understand that you and Sal go back a long way."

Before Kip could reply, the waitress quietly walked back into the room and set a bottle of Tsingtao beer down in front of him and filled his glass. He took a quick gulp and said, "Jeez, Sal, what is this stuff?"

"It's the only brand of beer they serve here. Like it?"

Kip frowned and took another drink. To Angie, he said, "He and I have known each other since our college days."

"So you trust him?" said Angie with a serious look.

Kip shot a glance at Sal who shrugged his shoulders. Kip said to Angie, "I'm not sure what you're asking."

"Do you have any knowledge of the Chinese culture?"

"No."

"Do you speak the language?"

"No."

"Have you been to China before?"

"No."

Angie slowly shook her head. "So despite knowing so little about this country, you've agreed to come over here and take on the problems of Shanghai Shores solely on the word of Sal."

Kip ran his fingers through his hair. "That about sums it up."

"Okay then. After hearing Sal's ideas about bringing you in, Reggie called me. I must say that he sounded the most excited about Shores since he first acquired the development. He asked me to consider coming back to assist you with the project. While honored with the offer, I wouldn't even consider it without meeting you first."

"That makes sense." Kip regarded her comments as a hopeful sign. "Your English is excellent. Where did you learn?"

"I studied English all through school in Shanghai. After graduating from Tonji University in 1996, I headed to California and received my MBA at U.C. Berkeley in 2000. I lived there for two years, enough time to polish my English in a way that would have been impossible to do over here."

"If I recall, Reggie said something about that in his speech at Moscone Center," said Kip. He drained his glass and held it up for the waitress to see. Looking back at Angie, he said, "By the way, do you always get cat calls from men in the audience when you're introduced?"

"No. That would never happen in China."

"Did it embarrass you?"

"Of course not. Actually, I kind of liked it." She turned to Sal and asked, "Have you told Kip about Mr. Avery yet?"

Munching on peanuts, he said, "Yep."

"Good. You'll need to be prepared for him," said Angie. "If I remember my American jargon correctly, you'd say he's *over the top* when it comes to arrogance."

Kip said, "Thanks. I'm forewarned."

Sal stood up and motioned with his hand. "Let's go ahead and sit at the table. They'll be serving soon."

Once they were seated, Kip grasped his chopsticks and nimbly popped a slice of pickled cucumber into his mouth.

Angie noticed. "Hey, I'm impressed! Foreigners usually end up fumbling when they first try to use chopsticks.

"I eat a lot of Chinese food in San Francisco."

"I see." She looked from Kip to Sal and said, "I think I'd like to join you this afternoon if it's okay."

Sal said, "We'd love to have you."

Kip thought this was a positive sign.

Angie said, "That would give us time to get better acquainted and talk about the project while on site."

Just then, a procession of waitresses walked into the room carrying steaming plates of food.

Chapter 7

Ten minutes after leaving the restaurant, Sal's driver pulled up to the main gate of Shanghai Shores. Looking around from the back seat, Kip said, "Very impressive. This is not how I envisioned the place to look."

Sal said, "Wait until we get inside, *Tuchi*."

Angie raised her eyebrows. "*Tuchi?*"

"That's the nickname I anointed him with when we were at Stanford."

She turned to Kip and said, "Let me guess . . . you have a name for Sal."

Chuckling, Kip said, "It's *Yani*."

"I won't even ask," she said, rolling her eyes.

The front of Shanghai Shores was screened off with a nine-foot security fence of wrought iron pickets between brick pillars spaced every twelve feet. The guards wore crisp military-type uniforms: dark blue with white belts around their waists and diagonally across their chests, walkie-talkies clipped to their breast pockets, and berets adorned with the Shanghai Shores logo in front.

A guard pushed a button and the gate lifted. The three guards on duty snapped to attention and saluted as the car entered.

Kip whistled. "That's some greeting. Is it typical to have military-looking guards manning the front gate for this kind of development?"

"Sure," said Sal. "You'll find the same setup all over, including the upscale housing developments for Chinese residents."

From the entry gate, the divided main road continued straight into the compound in an easterly direction. Single-family homes and townhouses bordered the road on the left, looking like a typical upscale subdivision in any American city. The Mediterranean-style homes had stucco siding and red tile roofs. The lush green front lawns and the overall landscaping scheme were nicely laid out. On the right side of the road, the view was starkly different. It looked like a wasteland of vacant building lots overgrown with weeds.

The car approached a circular roundabout with a water fountain then continued for another block before entering a landscaped parking lot for the clubhouse. It was a three-story building, also of Mediterranean architecture. Two thirty-foot tall palm trees were planted on each side of the main stairway that led up to the second floor lobby.

As the three were getting out of the car, Kip said, "Pretty impressive."

Sal and Angie looked at each other and smiled without saying anything. They walked up the stairs and into the spacious lobby, nicely appointed with marble tile floors, potted plants and rattan furniture. Several paddle fans were lazily circulating the air overhead. A uniformed young Chinese lady stood up from her chair behind the receptionist counter. "Hello, Mr. Estrada. Hi, Angie."

Sal said, "Andrea, is the third-floor conference room free?"

"Yes. May I bring up some tea for you?"

"Thanks. That'd be nice."

The three of them took the staircase up to the third floor. The top landing led to a lofted balcony overlooking the two-story restaurant below. Large picture windows framed the entire far side of the restaurant, allowing an unobstructed view of the ocean.

Kip said, "Jeez, what a beautiful view."

"You're looking at the East China Sea," Angie explained. "Shanghai Shores is actually facing out directly to what is called White Dragon Bay."

From the balcony, corridors led in opposite directions, either to the north or south wings of the clubhouse. Sal said,

"Because the development is only half built, the only two rooms used on the third floor are the conference room and an office dedicated to Ingram Capital when we occasionally make a visit. The rest of the occupied offices are down on the second floor. It's usually pretty quiet up here."

Sal led them into the north wing, walking through the first door to the right and into a plush conference room with a cherry-wood table set up to accommodate eighteen people. A white board was mounted on the far side of the room and a ceiling-mounted projector for video and PowerPoint presentations. A bank of windows on the east side provided a panoramic view of the ocean.

Sal asked, "So, what do you think?"

"Nice," said Kip. "What's this room used for?"

"Mostly for managers' meetings. But sometimes tenants use it for business meetings or private parties. The staff also uses it for general purposes."

Kip said "It's certainly first rate."

As soon as the three sat down at one end of the conference table, Kip pulled out his notebook. He turned to Sal and said, "The background information you sent me in San Francisco was helpful. Cutting through all of the details, what do you think our most serious problems are?"

Sal said, "First, we've had an unexplained loss of tenants and no one knows why. Shortly after Shanghai Shores opened, our occupancy rate reached seventy-three percent. Today, that's down to only twenty-seven percent. The Shanghai government insists that we get it back up to at least sixty percent, nothing less. That would generate enough profit for us to go ahead with a secondary offering and raise additional capital for completing Phase Two of the development."

Kip said, "Is that the area on the right side of the main road where there are empty lots?"

"Exactly," said Sal. "The second problem came from the development being poorly managed in the past. That then led to low staff morale and poor performance. However, you'll be able to quickly turn that around."

Angie cleared her throat. "Don't be so sure of that, Sal."

Sal shrugged his shoulders. "Anyway, then there's the ever present Rico Niu lurking on the sidelines ready to pounce and snatch the development away from Ingram. But, I'm not too worried about him."

Angie said, "Sal, you're underestimating what Niu could do."

"Please explain," said Kip.

"Well, for starters, Niu is Chinese. You two are not. Believe me, he knows how to do things the Chinese way which you couldn't even begin to understand. There's no question in my mind that he's made significant inroads to snatching Shanghai Shores away from Ingram."

Kip said, "Angie, I'm lost. How could Niu possibly take over Shanghai Shores after Ingram has funded its entire development to the tune of millions of dollars?"

"Look, I don't want to take up a lot of time trying to explain this. However, let me say that he's bribing officials from the Shanghai government as we speak."

"I hope you're wrong, Angie." Kip looked over at Sal. "Otherwise, I might be just wasting my time over here."

With an edge to his voice, Sal said, "Let's get back to the business at hand, okay?"

The receptionist rapped lightly on the conference room door and walked in with a tray holding a carafe of steaming water, cups, assorted teabags, and cookies. After serving everyone, she asked, "Mr. Estrada, is there anything else I can bring?"

"No, Andrea, that'll be all. Thanks."

Before she could excuse herself, Kip cleared his throat. "Miss, can you bring me a beer?"

Angie flashed a quick look at Sal. He avoided her eyes.

"What do you prefer, sir?"

"Anything but Tsingtao Beer."

"I understand." She nodded and quietly closed the door behind her.

Sal said to Kip, "You've already read my preliminary report outlining some of problems we discovered here."

"You mean the screw ups by the previous general manager?"

"Yes. Then we made the problem far worse by taking too long to recognize we had the wrong guy at the helm."

"*Yani*, I don't much care about him. He's history. My instincts tell me that this guy, Rico Niu, is the one stirring up the problems here, particularly the one where tenants are terminating their leases early."

Sal said, "How in the hell would you know that?"

Kip smiled and tapped the side of his nose with his forefinger.

Angie raised her eyebrows at Sal. "Is this guy really *that* good?"

Sal leaned over and wrapped his arm around Kip's shoulder. "Yeah, he really is."

Kip smiled. "Ah, shucks, fellers." The smile on his face dissolved into a serious look as he glanced at the notes in front of him. "Based on your breakeven analysis, Sal, I figure that we are presently renting thirty-five homes, but need to bring the occupancy up to at least eighty."

Angie looked over at Sal. "Why are you smiling?"

"When you hear him calling me, 'Sal,' you know he's into his zone. He's on automatic pilot." He turned back to Kip. "But, you're right. Getting eighty homes leased *is* the magic number."

"Angie, what's your take on this?" asked Kip.

"I don't know. You gentlemen have probably gotten it right."

Kip said, "That's it?"

Angie shrugged her shoulders. "Yes."

Sal said, "You'll learn that Angie's a sandbagger—she doesn't reveal what she's thinking right away. But when she does, you'd better pay attention."

Kip said to Angie, "Can you at least share your thoughts on the staff situation?"

"That's easy. The former general manager was a disaster. Seeing this go on fcr as long as it did, the Chinese managers took control of Shores. I'm guessing that some of them have carved out little fiefdoms for themselves by spending more time protecting their respective turfs than working as a team. I think you'll be able to see the personnel problems within a week or so."

"When Sal first asked me to come to Shanghai to bail Shores out," said Kip, "I told him he was nuts. I don't speak Chinese and haven't the slightest idea about the cultural differences here. I do know, however, that this project will require a mammoth amount of effort regardless of whoever tries to turn it around. Even before I start, I'm handicapped."

"Well, you have one thing going for you compared to most Americans who come over here to do business."

"And what's that?"

Angie looked directly into Kip's eyes and smiled. "At least you're smart enough to know you're in way over your head."

Chapter 8

Kip blushed with uncertainty. Before he could respond, the receptionist lightly rapped on the door and brought in a glass and a bottle of Budweiser for Kip. He thanked her and took a satisfying gulp. Setting the glass down, he asked Sal where the restroom was located.

"Take a left out the door and you'll find it half way down the hall."

When Kip left the room, Angie turned to Sal, "Does he have a drinking problem?"

"Yes, but for a damn good reason."

"Like what?"

"It's private."

"Oh."

When Kip returned, Sal said, "I've invited our Chief Engineer, Rory McKellar, and Maintenance Manager, Manny Okumu, to take us on a tour around the site. They'll be able to fill in the blanks about some of the problems we've discussed. You'll also get a rough idea of the layout of the development."

Kip said, "What can you tell me about the two men?"

"Well, Rory emigrated from Scotland to China about fifteen years ago. He's fluent in Mandarin. He's outstanding, someone you can rely upon when things get rough. In the past, he's managed infrastructure projects in China for large companies like Shell Oil, Coca-Cola and Siemens. About eight years ago, he married a wonderful woman from Beijing. They now have two kids, a son and daughter. He's big man, maybe six-four and three hundred pounds. No one messes with Rory, especially if his temper flares."

"And Okumu?" asked Kip.

"He's another exceptional man. He fled from northern Uganda when he was twenty-two and ended up in Hong Kong and eventually China. He never talks about his life in Uganda. I think it was a terrifying existence. I had heard that his older brother was hacked to death by a roving group of militiamen when Idi Amin was in power. As soon as Manny landed in Hong Kong, he spent all of his free time learning Cantonese and Mandarin. After a few years, he moved to Shanghai and was employed as Project Engineer by another expatriate housing development. We recruited him last year. He's deceptively bright, hardworking, and very reliable. He's also on the shy side."

Kip turned to Angie. "Have you met them?"

"Yes. It's comical watching the Chinese react when they overhear fluent Mandarin coming out of the mouths of a giant white man and a black man."

"Why's that?" asked Kip.

"For starters, there are very few black people in China. As such, Chinese people are curious when they see one. Manny even speaks a little Shanghainese, a dialect that very few Chinese can understand outside of Shanghai. You see, when Shanghai people don't want outsiders to understand what we're saying, we slip into Shanghainese. Anyway, I'm impressed with both of them. I suppose that—"

There was a sharp rap on the door. Rory walked in followed by Manny. Rory was an imposing man with a pale British complexion, ruddy cheeks and crystal blue eyes. His red hair was cropped closely to his head. In stark contrast, Manny was dark-skinned, only five-foot-six, but built like welterweight boxer. He wore a baseball cap and flashed a big smile full of pearly-white teeth.

Rory walked over and shook Sal's hand, "Hello, mate." He then gave Angie a hug, making her almost disappear within his clutch. "How's my wee lovely lassie getting on these days?"

"Just fine, Rory," said Angie smiling.

"Gentlemen," said Sal, "I'd like to introduce you to Kip Duchene. He's here from the States to take a look at Shores and give us some advice on the project. I want Kip to get an idea of the layout of the development. So, let's take a quick tour in the mini-van. I'd like you, Rory, to start us off by showing him around the infrastructure. And then, Manny, I'd like you to take us through some of the homes."

In the minivan, Sal said to Rory, "Just let my driver know where you want to go."

Rory leaned forward and gave directions in Mandarin, then turned to Kip. "I've asked him to start us off by slowly driving around the development without stopping anywhere specific. I'll try to describe to you what we're seeing as we go. If you've got a question, mate, just fire away. And the grand finale will take us to the waste treatment plant."

Smiling, Kip said, "Sounds good."

Rory unfolded a large plot plan and held it up for Kip to see. "The property is split in half with mirror images on the north and south sides. The north side is developed and the south side will stay undeveloped until they get funding for Phase Two."

During their tour Kip didn't see many residents except for a few kids on bicycles and a woman pushing a stroller. When they passed a fenced-in playground on the far north side of the development several youngsters were playing on the swings and a jungle-gym set while their moms sat on a bench chatting with each other. As the van looped back around close to the main gate, a two-story pea green building came into view. It reminded Kip of a barracks on a military base. He uttered, "What in the world is that?"

Rory chuckled. "That, my friend, is what we call The Green Latrine."

Kip arched his eyebrows. "The Green Latrine?"

Rory said something in Mandarin and the driver pulled over to the curb. He said to Kip, "Ah, yes. You see, the color of the building is a wee close to what you'd find in a baby's diaper."

Kip chuckled.

"While the clubhouse was being constructed, we used this building as our temporary offices. When construction was complete, the three women managing the finance, human resources, and administration departments convinced Ralph to let them and their staff to stay here instead of moving into the new offices over in the clubhouse."

"Why's that?" asked Kip.

Rory shrugged his wide shoulders. "I'm not really sure, mate. Maybe Angie can answer that."

Angie was nodding. "I can. The three women who manage those departments actually control the company behind the scenes. By staying in separate offices, they can operate more covertly and out of the scrutiny of general management."

Kip got a startled expression. "Jeez, I hope you're kidding."

"I'm afraid not."

Sal looked at Kip and turned up his hands with a shrug.

While Kip was trying to digest what Angie had just said, the van proceeded down the road and pulled into the parking lot to the plant facilities. While touring through the water treatment plant, waste sewage plant and electrical substation, Kip's spirits lifted at the sight of the spotless interiors and modern machinery in all three buildings.

When they stepped back outside in the bright sunlight, Rory said to Kip. "Well, that's it on my side. I'll turn the tour over to Manny now."

Kip said, "Thanks, Rory, I'm impressed."

Rory smiled. "Not to worry, mate."

After briefly speaking to the driver in Chinese, Manny said, "We have four types of homes here—townhouses, garden patio homes, larger executive homes, and finally our beachfront estates."

Kip said, "If I recall, there are one hundred and twenty-three homes already built and that makes up Phase One."

"That's right," said Manny. As he opened the door to the first home, Kip was transported to America by what he saw. The doors, windows and cabinets were all imported from the states. The appliances were made by named U.S. manufacturers. Before now, Kip would never have guessed that homes like these could be found in China of all places. The estate homes would be regarded by anyone as exceptional, whether at Shanghai Shores or Beverly Hills. These elegant homes faced the sea with spectacular panoramic views. It reminded him of the gray-green waters of the San Francisco Bay.

The entourage ended up walking along the boardwalk on their way back to the clubhouse. Kip said, "This makes me nostalgic watching the procession of cargo ships steaming up and down the coastal shipping lanes – just like where I grew up in Santa Monica." He turned to Sal. "I would think that this spectacular view would inspire people to want to live here."

Sal said, "I wish it was that easy."

As everyone was saying their goodbyes in the parking lot, Kip turned to Manny and Rory and shook their hands. "This was very helpful for me, gentlemen. Thank you."

Sal said, "Okay, then, let's head back to your hotel. Angie, your place is on the way so we'll drop you off, if you like."

On the drive toward downtown, Sal said to Kip, "The tour today was intended to help you get off to a good start tomorrow."

Kip said, "We'll see." He turned towards Angie. "I hope that we'll have a chance to work together. Obviously, I'm going to need a lot of help getting Shanghai Shores in shape."

"Thanks for your confidence. With your background, you'll have the opportunity to make some very positive changes. As for me, I regret not having any experience in property management, but will definitely think about your kind offer."

"That's fair," he said. In truth, he was thinking—*Not what I expected. I don't think she's interested in working with me.* He began to feel the first traces of sweat breaking out across his forehead. *I could use a drink.*

After Angie was dropped off, Sal said, "For tonight, we're going to have dinner with Reggie so he can properly welcome you to Shanghai. I think that he wants to share his own perspective of Shores with you. You'll enjoy meeting the man and seeing firsthand why he's so respected. In the meantime, you can take a short rest at the hotel. I know you're jetlagged."

Kip said, "Sounds good to me."

"I thought so. We'll meet in the lobby of the Jin Mao Tower. It's the tallest building in Shanghai. My driver will pick you up at five-thirty. As a matter of fact, I see that we're already at your hotel."

Kip looked out the car window and recognized the entryway of the Ritz-Carlton Hotel. As soon as he walked into his room he headed straight for the mini-bar. Opening a bottle of Scotch, he kicked off his shoes and stretched out on the bed. Marci's eyes stared up at him from the photograph propped up on the bedside stand. He reached over and held the frame to his chest. "I know, sweetheart . . . I'm trying." Feeling tears running down his cheeks, he said, "God knows, I'm really trying."

Chapter 9

Two hours later Kip sat alone in the backseat of Sal's car on the way to the dinner meeting at Jin Mao Tower. The route took him through downtown Shanghai on an elevated highway. Since the driver couldn't speak English, Kip was content to keep his thoughts to himself and gaze out the window at the surrounding sights. Modern skyscrapers jutted high above while rivers of bicycles flowed through traffic on the streets below. Kip slowly shook his head. *So far, China has been full of surprises. I wonder if Reggie Ingram will be another. Well, I guess I'm about to find out.*

The driver drove into a tunnel that connects the Puxi side of Shanghai with Pudong. Two blocks after they emerged on the other side, the car turned into an expansive arched portico and pulled to a stop in front of the main entrance. A uniformed attendant opened the door for Kip. "Good evening, sir. Welcome to the Grand Hyatt Hotel."

Kip smiled. "Thank you." He pushed through the revolving doors and immediately heard Sal's voice. "Oye, *Tuchi*, over here!"

As the men embraced, Kip said, "Jesus, this is one impressive building!"

"Wait until you see the view from up there." Sal pointed up with his index finger. He then led Kip into an elevator and pushed the only button on the panel—54. "This'll take us up to the lobby of the hotel."

"*Up* to the lobby?"

"Yeah. There are business offices from the ground floor up to the hotel lobby on the 54th floor. Everything above there is part of the hotel, all the way to the 87th floor."

"So how do people get to the business offices?"

"If you would've turned left when you came into the building, you'd run right into another bank of elevators for the business offices. Just beyond, you can buy a ticket to ride up to the observation deck located on the 88th floor—a very lucky number in China."

"How so?" Kip raised his eyebrows.

"Well, the Chinese word for eight is pronounced 'bah,' which sounds a hell of a lot like 'fah,' the word for wealth. So, in China, eight is the luckiest number, but eighty-eight is even more so."

As the elevator doors swished opened on the 54th floor, Kip said, "Got it."

The hotel lobby before them was several stories high and offered breathtaking panoramic views of downtown Shanghai. The red-tinted sun was sitting low over the skyline. Kip followed Sal across the foyer to another set of elevators. A smartly-dressed Chinese woman greeted them, "Do you have reservations, gentleman?"

Sal said, "Yes . . . Cucina's."

"I see." She then looked more carefully at the two men. "Do you happen to be joining Mr. Ingram tonight?"

Sal looked at Kip and winked, then turned back to the attendant. "Yes."

"He is waiting for you in the cocktail lounge." She smiled and motioned with her hand toward the awaiting elevator. "Floor fifty-six. Please enjoy your evening."

As soon as the elevator doors closed, Kip said, "How in the hell did she know?"

"Reggie's got this place wired, *Tuchi*."

In the cocktail lounge, Kip immediately spotted Reggie sitting crossed-legged on a couch against the far wall. With pipe in hand, he looked far more imposing to Kip than he remembered from the investment seminar in San Francisco five years earlier. He said to Sal, "He's quite a distinguished looking man."

"*Si, como no.*"

Reggie stood up and flashed a big smile when Kip and Sal walked up, extending his hand to Kip, "Welcome aboard, old boy!"

"I'm pleased to meet you."

"The pleasure's mine, I assure you. And how are we feeling after the long flight?"

"Other than being a little jet-lagged, I'm doing okay."

"Well done, I say." He then turned to Sal, shook his hand, and patted him on the shoulder. Reggie motioned for the two men to sit in the other sofa facing him. "Would you like to try a London Special? This is my first bloody one of the day" He held up an almost-empty martini glass.

Kip said, "Whatever it is, I'll try one."

"I'll have my usual tequila and tonic," said Sal.

"Right you are." After ordering a round of drinks, Reggie turned to Kip and said, "I trust your stay at the Ritz-Carlton is satisfactory."

"It's very comfortable, thanks."

"Good show."

Sal said, "But he decided to venture out on his own this morning and walk around the hotel."

Reggie raised his bushy eyebrows and looked at Kip. "You don't say? I see you survived."

Kip chuckled. "Just barely."

"Very well, then. Under normal circumstances, I'd prefer that we take more time to get acquainted, but there is nothing normal about what's in front of us at Shanghai Shores."

"Well, I guess that's why I'm here."

"That's the spirit! Sal gave me a pretty good rundown about the alarming loss of tenants, but we haven't got a grasp on why. Unless someone is physically onsite and is bloody good at solving problems, we're just making this wretched thing worse. Kip, I'm a bit fearful of what you may uncover. But, considering your record in Silicon Valley, I'll wager that you'll save the day."

Kip said, "Maybe a little early for that. But after seeing the development, I'm excited about the challenge of turning the place around."

Reggie pulled the pipe from his mouth and laughed. "Well, that's a start, wouldn't you say? While you won't have an easy time of it, I believe that you're the man to help us get on with it."

"Thanks. I appreciate your confidence."

Reggie said, "Alright, then!"

As soon as the drinks arrived, Reggie held up his glass up and made a toast, "Here's to our success at Shanghai Shores. Gentlemen . . . Cheers!"

The three men clicked their glasses and savored the drinks. Reggie looked across at Kip and said, "Well?"

"An excellent drink. What's in it?"

"Pre-chilled Bombay Sapphire over ice with a customary wave of the vermouth bottle and topped off with a large green olive."

"Well, it's superb."

Reggie continued, "Kip, old boy, please know that you weren't called over here to simply help us improve the performance of Shanghai Shores. I'm not sure how Sal was able to convince you to accept the position." Smiling in Sal's direction, he added, "Actually . . . I bloody well don't want to know."

Kip and Sal glanced at each other and chuckled.

Reggie set his pipe down and got a serious look on his face. "In reality, we're dealing with a serious problem underpinning literally everything else at Shores, a problem that I wanted to personally discuss with you."

Kip sat forward. "Okay."

"On May first, the Shanghai government delivered a completely unexpected blow to us, putting us on notice that we have only one year to demonstrate our ability to complete the project. That's only ten months from now. As you saw today, Shores is only half developed. Because we're not yet generating a profit, we're unable to go to the capital market to raise more funds for finishing off the other half. Without an infusion of capital, we can't move forward."

Kip said, "What happens if we can't make their deadline?"

"Surely we don't want to know. There's an obscure law in China that allows the government to confiscate property from a land developer who hasn't completed construction within a reasonable time. If they decide to take action against us they would probably turn it over to a state owned enterprise or a favored Chinese company."

After taking another sip of his drink, he continued, "Through my political connections with the Shanghai government, I've learned that there is an unscrupulous Chinese man who owns a conglomeration of businesses in China. One is a homebuilding company in Kunshan, a city just west of Shanghai. This man regularly invites government officials to his model homes for relaxation with beautiful women."

"Are you talking about Rico Niu?"

Reggie raised his eyebrows. "You know who he is?"

"Yes. I happened to sit next to Eleni Wentworth on the flight over here. She shared what she knew about him. She also said that you two are friends."

Reggie cleared his throat. "My, my, my. She's a smashing good lady and well-connected in Shanghai. What a coincidence you sat by her. Did she part with any new tidbits about our Mr. Niu?"

"No, except that he was now making regular trips to Shanghai."

"Is that so?" Reggie's eyebrows lifted.

"That's what she said."

"You see, he was the only other bidder for Shanghai Shores. I understand that he was a bit put off when he learned that we were awarded the contract. Refusing to give up, the greedy little sod wants to take over Shores and build the rest of the homes himself. Evidently, he's made steady progress bribing government officials to do just that. He gets his money from his illegal gambling operations in Hainan Island. It raises the stakes a bit to hear he's now a frequent visitor to Shanghai. If Mr. Niu prevails in getting the Shanghai government to move against us, the financial loss to our shareholders would be quite devastating. Our reputation must be saved at all cost."

"Can the Chinese government really do that?" asked Kip.

"Unfortunately, yes. So what we have to do is get our occupancy rate up significantly in the next six months or sooner."

"What will the government expect by the deadline?"

Sal said, "They'll need to see clear proof that Shores has made major improvements in its performance and be convinced that we're prepared to raise additional capital. While that's being done, we need to cleverly derail Rico."

"So," said Kip, "I assume the 'we' is actually me?"

Smiling broadly with his pipe tilting upward, Reggie said, "By George, I think you've got it!"

The three men laughed. While joining in on the frivolity, Kip was worried about how he would pull this off—especially now that it seemed unlikely Angie Li would be on board to help.

A hostess came over and led the men to a window table in the restaurant. Reggie motioned for Kip to take the chair so he was directly facing the floor-to-ceiling windows. Sal and Reggie sat on each side of him. Kip was mesmerized by the panoramic view of downtown Shanghai. The reflection of the tabletop candle in the window momentarily transported him back to the romantic dinners he and Marci used to have. He could envision her enchanting him with her radiant smile. Snapping back to the present, he felt a wave of deep sorrow sweep through his body. Reggie and Sal were preoccupied in conversation. He hoped that no one noticed the tears that glistened in his eyes. But something told him Sal had.

After dinner, the men walked out of the restaurant. On the way through the cocktail lounge, Reggie pulled a business card out of a gold holder and wrote on the back. Tapping on it with his index finger, he said, "This is my private cell phone number I give to very few people. If you're ever in a bind, you're welcome to call me at this number at any time."

Kip pulled his wallet out and slipped Reggie's card into a slot. "I'm glad we had this chance to talk."

"Very good then. Well, I'm popping next door for a nightcap. Remember to call if you ever need anything." Reggie shook Kip's hand and retreated to the cocktail lounge.

Sal walked Kip to the elevator. "*Tuchi*, Reggie asked me to stay behind for a minute so we can catch up on some other business. Ah . . . How are you doing?"

"*Yani*, you worry too much, but thanks for asking."

"Good. My driver is waiting for you below to take you back to the hotel. For tomorrow, let's meet in the lobby at seven-thirty. We'll have breakfast and head out to Shores."

"Sounds good – see you then."

On the way back to the hotel, Kip felt sweat bead up on his forehead and his heart hammering in his chest. As the car descended into the tunnel, Kip had a sinking feeling— *Am I making the biggest damn mistake of my life?*

Chapter 10

The next morning, Kip and Sal met for breakfast as planned. As soon as they sat down, Sal went over how he planned to announce to the managers about Ralph Maddox and that Kip was hired as their new general manager.

While Kip stirred his coffee, he said, "This is going to be interesting."

"See any problems on your side?"

"No. I'm ready to dig in. What else do we need to discuss?"

"Last night Reggie told me that he'd heard that Niu was bribing government officials in an attempt to shorten the deadline they gave us."

"That possible?"

"In China? Yeah, it's possible."

Kip slowly shook his head. "I have to say, *Yani*, that learning about the rampant bribery over here is unsettling."

"You'll manage." Sal took a sip of coffee. "At first, Reggie shirked off the bribery news as gossip. But your revelation last night about Niu making frequent trips to Shanghai changed that. As a precaution, we need to be prepared for the government to bring the hammer down on us at any time."

"What about Reggie's contacts with the Shanghai government?"

"If Reggie wasn't so influential over here, Rico Niu would have already been named the proud new owner of Shanghai Shores."

"*Jesus*, doesn't China have any rule of law?"

"I know it seems that they don't. In reality, their legal system is improving even though China has a long fuckin' way to go to catch up with the rest of the world. The contacts that Reggie has in the government are quietly protecting us as best they can. But there are no guarantees."

"Okay," said Kip, "we used to be pretty smart thinkers when we were at Stanford. Surely we can beat Niu at his own game."

"Maybe. The playing field for foreigners in China is not level under any condition. Between widespread corruption and weak laws, we have a big task in front of us."

"That's for sure. So tell me more what you know about Rico Niu."

"Most of what I know is hearsay. I've heard stories that Rico's father abandoned him and his mother when he was just a kid. He grew up in poverty on a rural family farm in Anhui Provence."

"Where's that from here?"

"About 300 miles southwest. Evidently, Niu was a school bully and has stepped on people to get ahead ever since. After graduating from college, he headed for Hainan Island to make big money."

"He graduated from *college*?"

"That's right. Beijing University with a B.A. in economics."

Kip raised his hands. "And ended up a gangster?"

"Yeah, a very wealthy one at that. He made a fortune from gambling and prostitution. About five years ago he had more cash stashed away than he could spend. He solved the problem by laundering millions in mainland China through acquiring legitimate businesses, including the homebuilding company in Kunshan that Reggie mentioned last night."

Kip said, "If he's so damn rich, why would he bother trying to take over Shanghai Shores?"

"Face."

"*Face?* I don't understand."

Sal chuckled. "Okay, this concept may be more difficult for you to grasp than the lucky number bit. I haven't found anything that Chinese pay more attention to than having a good *face*. That means a lot of things"

"Like what?"

"Well, shit, take your pick . . . reputation, prestige, dignity, power, sense of worth, blah-blah-blah. If a person is proven wrong, is humiliated, or blunders a situation, he loses face. And that, *amigo*, is what Chinese will avoid at all cost. But, here's the hardest part. In most cases, Chinese will value *face* more than honesty. They will value *face* more than keeping a promise. Most Westerners can say, 'I made a mistake,' or 'I fucked up,' or 'I'm responsible.' But I've never heard a Chinese person utter those words."

Kip said, "That's going to take a while to sink in. What else do I need to know?"

Sal reached into his attaché case and slid a bundle of money across the table. "Here's 10,000 Yuan."

"What's this for?"

"You should have some local currency in your pocket."

"Got it."

Sal said, "Later today, you need to open a personal bank account. Also, get one of the staff to pick up a cell phone for you. I doubt your phone is set up to work over here." He then slid a map across the table. "Here's a good street map of Shanghai."

Kip took the money and map and placed them in his briefcase. "If there's a write-up on the managers, I'd like to review it before this morning's meeting?"

"*No hay problema.*" There's no problem.

Sal's driver pulled away from the hotel and drove his two passengers through downtown Shanghai and onto the wide circular onramp leading to the Nanpu Bridge. On the Pudong side, row upon row of high-rise apartment buildings were lined up like standing domino tiles. All faced south.

Sal said, "That's *feng shui*."

"I don't follow you."

"Those buildings you're looking at. They're laid out like that because of an ancient Chinese custom of harmonious design. It's called *feng shui*."

"Oh, yeah. The interior designer who did my penthouse said something about *feng shui*."

"Was that when Marci moved in?"

Kip winced.

After a moment, Sal broke the silence. "Sorry about that, *Tuchi*."

"Don't worry about it."

Wanting to lighten the mood, Sal said, "Well, you're finally getting to ride along the infamous Longdong Road."

Kip looked up ahead. "We're on it?"

"Yes."

"I'm so honored." Kip couldn't help breaking into a smile. *Longdong? I don't think I'll ever get used to that name.*

"This road is important in that it runs due east from downtown Pudong towards the coastline and Shanghai Shores."

Twenty minutes later, the car pulled off the main road and onto a two lane paved thoroughfare through the small village of Chaoyeng. From the village, the main gate of Shanghai Shores could be seen straight ahead. *I'm glad I came here yesterday so the place is a little familiar to me.*

There was considerably more traffic than the day before. Cars, minivans, and taxis were coming in and out. They passed a yellow school bus packed with young children.

Kip asked, "Where are they headed?"

"The kids here attend the Pudong International Academy, an American school just down the road a few miles."

The clubhouse was bustling with activity when Kip and Sal walked in. A tenant was standing at the counter talking with the receptionist. Several people were sitting in the waiting area while employees made their way to and from the back offices. Laughter came from someone down the hallway.

Sal led Kip upstairs and into the office previously used by Ralph Maddox. He picked up a folder on the desk and handed it to Kip. "Okay, *Tuchi*, here's the information on the managers you asked for."

"This'll take just a few minutes." Kip sat down and began to speed read the entries while jotting down some notes.

Sal said, "Take your time."

Kip looked up. "Done."

Sal said, "In China, news about the most trivial things will get passed on with lighting speed, particularly with the advent of cell phones. I'm sure the managers already know something's up for today."

Kip closed the folder and said, "Well, I'm ready when you are."

The two men left the office and headed down to the conference room. From the hallway, the buzz of people talking inside could be heard. As soon as they opened the door, everyone sitting around the table stopped talking and looked their way. Manny and Rory were sitting together. Kip nodded at them while he and Sal sat down at the head of the table.

Just as Sal was about to address the group, Jessie Han, Manager of Tenant Services, burst into the room out of breath and sat down, "Sorry I'm late."

Sal said, "Glad you could make it, Jessie."

Hearing several of the other managers snickering, she blushed and slipped into a seat next to Rory. He leaned toward her and whispered, "I think you've been busted, wee lassie."

Sal said, "Okay, let's get down to business. *Zao shang hao*. It's nice to see you today. On behalf of Ingram Capital, I am pleased to announce that we've made some important changes at Shanghai Shores."

While Sal was talking, Kip looked around the table to study the managers' faces. Some were attentive while others stared down at the table without showing any expression.

"On Friday, I accepted the resignations of Ralph Maddox."

All eyes in the room riveted on Sal, then to Kip. Several then looked at each other with raised eyebrows. No one had ever been fired since the first employee was hired five years earlier.

Shelly Tang, the personnel manager, gasped, "What?"

Sal continued, "He's no longer allowed in the building or anywhere else on the property."

Jessie Han said, "What happened?"

"Jessie, what happened to him is not important. All of you know that we've been losing tenants steadily in the past two years. We've got to stop this trend and bring our occupancy back up as soon as possible. And to do that, I've brought in the brightest man I know to turn this place around. Everybody, I'm pleased to introduce your new manager—Kip Duchene."

Kip nodded to the group.

Sal said, "Compared to the limited role that Ralph had, Kip will have full hiring and firing authority as Managing Director of Shanghai Shores. In other words, Kip will not require corporate approval to make operational decisions."

Sal took a short pause to let what he had said sink in. "At this point, I'll turn the meeting over to Kip."

With an air of confidence, Kip stood, flicked off a piece of lint from his sleeve, and buttoned his suit coat. "Thank you, Sal." He looked deliberately around the table, making eye contact with each person. "With your help, we can put Shanghai Shores back on the map. Since we're meeting for the first time, I'd like to ask each of you to introduce yourself and tell me a little about your job. Rory, would you mind starting us off?"

"No problem, mate," he said.

Kip took notes as each manager spoke. At the same time, he quietly studied their reaction to his presence. Some were enthusiastic, nodding their heads and smiling. Others avoided eye contact with him. From the corner of his eyes, he noticed that three of the women were whispering to each other as the introductions were being made.

After everyone spoke, Kip said, "Starting today, I'll meet with each of you on a one-to-one basis, listening to your ideas about the problems we face, and what you think can be done to make improvements. For now, does anyone have anything they would like to discuss?"

After an awkward silence in the room, Rory spoke up, "Kip, welcome aboard. We really could use a new direction here. From my point of view, the change was damn well needed."

"Thanks, Rory. Anyone else?"

Jessie Han raised her hand, "I agree with Rory. I think that Shanghai Shores is a special place. I love it here and look forward to working with you, Mr. Duchene."

"Thank you, Jessie." Kip was glad to see a Chinese person speak up. "Everyone, please call me Kip."

Someone giggled at the far end of the conference table. It was Patti Bo, the manager of information technology. "You're prettier than Ralph."

Caught off guard by Patti's remark, Kip and Sal broke out laughing.

Barely speaking above a whisper, Manny said, "Mr. Kip, the houses is undesirable."

Noticing his poor English, Kip said, "What do you mean, Manny?"

"Well, carpets is stained, cigarette burns on countertops, and cracks on floor tiles. I think people do not like houses like this. They rent in villas elsewhere."

"Maybe you could show me around some of the homes later," said Kip.

"That be good, boss."

Priscilla Mao spoke up, but in Shanghainese rather than English. Shelly Tang automatically translated, "She says that the operation is not doing so poorly. It's just that Shores is so isolated from the downtown area and it takes almost an hour to drive out here."

"Thank you, Priscilla." Kip added to his notes.

Patti raised her hand.

Kip said, "Yes, Patti?"

"When do you think you'll be meeting with me?" She was giggling half way through her question.

Another ripple of laughter came from the group.

Kip thought Patti was like the girl in high school who was not particularly beautiful but so full of life you couldn't help but like her. Her chubbiness and round face were easily forgotten when she laughed with sparkling eyes.

"Well, how about if I ask you to be first?" asked Kip.

Patti brought her hands to her chest and exclaimed, "I'm in love!"

The entire room erupted into laughter.

After everyone calmed down, Kip looked to the far end of the table at Beverly Shen, their in-house legal counsel, and said, "Beverly, I haven't heard from you yet. Do you have any comments to share?"

"Mr. Duchene—sorry—Kip, I'm very glad that you're here and I'll be pleased to assist you in any way possible. As you may know, I take care of legal issues for the development, including creditors. We can talk later."

Kip nodded. "That's fair." *Okay, she's obviously a savvy woman.*

Beverly distinguished herself from the rest of the managers. Rather than wearing plain slacks and blouses as the others did, she had on a smart well-tailored suit, wore tastefully applied make-up, and groomed her hair attractively. Kip noticed that most Chinese women on the street wore no makeup and had the same basic hairstyle, parted in the middle and hanging straight down or pulled back into a ponytail. Beverly also spoke perfect English.

Kip guessed that she was well educated and raised in an affluent family.

He looked around the table and concluded, "I'll try to get to as many of you today as possible. If not today, we'll meet within the next few days. Unless anyone else has more to say, let's adjourn."

As the group shuffled out of the room, Kip said to Sal, "Are you going to stick around for a minute?"

"Yeah. I'm curious to hear what your first impressions are."

While Kip and Sal were conferring in the clubhouse, Priscilla Mao, Naomi Chen, and Shelly Tang slipped into Priscilla's office in the Green Latrine and closed the door behind them. Priscilla turned to the other two and said in an uppity tone, "Mr. Duchene might dress and talk like some important white man, but he's about to get a dose of China that he'll long remember."

The women looked at each other and broke into laughter.

Chapter 11

"Well, I didn't expect that," said Kip.

Sal said, "Expect what?"

"For starters, I've never conducted a meeting where half the people in the room were looking off into space."

Sal reached over and patted Kip on the shoulder. "Just hang in there. You'll soon learn that most Chinese don't handle sudden changes very well. Believe me, *amigo*, it had nothing to do with your pretty face or your Armani suit."

Kip chuckled. "What then?"

"It's just another example of saving face."

"I'm still lost, *Yani*. We also save face in the States."

"Ah, there's a difference though. Chinese are most comfortable when things are predictable and there are no surprises. If they know what to expect, there's less chance that they'll look stupid. But if they're thrown into a new situation, many automatically react by not saying much. Otherwise, they could say the wrong thing and end up losing face."

Wiping beads of sweat from his brow, Kip thought, *Christ, it's humid. I could use a nice cold beer right about now*. "So it's that bad with this face thing?"

"Don't look at it as good or bad. It's just part of their culture. Believe me, *Tuchi*, Chinese people are just as confused about our way of life as we are about theirs. They notice Americans acting as though they're superior to them. Yet, they wonder how we can think so highly of ourselves."

"How so?"

"For starters, we don't respect our elders anywhere close to the way they do. There's violence in every American city – yet, you can walk around in any city in

China without fear of being assaulted. Half of the marriages in our country end in divorce. Our children are kidnapped and murdered right off the—"

Kip held up his hands. "Okay. I get your point." He pulled a handkerchief out of his pocket and mopped his forehead.

"You okay?"

While Kip was neatly refolding his handkerchief, he said, "What?"

"You're sweating, *amigo*, that's all. It's only 76 degrees in this air conditioned room."

"I'm okay."

Sal said, "Getting back to what I was saying, just be patient with understanding the people over here. Once the managers get to know you, I guarantee that most of them will work their butts off for you."

"I hope so. By the way, did you notice the whispering going on between . . ." Kip glanced down at his notes. "Priscilla, Naomi, and Shelly?"

"Yeah, I did. Whadaya think they're up to?"

"Hell if I know."

"Any hunches?"

Kip raked his hand through his hair and said, "Whatever it is, I know I'm not going to like it when I find out."

"Just remember, you've got a free rein to do whatever is needed."

"From what I've already seen, I'm going to have to do a lot."

"Good." Sal reached over and squeezed Kip's shoulder. "Say, are you up for another Italian dinner tonight?"

"Sure, but let's not make it a late evening. I'm still feeling a little jetlagged."

"No problem. One more thing before I head out. Until you get an executive assistant, I suggest that you consider using Jessie Han for now. Her English is excellent and she knows the tenants much better than the others. She also seems to have a good attitude."

"Okay, I'll talk to her."

Sal stood. "I'm outta here. Since the conference room is the only space currently being used on this floor, why don't you take a look around and pick an office for yourself?" He pointed down the hallway. "Maybe that corner one. It has a great view of the ocean."

"I'll take a look."

"By the way, we've arranged delivery of a new Buick sedan for you in a day or two. The minivan we took on the tour yesterday is also available anytime."

Kip said, "Good. I'll see you this afternoon then."

The two men gave each other a hug. Sal said, "I sometimes worry about you."

"It's nothing that a cold beer couldn't cure."

"Shhhit . . . It's only eleven-fucking-thirty in the morning."

"It's eight-thirty in the evening in California."

Sal slowly shook his head as he walked away.

While Kip and Sal were talking, Naomi listened in on their conversation in the Green Latrine with her office door closed. The first time she heard her name, she pressed the headset closer to her ears.

Eager to get started, Kip called Jessie and asked her to join him in the conference room. While he was waiting for her to come up, he peered out the window and watched Sal's driver open the car door for him in the parking lot three floors below. The distant horizon was obscured by the ever present smog that draped itself like a blanket over everything.

When Jessie walked in, Kip motioned for her to take the seat opposite to him. Smiling, he said, "Jessie, I've heard good things about you from Sal and wanted to compliment you for the excellent job you've done at Shanghai Shores."

"Really?" Her eyebrows shot up and she flashed a radiant smile.

"Yes. I called you up to ask if you'd be interested in temporarily assisting me until I can recruit an executive assistant. Are you okay with that?"

"Of course. My pleasure."

"Good. I only have a few requirements. Everything you see and hear is absolutely confidential. No sharing information with anyone."

"I understand."

"Second, whenever I'm meeting with one of the managers, please take detailed notes. You can do that?"

"Ah . . . there could be a problem with that."

"Why's that?"

"Shanghai people usually favor their own kind. They look down on people who are not Shanghainese." She drops her gaze down to the table.

"I'm not following you."

"I'm from Kunming."

"Where's that?"

"It's in the southwest part of China. I have to work harder than the locals to keep up because I'm an outsider. It's okay though, I'm used to it. I'm just wondering how they'll react when they see me taking notes in front of them."

Kip was grateful that Jessie had shared something he'd never know otherwise. He smiled at her. "Just leave that to me. Let's go ahead and get started. You can run down to your office and grab a notepad, then ask Patti to meet us in the conference room in fifteen minutes."

Jessie stood up smiling brightly. "Thanks. I'll try hard to please you."

Kip gently patted her on the shoulder. "I know you will. Ah . . . Jessie, could you also have someone in the restaurant stock the refrigerator up here with some Budweiser beer?"

"Sure."

"Good. Go ahead and have it delivered now."

Kip was taking notes when a man walked into the room carrying a cardboard box. He knelt down and set several six-packs of beer into the refrigerator and left. As soon as the door clicked shut, Kip pulled out one of the bottles, twisted off the cap and took a long pull. *Jesus, I needed that.*

When Jessie returned, she said, "Before Patti gets up here I wanted to tell you to not be fooled by her. Her silliness is just an act. She's actually very well educated in computer technology and could probably write a book on the subject."

"If she's so bright, why's she working at Shanghai Shores?   Surely she could get a better paying job elsewhere."

"Maybe not. Most educated people in China would prefer to work for a foreign company rather than a Chinese one. A SOE would be the worst kind of company to work for."

"What's a SOE?"

"State-owned enterprise."

"Got it."

"Anyway, foreign companies treat their employees much better than Chinese ones. So the brightest graduates will try to get jobs with a foreign company. Patti's no different. She's also been exposed to English-speaking people here at Shores. Most Chinese are taught English in school but few get the opportunity—"

Her explanation was interrupted when Patti raced in through the door. She was out of breath. "Sorry I'm late."

"You're fine." Kip motioned for her to sit across from him. Patti looked over at Jessie.

"I've asked Jessie to take notes for me," said Kip.

"Okay." She sat down and smiled.

"Patti, I'm looking forward to getting better acquainted with you. For now, I'd like to understand exactly what you do here."

Without hesitation, she started, "When I was hired two years ago, the company's computer systems were really outdated. So I upgraded the cabling, hardware and most of the operating and program software. I also did a makeover of the company's network infrastructure, complete with installing a backup T-3 circuit to provide redundancy." Raising her eyebrows, she paused and looked expectantly at Kip.

With a knowing smile, he said, "Go ahead, I'm with you."

His invitation opened a floodgate of highly technical computer jargon. At one point, Kip asked, "Patti, what kind of firewall is connected to our circuits?"

"A Cisco 1700."

Kip nodded his head. *I'm impressed.*

Periodically Jessie had to interrupt Patti, "Would you please spell that for me?"

After hearing about Patti's work, he asked about her personal life. She eagerly told about her life experiences, playing the parts of people in her life. She cleverly mimicked their voices and mannerisms, gesticulated with her whole body, and laughed at her own monologues. Kip concluded that he would enjoy working with this joyful Chinese woman. Before excusing her, he said, "I have one more question for you."

Still smiling, she said, "Of course!"

"Why do you think we're having problems here at Shores?"

Her eyes darted from Jessie to Kip. Barely above a whisper, she said, "Be careful."

"I don't understand."

"I shouldn't say more. Just be careful of Priscilla."

He decided not to press her further. "Thank you, Patti. That'll be all for now."

Reigniting her smile, she popped up from the chair. "I'm glad you're here." After she scurried out, the room was momentarily quiet.

Kip looked over at Jessie and said, "Any idea what she's talking about?"

"Sort of. Patti's in the position to know just about everything that's happening in the company. She took a big chance to warn you."

"That's good to know. Okay, let's see the personnel manager next." Looking down at his notes, he said, "That's Shelly Tang, right?"

"Yes."

"Okay, then send her up."

Ten minutes later, there was a light rap on the door and Shelly walked in. Kip guessed that she was in her mid-thirties. She had a pixie-cut hairdo with bangs in front and wore thick eyeglasses.

Standing to greet her, Kip said, "Shelly, please have a seat. I'm glad to have the opportunity to meet you and learn more about your responsibilities here. To get started, please brief me on what personnel procedures I should know as general manager."

Shelly's response was polite and informative. She began by going over the company's health insurance plan and providing names of the medical clinic and hospital that employees use for routine checkups and emergencies. She asked Kip for his passport so they could register him with the local office of public security.

"What's public security?"

"The police department." She explained that all foreigners in China need to register their whereabouts with the government and keep their issued residency slip in a safe place.

Kip handed her a folder and said, "Shelly, this is a copy of my personal health insurance policy from the States. In the unlikely event that I encounter a serious illness or injury, I want to be treated in the U.S. rather than China. In an emergency, my insurance will pay for me to be air evacuated back home. This information should be part of my personnel records."

Shelly said, "I understand."

"Thank you. I guess that's it for now. Obviously I'll have a lot of questions for you in the days ahead. Thanks for coming in."

"What about your passport?"

"Oh, yeah." Kip reached into his attaché case and handed it to her.

After Shelly left, Kip turned to Jessie and said, "Jessie, this would be a good time for you and me to talk. Other than the hassles of not being Shanghainese, how are things going for you?"

"It's okay," she said, shrugging her shoulders.

"How could it be better?"

"I'm not sure." She began to click the retractor button of her ballpoint pen up-and-down.

He changed his approach. "What do you think I should know about the operation at this time?"

"Well, I don't think that Ralph Maddox did a very good job here."

"Such as?"

"Well, the tenants are really upset with how Shores is being run these days. When I started five years ago, we used to have regular tenant meetings. It wasn't perfect, but at least the tenants felt that management was trying to make Shores a better place to live."

Kip said, "Are you saying that the tenant meetings have stopped?"

"Yes. Ralph always had something negative to say about the tenants and accused them of complaining about too many trivial things. Eventually, he decided to stop having tenant meetings altogether. In order to keep the tenants appeased, I started monthly teas so the women could at least get together and vent their frustrations."

"A good move on your part." He glanced at his watch and saw that it was almost noon. "Where can I get something to eat?"

"If you'd like, I can take you down to our restaurant on the second floor and introduce you to Paul Zhou, our restaurant manager."

"Why wasn't he at the managers' meeting?"

"Priscilla actually controls the restaurant and gives the reports instead of Paul."

"What else does Priscilla control?"

"Administration, security, transportation, infrastructure, and the restaurant. Indirectly, she also controls finance and personnel."

After excusing Jessie, Kip walked over to the window and looked out at the South China Sea. *Jesus, how could Priscilla be allowed to control so damn much? I'll rein her in or she's out of here.*

Chapter 12

That evening, Sal's driver drove Kip into a quaint neighborhood in the Luwar district, a ten-minute drive from the hotel. The surrounding two-story stucco buildings had shuttered windows and vines on the walls, reminding him of villages in southern France. As he was making his way towards the entrance of Casanova's Restaurant, Kip took a moment to savor the balmy evening and smell the syrupy fragrance of jasmine blossoms hanging from an overhead trellis.

"*Que estaś haciendo, cabroń?*" boomed Sal's voice as Kip walked into the darkened cocktail lounge.

Kip thought – *Okay, he's already had a few*. He looked around. "Nice place."

"Yeah, and the food's fantastic. So, tell me, how did the rest of your day go?"

Kip sat across from Sal and sighed, "Enlightening, to say the least."

"I want to hear all about it." He held up a finger. "Just a minute." He finished off his drink and handed the empty glass to the waitress. "We'll take two more of these." He turned back to Kip. "Okay, *amigo*, shoot."

"Well, I know for sure that we've got a big problem with personnel. What would you say if you knew Priscilla is controlling the company?"

"You're shitting me?" Sal raised his eyebrows in surprise.

"It's true. I could use a good spy in the company about now."

"Too bad Angie didn't jump aboard."

"Yeah, it was."

"Did you decide to have Jessie help you for now?"

"I did. She's smart and seems to be loyal. However, she's not strong enough for the long haul, particularly when I start cleaning house."

"I know, I know. Just be careful about how you do the shit. Remember, you're in China, and the labor laws favor employees over employers. I'd hate for you to get into an early pissing match and have you distracted from your biggest problem?"

"Which is?" Kip raised a hand.

"Rico fuckin' Niu."

Kip chuckled. "Not to worry. By the way, you promised this would be an early evening."

"Not to worry. I'll tuck you in bed myself." Just as the two men were saying *"Salud"* and clicking glasses, the hostess walked over. "Mr. Estrada, your table's ready."

The dining room walls were adorned with frescoes of traditional Italian scenes. The lights were dimmed along with the muted background sounds of clinking of glasses, people talking, and the strum of mandolin music resonating out of speakers. The hostess led the two men between tables through the packed dining room and showed them to a private booth on the far side.

A Chinese waitress, dressed in a crisp tuxedo shirt, white bowtie, and black trousers, walked over to them smiling and announced the specials of the day. After she set leather-bound menus in front of them and left, Sal said, "By the way, your Buick will be delivered on site sometime tomorrow."

"What color is it anyway?"

"It's one of three colors. That's all I know."

"What three colors?"

"Black, black or black."

Laughing, Kip reached across the table and swatted him on the shoulder.

Sal said, "At least you can choose whatever driver you want to use. I think one of them even speaks English."

"Thanks, I'll look them over."

"Another thing. You can stay at the hotel indefinitely or take one of the houses at Shanghai Shores. If you did, that would eliminate your commute and give you an inside view of the place."

"Yeah, I'd prefer to move out there."

"*Perfecto, Tuchi!*"

"Excuse me, gentlemen," interrupted a portly man with rosy cheeks who had walked up to their booth. He spoke with a heavy German accent. "My wife and I couldn't help but overhear you talking about Shanghai Shores. Well, we live there."

Kip and Sal stood and took turns shaking hands with the stranger.

"A pleasure, gentlemen. I'm Hans." He then nodded toward an attractive middle-age woman with chestnut hair sitting at an adjacent table. She smiled and nodded her head.

Hans said, "That's Trudy. Your first time to Casanova's?"

"It's mine," answered Kip.

"If I might, I suggest that you allow Matteo, the chef, to create a special off-menu dinner for you."

Sal flipped his menu shut and said, "Sounds good to me." He looked at Kip.

Kip nodded.

"Ah, *sehr gut*," said Hans smiling. "Trudy and I have been coming here for several years. You're in for a treat. So if you'll excuse me, gentlemen, I'll get back to eating and get the word to Matteo."

Kip said, "Thanks. By the way, when your schedule allows I'd like to get together with you and pick your brains about your experiences at Shanghai Shores."

Hans raised his eyebrows. "You really want to know?"

"Yes."

"Consider it done then."

Ten minutes later Kip and Sal started their specially prepared meal by sipping Campari. Kip said, "This is a tad too sweet for me."

"It's good for your digestion."

"I'll stick to beer and this delicious antipasto." The platter between them had an assortment of cheeses, thinly-sliced prosciutto, olives and fresh vegetables. "Say, how are Maria and the kids doing?"

"*Qué la mádre*, they love it here!" said Sal, a little too loud. "Maria has her own maid and the kids are having a ball. Everyone misses family and friends back home, but they're okay."

While Sal was chattering away, Kip realized that the Chinese man sitting in the adjoining booth looked out of place. He wasn't conversing with his fellow diner, and he just poked at the food on his plate. His back was pressed against the bench seat opposite Sal with his head partially turned. *I'll be damn. This guy is listening in on our conversation.* Kip got Sal's attention by motioning with his head toward the man. "*Con cuidado.*" He hoped Sal understood why he was saying to be careful.

He did by quickly changing the subject. "Where in the fuck is our waitress anyway?" He swiveled his head around the room until he was looking face-to-face with the shocked eavesdropper a mere two feet away. The man's eyes widened and his mouth dropped open. Sal gave him his classic smile and said in a quiet voice, "Hello, *amigo.*"

Kip brought his hand up to his face while trying to keep from laughing. He failed.

Without saying a word, the man and his companion slipped out of their booth and headed for the stairway.

Sal turned back to Kip. "I think the man shit in his Chinese pants."

Still giggling, Kip said, "He was paying more attention to us than eating."

"What'd I tell you yesterday? It's hard to eat out without some local eavesdropping on what you say."

Turning serious, Kip said, "I hate to act paranoid, *Yani*, but I have a feeling they knew exactly who we were."

"I don't know. Say, did you notice the guy sitting across from him? He was sure an ugly fucker with all those scars on his face and a fucked up ear."

Kip said, "Yeah, I noticed. Well, let's forget about them long enough to enjoy our meal. I see the waitress heading our way with a platter of food."

For their main course, they were served white truffles, Florentine steak and several varieties of fresh pasta bathed in Pendolino olive oil and crushed garlic. The steamy aroma floating up from their plates made Kip's mouth water. He said, "Let's dive in."

When spumoni gelato was being served to them with the dark espresso coffee, Hans walked up to their table with a bottle in his hand. "Might I tempt you gentlemen with a nice glass of Grappa?"

Sal enthusiastically said, "*Amigo*, grab your pretty wife over there and slide on in with us."

Hans turned out to be a hilariously funny man. His uninhibited humor kept everyone at the table in stitches. When he told stories, he whimsically spoke with several accents: Italian, French, British and Russian. Trudy was an attractive, well groomed woman, but didn't say much. She laughed along with Hans' storytelling, swept up with laughter one moment, and embarrassed with Han's outrageous antics the next. The waitress brought over a second bottle of Grappa and said, "Matteo said this one's on the house."

Once Hans switched to speaking fluent Spanish, Kip thought – *Oh, shit, this is going to be one hell of an evening.* For a few hours, Kip was able to laugh without feeling grief for his beloved Marci.

Chapter 13

Kip was hanging up his suit coat at the office the next morning when the phone rang. It was Sal. "How'd you like Casanova's?"

"Other than the axe-in-the-head hangover, it was a great time. Hans is really something, isn't he?"

"He's a fuckin' wild man."

Kip said, "That, my friend, he is. What's up?"

"I've been thinking about what you said about Priscilla last night. *Tuchi*, you'll need to be very careful how you deal with her."

"What's your suggestion?"

"It's going to take you awhile for you to learn how to resolve conflict the Chinese way. Maybe ask Jessie what she thinks. Back home, you'd handle this kind of problem without screwing around."

"You bet your ass I would. So?"

"So, it won't work over here."

"What if I put Priscilla on probation?"

"Ah, shit, *Tuchi*. Don't even think about it. That'd be fuckin' worse."

"How?"

"She'd lose *face* big time. You don't want that to happen."

"Okay, I'll figure something out." Kip wasn't about to tell Sal that he'd already decided how to take away Priscilla's power.

At 9:15 a.m., Jessie poked her head in the door and asked Kip if he needed anything.

"Yes, please get me the personnel files on Priscilla."

The smile on Jessie's face vanished and her eyes nervously darted away from him. "What's the matter, Jessie?"

"Ah . . . I don't think Shelly will hand them over to me."

"By the time you get to her office, she will."

Jessie nodded and walked out with an audible sigh.

Kip picked up the phone and called Shelly. "Hi Shelly, this is Kip. I want to review Priscilla's personnel records. No, Jessie is on her way over there to pick them up. Says who? Well, things are different now. Go ahead and seal the records in an envelope and give it to Jessie. Is that understood? Good. What's that? Oh, that. I'll pick up my residency permit at public security later today."

Twenty minutes later, Jessie walked back into the office with a smile on her face and handed Kip the envelope.

He said, "I've been reviewing the list of employees. It seems as though Priscilla, Naomi, and Shelly are rather close. What can you tell me about this?"

Jessie glanced furtively at the door, walked over, and closed it. She sat back down and said, "Please don't tell anyone I told you this."

"I won't – go ahead."

"Well, the staff calls them *The Gang of Three*. Do you know about the *Gang of Four* in China?"

"A little, but please explain anyway."

Sitting back into her chair, she said, "Let's see. After Chairman Mao died, his wife, Madam Jiang Qing, and three Party members from Shanghai conspired to seize power."

"When was that?"

"Sometime in the late 1970's. Anyway, the four were tried and found guilty of conspiracy against the State. The staff sees similarities with Priscilla, Naomi, and Shelly. It's obvious to us that the three have methodically taken control of the company. After someone joked about them as the *Gang of Three,* the name stuck ever since."

"Jessie, what would happen if I fired them?"

"Oh, that would be a big problem, I think."

"Why?"

"It's complicated. It would cost the company a lot of money. The three women were hired about the same time five years ago. According to labor laws, we would need to pay them one month's salary for every year employed."

"We could manage that."

"Well, there's more. I know that they would also file grievances against the company with the Shanghai Labor Bureau, claiming they have been financially and emotionally injured. In China, government officials typically favor the worker in any dispute with an employer, particularly if it's foreign owned."

"Anything more?"

"Yes. I'll bet that they've compiled information against other employees and the company and would threaten to expose the information to government authorities if they're ever threatened with being fired."

"Are you serious?"

"I'm sorry. This is the way things are done in China."

Kip closed his eyes and slowly shook his head. "*Jesus*, I just can't believe this."

His instinct told him to do something decisive about the *Gang of Three* despite what Sal and Jessie had advised. Yet, how could Shanghai Shores be turned around in less than a year by going slow? While Kip was mulling over this question, Jessie silently waited for him to say who he wanted to see next. He finally looked up. "Give Rory a call and ask him to meet us in the conference room."

In stark contrast to Kip's business attire, Rory walked into the room wearing a straw cowboy hat, dark green polo shirt, tan shorts, and New Balance tennis shoes. After the two men shook hands, Kip said, "Go ahead and take a seat. I've asked Jessie to take notes for us. Do you mind?"

"Not a bit." Rory slipped off his hat and wiped his sweaty face with a handkerchief before lowering his formidable frame into a chair.

"Rory, what's the present condition of our utility systems?"

"You don't want to know, mate. 'Tis bad."

"Tell me anyway." Kip flipped his pencil on the table and sat back.

"In a wee nutshell, the maintenance of our equipment has been sorely neglected due to a tight budget and poor management. In China, you'll see that equipment is not maintained very well. People here tend to run a piece of machinery into the ground. Once it breaks down, they go about a fix with crude methods."

Jessie absentmindedly nodded in agreement without looking up.

"We've got patchwork repairs in all of the plant facilities. Our satellite TV system is falling apart. Ralph let our water and electric bills become seriously overdue. You dinnae mess about with these government companies over here. Someone's paying off officials at the utility companies; otherwise they would've marched in and shut us down long ago."

"That's not what I was hoping to hear," said Kip, while nervously running his hand through his hair.

"No worries, mate. I've been in bloody worse situations and did very well for myself." Rory smiled.

"Good to hear. Rory, go ahead and prepare a comprehensive analysis of the problems and your assessment of what needs to be done to correct them. I'll also need an estimate on what'll it cost to do the fixes."

"Consider it done, mate."

"Okay, then. That'll be it for now."

After Rory left, Kip said to Jessie. "I've decided to move out to Shores and stay in one of the houses. Do you have any suggestions?"

"Oh, I think that's a good idea. Being *da laoban*, you have to show good face."

"*Da laoban*?" Kip raised his eyebrows.

"It means the 'big boss.' I think you'd like the Marbella Estate the best."

"What's that?"

"It's one of the six large homes along the boardwalk facing the ocean. She stood up and pointed. It's also right next to the clubhouse so it would be convenient for you."

Kip looked in that direction. *Jeez, that's a hell of a lot of house for only one person. I'll bet it's at least 5,000 square feet.* "Okay, bring me a set of keys to several houses and I'll make a decision this afternoon. How long will it take to get a house set up for me?"

"Unless Manny's crew needs to go in to repaint or make repairs, we can have one ready for you within twenty-four hours."

Later that afternoon, Kip and Jessie looked through a number of houses before ending up at the Marbella Estate. As soon as Kip walked into the family room and saw the panoramic view of the East China Sea, he envisioned himself living there. The room was open to the sunroom on the right and a modern kitchen to the rear with sweeping countertops and an eating bar. With Jessie in tow, Kip walked into the kitchen. "Nice layout."

"It is. The expats also love the American-made appliances. Chinese people, however, don't like Western-style kitchens like this that are open to other rooms."

"Why's that?"

"We regard the kitchen as a work area that should be closed off by walls from the living quarters. Besides, with Chinese cooking we have a lot of steam, splattered oil, and cooking smells – that's not so good when you're entertaining guests." Jessie then showed Kip the rest of the house and they ended back in the sunroom. It jutted out to the rear deck with five angled walls, each affording a different view of the ocean.

Kip thought, *if I have to live in this godforsaken country, this is the place.*

On their way back to the clubhouse, Kip told Jessie that he liked the Marbella Estate and asked her to have it ready for him by the weekend.

At his desk, Kip thought that the architect was clever in designing the master plan. Homes closest to the ocean were the most luxurious and were all one story. Further back, homes were two stories. The three-story townhouses ran along the inner most part of the compound away from the shoreline. Like seats in an amphitheater, the homes were tiered in a way to offer most of them a view of the ocean. He was impressed.

Half way through the stack of telephone messages, Kip saw that Milt Avery had called. He was the field officer attached to the U.S. Consulate Office in Shanghai that Sal warned him about. He decided to call the man. On the third ring, an unenthusiastic voice answered, "Avery here."

"Mr. Avery, this is Kip Duchene at Shanghai Shores."

"Oh, yeah, the new guy trying to stop the ship from sinking. I'd like to get together and help you straighten things out, that is if it's not too late. When can we meet?"

Regretting that he called, Kip swept his hair back with his free hand and said, "How about sometime next week?"

"Why not today?"

"Mr. Avery, I just arrived three days ago and can't see you until next week."

"I still think you'd be smart to meet me today." Kip didn't reply on the other end. Breaking the awkward silence, Avery finally said, "Well, if you insist, I can come over on Monday morning."

"Two o'clock?"

"That would be fine. You know, the U.S. government is behind you all the way. See you then." Avery abruptly hung up.

Kip thought—*What a jerk.*

The phone rang. Fearing that Avery might be calling him back, he looked at the caller ID and smiled. *Good, I can always count on Sal to pep me up.* "Hi, *Yani*, what's up?"

In a strained voice, Sal said, "Have you heard about the girl in Haikou?"

"No. What girl?"

"News just broke that a kidnapped 13-year-old girl was found on a street corner in the downtown area. She's the daughter of an American scientist who had given a speech at some conference in a nearby—"

"Wait a minute!" blurted Kip. "I remember reading something in the *Shanghai Daily* about an expert in water pollution who was supposed to give a speech in China. You think he's the guy?"

"Has to be. The man took his wife and daughter with him. They planned to vacation in Sanya after the conference. Anyway, the girl was snatched off of the streets yesterday."

Kip said, "Well, at least she was returned."

"Yeah, *Tuchi*, she was." Sal's lowered his voice. "But whoever took her had her left leg amputated just below the knee. Evidently, the surgery was performed by physician because of the way the wound was sutured and dressed."

"Ah, jeez." Kip put his hand to his face imagining the terrifying experience of the girl.

Sal said, "An hour later, the father got a hand-delivered note in his hotel room."

"What'd it say?"

"Remember Belgrade."

Chapter 14

Kip said, "I don't understand."

"I don't understand either. The only connection I can make between Belgrade and China is when we bombed the Chinese Embassy during the Kosovo War."

"I thought China was supposed to be safe?"

"It is. This is just some sort of weird shit."

"Where in the hell is Haikou anyway?"

"It's the largest city on Hainan Island. It's also where Rico Niu lives"

"*Jesus*, is he a suspect?" Kip stood up and paced back-and-forth.

"No, and he'll never be named."

"Why in the hell not?"

"Niu controls the local police by making generous bribes, so I'm told."

Kip stopped. "You've got to be kidding."

"Not at all. And here's something else. Two years ago, there was a similar report that the daughter of an official from the Pentagon was kidnapped in the city of Chengdu. When she was returned, her left leg was amputated just like this girl. That case is still unsolved." After a brief pause, Sal said, "Be very careful, *Tuchi*. If Rico is involved in this shit, the man's more fuckin' dangerous than I thought."

After hanging up, Kip thought about what Sal said. *Surely things can't get any worse.* He pulled out the lower right-hand drawer of his desk and grabbed a bottle of vodka he'd stashed. He splashed several ounces in his coffee cup and washed it down while questioning his decision to come to China. After spritzing his mouth with breath freshener, he called Jessie. "Please ask Beverly to meet us in the conference room."

Beverly Shen walked in wearing a pinstriped business suit, neatly-pressed white blouse, and black high heel shoes. Beverly and Jessie greeted each other with smiles and animated conversation. He said, "Do you prefer to be called Beverly or Bev?"

"Most people call me Bev."

"Good. If you don't mind, I'd like to jump right into the legal issues. Could you give me a brief summary of where we currently stand?"

"Well, the creditors are our greatest problem. Actually, I think they could shut us down."

"How's that?"

"Ralph ignored our creditors, so I tried to pacify them as best I could. But no matter what I've been able to do, they will not let the Chinese New Year pass without getting something."

"When's that?"

"January 29th."

"Why Chinese New Year?"

"Well, people all through China take a week to ten days to celebrate the New Year. They return to their home villages by the millions on buses, trains and by air. In advance of the holiday, it's traditional for people to try to collect money that's owed to them. Some people won't hesitate to resort to violence in order to get their money."

"Don't Chinese people also try to pay off their debts? You know, for honor."

Bev and Jessie looked at each other and broke out laughing.

Kip shrugged his shoulders. *I wonder what's so damn funny?* He flipped his notebook open. "Bev, how much do we owe?"

"Naomi estimated about $2.5 million."

Kip raised his eyebrows. "Are we talking U.S. dollars?"

"Yes. I know it's a lot."

"Okay. Let's get back to why you think our creditors could shut us down?"

"Well, count on them to block our main gate sometime in early January. They'll put up angry signs and denounce Shanghai Shores for owing them money. As long as they're demonstrating, no one will be able to get in or out of Shores."

"The local police will disband them, won't they?"

"Actually . . . no," said Bev. "If we call them, they may send over a squad car at the most to observe from across the street. However, the policemen will just sit in the car and do nothing unless a bad fight breaks out."

"*Jesus*, you can't be serious. How do you know all this?"

"It's happened before to us."

Kip just shook his head.

Bev continued. "Unless we can satisfy our creditors before the New Year, I think they'll storm our gate and resort to violence."

"Okay, Bev, I get it. Here's what we can do to help prevent that. First, rank the creditors by how tough they'll be to satisfy. Hopefully, some can be put off without making any payment. Others will require at least a token payment. The worst will demand larger payments."

She said, "Okay. We're also behind in making payments to the power bureau. I worry about this a lot."

"What are the consequences?"

"Some low-level government bureaucrat could decide to make a name for himself by giving notice that our electric service will be turned off unless we pay in full. It could happen. As a matter of fact, I'm sure it would have happened already if it wasn't for Mr. Ingram's presence in Shanghai."

"Do you have any suggestions?"

"Yes. The best way to resolve a problem in China is to show up in person. It gives the other person good face. As soon as possible, I also suggest that you arrange to meet

with some of our senior officials in the Shanghai
government and the most worrisome creditors. We need to
let them know that you have been hired to turn Shanghai
Shoes around and that you are committed to getting our
creditors paid as soon as possible. You should also bring
along gifts."

"Like what?"

"Maybe a good bottle of liquor."

"Okay. Moving onto a completely different subject, I'd
like to know what you think of Priscilla."

She stole a quick glance at Jessie and back to Kip.
"Priscilla is a hard worker and has assumed a lot of
responsibility at Shores in the absence of good leadership
by Ralph. At this late stage, I think that she may be difficult
for you to manage."

"Why's that?"

Bev sat up more erect in her chair. "Blame Ingram
Capital for putting a man like Ralph Maddox in charge, not
Priscilla. She's in her fifties with no college education and
only knows the old ways of thinking. The rest of the
managers here are younger and are college graduates. They
can understand Priscilla because she's the same age as their
parents. She's going to continue to grab whatever control
she can for as long as possible."

"What do you think would happen if she got fired?"

"Oh, that would be bad. Please understand that she's
more powerful than any of us, including you."

Kip raked his hand through his hair. "I can't pretend to
understand."

"I know," said Bev. "Just be very careful about how you
handle her."

"Thanks for being so willing to share your thoughts
about this. I appreciate it."

Heading for the door, she stopped and turned around.
"Please keep this confidential."

After the meeting, Kip went into the office and tried to
make sense of what he'd learned from Bev. The problems
at Shores were far more complicated than he ever imagined.

I'll be damned if I'm going to let Priscilla interfere with what I have to do here any longer. He reached for his bottom desk drawer.

In his Haikou office, Rico Niu listened intensely to the caller on the other end of the line. He had previously asked his source at Shanghai Shores to find out if the new manager had a daughter. He was disappointed to learn that Kip Duchene wasn't even married. But what he heard next transformed his frown into a wide smile. "Good work!" he said and hung up.

Rico turned to his bodyguard sitting across the desk from him. "Tao, I'll have another job for you soon."

Chapter 15

From a deep sleep, Kip jolted awake when the hotel room exploded with bright light. Just as suddenly, it plunged back into darkness. Disoriented, he faced the door to see who was there, but the flash of light had blinded him. He blinked repeatedly but couldn't see anyone. With adrenaline flooding through his body and his heart hammering wildly in his chest, he fumbled for the bedside lamp. Before he got a chance to turn it on, another flash of light lit up the room. *Shit, it's only lightning. Jesus, I hate China. I hate the backward ways they do things over here. I hate the idea of saving face. I hate that Priscilla's holding Shores captive.*

Kip felt helpless, trying to avoid slipping into a sinkhole of depression. He turned on the light and reached for the photo of Marci—*Hi, Princess. I'd give anything to hold you right now. I miss you more than ever.* Fighting back tears, he kissed the photograph and set it back, just as another flash of light filled the room, followed by an ear-splitting thunderclap. He jerked.

God, my nerves are shot. He slipped out of bed and padded over to the mini-bar.

The next morning Kip stopped half way up the clubhouse stairs, looked around, and took a deep breath. *My God, the sky's deep blue today.* A high pressure system had pushed the previous night's storm west towards Nanjing and brought with it a fresh onshore breeze.

Jessie was waiting in his office when he walked in. "Good morning, boss. What's on the schedule this morning?"

"Please ask Naomi to meet us in the conference room. Tell her to bring along the financial statements. "

Kip and Jessie were already seated when Naomi walked in with a pasted-on smile.

Kip motioned with his hand. "Please go ahead and sit down."

Naomi frowned when she saw Jessie.

Kip said, "I've asked Jessie to take notes for me. Naomi, when working with a troubled company, I first look at the way financial affairs have been managed. For this reason, I'll need your help to understand the system you use."

As Kip was talking, Naomi's eyes darted around the room, avoiding direct eye contact with him. She kept spinning a pen around in her hand nervously. Whenever Kip asked a question, her answers were brief and to the point. Kip thought – *Okay. She's going to be a real pain.*

Undistracted, he plowed ahead. "As such, there's no manager at Shores more important to me than you. Do you understand?"

"Yes, of course I do," said Naomi tersely. "I think you'll see that the financial reports I've prepared are well done."

"I have no reason to doubt you." Feeling irritable at Naomi's arrogance, he stood up and walked over to the window. After taking a moment to calm himself at the sight of the tranquil sea, he turned back toward her and asked, "Who manages the cash?"

"I do."

"Before coming over here, Sal sent me a copy of the annual financial statements from 1998 through 2004. In studying them, I had a hard time reconciling the figures. They don't seem to follow GAAP."

"What's that?"

Kip's arched his eyebrows in amazement. "You don't know?"

"Whatever it is, we don't need it in China," said Naomi with clenched teeth.

Losing it, he flew back to the table and slapped his open palm down on it. The unexpectedly loud report made Naomi flinch. He barked, "I don't give a damn!" After taking a deep breath, he said in a calmer voice, "For your information, GAAP means 'Generally Accepted Accounting Principles.' It's *the* accounting standard throughout the financial world. And, Naomi, that includes China. Do you understand?"

Naomi stared straight ahead.

He opened a file folder and handed her a copy of GAAP translated in Chinese. "Go ahead and take this. It was prepared by KPMG China as a guide to help Chinese companies comply with GAAP standards. I suggest you learn what it says from cover to cover as soon as possible. That'll do it for today."

As she stood up, she set a manila folder down with "2005" printed on the tab. "These are the financial statements you asked for that covers January through May."

Kip said, "I'll study these and tell you what we need to do to clean them up."

Just as Naomi reached the door, she mumbled, "X*iao hu ning,*" just loud enough to be heard.

Kip asked Jessie, "What'd she say?"

"It was nothing."

"*Jessie*, what did she say?"

"It's a Shanghainese insult that means 'stupid outsider.'"

He slowly shook his head. "I didn't think Chinese people were so quick to insult."

"Believe me, Kip, we're not. Most of us will do anything to avoid conflict. I really don't understand why Naomi thought she could get away with being so disrespectful to *da laoban*."

"Well, let's get back to business. Anything on your end?"

"The new Buick ordered for you was delivered this morning. Priscilla told me it'll be ready this afternoon. You need to make a decision on a driver."

"Have you met the man who speaks English?"

"I know him, but not well. He's Shanghainese and kind of hip in a way. You need to talk to him yourself."

"What's his name?"

"Benjamin Wu."

That afternoon, Kip and Jessie were in his office when there was a knock on the door. He called out, "Come in."

A nice-looking man with closely cropped hair walked in. In a deep, resonating voice, he said, "Hello. My name Benjamin."

Kip noticed that the man was wearing a small gold loop earring in his left ear. *Well, that's the first I've seen in China.* He shook Benjamin's hand and said, "Please have a seat."

After they spent ten minutes talking, Kip said, "Let's go ahead and put you on as my driver for the rest of the month. If everything works out okay, then we'll make it permanent."

"Okay, boss, that good for me. I treat you right."

"Good. Check out the new Buick and make sure everything's in order. I'm not interested in how quickly we can go from one place to the next, but I am a stickler for safety. Do you understand?"

"*Mei wenti*, boss."

Jessie looked over at Kip. "That means no problem."

I think that I'm going to like Benjamin. After Benjamin left, Kip said, "I want to talk to Priscilla next—please give her a call."

Kip had already decided not to wait for the slowness of the 'Chinese way' to unfold. He was going to handle Priscilla head-on. Heeding Sal and Bev's warning, he reluctantly ruled out firing her on the spot.

A few minutes later Priscilla walked into his office smiling. She was dressed in a colorful blouse and full black skirt. Unusual for most Chinese women, she wore lipstick – a deep red. She spoke rapidly with a confident tone in her voice, using Mandarin rather than Shanghainese for Jessie's benefit. Before sitting down, she reached across the table and shook Kip's hand.

Ah, she's clever to try to take control – thought Kip. "Jessie, please tell her that I'm pleased that we have the chance to meet."

After Jessie and Priscilla exchanged comments, Jessie said, "She said to tell you that she personally welcomes you to Shanghai." Jessie then turned back to Priscilla and translated Kip's greeting.

Looking directly at Kip, Priscilla smiled. "Ah, *xièxie*."

Kip said, "Jessie, what I'm about to say is very important. So translate as precisely as possible."

She nodded and flipped open her notebook.

"Please tell her I've reviewed the management structure in the company and have decided to make some changes. It's clear to me that she's carrying too much of a load. Rather than managing five departments, she will be more effective by managing three or four. While I appreciate—"

Jessie interrupted, "Please let me translate to her what you've said so far. Otherwise, it's too difficult for me to keep up."

"Sorry. Please go ahead."

After Jessie translated, Kip resumed, "While I appreciate the spirit of what she's trying to do to help the company, I've decided to transfer the Utilities Department from her to Rory. As chief engineer, he should be managing that area anyway. Please tell her that I look to her for support, regardless of how difficult these changes might be. Go ahead and translate, then I'll continue."

Hesitating, Jessie said, "Ah, are you sure you want me to say this to her?"

"Yes."

As Jessie talked, the smile vanished from Priscilla's face. When Jessie finished, Priscilla quietly said, "*Wo jie da.*"

Jessie said to Kip, "She said she understands."

"Good! Tell her that I'll talk to Rory today about this and thank her for understanding—that should be all for today. You can go also, Jessie. Good job."

Jessie smiled. "Thank you." After she translated for Priscilla the two women walked out of the room.

Jeez, that was a lot easier than I thought—mused Kip. *That deserves a little celebration.* He pulled out his bottom drawer.

Chapter 16

Kip gave Sal a call after work. "*Oye, Yani*, do you have a minute?"

"For you, I do. What's up?"

"I wrapped up interviewing all of the managers today. In talking with them, I've learned that the company is in worse shape than we thought."

Sal said, "I'm not surprised. So what did you find?"

"Well, first, the two saleswomen under contract from a local real estate agency spend more time playing video games on their computers than trying to lease homes. So I called the agency and terminated our agreement with them. The guy I talked to didn't seem to mind. I want to replace them with only one person as soon as possible, but someone with more than two brain cells that talk to each other."

Sal chuckled on the other end of the line.

Kip continued, "If there's anyone you can recommend, let me know. We need to jumpstart our sales efforts . . . like yesterday."

Sal said. "I might have the perfect person for you. Do you remember me telling you about Reggie's daughter, Heather, the time he gave that speech at Moscone Center?"

"Barely."

"Well, she's all grown up now and smarter than ever. After graduating from UCLA, she got her MBA in international management and went on to get a law degree. Right now, Heather is interning at our office in Shanghai so she can polish up her Mandarin. She's also fluent in French and Japanese."

Kip said, "She sounds bright enough, but I really don't see how she'd fit in at Shores."

"I think she would, *Tuchi*. She's been recruited by a top-tier law firm in California but won't start for six months. You'll want someone to boost sales right away, someone you can trust. Since her undergraduate degree was in marketing, she'd be ideal."

"I suppose we could at least talk."

"As a matter of fact, she kind of reminds me of Marci."

Kip felt his stomach tightened. "What do you mean?"

"In looks. Heather has blond hair, green eyes, and the same kind of smile as Marci. Besides her brainpower, she's also unspoiled by Reggie's fame and wealth."

"Okay. Go ahead and have her call me. The second thing I wanted to talk to you about is our financial controls. *Yani*, they don't exist."

Sal said, "Sure they do. Ralph sent us financial statements every month. We assumed that they were accurate."

"Well, they weren't – not even close. I'll predict right now that the books have been doctored by Naomi Chen. When I mentioned GAAP to her, she didn't even know what the hell I was talking about. She's totally incompetent."

"You're fuckin' kidding me!"

"Not in the least. It'll probably take me a couple of weeks before I find out how bad it really is. By the time I'm finished, I think we're going to be looking at financials that are unimaginably ugly."

Sal said, "Well, fuck me. Is there anything good you can tell me?"

"Jessie's been a lifesaver."

"Great. Do you think she'll be able to work herself into the Executive Assistant position?"

"Not really. I'll need someone much tougher and probably a Shanghainese."

"Okay."

Kip said, "Listen, before we hang up, there's one more thing you should know. During my session with Priscilla I told her that I'm paring down her responsibilities in the company."

"Meaning?"

"I told her that I'm transferring management of the Utilities Department from her to Rory, effectively immediately."

"You're shitting me! What the hell happened?"

"Obviously, she wasn't too happy about it, but seemed to take the news okay."

"I'm not so sure, *Tuchi*."

"Well, it wasn't a problem."

That same evening, Rico Niu was in town trying to speed up the takeover of Shanghai Shores. He had invited senior government officials for drinks and a lavish dinner at an upscale restaurant. Rico started the evening by bringing out bottles of rare 50-year-old Moutai, the traditional drink of China. No one's glass stayed empty longer than it took a waiter to refill it. The owner of the restaurant was a college classmate of Rico and assured him that the meal to be served will be long remembered by all of his guests.

While the officials were busy making verbose toasts, Mr. Tao walked up behind Rico and whispered something. Rico took the cell phone handed to him and quietly slipped out of the room. In the hallway, he said irritably, "Yes, what is it? This is not a good time to be calling me."

The person on the other end of the line told him that the new manager at Shores was digging into the altered financial records. Niu thought about this disturbing news for a moment and concluded that he had to accelerate the takeover. "Okay, go ahead with my plan to get Mr. Duchene's attention."

Chapter 17

Dressed in a freshly ironed white shirt, Benjamin pulled up to the hotel entrance to pick up his new boss. He quickly ran around to other side of the Buick to open the rear door for Kip and said, "You look like movie star, boss."

"I think you been drinking too much, Benjamin."

"Oh yes, boss. Plenty tea from Wuyi Mountains."

Kip chuckled as he slipped into the back seat. "Let's head straight for Shores."

"Okay, boss."

They crossed the Nanpu Bridge. Armed guards were stationed on each end of the bridge, both frozen in place and looking straight ahead. They reminded Kip of the stoic guards in front of Buckingham Palace.

As the car slowly made its way through Chaoyeng outside of Shores, Kip noticed three old Chinese women. They were sitting on low stools and preparing some kind of vegetable. "What are they cutting, Benjamin?"

"*Zhu sun.*"

"What's that?"

"You say bamboo."

The three women were engrossed in animated conversation. Kip thought—*Jeez, they must be at least eighty years old.*

When they approached the entrance to Shanghai Shores the gate didn't automatically open as usual. Caught by surprise, Benjamin had to bring the Buick to an abrupt stop. He leaned out the window and started arguing with the guard on duty. Within a minute, they were cordially speaking as if nothing had happened. Benjamin turned around and shrugged his shoulders. "So sorry, boss. You have resident permit? Guard say need permit to come in."

Shit! I forgot to pick up the fucking thing. Kip said, "You tell that idiot that I'm the boss here! If that gate doesn't open right now, I'll fire his ass!"

Benjamin hesitated, giving Kip a blank look.

Kip said irritably, "Go ahead and tell him."

Benjamin leaned out the window and translated Kip's message. Standing his ground the guard yelled back at Benjamin, his face turning red. With a sigh, Benjamin turned back to Kip. "Guard say Priscilla boss, not you. If Priscilla say okay, then okay."

While Benjamin was explaining the situation to Kip, the Buick was bumped from behind. Kip jerked his head around–W*ell, what a fucking coincidence. The police are here!* A dusty patrol car had quietly pulled up behind them and barely nudged the Buick's rear bumper to announce its presence.

Two officers got out. The one who drove was smoking a cigarette and flipped it off to the side of the road as he sauntered up to the guard. The other officer braced his forearm on top of the passenger side of the Buick and leaned down to look at its occupants. After the driver finished talking with the guard he walked over to the Buick to say a few words to Benjamin, returning to his patrol car in no hurry.

Benjamin said, "Boss, I not know what. Police say follow him to police station. He say some crackdown in China. We get okay right away. *Mei wenti.*"

Kip was dumbfounded. "Well, there *is* a problem. Did you tell him who in the hell *I* am?"

"Yes, boss. No choice. So sorry." With that, Benjamin pulled the Buick around and followed the patrol car back out through the village.

Kip flipped open his cell phone and dialed Sal's number. On the first ring, Sal said with a cheerful voice, "*Que pasa?*"

With a vice grip hold on the phone Kip bellowed, "I-HATE-THIS-GODDAMNED-PLACE!"

"Whoa, *Tuchi*, calm down. What the hell happened?"

Taking a deep breath and slowly exhaling, Kip told him what was happening.

"Sounds like Priscilla's involved in this."

"I don't give a crap who's involved. I'm out of here on the next flight home."

"I'll call you right back." Sal hung up without waiting for Kip to reply.

Within a few minutes, Kip's phone rang. He said, "Okay, what the hell's happening?"

A velvety woman's voice said, "Ah . . . Kip, it's me, Angie. I'm heading out the door right now to catch a taxi. I'll be at the station as soon as I can. Everything will be okay."

Hearing Angie's soft words had a calming effect on Kip. He quietly said, "Thank you."

At the local police station, an officer in the crowded reception area told Benjamin that he and his boss were to take a seat. Everyone stopped talking when the tall foreigner and a Chinese man started to look for a place to sit. In one section, people scooted closer together, opening a gap in the bench for Kip and Benjamin.

The room was gloomy. Flickering fluorescent lights overhead did little to brighten the place. Walls were glossy gray, paint bubbling in some places and peeling in others. A ceiling paddle-fan hummed with electricity, but its blades were frozen in place. The windows looked like they hadn't been cleaned in a long time.

Just as Kip was thinking what a mistake it had been coming to China, he was jarred into the present as the front door burst open. A uniformed officer shoved a handcuffed Chinese man into the waiting area. The man's face was swollen with splotchy reddened areas and caked blood between his nose and lip. As they disappeared through a door on the far end of the room, the man could be heard sobbing.

A few minutes later, the front door opened again. Kip expected to see another person being brought in. Instead, it was Angie, dressed in a light-gray sweat suit with white tennis shoes. Her hair was pulled back in a bun with errant strands brushing across her face. Despite her casual attire, she looked beautiful to Kip. As soon as she spotted him sitting on the bench, she smiled and walked over. Without thinking, he stood up and embraced her, realizing immediately what he'd done. "Jeez, Angie, I don't know where that came from. I guess I'm not thinking straight."

"Well, that's one of the lamest come-ons I've ever heard," she said with her hands on her hips.

Her attempt to make light of the situation went unnoticed by Kip. He said, "When can I get out of here?"

"Just sit down. This should take only a minute or so." She walked over to the reception counter and talked to a bored-looking officer sitting on the other side. During their conversation, the man partially stood up to peek over the counter at Kip and then sat back down. He and Angie talked for another five minutes before she reached into her purse and counted out money. The officer stamped a receipt and handed it to her along with a clasped envelope. She said, "*Xièxie.*"

Smiling on her way back to the bench, she pulled out Kip's passport and residency permit and waved them. "Are these yours, boss?"

Kip stood and walked towards Angie with Benjamin following close behind. "Can we leave now?"

"Yes."

Benjamin was opening the door for them as Angie said, "If you'd like, I have time to go back to Shores with you. Maybe I can find out how this happened."

Smiling for the first time, he said, "Thank you,"

When the Buick approached the entrance of Shanghai Shores twenty minutes later, Benjamin need to slow down before for the gate swung open. Kip watched in amazement. *God, I don't understand these people.*

In the office, Angie looked around and said, "I thought by now you would have moved out of this office and into a nicer one."

"I haven't had time."

Angie arched her eyebrow. "I see. Well, I'm going to slip into the office next door and start making calls to see what I can learn."

"Thanks." Kip sat at his desk and tried to sort out what had happened. He didn't get very far into his thoughts before his cell phone rang. "Hello?"

"*Pendejo*, are chu still locked up in the *cárcel*?"

Not being able to suppress a smile, Kip said, "No, I'm not in jail. Angie straightened things out in a few minutes. She offered to stick around long enough to learn who pulled this shit."

"Are you still divorcing me, *Tuchi*?"

Kip heard Sal stifle a laugh on the other end. "No, I'm here, aren't I?"

"Good. Let's have lunch down at the seafood restaurant in San Jia Gang. I want to hear the details of your in-car-cer-a-tion."

"There's nothing much to tell. But, yes, that would be nice."

"If Angie's still around, you're welcome to invite her."

At noon, Sal was escorted into the private dining room where Kip and Angie were already seated. As soon as Sal laid eyes on Kip, he started to chuckle, then broke out in uncontrolled laughter. He managed to say, "Let me see your wrists, *Tuchi*. Did the cuffs leave any marks?"

Angie covered her mouth giggling.

Holding out his wrists, Kip said, "Not this time, shithead."

All three broke out laughing.

During lunch, Angie revealed to Sal that Priscilla orchestrated the whole episode.

Sal looked over at Kip and winked. "I told you so, *Tuchi*."

Smiling, Kip scratched the bridge of his nose with his middle finger, knowing that only Sal would understand his gesture.

He was wrong. Angie rolled her eyes. "Now, now, boys."

Chapter 18

When Kip walked into the office the next morning, he was confused by what he saw. Except for the furniture, everything was gone, including all of the files, stationary, and office equipment. Even the wastepaper basket was empty. His first thought was—*Oh shit, not Priscilla again.*

He poked his head back out of the office and looked around the hallway. All was quiet except for muffled noises coming from somewhere down the corridor. Following the sounds, he walked into the second office from the end. Angie was sitting behind a desk stacked high with file folders. Several strands of her hair had fallen across her face. "Good morning, Mr. Duchene."

Shocked at seeing her, he said, "Why are *you* here?"

"I answered the ad in the newspaper."

He raked his fingers through his hair and had a pained expression on his face. "*Jesus*, please don't kid me."

She gave him a warm smile. "I'm not Jesus. And I'm not kidding you. In only four days, you've made an incredible mess of things in trying to be the *da laoban*. You might have been the darling of Silicon Valley, but in China, you're out of your league. I think you need my help."

He smiled in return and nodded.

"So how do you like your new office?" She swept her arm towards the adjoining room.

He walked in and was overwhelmed by what he saw. "How the hell?"

It was a large corner office with a commanding view of the ocean. His desk was placed in the far corner angled to face the door. An intricate clay sculpture of a colorful dragonfly was displayed on the credenza. He walked behind his desk to examine the artwork more closely. "Angie, this is magnificent. Where did you get it?"

"Manny dropped it off early this morning. He made it when he lived in Uganda. Just so you know, a dragonfly in China is a symbol of good luck."

"Well, it's an exceptional gift." He set his attaché case on top of the desk and sank into the executive chair. "How'd you do this so fast?"

"I'm Chinese." She perched herself on the arm of the side chair, close enough for him to pick up the subtle fragrance of her perfume.

He said, "I thought you weren't interested in working with me?"

"I wasn't. But under the circumstances someone needs to keep you out of jail. But seriously, you're trying too hard to use your American ways of doing business over here. Believe me, Kip, it'll never work. Maybe there's a chance I can help you."

"I'd like that."

Angie slid off the arm of the chair and sat down. Crossing her long slender legs, she said, "You really need a quick primer on how to do business in China."

He held his palms up. "Now's as good a time as any."

Collecting her thoughts, she started, "Okay then. When you think you've heard one thing over here, it probably means something entirely different. Being Chinese, we can sense the subtle tones and hidden meanings when another native speaks. You can't."

"Meaning?"

"Let's see . . . okay. While going to school in Berkeley, I found that my classmates freely talked about what they thought. At first, I ended up wasting a lot of time trying to figure out their hidden meanings. I eventually learned that there *weren't* any. I was hearing what the person intended me to hear—plain and simple."

"So?"

"That kind of open communication doesn't work in China. Our survival through generations has depended on subtlety. It's a form of self-protection. Since conflict can cause someone to reveal true feelings, we avoid it whenever possible. It's deeply engrained in our society."

"Sorry, but I still don't understand."

"Well, let's say you get mad at somebody. Once you do, you've lost control—you've revealed your inner thoughts to the other person. To avoid this, Chinese will skirt around our intentions, keeping the other person guessing."

Kip chuckled. "What about Patti? She seems remarkably open."

"She's just different, that's all. Anyway, are you with me so far?"

"I think so." Kip reached into his attaché case and pulled out a notebook and pen. "Go ahead."

"Okay. The next thing that Americans have difficulty understanding is the practice of *saving face*."

Kip held up his hands in protest. "Jessie already explained that one to me."

"Good. Just remember that Chinese people are apt to say 'yes' to any question in order to avoid offending the other party. In reality, the person had no intention of agreeing in the first place. Kip, that kind of face-saving behavior is in the very fiber of how we communicate. On the other hand, we tend to regard Americans as being brash."

Raising his eyebrows, he said, "Are you serious?"

"Absolutely. American businessmen come to China thinking that they're going to take advantage of our vast marketplace of 1.3 billion people. Many believe that the Western way of doing business is superior to ours. They push hard to secure the deal while ignoring the importance we place in developing personal relationships. Some go home triumphantly with signed contracts in hand. However, many of those contracts are meaningless to their Chinese counterpart and will never be honored by them. When this happens, Americans naturally conclude that Chinese are dishonest."

"That's something I do understand."

"Well, remember this. Americans who prosper in China typically live over here, learn to speak the language, and regard their business endeavors with Chinese as a long-term process. Sal is a good example of this. He and others try to conduct business through the eyes of Chinese rather than rigidly holding onto a superior, know-it-all American attitude."

Kip snickered. "That's a little exaggerated, don't you think?"

"No, I don't," said Angie. "Don't let them see your true emotions. Don't lose your temper when you're dealing with Chinese." Angie looked up at Kip and smiled. "That includes doing stupid things that cause you to end up in jail."

"Don't rub it in. One of the most important things I need to do is figure out how to stop Rico Niu from taking over Shores. What do you know about him?"

With a serious expression on her face, she said, "Be very, very careful of Mr. Niu. He's had people killed for trying to go against him. I even heard a buzz about a possible connection between him and the two American girls who were kidnapped."

"The man must be seriously sick."

"Believe me, he is. Here's what I know about him. He lives in a guarded high-rise condo in the posh marina district of Haikou."

"Where's Haikou anyway?"

"It's a city on the north end of Hainan Island. I've heard that he owns the Haikou police, thanks to his generous bribes. Ironically, his name frequently appears in print or on television, portraying him in a positive light. As an example, he could be giving a news conference at a grand opening for one of his housing projects—things like that. There's also been a lot of coverage in the news about his lawsuits against foreign businessmen. It's ironic that most Chinese people actually cheer for the man when the Court rules in his favor, particularly when the other party is Japanese. The fact that he doesn't play by the rules is less significant than that he's Chinese. Just like you say in your country, blood is thicker than water. Does that make sense to you?"

He flipped his pen on the desk. "Unfortunately, yes."

Angie smiled. "Okay, enough of the cultural education for today. Jessie has already filled me in on what's happened so far. Kip, I think that she's done a really good job for you."

"Yeah, she has."

Angie stood. "I'm going to grab my notebook and will be right back so we can get started."

While she was walking into her adjoining office, Kip thought—*How could so many things go from being shitty one morning to this great the next. Maybe this is a sign of things to come?*

When Angie returned, she asked, "What next?"

"Sal suggested that I interview Reggie Ingram's daughter, Heather, for an interim position as our sales manager."

"I thought we already had a couple of representatives from the real estate agency."

"We did. Seeing they were useless, I fired them."

"My, my." Angie looked up from her notes. "Well, it's always good to have a Westerner involved in sales in China. She'll probably do well here."

"If I hire her, she'll be working with us for only six months. But, that should be all we need to boost sales before someone permanently can be hired. If we're to pull this ugly puppy out of the drink, we'll need to write up a lot of new leases, and fast."

"Would you like for me to set up your interview with her?"

"Please—give Sal a call for the details. In the meantime, I'd like to meet with Manny Okumu this morning."

"I thought you already talked to everyone."

"I did. But we didn't get a chance to cover everything. I'd like for you to attend these meetings and take notes. After the meeting, it would be important to hear your opinions. "

"Got it. Are you ready to see Manny now?"

"Yes."

Angie walked back into her office. While listening to her on the phone, Kip felt less lonely than since he'd arrived in Shanghai. As soon as he heard her hang up, he said, "Angie?"

She called out from her desk, "Yes?"

"I'm pleased that you're here."

"So am I."

Rico Niu was heading out of his Haikou office for lunch when his cell phone chimed. He opened it and said with a bored voice, "*Wei.*" Hello

The caller reported that Angie unexpectedly showed up at the police station and bribed an officer before Kip could be charged. Rico interrupted her, "So you're telling me that Duchene was released?"

Speaking hardly above a whisper, she said, "*Shi da.*" Yes.

Rico said, "I guess it's time to send Mr. Tao up there to have a private talk with you." He flipped the phone shut with a loud snap.

Chapter 19

"Sounds good." Kip glanced at his watch. "Well, I had better get back to work. Thanks for coming in. I look forward to your call."

The group stood and said their goodbyes. As Heather was heading out the door, she turned back to Kip. "By the way, I remember seeing an article in the San Francisco Chronicle about your wife. Please accept my condolences— I'm so, so sorry." Tears rimmed her eyes.

Taken completely off guard, Kip pursed his lips together and nodded not knowing what else to say. Angie escorted her out. Hearing the women chatting as they made their way down the hallway, he pulled out his bottom drawer and filled half of his coffee mug with vodka.

When Angie returned, she walked into his office and said, "Kip, I didn't know you were married. May I ask what happened?"

Kip held up his hands. "I'm sorry, Angie, it's a personal matter."

Kip slipped Eleni Wentworth's business card out of a plastic card holder and dialed her number. "Eleni, this is Kip Duchene. We met on the Shanghai flight last week."

"Of course. It's nice to hear from you. I've been wondering how your first few days at Shanghai Shores went."

"I could write a book."

"God, I can imagine. Did you happen to hear about the girl in Haikou?"

Kip said, "Unfortunately, yes."

"I'll bet Rico Niu was involved somehow."

"Yeah, I agree. Eleni, the reason I'm calling you is to ask a favor."

"Sure. Anything."

"I'd be grateful if you could come out here and give me an unvarnished opinion on how we can boost sales."

"I'd be pleased to. When did you have in mind?"

"I'm not sure. I'll give you a call when I have a better idea of timing."

"Anytime."

"Thanks, Eleni."

After hanging up, Kip heard Angie call out from the outer office, "Who was that?"

"Nothing important, Miss Nosy."

"I see we're a bit touchy today."

Kip didn't reply.

Angie said, "By the way, Jessie called earlier to say that the Mirabella Estate is ready for you to move into."

"Please thank her for me. I'll wait until tomorrow."

"Okay."

"While I'm thinking about it, please give Naomi a call and ask her to deliver a copy of all of our financial statements. I want to review them over the weekend."

"Anything else?"

"Yes. This would be a good time for me to meet with Bev again. Ask her to come up."

Kip spritzed his mouth with breath freshener just before Angie escorted Bev into Kip's office. He motioned for them to sit down across from him on the sofas.

As they were getting settled, Bev said, "Kip, I've brought a copy of the spreadsheet listing our debts. It's divided by secured and unsecured creditors."

He took a moment to scan the list. "Did this come from Naomi?"

"No, I prepared it myself."

"Good. I see that you also sorted the creditors by the amount owed along with an aging of the accounts. What about pending lawsuits against us?"

"There are nine. I keep in close contact with Chairman Zhang Guofeng. He's—"

"Sorry to interrupt. For Chinese names, do you say the family name first?"

"Yes. Chairman Zhang is the head of the Political Committee for the Pudong Municipal Government, an important government official. He presides over all lawsuits that are filed in Pudong Courts, most of which flow through the system without his intervention. Because we're a foreign-owned company, the process ends up being a little bit more complicated. In a way, he's like a mediator who tries to find a way for the parties to reach a settlement out of court."

Kip said, "What is our relationship with him?"

"Good. Anytime he phones, I always take it. When he requests that we meet, I offer to go to his office. Since this kind of cooperation is so unusual in China, he shows his appreciation by giving us reasonable breaks whenever a situation warrants. Otherwise, we wouldn't be in a very good place right now."

"Very good."

"When you can, I suggest that you meet with Chairman Zhang. It would benefit us to give him *good face*."

"Anytime. Just set it up through Angie."

Thirty minutes later Angie buzzed Kip on the intercom. "Heather's on the line and asked if you could meet her after work today."

"Sure. Six-thirty in the lobby lounge at Ritz-Carlton."

Kip then called Sal to bring him up to date about Heather.

Sal said, "That sounds like she may accept."

"Let's hope so."

"Say, *Tuchi*. I'm catching hell from Maria about you not coming over to see us. How about this weekend?"

"I'd love to, but I'll be swamped reviewing our financials. I promise to come over soon."

"Okay. Let me know if you need anything and good luck with Heather."

Unsure how he would react to seeing Heather again, Kip arrived early so he could order a double vodka tonic. By the time she walked in, he was feeling the soothing effects of the drink.

Heather attracted a lot of attention from men in the lounge on her way in. Without taking notice she sank into the overstuffed chair across from Kip. "They've done a nice job decorating this place."

He looked around. "Yeah, they have. Care for a drink?"

"No, thank you." After the two chatted for several minutes, Heather said, "Kip, I thought about your offer and would be delighted to accept. I like tackling big challenges."

"Well then, you'll surely like what's in front of you at Shanghai Shores."

Later that night in his hotel room, Kip thought— *we're on our way.* Slipping into bed, he looked over to the photo on his bedside stand, kissed his fingers, and touched them to Marci's image. *Good night, my love.*

As soon as Kip turned off the bedside lamp, he quickly drifted off into a sound asleep. But an hour later, he was jarred awake by the phone ringing. When he picked up the receiver, a young woman's voice said, "Meester Doocheenee, you like massagee?"

He hung up without saying a word, rolled over, and tried to remember what he'd been dreaming about.

A black limousine coasted to a stop on a side street a block away from Shanghai Shores. Mr. Tao opened the rear door and stood, motioning for the woman waiting at curbside to get in. Once she did, Mr. Tao sandwiched her between him and Rico Niu. As soon as the door closed,

Rico said, "I'm glad to hear that Duchene is moving to Shores. Do you have any questions on what you're to do?"

In a quiet voice, the woman said, "No."

"Okay, then. You remember what I told you what would happen if there are any more slip-ups."

With a shaky voice, she said, "Y-yes, I remember."

"Good." He picked up an envelope stuffed with money and slid it across the leather seat to her.

Chapter 20

Kip woke up Saturday morning excited about moving into the Mirabella Estate. He called Benjamin before showering and told him to use the minivan instead of the Buick. "We need to stop at that supermarket on Longdong Road so I can pick up things for the house."

"Yes, boss."

Two hours later they were loading three shopping carts of goods into the rear cargo area of the van and heading toward Shanghai Shores. While passing through Chaoyeng, Kip looked for the three old ladies and smiled to himself when he spotted them huddled together in conversation by the side of the road. All three had white hair. Two stood less than five feet and the third one may have been just a few inches taller. Despite being surrounded by Chinese people all day, Kip was attracted to these villagers. Before coming to China he had a vision of how people looked in this country. *For me, these villagers are them.*

After the two men unloaded the van and got everything into the house, Kip said, "Benjamin, go ahead and take the rest of the day off."

"Okay, boss. If need me you call me."

"Just enjoy your family today."

"Thanks, boss."

Kip closed the front door and slipped out of his Birkenstocks. He walked through the house in his stocking feet and more closely inspected every nook and cranny. When he got to the kitchen he grabbed a can of lukewarm beer out of the refrigerator, pulled open a bag of tortilla chips, and walked out onto the deck. He savored the first swig of beer, letting it swish around in his mouth before swallowing. The view of the East China Sea and smell of salt air reminded Kip of the San Francisco Bay. *What do you think about this, my love?*

He was tempted to have another beer, but decided to go back inside and get the house organized. Three hours later, he was satisfied that everything was in place. He picked one of his favorites Stan Getz' CD and slipped it into the CD player. *This is cool. The speakers put out a nice sound.* The mellow tenor saxophone transported him back to Santa Monica where he'd listen to his dad's record collection. He thought—*What the hell. Why not?* He grabbed another beer out of the refrigerator. This one was ice cold.

After his third beer, he decided to plunge into the financial records that Naomi reluctantly provided. Two hours later, he had a full-blown headache. He discovered that some of the records were still missing. The balance sheets, profit and loss statements, and cash flow analysis were all a jumbled mess. Studying the irregularities, Kip had good reason to believe that money was being funneled away from the company. *The Gang of Three has to be behind this.* He slipped the financials into his attaché case and headed back to the refrigerator.

On Monday morning, Kip blurted from his office, "It's show time, Angie!"

Angie peeked her head around the doorway. "Are you always this cheerful on a Monday morning? And what does *show time* mean?"

"It's time to start turning this behemoth around."

"If you say so, boss."

"Be nice." Kip wagged his finger at her.

"I don't know how."

Kip smiled and nodded. "I figured. By the way has Heather's office been set up yet?"

"Housekeeping did it over the weekend."

"Good. Please ask her to be prepared to address the managers for our meeting this morning."

The meeting went better than Kip expected. Not only did Heather cause a stir when she walked into the room, she addressed the managers in Mandarin—*A damn smart move*. While not understanding a word she said, he was swept up with a feeling of warmth and sadness by being reminded of Marci. He was also impressed with the degree of confidence she exuded. After he adjourned the meeting, he thought—*Heather's going to be good for the company*.

Jessie stayed behind in the conference room after everyone else filed out. She ambled over to Kip and said, "Do you have a minute?"

"Sure, take a seat." He motioned with his hand.

In a low voice, she said, "I think that Priscilla may try to make trouble for you."

"How's that?"

"I hear things, that's all. Since I'm not Shanghainese, it's a little more difficult for me to find out what's happening. Please be careful."

"Thanks for the warning, Jessie. I'll keep a close eye on her. And, Jessie?"

"Yes?"

"You did an outstanding job assisting me last week. Thank you."

"I really enjoyed it." Smiling broadly, she stood up and walked out of the room.

Back in his office, he called out to Angie, "Is there really that much of a difference between Shanghai people and other Chinese?"

She laughed and poked her head around the door. "Why do you ask?"

"I just sense that Shanghainese are a little like the people of New York City. They pride themselves as being different than everyone else."

"Yes, it's true. It's ingrained in us that we're superior to other Chinese, even better than the almighty Beijing people. We even have a name for outsiders, '*wai de ren*'."

"Interesting," said Kip.

Angie sat down in the side chair and crossed her shapely legs. "Can we take a minute to go over the schedule?"

"Shoot."

"Let's see, Heather wants to talk with you when you're free. She's picked out a townhouse and wants to move in tomorrow."

"No problem."

Angie looked down at her notes and proceeded to tell him his schedule for the week along with the most pressing problems that need his attention.

Kip said, "The only thing you didn't have listed is my meeting the infamous Mr. Avery?"

"Oh? I didn't know. Poor you."

"Well, I need to get it over with. Please plan to join us when he gets here."

"Can't wait."

An hour later, Kip placed a call to Heather. "So you found a place to live?"

"I did. I really like the privacy of the townhouse and it gives me a great view of the ocean from my third floor bedroom."

"I'm glad. As soon as possible, I'd like to introduce you to an acquaintance of mine who owns a real estate agency in Shanghai. She specializes in placing expats in rental units. Anyway, she's agreed to come out here to take a look at what we have here and to possibly make some suggestions."

Heather said. "Would she be Eleni Wentworth?"

"Yes, do you know her?"

"No, but my dad has mentioned her several times."

"Well, now you'll have a chance to meet her."

Later that morning, Kip accepted Sal's invitation for dinner at his house on Saturday.

Chapter 21

Right after lunch, Jessie called and asked Kip if he would like to take a tour of the clubhouse. He figured that they'd get back in time for his meeting with Avery. They started off in the reception area and then went to the restaurant and cocktail lounge.

Jessie said, "Kip, I want to introduce you to Paul Zhou, the restaurant manager."

Paul was wearing a dark suit, white shirt and silver tie. He was a nice looking man, maybe thirty. He seemed a little nervous but had an easy smile.

Next to the restaurant, Kip was shown into the convenience store, stocked with an assortment of foods items imported from the Unites States, England, and Japan. *Looks like a 7-Eleven.* They then walked down a hallway with offices on each side. Kip said, "Jessie, why are so many of these offices empty?"

"Well, the clubhouse was built to serve the entire development of 264 homes. Since Shores is only half built, we don't need all the offices until Phase Two happens. Then there's the *Gang of Three* refusing to move over here from the Green Latrine."

Kip shook his head without comment.

Next, they headed down the stairs to the ground floor. Jessie showed him through a well-equipped fitness center and then out through the double glass doors to the swimming pool.

"Very nice." Kip looked at his watch. "Ah, it's getting late. I had better get back. Thanks for the tour."

She blushed and said, "It's my job."

A minute later, Angie buzzed him to say that Mr. Avery was waiting for them in the conference room.

Kip said, "Then let's do it."

Kip and Angie greeted Mr. Avery and they traded business cards. Avery was in his early fifties, only five-six, dressed in a conservative black suit and plain necktie. His face appeared freshly scrubbed, and he wore crystal-clean glasses with plastic rims. He flashed a phony smile that went on-and-off at will.

Avery wasted no time stating his purpose for the visit. "Mr. Duchene, now that you've been here a week, you can see that Shanghai Shores is a mess."

Kip scratch his temple and said, "Oh?"

"Yes. I've offered to help clean it up in the past, but to no avail. Ingram Capital believed it could run this development without the capable guidance of the U.S. Department of Commerce. Well, they were obviously wrong. With your arrival, I hope that we can turn over a new leaf and begin true cooperation."

Kip took a breath and let it out slowly. "Mr. Avery, I'm grateful for your interest in Shanghai Shores. It'll take me another three weeks to sort through what we have here. When that happens I'd be willing to meet again and explore how we can work together."

Avery said, "I'm afraid that'll be too late."

"Excuse me?" Kip arched his eyebrow and flashed a look at Angie.

"Through our back channels, we understand that Rico Niu is making further headway with Shanghai officials to take over the project. We can't let that happen."

"*That*, I can agree. Since Shanghai Shores was entirely funded by Ingram Capital, they're relying on my expertise to turn the company around, not the U.S. Consulate." Standing up, Kip extended his hand towards Mr. Avery and said, "But I'll keep you closely informed."

"You do that." With a reddened face, Avery turned and walked out of the room.

"Oh, my, my!" said Angie.

"What?"

"I pegged you wrong. I thought you were the intellectual type who prefers to sit behind a desk and give orders. If that was any indication how you're going to handle things, I'm frankly impressed."

"Well, the man's a real jerk. By the way, Naomi didn't turn over all of the financial records that I requested last week."

"I didn't know. I'll see what I can do," said Angie and she walked into her office.

Kip glanced at his to-do list and placed a call to Eleni. She agreed to come over the following afternoon. As soon as he hung up, the phone rang. "Hi, Kip. It's Bev."

"Hi. What's up?"

"Are you free to meet with Chairman Zhang tomorrow morning at 9:30?"

He looked down at his calendar. "No problem."

Bev said, "Thanks, this is really important for us. You know, Ralph never bothered to meet with any of the government authorities and it caused us to lose face."

"Bev, I actually look forward to it – something to tell my grandchildren about."

"Oh, I thought you weren't married."

Chuckling, he said, "It's just an American saying."

"Okay, see you tomorrow." She hung up.

Angie walked back in and said, "I talked to Naomi. Reluctantly, she agreed to send over more of the financial records later this afternoon. She's really holding onto them tightly"

Kip said, "Just make sure we get them all."

After dinner, Kip poured through the missing financial statements Naomi handed over. They spelled out more bad news. *Enough is enough. Time to bring in one of the big accounting firms. If we're lucky, PriceWaterhouse has an office in Shanghai.*

Needing some fresh air, Kip pulled on a sweatshirt, poured a glass of wine, and went out on the deck. He enjoyed the solitude of sitting in darkness, listening to the waves lapping on the shore, and watching the sights. With their red, green and white running lights aglow, cargo ships slowly passed through the shipping lanes.

Kip's mind drifted to his penthouse apartment in San Francisco, a place that was quickly becoming a distant memory. It was only ten days ago that he locked his front door and headed out to the airport. He met Angie at the seafood restaurant only eight days ago. It seemed like a million years ago the last time he and Marci laughed together.

That night Kip tossed in bed with interrupted sleep, reliving a nightmare about Marci that gave no indication of going away.

By midnight, Rico Niu's face had turned bright red from drinking alcohol. He had good reason to celebrate. A group of government officials from the Shanghai Real Estate Planning Bureau were being entertained at his enclave in Kunshan. Rico knew he was winning them over regarding Shores. Maybe even more important, he got a surprise telephone call from his informant. He was ecstatic to learn that Reginald Ingram's daughter just accepted a position at Shanghai Shores.

"Tao, we can start planning our next move. Let's see how much the old man wants to hold onto Shanghai Shores."

Chapter 22

Moving into the Mirabella Estate made Kip's life easier. The walk from his house to the clubhouse took about 30 seconds compared to the one hour drive from the Ritz Carlton. He could be at his desk by 7:00 a.m., two hours before the other employees arrived. Most of them commuted by using the company shuttle van, municipal bus, subway train, or bicycle. Bev and a few others were privileged enough to own their own cars.

At eight forty-five, Kip walked out of his office and down to the parking lot where Benjamin was dutifully waiting for him beside the Buick. While opening Kip's door, Benjamin said, "We drive to see Chairman Zhang now?"

Kip slipped off his suit jacket and folded it neatly on the other side of the back seat. He said, "Yes. You know where to go?"

"I know, boss. *Mei wenti.*"

Kip smiled—*Everything with Benjamin was no problem.*

As the Buick headed toward downtown Pudong along Longdong Avenue Kip looked out the window and watched the throng of bicyclists pumping their way to work. Some had carts attached to the back of their bikes, piled high with paraphernalia such as bamboo reeds, cardboard, or Styrofoam extrusions. Some bicyclists wore slacks and sport coats while others rode comfortably in their pajamas. Kip smiled.

Thirty minutes later, the car pulled over to the curb in front of an austere looking government building set back from a twelve foot high wrought-iron fence with pointed spears on top. Bev was waiting for him in the doorway of the security shack. Her broad smile suggested that she was glad to see him. "Welcome to the heart of the judicial system of Pudong."

Kip stepped inside and said, "Hi Bev. I look forward to my first meeting with a real Communist Party member."

With a twinkle in her eye, she said, "Scary, huh?"

Kip chuckled. "Let's do it."

"We have to clear security first before going in."

A uniformed guard walked up to them and asked for their passports. He then said something to Bev. She motioned to the chairs along the wall. "We can sit over there until we're cleared."

After they took their seats, Bev said, "Do you know much about Chinese protocol?"

Kip shook his head. "None."

"The check-in process will take a while. If you like, I can give you a crash lesson on a few points."

"Yeah, I'd like that."

"Okay. Hand me one of your business cards."

Kip flipped open a gold-plated card holder and passed a card to Bev. After studying it for a moment, she said, "Gosh, this is really good. Whoever did the Chinese translation on the back side knew what they were doing. Most are not very good."

"I'm glad to hear that."

She continued, "Okay, the first thing to remember when you're introduced to a Chinese person is to hand the person your business card with the Chinese side up. Position it so they can read it, not you. If you're being introduced to more than one person, always pass your card to the most senior person first, then the second most important person, and so on."

"How would I know who's most important?"

"Ask the Chinese person accompanying you. Anyway, use both hands to hold your card when passing it. The other person may, or may not, shake your hand at that time—maybe just a nod. When you take the other person's card, be sure to examine it while showing interest in what it says."

Kip asked, "Why's that?"

"It's a good way to show a sign of respect for the person's position. God, one time I saw an American guy use a Chinese official's card to pick his teeth."

Kip chuckled. "Okay, what if the card is in Chinese?"

"Fake it by pretending to read it anyway." Bev smiled. "The next thing to remember is to lower the sound of your voice and make physical movements in a subtle manner. Many Chinese think that Americans are too loud, impatient, and brusque."

Kip said, "Oh?"

"Yes. The good news is that you're a gentleman and shouldn't have much trouble adapting. Another thing, please don't make the mistake of bowing—that's Japanese, not Chinese. Always address people politely, even when you want to throttle their neck. No matter what, stay cool and—"

Bev was interrupted by the guard handing the passports back to them. She said to Kip, "Okay, we can go in now."

While they were walking across a large concrete expanse in front of the imposing building, Kip said, "Thanks for the lesson."

"My pleasure."

Kip and Bev were the only ones walking up the forty-foot wide steps leading to the building's main entrance. The building was five stories high, clad in gray marble with a series of support columns spaced every twenty feet across the entry area. Kip pointed to a red emblem centered high on the building. It was surrounded by a wreath cluster with five gold stars and a silhouette of the Tiananmen building in the middle. "What's that?"

Bev said, "That's our national emblem. It gives tribute to the working class of China."

They entered the stark and cold lobby, their footsteps echoing on the polished marble floor. Only a few people could be seen in the cavernous area. Bev led Kip confidently through the place, leaving no doubt that she'd been there many times before.

They rode the elevator up to the fourth floor and made a series of turns through a confusing maze of hallways. Bev walked into a room that was furnished with a couple of couches facing each other. Cigarette butts overfilled the large glass ash tray on the coffee table. In the corner of the room, a dark-stained bookcase held an assortment of Chinese artifacts, canisters of tea, and old books.

In the back of the room, a doorway opened into a private office. As soon as they entered the outer office, there was the sound of a chair scraping on the wood floor somewhere in the inner office. A tired-looking Chinese man walked through the threshold while slipping into his suit coat. Chairman Zhang was dressed in a dark suit, white shirt and blue tie. His clothes were tastefully neat but not stylish or expensive looking. His hair was parted just off center with the left half falling partially down onto his forehead. He wore professorial-looking glasses with clear plastic rims.

He greeted them with a warm smile. Bev introduced Kip while the two men were exchanging business cards. Kip studied the Chairman's card and nodded. Chairman Zhang motioned for them to sit and placed Kip's card directly in front of him on the coffee table. Seeing this, Kip did the same with the chairman's card.

After the pleasantries were made, Bev told the chairman about Kip and his reputation in the States for turning troubled companies around. They spoke entirely in Shanghainese. As Bev spoke, the chairman nodded and periodically turned to Kip and smiled. The Chairman talked for about five minutes without pause. Bev shot Kip a look of exasperation, as the Chairman's long-winded speech didn't allow her time to fully translate. She said nothing though, but simply took out her note pad and wrote as fast as she could.

When he finished, she turned to Kip and explained what he had said about Pudong's judicial system and his role in mediating difficult cases. "Chairman Zhang concluded by complimenting me for always showing up and keeping him informed. He then said that he was pleased to meet you and to learn that Ingram Capital brought you in to clean up Shores. He said that he wishes you luck because it would cure him of his number one headache."

Kip said, "What's that?"

"*Shanghai Shores*, of course!"

Caught off guard, Kip broke out laughing. He thought— *The Chairman has a sense of humor.*

Kip handed Chairman Zhang a velvet gift bag and said to Bev, "Please tell the chairman that this is good medicine for curing headaches."

It was an expensive bottle of Scotch. As Kip and Bev turned to leave, they got a glimpse of the chairman in his inner office, pulling the bottle out of its sack and chuckling.

As they retraced their steps through the maze of hallways, Bev said, "I think Chairman Zhang likes you."

Chapter 23

"May I come in?" asked Angie as soon as Kip got back to his office.

"Sure."

"You received several messages. First, Mr. David Liu from PricewaterhouseCoopers in Shanghai called and said he was returning your call. Eleni Wentworth called to confirm your appointment with her at two o'clock today."

"Good. Make sure Heather is reminded."

"Shelly dropped off a copy of the personnel records but she was clearly not happy about it. Manny walked Heather through quite a few of our houses. She suggested which of them should be renovated first. Replacement carpet and paint have been ordered. We'll get the first shipment of paint tomorrow. Sal called a few minutes ago but left no message."

"I'll call him back later."

"Jessie wanted to know if it was okay with you to schedule a maid for your house on Mondays."

"Tell her Mondays are fine. For the meeting with Eleni, let's meet down in the restaurant. The atmosphere is better there. Paul should be alerted."

After Angie left his office, he picked up the phone to call Mr. Liu of PWC. They agreed to meet at Shores on Friday.

At 2:00 p.m., Angie informed Kip that Eleni was waiting in the lobby.

"Okay, please call Heather and tell her to meet us in the restaurant."

Kip introduced everyone as they were being shown to a table. Paul had made a special effort to accommodate them, including a small floral arrangement placed in the middle of the table. *A nice touch*—thought Kip.

Without much ado, they got down to business. Kip handed Eleni a graphic chart showing the decline of rentals at Shores for the past two years. He outlined their tentative plans to ramp up leases, including the renovation of the houses.

Eleni's knowledge of the Shanghai real estate business was obvious as Angie and Heather took copious notes of what she had to say. "After hearing your plans, Kip, I think that you're already headed in the right direction. Without exception, you can *never* show any of your homes that are not in perfect condition. That would be the kiss of death for getting new tenants. And lastly, don't be surprised if you find out that Rico Niu is directly controlling some of your senior staff members and getting daily reports of your activities."

Kip said, "You serious?"

"Yes. With Niu, anything's possible."

Kip said, "Well that seems like a stretch to me."

"I understand your skepticism," said Eleni. "I just think a little caution is warranted. Remember, in China money can buy a lot of favors when you spread it around. Believe me, Niu is well known for slipping people money to get his way. I'd be surprised if he wasn't bribing a good number of your employees already. "

Even though Kip had only met Eleni on the plane ten days ago, she felt like a longtime friend. After the meeting concluded he escorted her to the parking lot. "Eleni, I can't thank you enough."

"It's not a bother. I hope I didn't say anything that discouraged you."

"Not at all."

"Kip, how are *you* doing?"

"Other than learning how to survive in the minefield of China, I'm okay."

"Good. I'm thrilled to see what you've done here in such a short time." After getting into the car, she lowered the window and said, "Maybe this dark horse of Shanghai isn't going to fade after all."

Kip stood at curbside until her car was out of sight. While walking back into the clubhouse, he smiled.

Kip spent much of the remaining day reviewing all of the changes that he'd put in place. Angie's capacity to take on a heavy workload allowed him to focus on more pressing issues. Eleni's warning about Shanghai women didn't seem to apply to Angie. While not being able go anywhere without attracting a lot of attention from men, she showed no interest in them. That included Kip. What he did feel from Angie was a growing sense of loyalty and respect. For him, that was plenty.

On Friday morning, Angie ran through a status report of the week's activities and reminded Kip of his schedule for the day. "Bev said that she got a call from Chairman Zhang saying that he enjoyed meeting you. She also said that he enjoyed the headache remedy. What's that about?" She looked up with an arched eyebrow.

He smiled. "Just men's stuff. Go ahead."

"I'll find out anyway."

"Can we get back to business?"

"Okay."

Kip looked down at his notes. "Remember that Mr. Liu from PriceWaterhouse will be here at ten. I want to talk privately with him before you call Naomi up to join us."

"Good idea. By the way, Heather is excited about something and wants to see you."

"Send her up."

Five minutes later, Heather walked into his office holding a folder. "I have some good news for you. Manny's crew and the flooring company were able to finish the townhouse model and may get a garden home done by this afternoon. He brought in a couple of temporary workers from the village to help out. They're all doing such a terrific job."

"That *is* good news."

"Well, there's more. The administrator of the Pudong International Academy is a good friend of Eleni. His name is Daleep Gupta."

Kip said, "Must be Indian. Is that the school for expat kids a couple of miles from here?"

"That's the place. Anyway, Eleni ran into Mr. Gupta at a reception last night and presented him with the idea of leasing a block of homes at Shores."

"Why would he do that?"

"Eleni said they needed housing for their teachers who want to live closer to the campus rather than making a long commute from downtown Shanghai. Anyway, he dismissed the idea at first. He told her that he'd heard that many of our tenants had moved out in the last two years because they were unhappy with the way Shores was run. After she told him about you coming in to turn the place around, he agreed to at least meet with us. In following through, I've arranged for him to meet with us next Tuesday to consider the idea."

"Fantastic!" Kip leaned over his desk and gave Heather a high five.

Blushing, she said, "Thanks. I also have some more good news."

Kip smiled. "Don't keep me waiting."

"Yesterday afternoon I met with a couple who happened to drive past our main gate. They just arrived from Norway and loved the fresh air and openness of Shores. I think that I can lease one of our garden homes to them."

"Music to my ears," said Kip, beaming.

"Mine too." She stood up and headed out the door.

Chapter 24

Angie called out from her room, "Mr. Liu from PWC is here. I've put him in the conference room."

"Okay, thanks."

A few minutes later, they walked in the room together. Kip extended his hand and said, "Mr. Liu, I'm pleased to meet you."

"Please call me David." They exchanged cards and sat across the table from each other.

David Liu spoke fluent English and wore a tailored pinstriped business suit. After tea was served, Liu proceeded to give Kip an overview of the services that PWC could provide and thanked him for considering his firm.

Kip laid out a grim assessment of their financial controls. He started by sharing his concerns about how the finance department has been handling cash. Kip then slid a copy of their latest financial statements across the table. His notes were scribbled in the margins.

As Liu perused the statements, he slowly shook his head without looking up. "Well, you're right about how seriously flawed these statements are." He then turned his attention to Kip. "At a glance, I can see that the financial irregularities are widespread, disturbing, and violate Chinese accounting laws. Your finance manager is either incompetent or dishonest. My guess is that she's both. Despite the gravity of the situation, we would need to handle this very delicately. The last thing we want would be for your manager to know that we're onto her. We'll need to be patient and take it one step at a time."

"Of course," said Kip. "Actually, I'm comfortable with going ahead with you now. You're welcome to draw up the engagement papers when you get back to the office and have them sent by courier to me for signature."

Liu smiled. "Kip, I'll personally handle your account."

"Good." Turning to Angie, Kip said, "Please call Naomi and ask her to come up to join us."

Liu said, "This'll be most interesting."

After Naomi walked in and introductions were made, Liu suggested to Kip that he speak with her in Shanghainese, explaining that it would be easier for him and Naomi to talk. In a soft, confident voice, Mr. Liu outlined what he needed her to do.

Angie simultaneously translated for Kip, whispering that Mr. Liu informed her that Kip had retained PWC to oversee their financial operations, audit the books, and provide advice to the company from time to time. Kip looked over at Naomi and saw that she was clearly not pleased with hearing the news. He thought he also saw the look of pure, unmitigated hate in her eyes. The session with Naomi lasted less than fifteen minutes.

As soon as Liu left, Angie walked back to the office with Kip, "Boss, this is getting exciting, isn't it?"

"Yes, it is. It's time to buckle your safety belt."

"Huh?"

"You'll find out soon enough," said Kip.

That afternoon, Kip called Angie on the intercom. "Let's take a walk over to the Green Latrine and make a surprise visit to the Gang of Three."

"Just a minute." She dashed around the edge of the doorway with a concerned look on her face. "You sure you want to do that? They won't be happy to see you just showing up without prior notice."

Kip smiled. "That's the idea. Besides, I'm the damn boss around here."

"Okay. But before we head over, can we talk about Rico Niu for a minute?"

Kip leaned back in his chair and clasped his hands behind his head. "I'm listening."

"A janitor who cleans up Rico's office in Kunshan happened to see a copy of our financial statements on his desk."

Kip sat upright. "Ours? As in Shanghai Shores?"

"Yes."

"How could a janitor understand English?" he asked while flipping his notebook open.

"In compliance with Chinese accounting regulations, we convert all of our statements into Chinese."

"How did you hear about our financials showing up in Rico's office?"

"From the janitor's niece. She's a classmate of mine. This is how information gets passed around in China."

"I'll bet Priscilla's involved in this somehow." After scribbling a few notes, he closed his notebook and stood up. "Time for our little surprise visit."

As soon as Kip and Angie were seen walking into the Green Latrine, the office staff stopped what they were doing. All had nervous expressions on their faces and none smiled. Several whispered among themselves. Ignoring the chilly reception, Kip walked past the several rows of desks and into the first office he came to.

Shelly Tang, the personnel manager, looked up from her desk and flashed a surprised look, then quickly smiled. "Hi, Kip. I didn't know you were coming."

"We're just walking through so I can familiarize myself with the offices here."

Shelly motioned to the chairs in front of her desk and said, "Very good. Please make yourselves comfortable."

For the next ten minutes, Shelly answered Kip's questions about her department and her own life. He learned that she was married and had a two year old daughter. Kip then stood and said, "Well, it's been a pleasure, Shelly. Can you point me to Priscilla's office?"

Shelly said, "Sure." She walked out to the hallway and pointed to the last door on the right. "That's her office."

Priscilla was sitting behind her desk, and a man in a police uniform sat across from her. She flashed an expression of shock when she looked up and saw Kip and Angie standing at the door. She then smiled awkwardly and said something to Angie in Shanghainese.

Angie nodded and turned to Kip. "She said she was pleased to see you and wanted to know if she could do anything for you."

"Please tell her I was just stopping by to say hello and wanted to tell her what a great job she was doing." *Please, God, don't punish me for lying out of my ass.*

After interpreting Kip's message and listening to Priscilla's reply, Angie said, "Kip, this is the chief of the local police, Officer Jiang Renren." She turned to the chief and formally introduced him to Kip. Officer Jiang stood as the two men exchanged business cards and shook hands. Kip towered over Jiang by more than a foot.

Kip smiled down at him and said, "Angie, please thank Chief Jiang for the kind hospitality I received at his station during the mix-up with my residency permit."

She translated and the chief immediately raised his eyebrows and smiled. "*Xièxie.*"

On their way down the hallway, Angie turned to Kip and said, "Okay, *dà laoban*, you're starting to catch on really fast."

Kip smiled and said, "*Mei wenti.*" No problem.

They then walked up to the second floor where the finance department was located. Shelly must have already alerted Naomi, because she and her staff were seated at their desks, all with saccharine smiles plastered on their faces. Naomi's smile was the biggest. She introduced Kip to the four staff members in the room, explaining what each of their duties were. As they walked from desk to desk, Kip noticed that one of the clerks had a cash box stuffed with currency sitting open in her bottom drawer. He also saw that the company's safe was ajar.

As Kip and Angie left the building and were walking toward the Buick, he said. "Well, that was revealing, wasn't it?"

"I don't know. I thought that Naomi pulled it off fairly well—gag, gag," She pointed a finger in her open mouth with her tongue out, pretending to be vomiting.

Kip chuckled and said, "You should be on stage."

Angie slipped into the Buick with a satisfied smile on her face.

Kip called Jessie up to his office for a briefing on the tenants. He asked, "I'm curious about Hans Friedrich. What do you know about him?"

"Well, he and Trudy live just down the street from you in one of the executive homes. They have a teenage girl. Hans gets a little wild sometimes but he's always respectful and a good family man. Sometimes Trudy has to come over to the clubhouse and help Hans back home after he drinks too much. I heard that once he and Manny were dancing to African tribal music in the bar. Manny's so shy, it's hard to believe. But it happened. The Friedrich family used to live in South Africa where Hans learned several African dialects. As such, he and Manny have forged a nice friendship."

Remembering their night at Casanova's, Kip wasn't surprised by anything that Jessie was telling him about Hans.

After getting home that evening, Kip changed into a warm-up suit, feeling pleased with the recent progress that had been made. He then poured a tequila and soda and walked out to the deck. The sun had already gone down. A high pressure system had settled over Shanghai, giving the area a temporary respite from coastal winds.

He pondered the change of events that had brought him here. When he'd first agreed to come to Shanghai, he did so only as a favor to Sal and nothing more. Shanghai Shores was a small project compared to the scope of his work at The Duchene Group. The thought of going to China was unsettling for him at first. He didn't know much about the country or its people.

But that was beginning to change. Despite coping with bouts of depression, he thought about the incredible experiences he'd had in just the last two weeks. Returning to the deck with his second drink in hand, Kip wondered about Angie. He thought about how valuable she'd become to him, yet she kept at a distance from him. His musings were interrupted by his phone chirping. It was Sal reminding him about dinner at his place the next evening. Kip assured him that he'd be there. Sal asked how things were going at Shores.

"Something changed today, *Yani* – there's a spark of optimism now flowing through the place. People are smiling and joking around here. Heather thinks that she may sign up a new tenant next week. Anyway, I'll catch you up on everything tomorrow."

"Hey, that sounds encouraging. See you tomorrow."

Flipping the phone shut, Kip thought—*With a huge amount of luck, we just might pull this beast out of the mire.*

Chapter 25

Kip woke up the next morning looking forward to visiting the Estrada clan. He missed seeing Maria, Sal's beautiful and fiery wife, and the three kids. *Let's see, Lora should be almost thirteen now, Tony would be eleven and little Carla eight. Maybe I've put off the visit because it's too hard seeing Sal and Maria's affection for each other. God, I miss Marci so damn much.*

On the drive over, Kip asked Benjamin to pull over to a roadside flower stand so he could buy a bouquet for Maria. They then headed off to the Jinqiao district of Pudong and stopped at the security shack of the gated community where they live. The guard gave Benjamin directions.

Sal's home looked palatial from the curb with two-foot wide Corinthian columns framing the front porch. His garden was well maintained with a wide variety of decorative plants and flowers.

As Kip was getting out of the Buick, he saw that someone pulled the curtains aside at the front window and then disappeared. Before he could reach the porch, the three kids bounded out of the front door and made a beeline for him. He had to raise the bouquet of flowers above his head so it wouldn't get crushed. All three were talking to Kip at once when they stepped into the foyer.

"Is that you, *Tuchi*?" Sal called out from down the hallway.

"*Oye, Yani*. Nice place you have here," replied Kip.

Sal said, "Hey, you kids, get off of your ugly uncle before he falls down and hurts his little tutu." Laughing, the children untangled themselves from Kip and raced off while the two men embraced.

From around the corner, Maria set her apron down on a barstool and walked into the foyer. "Okay, you two behemoths, break it up."

Kip handed her the flowers with ribbons curling down from its base. "Jeez, Maria, you're getting more and more gorgeous every time I see you."

She smiled. "Thank you. And the flowers are so beautiful." Holding the flowers in one hand, she wrapped her arms around him and started to cry.

"What's the matter?" said Kip with a worried look on his face.

"I don't know." She stammered. "It's just that I feel so sorry for what you've had to go through with Marci."

Kip held her tight, feeling tears welling up in his own eyes. He looked over at Sal with a wan smile on his face.

Taking the hint, Sal said, "Come on, *cabrón*, I'll take you through the place."

While the men were meandering from room to room, Kip said, "The aromas drifting out of the kitchen are making my mouth water. I miss Maria's home-cooked meals."

Sal said, "Well, she's cooking up one of your favorite Mexican dishes, and it won't be ready for a while. How about a drink?"

Kip smiled. "Need you ask, *amigo?*"

Kip regarded Sal's family as his dearest friends in the world. He's always felt content being around them.

After a chaotic dinner where everyone but Kip was talking at the same time, the family retreated to the family room. It took about ten minutes before the kids got bored listening to adult conversation, so they slipped off to their rooms upstairs. As the tequila continued to flow into the night, Maria, Sal, and Kip began to sing Mexican love songs in sync with the CDs they were playing. When one of the songs ended, Sal turned to Kip. "Ever think of taking singing lessons?"

"I thought I sounded pretty good."

Maria laughed and reached over to give Kip a kiss on the cheek. "Don't listen to him. I know you're trying, sweetie."

Kip thought—*This is a perfect evening.* It reminded him of the times he and Marci used to go over to Sal and Maria's home in Mill Valley.

His thoughts were interrupted when Maria turned serious. "With all the news about that poor American girl who had her leg amputated in Haikou, I've been keeping a closer eye on the kids."

Kip said, "Do you really think they're in danger?"

"Well, I think that Rico Niu was somehow involved. If he's so intent to taking over Shanghai Shores, who knows what he'll do? Maybe I can relax once he's in jail where he belongs."

Sal wrapped an arm around her shoulders and pulled her close to him. "It'll be okay, *mi amor.*"

Despite Sal's comforting words, Kip saw the worried glint in his eyes.

Energized from his visit with Sal's family, Kip got up early on Monday and was at his desk by 6:30 a.m. He kept thinking about Sal's worried look when Maria brought up Rico Niu. *I wonder if he's holding something back from me?*

At nine sharp, he heard Angie going through her morning routine in the outer office, hanging up her coat behind the door and putting her purse into one of the desk drawers. He liked the idea that she made arrangements for coffee and tea to be automatically set up in Kip's office for the start of their day. As they discussed the day's schedule, Kip drank coffee and Angie sipped tea.

"Do you always slurp your coffee?" asked Angie. She was sitting on a couch across from him with her notebook open.

"If you don't mind, I enjoy my coffee. For God's sake, let's talk about business."

Angie looked down to her notebook with a satisfied smile on her face. She spent the next few minutes reviewing the week and answering his questions. She then set her notebook on the coffee table and said, "I have a bad feeling about Rico Niu."

"What do you mean?"

"I dunno. It's just a weird feeling. Maybe we should be extra careful."

"Yeah, I guess we should."

Just before lunch, Heather came dashing into Kip's room waving a file folder and beaming. Her blotchy neck was a giveaway that she was excited about something. "We've signed up our first new tenants!"

Kip said, "Fantastic! Who are they?"

"Jan and Clara Eikland"

"Congratulations!"

Overhearing the commotion, Angie ran into the room. "Hey, girl. Way to go!"

While the two women were doing a high-five, Kip said to Heather, "When do they move in?"

"The first of the month. After doing a walk-through, they gave me a list of things that they want done, all of which were reasonable."

Kip said, "Well done."

"Thanks."

"By the way," said Kip, "what time is Mr. Gupta coming in tomorrow?"

"He'll be here at ten."

At three o'clock, Kip and Angie piled into the Buick and headed off to meet with a manager of the power bureau. Worried about their delinquent bill, Kip had asked Angie to arrange the meeting. On their way over, Kip said, "So I don't put my foot in my mouth, what advice do you have for me for the meeting?"

"Mr. Duchene, I'm glad you asked," said Angie as she crossed her legs.

Kip eyes flicked over at her knees and back, trying not to reveal that he'd noticed.

She continued, "Well, Chinese protocol can be really confusing for foreigners. First, please remember that the most senior person from each side typically opens the meeting with some kind of speech. Subordinates say nothing at this stage of the meeting. For today's meeting, let the general manager speak first."

"For *good face*?"

"Exactly. Under no circumstances should you interrupt him in the middle of his speech. He'll sit in the middle of the table directly across from you. Typically, these meetings start off on the flowery side. So it'd be good for you to be effusive about how much you respect them— blah, blah, blah. But, I can't guarantee that someone on the other side won't say something incredibly offensive—you know, like right in your face. Don't lose your cool if it happens, no matter what. Most American businessmen find it difficult to be humble. So, if you want to be effective in China, you'll learn to be humble."

"Got it." Kip looked through the windshield when Benjamin started to slow the Buick.

The power bureau was located in a drab, institutional-looking, three-story building. Benjamin had to check in with a guard at an entry gate that led into a courtyard parking area. As they walked up the interior staircase, Kip noticed that the risers of each step were slightly different in height. They were made of concrete with dubious workmanship. The hallways were narrow and poorly lit. A few times, Kip had to actually stoop while they were walking in order to keep from knocking his head on one of the cement support beams overhead. At the end of the corridor they were shown into a cluttered conference room with files stacked haphazardly on a rear credenza.

A lady came in and poured hot tea into the thinnest plastic cups Kip had ever seen. He didn't dare try to lift his cup for fear that it would collapse in his hand.

After a twenty minute wait, four men and a woman bustled into the room, speaking with excited voices. They walked around the table shaking hands with their visitors and making excuses about why they were late.

Kip thought—*What a bunch of bullshit.*

During the hubbub, the power bureau people took special notice of Kip. He was dressed in a freshly-pressed dark Armani business suit, crisp white shirt, and silk lavender tie, looking the part of a celebrity. None of the people taking their seats were accustomed to seeing such a well-dressed visitor.

Angie was quick to realize that the man sitting across from Kip was *not* the senior official present. She knew that state-owned companies would occasionally try to mislead guests at a meeting if they thought it suited them. After looking around, she wrote on a piece of notebook paper and discreetly slid it in front of Kip:

> Don't let on, but real boss is sitting
> at the end of the table to your right
> and not across from you.

Kip looked down at the note and nodded. While the acting boss was making a speech, he scanned the room to observe the head man. *Now I see him. He's dressed better, and he isn't smiling stupidly like the others.*

In the meantime, Angie was writing down the essence of the speech. Shortly after the man finished, three of the other representatives started to talk at once, all expressing an angry tone of self-importance. Remembering what Angie had said, Kip forced himself to say nothing. Besides, he couldn't understand a word they were saying.

As the meeting concluded, the man sitting across from Kip slid a document across with a red star insignia stamped on it.

Before Kip could ask what it was, Angie whispered, "I'll tell you later."

"Okay. Before we leave, let the gentleman at the end of the table know that I'd like to personally invite him to Shanghai Shores sometime as my special guest."

She raised her eyebrows and smiled.

Kip watched her walk over to the man. As they talked, the official peered over her shoulder to look at Kip, giving him a subtle nod.

Half way down the stairs, Angie said to Kip, "Boss, you really pulled that off really well. The meeting went better than I thought, and the department manager I talked to was impressed with you."

He said, "Good. So what is the document they gave us about?"

"It's a demand letter, giving us three months to pay off our past debt of about $65,000 to the power bureau."

Kip stopped on the stairs. "You've got to be kidding! If I remember right our financial records show our debt to them to be only a fraction of that amount."

"We'll have to figure it out later," said Angie.

Later that evening, Kip called Sal, "*Oye, Yani*, we closed our first new lease today."

"*Que la mádre!* That's fantastic news. I'll make sure that Reggie gets the word. Even though it's only one lease, it's a good fucking start. He'll be thrilled."

"By the way, thanks for the great time over at your place. I really needed it."

"We're family, *cabron*. Maria and the kids also enjoyed having you over. They love you, *hermano*."

"I know. I can't tell you how good it felt. Listen, I do have another question for you. I met with officials at the Shanghai Power Bureau today. While we were there, they gave us a ninety-day demand letter for an estimated

538,000 RMB. That's about $65,000. I think that we'll finally get proof that someone has been embezzling money from the company. Since it's going to take us awhile to set aside that kind of money internally, does Ingram Capital have any contingency funds to take care of this kind of situation?"

"I'll check into it and get back to you."

"Okay, thanks. I'll see you soon."

While pouring himself a drink, he thought—*No matter how this turns out, I think we're fucked.*

Chapter 26

Angie buzzed Kip on the intercom, "Daleep Gupta from the Pudong International Academy is here."

"Good," said Kip, slipping on his suit coat. "Has Heather been called?"

"Yes."

"Okay then, let's not keep the man waiting." Before he and Angie made it down to the conference room, Heather rounded the corner from the opposite end of the hallway. The three of them walked in together.

After shaking hands, Kip welcomed Gupta and introduced him to Heather and Angie. He was a distinguished looking gentleman in his late forties and spoke precisely with a British accent.

After tea was served and small talk out of the way, Kip asked Gupta to give them a background of the academy and to elaborate on the faculty's need for housing. Gupta made a crisp presentation about the school and concluded his remarks by saying, "The housing issue is quiet simple. Our faculty works hard and puts in long hours. Their biggest complaint is the one hour commute from downtown Shanghai to the campus. If there's a traffic snarl, then it could take considerably longer."

Heather said, "Well I sure know about that. It took me a good hour to drive from Puxi the first time I came here to interview. It feels great now to step out of my front door and be in my office a few minutes later."

Gupta said, "You live here?"

"Uh-huh."

"I guess you have to say you love it."

"Uh-huh." Heather was smiling and nodding her head.

Gupta laughed. "Before getting in my car to come here this morning I looked at my watch. Seven minutes later I was walking up to your reception area downstairs. If this development proves to be a suitable place to accommodate housing for my staff, then I'll be a hero."

Kip chuckled. "So will I."

Everyone laughed.

Kip turned the meeting over to Heather, who in turn, gave a PowerPoint presentation with charts, illustrations and colorful photographs of Shanghai Shores. The first frame projected on the screen was a regional map showing the location of Shanghai Shores in relation to the Pudong International Academy, the Pudong International Airport, and downtown Shanghai via Long Dong Road. She went through a series of photographs of the various types of homes, including the waterfront estates, executive, garden, and three-story townhouses. She then showed photos of the restaurant, cocktail lounge, convenience store, gym, swimming pool, conference room, and playgrounds for the children.

She wrapped up with a radiant smile and turned toward Kip. "If Mr. Gupta is interested, I'd be glad to take him around the development."

"Absolutely," said Kip. He faced Gupta. "Do you have the time for Heather to give you a quick tour?"

"Why, yes. That would be a pleasure."

Kip nodded.

Just before noon, Heather phoned Kip and let him know Gupta had left. Kip suggested that she meet with Angie and him for lunch in the clubhouse restaurant.

As soon as they sat down, Kip noticed that three mugs of beer were delivered to their table. "What's this about?"

Smiling, Heather picked up her glass and waited for Kip and Angie to follow. "We have a chance to lease TWENTY-FOUR of our houses with Pudong International Academy!"

Kip and Angie looked at each other in shock.

Heather continued, "Mr. Gupta wasn't as formal when we walked around. He said that if they could get a special deal with Shores, they may consider leasing a block of twenty-four homes: fifteen townhouses, seven garden homes and two executive homes."

Kip smiled coyly. "And no estate homes?"

Angie said, "I wasn't even there and know the answer to that. It's called $12,000 a month lease payments."

"Now aren't you smart," he quipped.

Heather said, "Anyway, if we could put a deal together the teachers would start to move into the twenty-four homes on Sunday, January 1st. That would give them one full week to get settled before classes begin."

Kip said, "That would boost our occupancy to forty percent in one damn big swoop. Can we get the twenty-four units ready by January 1st?"

"I've already talked with Manny," said Heather, "and he said that we could—no problem."

"Okay, what has to happen in order to sign them up?"

Clearing her throat, Heather said, "Well . . . er, that's our challenge. Mr. Gupta is skeptical about our ability to bring Shanghai Shores up to the standards he requires. First, he pointed out that we have a terrible reputation."

Heather looked from Angie to Kip before going on. "He said that there are too many stories floating around Shanghai that we're so poorly managed we may lose the development due to government intervention."

Kip groused, "How in the hell would he know that?"

Angie put her hand on his sleeve and said, "How many times have I reminded you that this is China. Everybody knows everything here."

Heather continued, "He was mostly concerned that our tenants are unhappy, some of whom are planning not to renew their leases."

Kip said, "Christ! How much time do we have to satisfy Gupta?"

"December 1st."

Kip stood up and walked over to the window. While he was gazing out to the sea, Heather and Angie looked at each other. Angie shrugged her shoulders.

He then returned to his seat and said, "Okay, that gives us a little over four months. Now I know that seems like a long time, but believe me it's not. First we have to overcome the problem of tenant dissatisfaction. Hopefully we can improve it enough to satisfy Gupta. He's more apt to want to see a positive trend rather than a miracle. Anyone disagree?"

Heather and Angie looked at each other and shook their heads.

"Good. At the same time, Rico Niu is doing everything possible to bribe government officials and he seems to be making steady progress. I haven't figured out yet how to neutralize him, but believe me, I will. Then there are all of the sticky issues of managing our debt load. I'm worried that those idiots at the power bureau will renege on their notice to give us three months to get current. And let us not forget our little threesome in the Green Latrine."

Angie and Heather laughed.

"Yeah, I know," said Kip. "We have to try to keep our sense of humor through all of this. In the meantime, we should start thinking about scheduling a tenants meeting as soon as possible."

Heather said, "Okay. I'll ask Jessie to help with the arrangements."

"Perfect. Say, that PowerPoint presentation you gave to Gupta was impressive."

"Thanks." Heather gave Kip a warm smile.

"Where did those beautiful photographs of Shores come from?"

Angie nodded toward Heather. "She took them."

Kip raised his eyebrows. "Well done. By the way, I meant to ask how the townhouse is working out for you."

Heather brushed some loose strands of hair away from her face. "I love it. It's cozy and private."

After Paul served their meals, Kip said, "Don't say anything now, but I'm going to name Paul as our food and beverage manager and invite him to the managers' meetings when the time is right. It would be good for the company."

"You know you're going to have a fight with Priscilla on that, don't you?" said Angie.

"Don't worry. I have plans for her."

After Kip returned to his office, he picked up the phone and thanked Eleni for introducing Mr. Gupta to them. He then walked down the hall to an unused office and nonchalantly stepped inside. Flipping open his cell phone, he called Sal to inform him about the proposed deal they were working on with the Pudong International Academy.

"Well fuck me!" Sal exclaimed. He then congratulated Kip and said that he was pleased that Heather was making a difference.

Kip was not surprised when Sal promised to send over a bottle of Gran Patrón. He then cleared his throat and said, "Sal, I think my office phone is bugged. Right now I'm calling you on my cell phone."

"Where are you calling from?"

"I'm holed up in an unused office several doors down."

"Good thinking," said Sal.

"After we hang up I'm going to head back to my office and call you on my land line. Here's what I want you to say . . ."

Chapter 27

Kip was walking through the outer office when Angie looked up from her computer. She said, "Do you have a minute?"

"Sure."

She followed him into his office and sat in the chair in front of his desk. "After you talked about your plans to promote Paul, I picked up some tidbits about why Priscilla is managing the restaurant. She once owned a hotpot restaurant in Qingdao and used that information to convince Ralph that she should temporarily manage our restaurant."

"When was that?" asked Kip.

"When Shores first opened. The problem occurred when she refused to give it up later. Ralph was too lazy to deal with her antics, so he decided not to make the change."

"Didn't Paul object?"

"Hardly. He wouldn't for fear of losing his job."

"She doesn't have the power to do that," said Kip, flipping a ballpoint pen onto his desk.

"In reality, she has more power here than anyone, including you. You've already gotten a good dose of that."

"Yeah I have. Listen, I need to make a private call. Would you mind closing the door on your way out?"

She stood with a confused look on her face. "Oh . . . okay."

Kip picked up the phone and dialed Sal's number. After finishing his conversation with Sal, he got up and went over to open the adjoining door to Angie's office. "You can come in now."

Angie looked up from her desk. "Did your little private call happen to involve a woman?"

He chuckled. "Why in the hell would you say that?"

"I don't know. You've never asked me to leave before when you've made a call."

"For your information, I didn't call a woman." Kip sat at his desk and opened his notebook. *How about that. Was that a little jealousy?*

After flipping through several pages, he said, "We need to schedule a second meeting with Mr. Liu. Our present accounting software package needs to be scrapped and replaced with one that complies with GAAP."

He jotted down a telephone number on scratch paper and slid it across his desk. "Go ahead and call Mr. Liu to set up the meeting. Then let Naomi know about it, but be discrete about how much you say to her."

"Anything else?"

"Yes. In about an hour, I want you to ask Bev and Priscilla to meet us in the conference room. We should talk about yesterday's meeting with the Power Bureau. But before they come over, instruct Naomi to give Priscilla a copy of an itemized billing statement of our electric bill."

"Got it."

An hour later, Angie announced from her outer office that the women were waiting in the conference room.

Slipping on his suit coat, he said, "Good, let's go."

After everyone was seated, Kip said, "Thanks for coming. My first question is this. Are we guaranteed that the power bureau will give us three months to bring our account current?"

After Bev translated for Priscilla, they both agreed that they had absolutely no guarantee of anything. The power bureau could come in and cut off their supply of electricity anytime they pleased.

Kip shook his head in frustration. "We also need to reconcile our payments to the power bureau. Did you bring our records over?"

Bev and Priscilla looked at each other. Bev said, "Ah, Kip . . . I'm afraid that Naomi was not able to find the power bureau files."

His face reddening. "How convenient."

No one said anything.

Kip took a deep breath and exhaled. "Okay, here's the bad news. Right now, we can't afford to pay off our electric bill. Under the circumstances, does anyone have a suggestion on how to best handle this with the power bureau?"

Bev translated for Priscilla. She stammered something in response. Bev said, "Priscilla thought we were planning to pay them off in full."

Kip thought—*Fantastic! I finally got the bitch!* In a calm voice, he said, "I wish we could."

Priscilla looked confused.

Kip stood up. "Okay, we can figure this out later. Bev, please thank Priscilla for me, but stick around for a minute after she leaves."

After Priscilla left, he said to Bev and Angie, "Those power bureau files have probably been taken off site by now, and I doubt that we'll ever find them. Bev, I want you to run over to the power bureau and ask them for copies of our payment records covering the last two years. Don't call them in advance."

"Right now?"

"Yes."

After the meeting, Kip told Angie to ask Heather to come up.

She said, "What's up, boss?"

"I'll explain after Heather gets here."

Five minutes later, Angie called out, "Heather's here."

Kip led them down to the spare office.

Angie looked around at the dusty office furniture inside and chuckled. "Well, this is interesting."

Heather added, "It sure is. What going on?"

Kip said, "You'll understand in a minute." Just as the door clicked shut, Kip raised his arms in triumph. "Okay, ladies, I've got Priscilla!"

Angie said, "What do you mean?"

"Where do you think Priscilla got the idea that we were prepared to pay off the power bureau?"

"I dunno. I didn't think much about it at the time."

Heather settled in a seat and said, "Hey, guys, I'm totally lost."

Kip said, "Sorry about that. Here's what happened. Earlier this afternoon, I called Sal from my office and asked him if he could arrange for Ingram Capital to pay off our power bureau bill. He said they would."

"Sorry, but I'm not following you," said Angie.

"I'm surprised. You usually figure these things out before anyone else. My call to Sal was to set up a ruse. I suspected my telephone was being bugged and wanted to find out for sure. So, Sal and I staged the whole thing, hoping that Priscilla would be listening in."

Laughing, Angie said, "You sly fox, you!"

Heather said, "What a trip!"

"Thank you very much." Kip stood up and bowed.

Angie rolled her eyes and said, "It wasn't really *that* great."

"Maybe not," said Kip with a boyish grin. "Angie, just how prevalent is wiretapping in China?"

"It's prevalent."

"Tell me more," said Kip.

"Well, the practice of bugging a person's home or office is certainly not rare, particularly if the government's involved. Because government officials tend to be paranoid of outsiders, they believe that it is their patriotic duty to target them for wire-tapping and shadowing their movements. Simply put, we have no right to privacy in China. So what are you getting at?"

"Just this. From now on we need to be very careful about what we say. If we suspect that a room may be bugged, we don't talk about Rico Niu, the Gang of Three, or anything confidential. While we were being so smart in our planning to defeat Niu, all of our conversations could have been bugged."

Heather said, "Are you sure?"

Kip said, "No. But hearing unexplained clicks on the phone, I started to wonder. So for now let's just assume we are just to be on the safe side. We should quietly give each other a signal when we need to discuss sensitive subjects. We'll meet in this room to talk. In its present disheveled condition, no one would bother to plant a bug in here."

"Very clever, boss," said Angie. "Are you sure that you weren't Chinese in a previous life?"

"Shit!" Heather blurted. "This is like watching one of those old whodunit movies."

"Yes, but this is even better," said Angie. "My devious Shanghainese mind understands what Kip is thinking. Also, we really blew it with Benjamin."

"Why's that?" asked Kip.

"Well, he's been hearing everything in the car, including our telephone conversations. A few times I thought I saw his eyes react to what we were saying, but scoffed it off as overreacting."

"I'm still not following you," said Kip.

"Benjamin was hired by Shelly."

"So?"

"In China, that means she controls him. He's indebted to her."

Kip said, "So that suggests he's spying for her?"

Angie rolled her eyes. "Duh."

Heather laughed. "You guys are killing me. Do you always spat like this?"

Angie said, "Heather, it's hard to avoid it when working for someone who's as clueless about China as Kip."

"Let's get back to business," said Kip. "Why don't we just change drivers? I told Benjamin that he was just temporary anyway."

Angie said, "I can tell you that most employees have a very high regard for one of the other drivers, Mr. Zeng. He works hard, is incredibly loyal, and minds his own business. He lives in the nearby town of Chuansha."

Heather said in a quiet voice, "I wouldn't make the change."

Kip and Angie looked at her with surprised expressions.

She continued, "Why not keep Benjamin on as if he's done nothing's wrong? Then let Benjamin overhear us talk about things we want him to pass on to Priscilla. You know—deliberately mislead him."

Kip said, "Jesus, Heather, now I know why you want to practice law. You're devious."

Angie nudged Heather with her elbow. "That a way, girl."

Kip said, "Okay, ladies, any other ideas on how we should proceed from here?"

Angie explained, "We need to think as if we're at war, because we *are*. In my ancient history class we read about General Sun Tzu, one of our most influential military figures. More than 2,000 years ago, he wrote a book: *The Art of War*. People from all over the world have used his text to study the principles of war. We don't need to read his book, but we do need to look at Rico Niu and the *Gang of Three* as our enemies. You see, one side will be victorious and the other will lose. None of us wants to be on the losing side."

Heather said, "When I studied Chinese history I remember one of the things General Sun Tzu said."

"You know about him?" asked Angie.

"Yes. He once wrote that if you believe that you have enough soldiers to win, go out and increase that number tenfold—then go forth and bury your enemy. Taking his advice, we should mount an attack against Niu and the *Gang of Three* many times stronger than we believe will ever be needed. Right now, we're far from being ready."

Kip said. "Without knowing a thing about Chinese military history, our first strategy should be secrecy—you know, surprise the enemy. No one other than Sal and Reggie should know about our plans. Anytime we talk about this, we should assure ourselves that we're not being bugged. Heather, you should assume that your townhouse is also being bugged."

She chuckled. "That seems like a stretch to me."

"Think about it—you're the daughter of the Chairman of the Board. You've taken on one of the most important positions here to boost sales. As a matter of fact, I want you and Angie to be extra careful. With Rico Niu, we shouldn't rule out anything."

Angie said, "Believe me. I can take care of myself."

Kip held up his hands. "Ladies, please just be careful."

Angie turned to Heather and sighed, "I think he cares."

"Come on, knock it off," barked Kip. "So, getting back to what I was saying, I suggest we assume that obvious places are being bugged and the information is being handed over to Rico Niu. If we're able to make plans without tipping anyone off, then we hold a great advantage over him."

Absorbing what Kip had shared, Heather said, "You know, I have to say that I wouldn't have ever thought that we could have been bugged in a million years. The idea that someone might be listening to my private conversations frankly pisses me off."

"Get used of it, girl. You're in China," said Angie.

Kip said, "Okay, then. I'll check into how we can get the entire development swept for listening devices without anyone knowing what we're doing."

In the close quarters of the unused office, Kip was privately enjoying the intermingling scents of the two women's perfumes. With the meeting over, Heather headed down the stairs while Kip and Angie went back to their offices. Before Angie sat at her desk she noticed a flower arrangement sitting on top of her credenza. Thinking someone made a mistake, she pulled out a card wedged between the stems and read it:

Dear Angie,

This is just to let you know how much I appreciate your hard work. I know it's not easy trying to teach me how to understand the "Chinese ways."

Warm regards,   Kip

Overwhelmed with emotion, she walked around her desk and headed into Kip's office.

When he looked up from the notes he was making, he saw that Angie had tears trickling down her cheeks. With an alarmed look on his face, he said, "Angie, is something wrong?"

"Nooooo," she sobbed.

He stood up and walked over to her. "Come on, what's wrong?"

She said, "No one's ever given me flowers before."

His shoulders relaxed and he smiled. "Really? I just wanted to say thanks."

Wiping tears away with her hands, she said, "Sorry. I just got a little carried away, boss, that's all. The flowers are lovely—thank you." She then scurried back into her office.

That evening, Kip thought about Angie's reaction to the flowers. His mind automatically went to Marci. *If you're here, I'd tell you how much I miss you and love you.* Feeling alone and depressed, he pulled out a bottle of Merlot from his wine rack, grabbed a stemmed glass, and walked out to the deck. After getting settled and taking his first sip of wine, Kip noticed that a storm was approaching the coast from the East China Sea. Far out on the horizon, an ominous bank of dark clouds could be seen with periodic flashes of lighting. *Too far out to hear thunder.* The onshore winds were kicking up three-foot waves against the seawall. Feeling the salt air stinging his face, he compared the storm with how he was feeling inside—dark, foreboding, and turbulent. He mused about how to uncover the problems at Shores in time. The chances of success seemed almost insurmountable. He finished off the first glass and thought—*Fuck it. I might as well have another.*

From his Haikou penthouse apartment, Rico Niu was talking on the phone. He smiled and had an excited lilt to his voice. "Okay, let's start keeping a closer eye on her. Follow her everywhere she goes. It's good to know she rides a bicycle through the villages around Shanghai Shores. I'll figure something out—something real nice and sweet. *Zàijiàn.*"

The person on the other end also said goodbye and hung up.

Chapter 28

The next morning, Jessie waited patiently in the doorway of Kip's office while he was talking on the telephone. As soon as he hung up, she walked over and asked, "How does next Wednesday evening look to you for our first tenants meeting?"

He flipped open his appointment book. "Sounds good— let's do it."

"Okay, I'll make all of the arrangements."

As she started to head back out, Kip called, "Say, wait a minute."

"What?"

Kip looked more carefully at her. "That's a nice shade of lipstick you're wearing."

Jessie smiled and dashed out of the room.

I'll be damned. Probably Heather's doing. He brought his hand up to his sweaty forehead and squeezed his temples between his thumb and fingers. *Aspirin's finally working. Maybe I should cut down a little.*

He worked late that evening. While looking at his watch, he thought—*It's 7:30 already. I could use a drink. Just a couple though.* He gathered the files spread across his desk, locked them in the bottom drawer, and headed downstairs to the clubhouse lounge.

"Hey, Kip, over here!" Hans Friedrich was sitting at a far table with his wife, Trudy, and another couple he didn't recognize. "Pull up a chair. Whadaya drinking?"

He hesitated for a moment—*Ah, what the hell.* "Tequila and soda on the rocks with a wedge of lime."

After ordering a round of drinks for everyone at the table, Hans said, "Kip, let me introduce you to Henry and Lisa Young."

Duchene leaned forward and shook their hands. Henry was a handsome Chinese man in his early forties. He had salt-and-pepper hair parted in the middle. Lisa was a petite Chinese woman and remarkably beautiful. Her facial skin looked like fine porcelain in contrast to her jet-black shiny hair. Both were impeccably dressed and well groomed.

Henry nodded at Kip. "I'm pleased to meet you. I've heard a lot of good things about you from Hans."

Kip glanced at Hans and winked. Hans smiled back, revealing a gap between his front teeth.

Henry continued, "Lisa and I are glad you're onboard here. This thing's been hell on the tenants."

Kip said, "Sorry you had to go through that."

Hans said, "Lisa's been the shining light at Shores. Despite the problems here, she's stepped up to boost tenant morale by hosting informal parties."

Kip turned to Lisa. "I hope you're not planning to leave anytime soon."

She said, "Oh, no. Despite the problems, we love it here."

"That's good to hear." Before sitting down, Kip walked around and gave Trudy a hug. Compared with Hans' rotund body, she worked out daily and her slim waistline proved it. Leaning closer, Kip inhaled with his eyes closed. "Let me guess . . . Jacobs' Daisy Perfume."

She chuckled. "Kip, you're amazing."

He cupped his hand next to her ear and whispered, "Has Hans been behaving himself?"

"Yeah, in my dreams."

The waiter arrived with a full tray of drinks. Hans then raised his glass and said, "*Salud, para dinero y amor.*"

Henry said, "What does that mean?"

"Cheers to money and love," said Kip and took a satisfying swallow of his drink. "Other than German,

English, and French, Hans also speaks a pretty mean Spanish."

Over the next hour and a half, Kip found Henry and Lisa to be a delightful couple. Henry had a low-keyed manner and laughed easily while Lisa playfully bantered with the others around the table. Hans' stories of his zany adventures made everyone laugh out loud. Trudy was content to join in the laughter without saying much herself. By the time Henry and Lisa decided to leave, the three men had finished off their fifth drink.

Hans hadn't shown any sign of drinking other than his cheeks getting rosy. But as soon as he tried to stand up he started to wobble and had to flop back down in his seat. Kip motioned for Paul, the restaurant manager, to come over. "Paul, let's help get Hans home."

Paul said, "Sure, boss."

Between the two men, they propped Hans up between them and walked him the fifty yards between the clubhouse and his home down the street.

Ten minutes later, Kip let himself in his home and made a beeline for his bed. At 2:15 in the morning, he was awakened by an irritation on his neck from his starched shirt collar. *Ah, shit. I forgot to get undressed again. Fuck it.* He slipped back into a deep slumber.

As soon as Angie got to work on Monday, she bounded into Kip's office and said, "I have some news about Rico Niu!"

Kip winced. He brought a finger to his lips and pointed up.

Angie slapped her forehead with the open palm of her hand.

He winked at her. "I couldn't care less about Mr. Niu."

Understanding what he was doing, she went along and said, "Whatever," then walked out.

Despite the slipup, Kip couldn't help but smile hearing Angie banging around in her office putting her things away in record time. *She's mad at herself, all right.* Allowing a few minutes to pass, Kip walked through the outer office and motioned with his finger for her to follow. Neither one of said a word as they walked down to the unoccupied office.

Once inside, Angie flopped down in one of the chairs and said, "Sorry, I forgot."

"Don't worry about it. Tell me about Niu."

She sat upright. "Okay. One of my classmates is a hostess at Eight Dragons."

"What's that?"

"It's a popular restaurant for locals in the Lujiazui Area of Pudong. Anyway, Rico Niu and the local police chief, Inspector Jiang, dined there together last night."

Kip arched his eyebrows. "No kidding."

"And guess who was with them?"

"I give up."

"None other than our very own Priscilla Mao."

He said, "Fantastic! That's the direct link between Niu and the *Gang of Three* we've been looking for. Wasn't Inspector Jiang the guy we saw in Priscilla's office the other day?"

"None other."

Making notes, he said, "Angie, how reliable is this?"

"Chinese people usually get this kind of thing dead right. I've told my friend all about what's happening here. She already knew what Inspector Jiang looks like. And most people in China would recognize Niu."

Kip looked at Angie and frowned. "Why?"

"He's famous, that's why."

"How did your friend know it was Priscilla?"

"When she was checking the reservation list, she saw Priscilla's name listed with 'Shanghai Shores' as the company name. You should know by now that Chinese are really snoopy." Angie smiled and fluttered her eyes.

Duchene slowly shook his head. "Like I need to be reminded." He closed his notebook. "Okay, Niu must be stepping up his bid to take over Shores. With Priscilla's involvement, this is a classic Trojan Horse kind of attack."

"A what?"

"Nothing."

"Whatever," Angie said with a smirk. "Is there any chance that you know anyone in the gambling business?"

He looked up. "Why do you ask?"

"Well, shouldn't we be trying to find other people who regard Niu as a problem?"

Kip flipped his pen onto the dusty desk. "Go on."

"Well, right now, we're too small. If we can build a coalition of people with like minds to go after Niu, we'd have a better chance to beating him. The best place to find an enemy of an enemy is to look within the industry they operate. In Rico's case, it's gambling."

"You Machiavellian little devil."

"Naturally, I'm Chinese." She smiled and crossed her long legs.

He noticed. "Well, it's a damn good idea and I happen to know someone in the gaming business in Las Vegas. I'll ask him if he knows anything about Niu."

"What does he do?"

"He's a major figure in professional poker—even wrote a best-selling book on it."

"There you go then," said Angie.

Kip said, "Okay, let's talk about a tenants meeting for a minute. Forget the clubhouse. I've decided to have it over at my place."

"You mean your home?"

"Absolutely," said Kip with excitement in his voice. "The Marbella will give us a cozier atmosphere. Talk to Paul about catering it. Oh yeah, make sure there's plenty of booze."

"Wow. This is getting exciting."

"One more thing. I want all of the managers there to give a very short speech. The tenants should know who does what. That includes you."

"I feel so privileged," she said, rolling her eyes. "Anything else?"

"No, that's it for now."

Chapter 29

After Angie left, Kip stayed behind. *Let's see, I think it's 5:30 p.m. in Las Vegas.* He flipped open his cell phone and dialed Mike Lerner, a classmate from Santa Monica High School. "Hey Mike."

"Who's calling?"

"It's Kip."

"Hey, Kipper. It's nice to hear from you! You sound like you're calling from the other side of the world."

Kip chuckled. "I am. I'm doing a difficult turn-around job for Ingram Capital at an expatriate housing community in Shanghai."

"Shanghai? What the fuck are you doing in Shanghai?"

"I'll fill you in some other time, Mike. But right now I have a problem."

"Anything I can do to help?"

"I sure hope so. The Shanghai government may attempt to confiscate the property back from Ingram and hand it over to a notorious Chinese racketeer. Since he's a kingpin in gambling, I was hoping that you could give me some advice."

"What's the guy's name?"

"Rico Niu. He's from Hainan Island in—"

"Ah, shit. Kipper, you've got a problem all right. He's a bad dude known for his strong-arm tactics. He doesn't play by the rules in the gaming industry. You probably already know that Hainan is a rogue island state and far from the reaches of Chinese leaders in Beijing."

"That's what I've heard."

Lerner went on. "Niu is king there. He has deep enough pockets to lavish government officials on the island with bribe money. As a result, they protect the man. Any complaint against him gets thrown out of court."

Kip said, "I'm not surprised. It's finally sinking in that the rule of law in China sucks."

"That's right, my friend. So tell me, how exactly is Niu connected with taking over your housing development?"

"Niu launders his gambling money on the mainland. One of the legitimate businesses he's acquired is a homebuilding company in Kunshan, a city just west of Shanghai."

"I hadn't heard," said Mike.

"Well, he has. Based on our information, he has set his sights on using the Kunshan operation to build the rest of the homes at Shanghai Shores."

"What's that?"

"Oh, it's the name of Ingram's development. Using the same tactics Niu has used in Hainan, he's bribing local Pudong government officials to help facilitate the take-over."

"What are the chances that he can succeed?"

"Reasonably good. The development has been poorly managed in the past. As a result, the occupancy rate of tenants is declining. This has prevented Ingram Capital from going to the secondary market to raise the funds needed to finish construction of the project. There's an obscure law in China that gives the government the right to take back property under these circumstances."

"It surprises me to hear that an Ingram Capital project has been mishandled. Reggie is known for turning rags into riches, not the other way around."

"Well, it's rather a complicated story."

"I can imagine. Okay, here's what I can do. I know Danny Tong, the second most important guy in the gaming business in Macao. By working quietly behind the scenes, he's orchestrating to have Macao overtake Las Vegas as the number one gambling destination in the world."

Kip said, "He must be a powerful figure."

"He is." Lerner paused, as if weighing his options. "Okay, I'll talk to Danny about your situation. Without question, he'll know a lot more about Rico Niu than either of us. As soon as I hear back from him, I'll give you a call. How can I reach you?"

"Just call me on this number."

"No problem. Ah, Kipper . . . how are *you* doing?"

"Hanging in there." Kip shifted in his seat.

"I'm so sorry. You know, I hardly recognized you last year at Marci's services. If ever I saw a man whose had his heart torn out, it was you."

Wanting to quickly get off the phone, Kip said, "Well, let me know if you find anything on this."

"Will do. Talk to you soon, buddy."

"Thanks again," said Kip and hung up. He pulled a handkerchief out of his pants pocket and wiped the sweat off of his forehead. *Okay, I have a feeling that we've just started round one, Mr. Niu, you big prick.*

While Kip was reviewing financial reports later that morning, his desk phone rang. "Hey, *Tuchi, que pasa?*"

"Everything's good here."

"Listen, Reggie's invited us to his penthouse tonight. He's—"

"*Yani*, I'll call you right back."

Kip walked down to the spare office and flipped open his cell phone. "Sorry to cut you off."

"I know, I know. I can be fucking stupid at times. Forgot about the bugging thing."

"Do I hear a little humility?"

"You hear no such fucking thing. What I was saying was that Reggie wants us to attend a social gathering at his penthouse tonight."

"He has a penthouse in town?"

"Yeah. Wait until you see it. It's in an exclusive high-rise apartment complex in Pudong. From his place, you can see all of downtown Shanghai with the Huangpu River right below. Anyway, he'll be having some honored guests from

Dubai along with some friends from Shanghai. It would be good if you could make it."

"I guess so. What's the occasion?" Kip flipped open his notebook and started to jot down the information.

"Ingram recently put together an investment fund in Abu Dhabi. This came as a result of Reggie's long-time friendship with the royal family of United Arab Emirates. One of the family members will be there along with two associates, an architect and a financial guy."

"What's the address?"

"Don't worry about it. I'll ask my driver to give Benjamin a call. He'll give him directions."

"What time?"

"Six thirty. It's on the 48th floor."

"Okay. See you tonight then," said Kip.

Kip tried to think how much Sal had a chance to say over the land line in his office. *Oh, well. I doubt that any harm was done.*

Angie popped her head in the door. "I didn't know you had an appointment with Milt Avery."

Still smarting from his first meeting with Avery two weeks before, Kip snapped, "What are you talking about?"

"He's waiting for you in the conference room."

"Tell him I'm busy. And tell him not to ever return without calling first."

Seeing Kip's jaw muscles tighten, she said, "I'll take care of it."

After she left, Kip stewed about Avery—*What a complete asshole.*

Thirty minutes later in Haikou, Rico Niu received a telephone call from Priscilla. He said, "Uh-huh. I see," while leaning back in his chair and filing his fingernails. He listened for another minute before sitting upright. "Okay then. Good work." He hung up with a smile that revealed a perfect set of whitened teeth.

He called his disfigured bodyguard, Mr. Tao, into his office. "Make contact with our man in Pudong and tell him that he can go ahead with our plans"

Tao asked, "When?"

"Tonight. Duchene will be heading over to Ingram's penthouse."

"What time?"

"Don't fucking question me." Niu flashed a chilling look at Tao. "Just have Mr. Long wait outside the main gate to tail him when he leaves. In your special way remind Mr. Long not to fuck it up."

A smile crept across Tao's scarred face.

Chapter 30

Reggie's penthouse was only a few blocks from the Jin
Mao Tower. Driving the minivan, Benjamin pointed. "Boss,
we go there."

Duchene looked up and saw that the development was
gated consisting of three high-rise buildings. At the entry
gate, the guard checked Kip's name on a guest list and
waved Benjamin through, telling him to drive to the portico
of the second building.

As Benjamin opened the car door for Kip, he said, "Ah .
. . boss?"

Kip got out and was buttoning his suit coat. "Yes?"

"I think some guy follow us."

Kip looked at Benjamin. "You sure?"

"I think yes, boss. I see car have only one headlight. I
turn, he turn. He follow me one street back. I no get good
look. I think he in black Toycta. Not so good."

"Maybe you should call the police."

"No, boss. We okay. You need know."

"Okay, thanks for being alert." Kip had a frown on his
face as he mounted the entry steps and entered the building.
I wonder if Rico's involved in this?

"*Que estás haciendo, hermano?*" echoed Sal's voice
from the far side of the elegant lobby.

"No problem." Kip gave Sal a hug and exchanged a
couple of slaps on the back. "I'm looking forward to seeing
Reggie's place."

"It's out-fucking-rageous, *Tuchi.*"

Kip chuckled.

On the way up in the elevator, Sal looked in the mirror and realigned his tie. Kip caught him practicing his smile. "*Yani*, you're pretty enough."

Sal did a salsa dance step in place and sang out, "*Doncha know it?*"

Kip smiled and slowly shook his head.

As the elevator doors slid open on the 48th floor, the two well-dressed men stepping out could hear the kaleidoscopic sounds of the party resonating from down the hallway.

Kip said, "I thought this was going to be an intimate affair. The place looks packed."

"When Reggie gives a party in Shanghai," said Sal, "he invites a lot of his friends, business contacts, and government officials. He's a wise old fox who deliberately selects certain guests for every affair and puts them together to see what happens."

Kip said, "This'll be interesting."

As they entered the crowded foyer, Sal said, "*Tuchi*, you can think of Reggie's bashes as Shakespearean productions, and he plays King Lear to perfection."

"Ah, there you are, my two handsome knights in armor," beamed Reggie, walking toward them with a clenched pipe in his mouth. "Sal, I already bloody well know what you're drinking. Kip, my bartender makes a wicked London Special, even better than what you had at the Jin Mao Tower."

Thinking of what Benjamin said about being followed, Kip smiled. "I could use one."

Reggie pointed to the bar surrounded by guests vying to get the bartender's attention. "Okay, pop on over and I'll find you chaps later."

Sal asked Reggie, "Where're the gentlemen from Abu Dhabi?"

"I'm afraid they'll arrive a trifle late. Their flight in was delayed."

With drinks in hand, Kip and Sal wandered around the expansive flat. It was decorated like an English country estate, with floor-to-ceiling polished wood paneling and wainscoting, fine-crafted furniture, and oil paintings depicting classic English scenes. The formal dining room, wet bar, and kitchen was located on the right side of the foyer. On the left was a step down living room with a twenty-four foot vaulted ceiling. Muted jazz filtered through every room. From the rear of the foyer, a grand curved staircase led up to the second-floor bedrooms.

Looking around, Kip said, "I wouldn't have guessed this kind of place to be in Shanghai."

Sal put his arm on Kip's shoulders and led him away. "I told you. Hey, look at the view from over here."

The two men peered out floor-to-ceiling picture windows that provided a panoramic view of the Huangpu River just below and the lights from downtown Shanghai beyond.

Kip finished off his drink. "I'm impressed." Holding up an empty glass, he said, "You ready for another?"

They worked their way back toward the bar through clusters of people, most of whom were Chinese, either government officials or young venture capitalists. Kip said, "Shouldn't we introduce ourselves to some of these guys?"

Sal said, "Nah. They've all been invited for a certain reason. Reggie will bring one group after another over to us and open the conversation, then move on to make other introductions. You'll understand later."

"If you say so." Kip handed his glass to the smiling bartender. "I'll have another London Special."

While their drinks were being made, Kip turned around and saw Reggie circulating around the room with his Chinese executive assistant. Beginning to feel mellow, Kip smiled to himself—*Not as beautiful as Angie.*

"What the fuck are you smiling about?" chided Sal.

"Ah, nothing." Kip picked up his fresh drink and nodded toward the living room. "Look who's heading our way."

With his assistant in tow, Reggie was guiding a distinguished looking Chinese man toward them. Reggie got a surprised look on his face when his guest recognized Kip and made a fuss saying hello and enthusiastically shaking his hand.

Kip smiled back and attempted to greet the man in Chinese. "*Ni hao ma?*"

"*Ah, hen hao! Xièxie.*" Very good. Thank you.

Chairman Zhang laughed, then turned to Reggie and rambled off something in an excited voice. Understanding, Sal also laughed and patted Kip on the shoulder.

Translating, the assistant turned to Reggie and said. "Chairman Zhang said that Kip is his good friend even though his Chinese is quite terrible."

Reggie chuckled.

She continued, "The Chairman said that Kip and Miss Beverly Shen, our legal counsel, visited him a couple of weeks ago and he immediately took a liking to Kip."

"Well done, old boy!" beamed Reggie. He tilted his pipe up between his teeth. "Chairman Zhang represents the new breed of senior government officials in China. They are well-educated leaders who are working for justice and dedicated to making China a better country for its people."

After hearing the translation, Chairman Zhang said to Reggie, "*Ah, xièxie—xièxie,*" and reached out to shake his hand with both of his. After Reggie headed off in another direction, the Chairman lowered his voice and spoke close to Sal's ear. He then faced Kip and smiled. "*Zàijiàn, péngyou.*"

Kip answered, "*Zàijiàn*, my friend."

After Chairman Zhang wandered off, Kip asked Sal, "What the hell was *that* all about?"

"He said that Rico Niu is honing in on Shores and suggests that you be very careful. *Tuchi*, the Chairman hears just about everything that goes on in Pudong."

An hour later, the group from Abu Dhabi made a grand entrance to a spontaneous applause, led by Reggie. Kip assumed that the three men would be dressed in the traditional *Thobe* robes and *Ghutra* head wraps, but they were impeccably dressed in western business suits. They looked to be in their late thirties.

Reggie warmly greeted them, extending his hand to the senior member of the group, "*Salaam alaykum.*"

Smiling, he replied, "*Wa alaykum as-salaam.*"

Previously instructed by Reggie, a waiter brought over a tray of their favorite fruit juices. With drinks in hand, Reggie escorted his honored guests directly over to Kip and Sal. He turned to the Arabs and said, "Gentlemen, permit me to introduce you to the two good chaps on our team I spoke to you about earlier. This is Mr. Kip Duchene and Mr. Sal Estrada."

They replied warmly, speaking with refined British accents. Their eyes sparkled with a look of excitement and open curiosity.

A few minutes later, Reggie said, "Well, Mohammed, are you ready to be introduced to our guests?"

"Yes, anytime."

Setting his glass down on a side table, Reggie walked over to the curved staircase and took a couple of steps up. He turned around to face his guests and draped an arm over the curved banister. Speaking over the din of the party, he called out, "I daresay, you all look to be having a jolly good time, what?"

Within a few seconds, everyone stopped talking and turned their attention towards Reggie. "My mum once told me that a cracking good speech is inversely proportionate to the length of time it takes to give it. Since she's never led me astray, I'll make this quite short so we can get on with it."

People chuckled while others were translating what Reggie was saying for Chinese guests.

Clearing his throat, he said, "Well now, we're indeed honored this evening to be in the presence of three very distinguished gentlemen from one of the two most exciting cities of the world—Dubai."

Motioning his hand, he said, "Mohammed Karoo, Khalid Yacoub, and Sharif Al-Fulani."

A polite round of applause rippled through the room.

Reggie continued, "Many people would mistakenly believe that Dubai had realized its unparalleled growth and wealth through oil revenues alone, when in fact only 6% of its GDP is oil related. The bulk of revenue comes from its free trade zones and tourism. It boasts the tallest hotel in the world and has built incredible off-shore residential islands, such as the Jumeirah Palm Island and the World Archipelago. The key to these accomplishments comes from a keen sense of imagination and brilliant innovation. That's what these gentleman represent, all of whom have played a vital role in Dubai's success. Please help me welcome Mohammed Karoo of the Karoo Empire of the Gulf region. Mohammed?"

As people were clapping, Mohammed traded places with Reggie on the stairs and nodded. "You know, I'd much rather have the honor of introducing Reggie than ever having to follow him."

People smiled and chuckled.

"Having said that, I appreciate Reggie's kind introduction." Gazing over the room, he continued, "In the United Arab Emirates, Reginald Ingram has become our brother." He paused for a moment and looked over at Reggie and winked. "Well . . . a much older brother."

Everyone laughed.

He told the story of how his family met Reggie and how he freely gave advice to them without ever asking for anything in return. Mohammed proved to be a very articulate and eloquent speaker. Over the next fifteen minutes he shared the vision of Dubai and the UAE in general and provided an astounding preview of their future plans. He finished by saying that his company had chosen Shanghai as the next place they planned to invest their capital, and how they looked forward to engaging in joint projects with Ingram Capital.

Reggie returned to the stairway to thank Mohammed. With a twinkle in his eyes, he looked out to the guests and said, "Oh my, I almost forgot to tell you what the other great city was . . . Shanghai, of course!"

His comments got a big applause, particularly from the Chinese in the room. The party carried on with abundant food, drink and stimulating conversation. Many of the guests crowded around the three Saudis.

Reggie worked his way back over to Kip and Sal and said, "I haven't had the chance to let you chaps know why I wanted you to meet my Arab friends tonight. As you just heard, Dubai has done some spectacular things in creating innovative housing communities. I was thinking that one might have a spot of fun to explore a joint venture in Shanghai with these men. Kip, it wouldn't hurt Shanghai Shores if it were known that Ingram Capital was spearheading an off-shore housing development with the Saudis group."

Kip asked, "It that even possible here?"

"Ah, yes. You see, Shanghai was once covered by the ocean. Over time, the confluence of the great Yangzi and Qiangtang rivers had gradually built up a spit of alluvial land that is now called Shanghai. Each year, the eastern shoreline of Shanghai grows at a rate of about ten yards per year. The surrounding ocean is very shallow, perfect for an off-shore housing development along the lines of what they've done in Dubai."

Kip said, "Impressive. This would be a world-class destination then."

"Quite right," said Reggie. "Recreational boating in China is about to see a bloody boom. Experts predict that within a few years, China may account for ten percent of the luxury boating market in the world. The opening of the Shanghai waterways to pleasure boating is expected to create a great opportunity. An offshore housing development with every home having its own boat dock would provide that opportunity. So, gentlemen, you now know that I'm keen on this. Let's think about it and be prepared to further the idea with our Saudis friends in the days ahead."

Kip said, "Reggie, I see that you think small."

"If that's what one calls it, then *small* it is!"

Seeing that the party was winding down with guests starting to leave, Kip and Sal said goodbye to the three Saudis, some of their new acquaintances, and Reggie. On the way to the elevator, both of them automatically flipped open their cell phones to call their drivers.

In the lobby, Sal said to Kip, "Chairman Zhang must have really liked you the way he carried on up there. He's a powerful official to have on our side."

"Sure is. Even though our first meeting was relatively brief, we seemed to hit it off."

"Say, that reminds me. My parents are planning to come here for the Christmas holidays. It'll be a good break for me."

"A break from what?"

"Mostly because Maria is not thrilled with the amount of time I've been traveling around China. But, it should ease up once I get a better handle on our investments."

"You know if you and Maria ever wanted to get away for a weekend, let me know. I'd love to have the kids stay over at my place so I could spoil them rotten."

"That'd be nice, *Tuchi*. I'll ask her."

Kip gave Sal a robust bear hug and stepped into the awaiting minivan at the curb. As Benjamin navigated through the darkened streets of Pudong, Kip periodically glanced out the rear window to see if the Toyota with one headlight was following them. It was impossible to tell from the throng of cars weaving in and out of traffic.

Before nodding off to sleep in the back seat, he wondered where their association with the Saudi group would take them. Then he thought of Rico Niu.

While Benjamin navigated the minivan through the darkened road in Chaoyeng, the brightly lit front gate of Shanghai Shores came into view several blocks ahead. The

LED dashboard clock read 12:19 a.m., the very moment a deafening sound of screeching tires, grinding metal, and shattering glass turned the tranquil evening into chaos.

Chapter 31

Kip's body slammed against the side door from the impact. He felt excruciating pain in his chest—like an axe had ripped into it. His mouth flew open, but he couldn't breathe. Disoriented, he saw spots, each one becoming larger with each passing second. *I'm dying!*

On the verge of losing consciousness, Kip began to suck in staccato-like shallow breaths in rapid succession. His head began to clear. He looked around trying to understand what happened. Movement to the right of the van caught his attention. A dark car with only one headlight made a U-turn and sped down the road in a cloud of dust.

What the hell! He tested his arms and legs, then patted his face and chest. *I think I'm okay.* Despite the pain wracking his body, he unfastened his seatbelt and leaned forward to check on Benjamin. He was slumped unconscious on the passenger seat with his head in a pool of blood. The window on the driver's side had a starburst pattern of fractured glass the size of a basketball where his head must have hit.

I've got to stop the bleeding. Shock was beginning to numb Kip's pain. He ripped off his tie and dress shirt, tearing away one of the sleeves. Leaning over the front seat, he took the sleeve and wadded it against the hemorrhaging head wound, then wrapped his tie around Benjamin's head to secure it in place.

By that time, villagers were pouring out of their houses and running toward the van. Someone yanked opened the door on the driver's side while talking rapidly in Chinese. Another person opened the passenger door. It took four men to slide Benjamin's limp body out of the van and lower him onto a blanket on the ground. Others ran up with more blankets and spread them across his unconscious body.

The side door of the van slid open and Kip felt hands tugging on his arm. He looked over and recognized one of the three old women. She gently led Kip out of the van and then reached up to wrap a blanket around his shoulders. He looked into the woman's deeply wrinkled face and said, "*Xièxie.*"

Smiling, she motioned with her hand. "*Bu keqi.*" It's nothing.

Over the din of at least fifty villagers talking at once, a blaring siren could be heard getting louder as it sped closer the scene. Kip began to relax, knowing that his driver was about to get medical attention. Without forewarning, Kip's body started to shake uncontrollably, forcing him to slump back against the van.

A moment later, the ambulance pulled up. Assessing the situation, the white-clad attendants went to Benjamin first. Kneeling on each side of him, they checked his vital signs and dressed his head wound. After an I.V. was started, they transferred him onto a gurney and lifted it into the ambulance.

One of the attendants circled around the van, roughly pushing onlookers out of the way. He then walked up to Kip and began to palpate his body for injuries while saying something in Chinese.

Kip waved his hand in front of him. "*Mei wenti—mei wenti.*" There's no problem.

From somewhere in the crowd, a female voice said, "He's asking if you have any pain anywhere." Kip looked up and saw Heather clearing a path through the gawkers. Hans was following right behind. When they reached him, she said, "Oh, God, you're hurt!"

Kip said, "I'm okay. Tell this guy that I'm just banged up a little, but otherwise okay."

She translated. The attendant spat something back to her and took a hold of Kip's elbow. Out of nowhere, Hans' large hands reached out and almost lifted the man off of his feet. Holding a finger up in front of the EMT's face, Hans barked, "No!"

The man shrugged his shoulders away from Hans and walked away while mumbling something incoherent. A moment later, the ambulance sped off down the road with its siren blaring and red lights flashing.

"You're really hurt, aren't you?" asked Heather.

Kip nodded. "Yeah, let's just get the hell out of here and go home. There's no way I'm chancing a Chinese hospital."

With the blanket still wrapped around Kip's shoulders, Heather and Hans got on each side of him and walked him to Hans' car. When they lowered him into the front seat, he let out a loud yell.

When Hans got behind the wheel, he looked over at Kip and started to giggle.

"What's so damn funny?" groaned Kip.

"Ya, this is a nice change, now isn't it? You're usually the one helping *me* home!"

From the back seat, Heather broke out laughing.

Kip said, "You guys are really something. Maybe I should have taken my chances with that EMT guy."

While Hans started the engine and pulled forward, Heather managed to control herself enough to utter, "Nice t-shirt, boss. I was wondering when you'd lose your shirt in China."

As the car passed through the front gate, both Heather and Hans were laughing.

Kip slowly shook his head but even that hurt.

By the time the car pulled into the driveway, Kip had broken out in profuse sweat, and he was beginning to feel nauseous.

Taking Kip's keys from him, Hans walked ahead and opened the front door. Once he and Heather guided Kip up the walkway and got him into the foyer, they could see Kip's ashen face and deep furrow lines of pain. Hans said,

"Maybe we should take you to the World Health Clinic. They have American doctors."

"No. I think I'll feel better once I take a shower."

Hans and Heather looked at each other and shrugged. Heather said, "Well, we're sticking around until we know for sure you're okay."

Kip slowly headed down the hallway and muttered, "Thanks."

Twenty minutes later, he walked stiff-legged into the family room wearing silk pajamas, a terrycloth robe and floppy slippers. Hans and Heather were sitting on adjoining sofas with worried expressions on their faces. Kip said, "Thanks for helping me. I think that I'll be okay now." Kip reached behind him and held onto the arms of a side chair, slowly lowering his body into a seated position.

"Would you like a cup of coffee?" Heather asked Kip.

"Sounds great. As a matter of fact, I could use a nice slug of Courvoisier in it."

"Will do," said Heather heading into the kitchen. "How about you, Hans?"

"Ya, ya," he said with a big smile on his face. He then turned to Kip. "Well, do I take you into the clinic?"

"You know, Hans, I think my body was just battered around a lot. After I got out of the shower and looked in the mirror, I saw an ugly bruise running diagonally across my chest, along with a lot of other purplish colors. I guess the seatbelt did its job."

Hans said, "Ya, a good thing."

"Well, let's see how it goes tonight. My guess is I'll be back in the office tomorrow."

Heather walked over with a tray of three coffees and set it down. "God, do men always have to act so damn brave? I think you should be in a hospital, not at work." She handed a cup to Kip.

After taking a sip, he said, "Thanks, Heather. This really hits the spot."

Hans said, "Kip, what can you tell us about what happened out there?"

"I'm still a little foggy about it." He looked over at Heather. "I went over to the Saudi reception at your father's place this evening." He then turned back to Hans. "When we pulled up in front, Benjamin told me that he thought we were being followed by a black Toyota with a missing headlight. On the way back to Shores I fell asleep. When we reached the frontage road, the Toyota must have tried to run us off the road. Before it could speed off, I was able to see that it matched Benjamin's description."

"Sounds like something Rico Niu would have done." said Heather.

Hans raised his eyebrows. "Who's Rico Niu?"

Kip rubbed the back of his neck with his left hand and rotated his head back and forth with his eyes closed. "Some other time, Hans. It's a long story. Just know he's a bad guy."

Hans slurped his coffee and joked, "So am I."

After being assured that Kip felt better, Hans decided to go home an hour later. He turned to Heather and said, "Are you going to be okay getting home?"

"I'll be okay." After she walked Hans to the door, she gave him a peck on the cheek. When she returned, she fluffed a throw pillow under her and stretched out more comfortably on the sofa. "Isn't it odd that Rico's never even been questioned by the authorities regarding the kidnappings of those American girls? The guy must have bribed a whole lot of corrupt government officials."

"I'm not surprised." Kip winced from the pain. "Sal and I talked about what we'd do if we ever got hold of him."

"Well, just be careful with your bravado stuff. I think that several others thought the same thing and they ended up dead."

The Percocet Kip had taken earlier was starting to take the edge off the pain. Feeling more relaxed, he noticed for the first time how lovely Heather looked sitting across from him. She was wearing sweatpants and a t-shirt. He thought she looked remarkably beautiful stretched out with her bare feet on the sofa. He said, "I'm curious. How did you get to the scene so quickly?"

"One of the guards who knew me called, saying that you had been in a car accident a few blocks from the main gate. So I called Hans knowing that he had a car. A minute later, he was at my front door. The rest is history."

"Well, I'm grateful."

Just then, there was a loud knock on the door.

Kip jerked. "What the hell?"

Heather stood up and headed for the door. "I'll get it."

As soon as she unlocked the door, Sal rushed in. "What the fuck happened?"

From the family room, Kip called out, "*Yani*, for God's sake, keep your voice down."

Sal rounded the corner with his eyes boring in on Kip. "Now you look even uglier with all those fucking bruises on your face. You can just start from the beginning."

"How'd you know?" asked Kip.

Sal glanced over at Heather.

She shrugged. "I thought you'd want me to call him."

By 3:30 a.m., Heather said, "Okay, guys, I'm wiped out. I'm heading home." She leaned down and gave Kip a soft kiss on the cheek, not quite like the peck she'd given Hans.

While she was walking to the front door, Kip called out, "After that, I'm feeling better already."

"I'm sure you are, Mr. Duchene." Chuckling to herself, she opened the door and stepped out into the humid night air.

"What the fuck was that about, *Tuchi?*"

"It's nothing. How about another special coffee?"

"Coming up." On his way to the kitchen, Sal said, "By the way, I'm staying here tonight to keep an eye on you."

"Not in my bed."

"In your dreams." Sal chuckled.

When Kip woke up after a fitful sleep, his entire body felt like someone had bludgeoned it with a 2X4. The wracking pain across his chest was unbearable. Two Percocets and a hot shower were intended to ease the discomfort. They didn't.

Sal was waiting for him in the sun room with a cup of hot coffee in his hands. "How ya doing?"

"I'll make it."

"What a crock of shit."

"Look, if I'm not feeling better by this afternoon, I'll go in and get checked out."

"Well, you go right ahead and do that. Because if you don't, I think I'll give you one of my loving bear hugs."

Kip winced. "Don't even think about it."

Sal stood up. "Can I pour you some coffee?"

"No. Thanks for babysitting last night."

Slipping on his jacket, Sal said, "You owe me, *Tuchi*."

"Yeah, I know."

"Trust me on this. We're going to find a way of getting even with that asshole, Niu, and it won't be pretty."

"Music to my ears."

Twenty minutes after Sal left, someone knocked on the front door. Kip looked at his watch and wondered who it could be at seven-thirty in the morning. He opened the door and saw Angie standing there.

She said, "Well, what did you do now?"

Backing away, he motioned. "Come on in. I'm glad to see you."

As they were walking into the family room, Kip said, "Would you like some tea?"

"Yes, but I'll fix it myself. Why don't you sit down and relax? I see that you're walking kind of funny. What's the problem?"

"Just a little sore."

When she walked into the family room after making tea, she handed Kip a fresh cup of coffee. After curling up in one of the overstuffed chairs, she eyed Kip. "I hate to say it but you look terrible."

"Just do me a favor and make sure that Patti stays away from me today. Laughing is the last thing I want to do."

"Yeah, a good idea even though you're not going back to the office."

"The hell I'm not."

Angie didn't respond. After taking a sip of tea, she looked more closely at Kip and said, "Boss, how are you really doing?"

"Okay."

"Heather called me as soon as she got back to her place last night. After she told me what she knew, I really wanted to come over right away but that wouldn't have helped you."

"Oh yes it would," said Kip.

She shook her head. "Is that all you men think of? Anyway, Heather told me how worried you were about Benjamin, so I went ahead and contacted the hospital before coming over. Other than suffering a concussion, he's going to be okay. They'll probably discharge him in a couple of days."

"That's a relief."

"I've also arranged for the van to be taken into a body shop this morning."

"Thanks." While reaching for his cup of coffee, he grimaced in pain and gingerly pressed the palm of his hand against his chest.

Angie said, "Okay, let me take a look at it."

"No, it's okay."

"Either you pull up your shirt or I will."

An hour later, Kip was holding his breath on the X-ray table at the World Health Clinic in Puxi.

Chapter 32

Jesus, this hurts!—thought Kip, still lying on the examining table and waiting for Doctor O'Connor to return with his diagnosis. The slightest movement caused a stabbing pain across the right side of his chest, enough to bring tears to his eyes. It helped to take slow shallow breaths through his nose. He picked up the tingly waft of antiseptic in his nostrils. Trying not to think about the pain, he forced his gaze to wander around the treatment room. Rolling his head to the left, he saw a six-foot wide base cabinet with a gleaming stainless steel sink set into the countertop. Various jars and boxed medical supplies were neatly arranged on top. The surrounding walls were adorned with medical posters, illustrating the body anatomy.

Kip's musings were interrupted when he heard a light rap on the door. Doctor O'Connor walked in wearing a starched white jacket with a stethoscope draped around his neck. He slipped a chest x-ray onto the back-lit viewer on the wall and smiled over at Kip. "Well, Mr. Duchene, you're a lucky man. As badly as you were banged up, I'm surprised that you didn't have a skull fracture or any sign of internal injuries." He pulled a ballpoint pen out of a plastic holder in his coat pocket and pointed to the left side of the transparent x-ray. "Can you make out these fine dark lines?"

Kip lifted his head up from the pillow to see and immediately let out a yelp.

The doctor said, "Yeah, it should hurt. You've got hairline cracks here, and here and here." His pen tapped on three consecutive ribs.

Kip grimaced, easing his head back on the pillow. "That's not what I was hoping to hear. What's the treatment?"

"Other than putting your right arm in a sling—nothing."

"Nothing?"

"Nothing except giving you something for pain. Mr. Duchene, you're going to get a taste of what women have to go through with childbirth, only you're going to feel the pain for up to a month. I suggest that you take at least a week off from work."

Kip smiled without comment. There was no way he was going to take any time off.

As the doctor was making a final adjustment on Kip's arm sling Angie walked through the opened door, her eyes darting over at Kip sitting up on the table. His forehead was covered with a sheen of sweat and rivulets coursing down both cheeks. She said to the doctor, "The nurse said I could come in. What's wrong with him?"

"Are you his wife?"

"God forbid, no."

Kip rolled his eyes and slowly shook his head.

The doctor laughed and proceeded to explain Kip's condition. Then he tore off a slip of paper from a pad and handed it to Kip. "Here's a prescription of Norco for pain. If you can, try to limit the dosage to one tablet three times a day. If the pain gets particularly bad, you can take two tablets. But know that these things can be addictive. There's a pharmacy on the first floor."

"Thanks, doc," said Kip, scrunching up his face as he eased himself off the table and stood up.

The doctor patted Kip on the left shoulder and said to Angie, "Mr. Duchene is one tough guy. You make sure to call me if his condition worsens, okay?"

She nodded as the doctor left the room and headed across the hall. They heard, "Hi, I'm Doctor O'Connor," before his voice was cut off to a muffle as the door closed behind him.

Angie walked in front of Kip and began buttoning up his shirt. With arched eyebrows, she said, "Cracked ribs, huh?"

On the ride back to Shores, Kip said to Angie, "Let's go ahead and have the tenants meeting tomorrow night as planned."

"You've got to be kidding!" said Angie.

"I'm not."

"Okay, I'll make a deal with you. Let's put it off for one week. It won't hurt anything, and you'll have a chance to a feel a little better than you do now. Okay?"

Looking down at the sling on his arm, he closed his eyes and nodded.

Chapter 33

Kip was surprised to see several arrangements of flowers sitting on his desk the following morning. He called out, "Who sent the flowers?"

Walking in from her office, Angie said, "They're from some of the tenants and staff."

"That's awfully nice."

"By noon yesterday, I think that every employee and tenant heard about the accident."

"Who told them?"

"You keep forgetting that this is China."

"How can I forget? Listen, any word on Benjamin?"

"I'll stop by the hospital sometime tomorrow to check up on his condition. Between Heather, Jessie, Paul and me, we're all set for the tenants meeting. Are you okay with a week from Friday?"

"Sure." Kip reached for his notebook and winced with pain.

"You okay?"

"Yeah, I just took a pain pill."

Handing Kip an envelope with Chinese writing on the front, she said, "This note was handed to a guard at the front gate. It's for you."

"Who's it from?"

"I didn't think you'd mind if I went ahead and opened it. It's from the three ladies in the village, wishing you a speedy recovery. By the way, Kip, did you know that one of them pulled you out of the van last night?"

"I vaguely remember. I'll have to personally thank her and return the blanket after it's cleaned."

Angie said, "Don't worry. I'll make sure the blanket gets returned."

"No, I want to return it myself."

Angie looked at Kip. "Yeah, that would be better." She then flipped open her notebook. "Let's see . . . a police inspector asked to talk with you tomorrow."

Kip flashed a concerned look at her. "Who, Inspector Jiang?

"No, some other guy."

"What does he want to talk about?" Kip said with an edge to his voice.

"Relax, boss. He just wants your version of what happened."

"Oh."

"By the way, the new tenants Heather signed up will move in tomorrow. That's all I have to report."

Looking at his own notes, Kip said, "Okay, thanks. I'll need a driver while Benjamin is recuperating. Please talk to Priscilla about that and have someone available by tomorrow morning. I can see the police inspector anytime tomorrow."

He then jotted down a note and slid it over to Angie.

I'll join you at the hospital when you go to see Benjamin.

"You sure?"

He nodded, then immediately winced. Beads of sweat were forming on his forehead.

Raising her eyebrows, she slowly exhaled, "If you insist."

The police inspector met with Kip at ten the next morning, and ended the interview by saying that he was satisfied with Kip's account of the incident. Translating, Angie said to Kip, "The inspector said they would try to find out who caused the accident."

After the inspector left, Angie said sarcastically, "Don't hold your breath. We can't even rule out the possibility of the police themselves being somehow involved."

Kip shook his head and pointed up.

They walked out of his office without saying another word and headed down to the spare office.

Inside, she sat down and lowered her head, whispering, "I'm so stupid!"

Kip sat in the chair across from her. "What did you say?"

Angie looked up and barked, "I'M SO STUPID!" She then smiled wanly and said with a syrupy tone to her voice, "Are you satisfied?"

Kip smiled. "Indeed, I am." He was soaking up Angie's rare display of humility.

That afternoon, Kip and Angie walked down from the clubhouse to the parking lot. She said, "I went ahead and arranged for Mr. Zeng to drive us to the hospital. With the van in the shop, we'll take the new Buick"

"Who's Mr. Zeng?"

"The best driver we have and he's very popular with the staff. He lives in Chuansha, a town just a few miles south of here."

"Does he speak English?"

"Not a word."

"Oh."

In contrast to Benjamin's habit of being a non-stop talker, Mr. Zeng didn't say a word during the drive to the hospital, leaving Kip and Angie to chatter without interruption. Zeng drove into a gated parking lot and paid a fee to an old attendant in soiled clothes wearing a threadbare Yankees baseball cap. Kip noticed that Mr. Zeng slowly eased the van over several speed bumps in the parking lot. *Okay, this man knows I'm hurt. I'm impressed.*

The hospital looked foreboding. It was a drab five story building with moldy stains bleeding down from barred window wells. The grey stucco siding was cracked everywhere. Someone must have recently patched it with fresh grout, making the building look like it had suffered from a fatal skin disease.

The noisy lobby was solidly jammed with people, many of whom were pleading for attention. Angie aggressively knifed through the crowd with Kip following right behind. He said, "What's that God awful smell in here?"

Without breaking stride, she said, "You don't want to know." She cut in front of one of the long lines and asked the receptionist what room Benjamin was in. The woman started to bark at Angie but stopped short when she saw the tall American man standing next to her with his arm in a sling. She looked at the computer monitor, typed a few strokes, and said in English while batting her eyelashes in Kip's direction, "Room 216."

"What the hell was that all about?" he asked Angie as they were walking away.

"Just showing off her English in front of a handsome American."

One of the patients jostling for a place in line bumped against Kip's side. He yelled, "Shit!"

In a flash, Angie was at Kip's right side. "Just follow me. I'll make sure that doesn't happen again."

"Thanks. By the way, why are we walking past the elevator?"

"We're going to take the stairs."

He stopped. "Ah, come on, Angie. I'm in a world of hurt."

"Unless you want your ribs to go from being cracked to being broken, we don't take the elevator. It's usually jammed with twice the number of people it was designed to hold."

He shook his head and resumed walking with her. "Lead the way."

By the time they reached the second-floor landing, Kip had beads of sweat glistening across his forehead. Angie noticed. "How are you holding up?"

"*Mei wenti.*"

"The way you say 'no problem' these days, someone might think you're Chinese."

"Fat chance. Let's find Benjamin's room and get the hell out of here."

Nurses on the floor wore crisply-ironed white uniforms while scurrying up and down the hallways. The walls were coated with a thick layer of light-green enamel, bubbling in some places and flaking off in others. Angie led Kip through a maze of hallways, stopping in front of Room 216. She slowly pushed the door open and stuck her head in. Curtains were drawn around all four beds in the room. Not knowing which bed Benjamin was in, she turned her head trying to pick up on the conversations. She then spun around to Kip, putting a finger to her lips. Whispering, she said, "Shhhh. I hear Benjamin's voice, but something's wrong . . . let me listen for a minute."

A moment later, Angie grabbed Kip's hand and backed out of the room. "We've got to get out of here."

In a half-run, they hurriedly retraced their steps along the corridor and back through the stairway door. Before they started down the stairs, Kip stopped and leaned over to rest his hands on his knees. "Hold on a moment. Shit, my chest is killing me."

With a frightened look, Angie pleaded, "We have to keep going." They didn't talk all the way down the flight of stairs and out to the car. Mr. Zeng pulled out into traffic. Still out of breath, Kip gasped, "What the hell happened back there?"

After glancing back through the rear window, she said, "Benjamin was talking angrily to another man by his bedside. Benjamin said that the Toyota wasn't supposed to crash into the van, just run it off the road."

"Wait a minute. He said what?"

"Benjamin must be working for Rico."

"Jesus, I can't believe this." He raked his hand through his hair.

"Well, you better start believing. He complained about being all cut up and said that he'd done exactly what he was told. He told the man that when he drove up to Mr. Ingram's place he let you know that someone was following them just as they planned. I guess they thought the forewarning would make the road incident more convincing to you."

Kip winced and said, "Sorry, but these guys are frigging crazy. What else did he say?"

"Well the other man said that it wasn't his fault, explaining that a rut in the road must have caused him to swerve too hard and hit the van. Benjamin then demanded that they pay him double because of his injuries. The man said that he would pass that on to his boss. Before the man started to leave, he warned Benjamin not to demand too much money otherwise—and get this—Mr. Niu might get mad. Benjamin said that he didn't care."

Kip said, "Okay, I get that part. Why did we have to make a mad dash out of there?"

"Just as the man was saying, 'It's your choice,' I saw his hand pull open the curtain and peek out. That's when it was time for us to make our retreat. I don't know if he saw me."

"I hope not." Trying to absorb what Angie had just said, Kip sat there thinking—*Okay, Mr. Niu, I've finally got your message. No matter what you do, I'm going to figure out how to crush your ass.*

A thousand miles south of Shanghai, Rico was secretly planning something entirely different—something that would make the bumping incident with the van pale in comparison. He was furious that he'd badly underestimated Duchene. He got a call from one of his drivers in Shanghai claiming that he thought he saw Angie eavesdropping in Benjamin's hospital room and that a tall man with an arm sling was standing behind her. Priscilla also reported that Duchene was making progress uncovering their involvement at Shanghai Shores. At that moment, Niu made the decision to permanently solve the Duchene problem.

His wife poked her head in the door and asked him if he was ready to eat dinner. With veins protruding from his sweaty forehead, he yelled, "Get out!"

Chapter 34

Kip was awakened by the rays of the rising sun. Shielding his eyes from the glare, he looked over at the bedroom window and saw that it was a crystal clear day with deep blue sky. He smiled—*Great. No smog or rain today. If the weather holds, we may have a good turnout for the tenants meeting tonight.*

He flipped the covers off his naked body and sat on the edge of the bed. *Well I'll be damned, there's less pain in my chest.* He padded into the master bathroom and stood before the floor-to-ceiling mirror. He lifted his right arm and turned to the right. His rib cage was covered in blotchy purple bruises with greenish-yellow edges.

After taking a long steamy shower and dressing, he decided to loosen up his stiff muscles by taking a short walk. Gingerly slipping his windbreaker through his left arm and over the sling on the other side, he walked out the patio door and strolled along the boardwalk. The exceptionally clear air allowed him the rare sight of the offshore island of *Changzing Dao,* usually obscured by haze. Passing cargo ships in the sea lane between the mainland and the islands appeared to look much closer than normal.

That afternoon Kip was holed up in his den preparing notes for the tenants meeting. Thirty minutes later, Angie knocked on the door and peeked in. "You feeling okay?" She was wearing a silk black pant suit that complemented her svelte shapely body. Her shiny black hair was pulled back in a ponytail.

Kip looked up at her and thought—*Wow, she looks so beautiful*. He smiled and lifted his arm in a sling. "Good as new."

"Yeah, like I believe you. When you're finished in here, I'll show you around so you can see what we've done."

"Okay."

While Angie and Jessie were busy organizing the housekeeping staff for the finishing touches, Paul walked through the front door with several relish trays wrapped in cellophane and slid them into the refrigerator. Bowls of peanuts, cashews and flavored crackers were placed around the room. Paul assigned three of his staff to serve the group, two bartending and the other circulating around the room to make sure that everyone was taken care of. In order to accommodate the expected turnout of tenants, extra chairs had been set up in the family room. It was a large room with a high vaulted ceiling and wet bar, which offered a commanding view of the ocean.

Except for Naomi, all of the managers had confirmed their attendance with Angie. Most said that they were excited to be invited, something that had never happened before. After Kip wrapped up his preparation for the meeting, Angie escorted him through the family room to show him how the room was set up. Kip looked around and nodded. "Good job."

Paul walked over to them and asked if he could do anything more before taking off. Kip smiled and draped his free hand on his shoulder. "Everything looks great. You know, Paul, I've been thinking that this would be a good occasion to formally introduce you as the manager of food and beverage. What do you think?"

Paul's eyes darted over at Angie then back to Kip. "Really?"

Kip nodded.

Paul flashed a big smile. "Oh, yes! Thank you, boss."

Kip walked over to Jessie and said, "As the tenants arrive, I'd like you to stay with me to make introductions."

Jessie was wearing a stylish white blouse and a gray skirt instead of her usual plain blouse and pants. She said, "Okay."

Kip looked more carefully at her. "Say, your hairdo looks nice. What's different?"

Jessie smiled and her face turned red. "Thanks for noticing. I've been admiring the way Heather wears her hair so I decided to get mine cut and permed for the meeting."

"Good for you."

The first tenants to arrive were Hans and Trudy. Just as Jessie was about to introduce them to Kip, he stopped her and said, "Thanks, Jessie. We've already met."

With a twinkle in his eyes, Hans smiled brightly. "*Jawohl!* Any chance you're serving some adult beverages tonight?"

Kip chuckled and pointed to the bar. He then turned to Trudy and said, "You look beautiful as always."

"Thank you, Kip."

As more tenants arrived, they received pre-printed name badges, were directed to the bar and invited to take a seat in the family room when they wished. As minutes went by, the room filled with the growing sounds of clinking glasses, multiple conversations and sporadic laughter. By 7:30 p.m., everyone was present. Kip nodded to Jessie and said, "Well, I guess you're on."

She stood in front of the room and got everyone's attention. Once the sound died down she welcomed the group and proceeded to give a succinct overview of Kip's professional background. Speaking with poise, she concluded by saying, "I am very happy to be the one to introduce you to our new manager, Kip Duchene."

With a smattering of applause, Kip stood before the tenants in his custom-tailored Armani suit and said, "After accidentally meeting Hans at a downtown restaurant, I've put off having this tenants meeting for as long as possible."

Everyone who knew Hans chuckled.

"Then after drinking with him in the clubhouse lounge last week, I thought about canceling the meeting altogether."

Another ripple of laughter floated through the room as the group looked towards Hans. Always a showman, he lifted his formidable frame up from the seat and took a grandiose bow. Despite the raucous applause, Trudy reached up and pulled him back down into his seat.

Kip shrugged his shoulders and said, "But, Jessie informed me, in her typically polite way, that it was too late to back out of the meeting, whether or not I had to wear this arm sling. So here we are."

Kip spent the next twenty minutes outlining problem areas at Shanghai Shores and what he intended to do to resolve them. He openly invited the tenants to make suggestions for improvement, and they did. He ended his speech by sharing his optimism for the future. He then introduced each of the managers, and they in turn, made short speeches about their departments. As the meeting was about to adjourn, Kip was surprised to see that it was already past 9:00 p.m. He extended an invitation for drinks for anyone who would like to stay after the meeting. He assumed correctly that Hans and Trudy would take him up on the invitation.

While the housekeeping staff was tidying up, a company shuttle pulled up to the curb in front to take the managers home. Kip said to Angie, "You taking the shuttle?"

"If you'd like, I can stick around for a while to help serve the tenants."

"That'd be great. Mr. Zeng can take you home later."

Kip lit the gas fireplace, put on an old Marvin Gaye CD from the 1980's, and encouraged everyone to relax in the overstuffed couches and chairs. With the meeting out of the way, Angie decided to have a glass of wine along with the four couples who settled in. The conversations that followed were laced with warmth and humor. Not surprising to anyone, Hans took the lead to entertain everyone with humorous adventure stories about his experiences in the bush country of Africa.

Slipping off her shoes, Angie sat across from Kip with her long legs tucked in under her. Between the effects of his medication and the few glasses of wine he drank earlier in his den, Kip felt less pain than he'd experienced since the accident. He also found Angie looking beautiful in a way he'd never noticed before. He could feel his heartbeat pick up when hearing the way her joyful laugh rippled across the room in response to one of Hans' insane stories.

By midnight, Hans and Trudy were the only tenants left. Trudy whispered to Kip, "I'm so sorry to ask, but would you mind helping me get Hans home again? I'm afraid that he might be more difficult to manage this time."

Kip looked over at Hans. The large man was splayed out on the recliner with a plastered smile on his face. Kip chuckled. "We can manage." Kip turned to Angie and said, "Ask Mr. Zeng if he could come in and help me out with Hans. With one arm, I'm in no condition to handle him alone."

Mr. Zeng proved to be surprisingly strong in taking the lead to get Hans up on his feet and into the van. Even though Mr. Zeng couldn't speak English, he and Kip were able communicate enough to maneuver Hans to his doorstep and into bed without anyone getting crushed. On the way back, Kip pulled out the Chinese dictionary he kept in the car and attempted to tell Mr. Zeng that Angie would need to be driven home. Mr. Zeng smiled in acknowledgment and nodded.

But when Kip got back home, he didn't see Angie. *That's odd. She didn't even say goodbye.* As he headed into the family room he saw her curled up on a couch sound asleep. He tried to wake her with a gentle nudge, but she just groaned something unintelligible and rolled over onto her other side. Giving up, he walked back outside and motioned for Mr. Zeng to go home.

Kip pulled a comforter and pillow down from the linen closet and tucked Angie in. She didn't stir. As an afterthought, he grabbed a Stanford sweatshirt and a pair of his jogging pants and set them on the coffee table next to her. She might want to change out of her own clothes in the morning. With her head poking out from the covers, Angie looked vulnerable and remarkably beautiful. For a second, he had an impulse to lean down and kiss her. Shaking that thought off, he tiptoed into the kitchen and turned on the range-hood light to give her just enough light to see around the room.

Exhausted from the meeting, he padded down the hallway and into his bedroom, leaving the door ajar. He slipped into bed, oddly comforted knowing that Angie was safely asleep in the family room.

Kip woke up early the next morning with the tantalizing aroma of bacon in the air. He bolted out of bed a little too fast and winced with pain. He took a quick shower, then slipped on a pair of khaki pants, a Polo shirt and sandals.

Angie was standing at the cooktop range preparing bacon and eggs. She was wearing Kip's baggy warm-up suit. She looked up when Kip walked in. "Okay, am I supposed to apologize or are you?"

"*You* are, of course."

"No, I think that, as host of the party, it was your responsibility to make sure everyone got home intact."

"Believe me, my dear, you're intact!" he said and started to laugh.

She ignored the innuendo. "How do you like your eggs?"

"Over easy, please."

While Angie was busy in the kitchen, Kip set out plates and utensils on the table in the sunroom. The sun had just broken over the ocean horizon, flooding the entire room with a soft apricot glow.

After they ate and were sipping on their second cup of coffee, Kip looked across the table at Angie. "Please don't get me wrong, but this is the most relaxed I've been in many months."

In a soft voice, she said, "Yes, it's nice for me also." After a pause, she continued, "Kip, would you mind telling me about your wife?"

Kip took a deep breath and thought, O*kay. I think I can do this.* "Marci was an angel to me and the only woman I've ever really loved. We got married in 2001 and had three-and-a-half wonderful years together." He told her about what had happened on the day of the accident. "Angie, I simply lost it and ended up sinking into a deep depression and drank way too much."

"God, I can't imagine. How are you doing now?"

"There are good and not-so-good days."

Angie said nothing in response.

After an awkward pause, Kip said, "You know, there's going to be some talk around here about us."

"Us?" She looked over the rim of her coffee cup at him.

"Yes, you and me. Hopefully, Mr. Zeng will keep his mouth shut, but who knows."

"Why would *he* say anything?"

"Well, he and I had to help Trudy get Hans home again last night. So on the way back, I told Zeng in my halting Chinese to wait in front so he could take you home. But, as soon as I realized that you weren't going anywhere, I motioned for him to go ahead and leave."

"Oh."

Kip said, "Well, we'll deal with it as best as we can."

They were both smiling to themselves as they cleared the dishes off the table.

Angie said, "Kip, I don't know if you knew, but my dad's recovering from cancer surgery."

"No, I didn't know. I'm really sorry to hear that."

"Thank you." She glanced down at her watch. "I should head back home to help my mom care for him. Obviously we're worried about him. Since they won't understand why

I'm in these baggy clothes, I should change back into my own."

"Okay. Please go ahead. I'll give Mr. Zeng a call."

"No, that won't be necessary. I can take a taxi—no problem, really."

"Mr. Zeng will drive you back and that's final. Besides, then you can explain to him why you stayed over last night."

Twenty minutes later, Angie had changed out of the baggy outfit and transformed herself back into a smartly-dressed executive assistant. Emerging from the powder room, she looked radiant. Her full lips were glossy pink in contrast to the light porcelain hue of her unblemished skin. With high cheekbones setting off brown almond-shaped eyes, Angie could easily be mistaken for the beautiful movie star, Li Gong. Kip walked Angie to the front door, neither one saying anything. Without forethought, he gently wrapped his arms around her and pulled her close to him. She melted into his clutch, dropping her purse on the floor. He could feel the warmth of her thighs pressed against his and the softness of her breasts touching his chest.

When they disengaged, Angie looked up and whispered in his ear, "Kip, thank you for being such a gentleman." She kissed his cheek before opening the door and scurrying down the front walk and into the minivan.

From the porch Kip watched her looking over at him through the side window and wondered what she was thinking. He thought—*What in the hell did I just do?*

Chapter 35

Unsettled by not knowing why he hugged Angie, Kip decided to take a walk to clear his head. It was a warm muggy morning at Shanghai Shores. Wisps of high cirrus clouds were slowly drifting southward across the sky. With flaps down and landing gear extended, a 747 jumbo jet was making a high pitched whine directly overhead on its final approach to the Pudong International Airport.

One of Kip's neighbors across the street waved and called out, "Good morning."

"Hey, Dan, how's it going?" said Kip.

"I wanted to tell you how much I enjoyed the meeting last night. How ya feeling?"

Kip lifted his right arm in the sling and said, "Getting better all the time."

"Good. You know, I'm glad you're onboard to try to straighten out the mess around here. It's been hard on us all."

Kip smiled. "Yeah, I know. We've got a great group of managers who just needed someone to point the way."

"Well, we're all rooting for you."

"Thanks. I think I'll take a walk to get a little exercise."

Dan patted his waistline. "That's exactly what I need to be doing. Too much eating out."

"Yeah, I hear ya. Take care." Kip headed down the street. During the remainder of his walk several other residents went out of their way to say hello. Just as he was thinking—*Okay, this is good*—his cell phone chimed. "Hello?"

"*Tuchi*, how did the tenants' meeting go?" asked Sal.

"Hey, I'm glad you called." Kip walked around the side of his house to the back patio and sat down in one of the lounge chairs. "The meeting went great. I've already gotten positive feedback from the residents."

"Good going. How ya feeling?"

Kip said, "Why does that sound like a loaded question?

"Shit, it's not!" Sal lowered his voice and said, "I just thought that you'd be on top of cloud nine since Angie spent the night with you."

"How in the hell did you know she stayed over?"

"I'd bet that everyone in Shanghai knows by now."

"Well, nothing happened. She just drank too much and crashed on the sofa."

Sal chuckled on the other end of the line. "If you say so. The other reason I'm calling is to alert you that Reggie would like us to meet with the Saudis on Tuesday afternoon at Shores. Is that going to work for you?"

"No problem. We'll be prepared."

"Good. By the way, I told Maria about your suggestion to have the kids over at your place. I was surprised that she said she loved the idea. You know how protective she is about the kids."

"Yeah, I know she worries even more with the news about those poor girls and the amputations."

"All the more reason to get rid of that fucker, Rico."

"We will." Kip looked out at the calm sea and cleared his throat. "Talking about Rico, you know that Angie and I went to the hospital to check on Benjamin."

"Oh yeah. How'd that go?"

He told him how Angie overheard Benjamin's conversation in the hospital room and the fact that he actually referred to Rico as the boss.

Sal said, "Sounds like bad news."

"*Yani*, it's actually not."

"How do you figure?"

"Well, think about it. We know that Benjamin's working for Rico, but they don't know we're on to them.

So, we should act as if nothing's changed and welcome Benjamin back with open arms. From now on, Benjamin will overhear information *we* want him to hear. That, in turn, will find its way back to Niu."

"Smart thinking. Do you know how Benjamin got connected with Niu?" asked Sal.

"I think so. Benjamin was introduced to the company by Shelly Tang, one of the Gang of Three—"

"Wait a minute," interrupted Sal. "Isn't she our personnel manager?"

"Yes. She's the one who hired Benjamin."

"Well shit then, that explains it. She controls his ass."

"Yeah, that's what I understand from Angie."

Sal said, "You sure you're not banging her?"

Kip flipped the phone shut, smiling as he heard another jet approaching from far off. *I think he's jealous.*

That night Kip had a hard time getting to sleep. He was still questioning his impulse to give Angie a hug, and was surprised by her unexpected response. He had replayed the scene many times in his mind, reliving the titillating pleasure of the moment. He wasn't really sure if the residual warmth could be explained by his loneliness or something else. *Marci, what am I supposed to do?*

The next morning Kip was a little nervous about what he should say to Angie when she got in to work. He knew that things would be different between them from now on. *I can't afford to get involved with anyone, particularly her.* Just then, he heard the familiar sounds of Angie rustling around in her office.

"Good morning, boss." she called out in a perky voice.

"Good morning," Kip replied. He felt trickles of sweat roll down his armpits. Deciding to get it over with, he walked into her office and motioned with his head. Angie followed him down the hallway to the spare office.

After he closed the door behind them, Angie asked, "Well, how was your weekend, Mr. Don Juan?"

Kip thought—*Okay, here it comes.* Trying to sound innocent, he said, "Whataya mean?"

"Well, after you took advantage of a lady in distress."

Yep, I'm in trouble all right. "Angie, I'm sorry. I never meant to offend you."

"Well, aren't you the humble one." Angie's glistening dark eyes looked directly at Kip. "What you did was . . . well, quite wonderful." She broke out in a smile.

"Okay, you got me," said Kip, letting out his breath.

"Kip, I think that you were very sweet, so let's just enjoy remembering the feeling of that moment for what it was. We've been under a lot of strain lately and we simply stole a slice of comfort. There was nothing wrong with that."

"Yeah, I agree." Wanting to quickly move on, he opened his notepad and said, "Getting back to business, what's up for this week?'

"Okay. Bev asked if you were ready to start meeting with the more troublesome creditors. Priscilla received another demand letter from the power bureau on Friday for the past due amount. Manny continues to make good progress in the renovation of our houses. This morning, I saw that Jessie had a lot of messages from tenants. It may be positive feedback on our tenants meeting, but I'm really not sure." She looked down at her notes. "So, I think that's it."

Kip wrote it all down in his notebook. "Good. I'll need a little time to get ready for our managers' meeting. And by the way, I'm glad there wasn't a problem about Saturday morning."

"I am too," said Angie as they headed back to their offices.

Just before the managers' meeting, Kip got a call from Eleni who invited him to have lunch. "Would it be okay if I asked Heather and Angie to join us?"

"Sure, as long as you trust them one hundred percent."

"That's not a problem. Where would you like to meet?"

"Let's meet halfway. There's a nice Korean restaurant just across the street from Jin Mao Tower. You'll recognize it by the green awnings."

"See you then," said Kip.

The meeting with the managers was particularly upbeat. Heather gave an inspiring update on occupancy. "You can see that we've finally made a turn-around last month, increasing occupancy from thirty-five to thirty-eight families."

The managers clapped enthusiastically, looking at each other with acknowledged pride. Kip was pleased that they finally had something to cheer about.

Heather wrapped up by saying, "By the way, I thought that our tenants' meeting was really successful. Everyone seemed to have had a wonderful time."

Naomi looked down without making eye contact with anyone.

Jessie reported that several residents had called her to say how pleased they were with the tenants' meeting. Patti gave her report on a newly installed computer networking system.

Kip briefed the group about the Saudis visiting Shores the following day and said that Mr. Ingram and Sal would be joining them. "Shelly, inform Priscilla that the guards should be properly notified about these important visitors. Angie can provide her with the type of car they'll be arriving in and its license plate number."

After Shelly translated, Priscilla said not to worry.

As Kip and Angie were walking back to their offices, he said, "Listen, Eleni called earlier and invited me for lunch today. If you and Heather aren't tied up, I would like for you to join us."

"Thanks. I'll tell Heather. I'm sure she'll also want to go."

Chapter 36

The Korean restaurant bustled with activity. Mouthwatering aromas of garlic and exotic spices permeated the air. The Chinese waitresses wore traditional Korean *Hanbok* dresses with high waist lines and flared colorful skirts. Kip saw Eleni in the back of the large dining room waving to get his attention. Leading the way, he wove through the tightly-spaced tables towards the corner booth.

Eleni stood to greet them. "I grabbed this booth since it's more private for us to talk. How's everyone anyway?"

"Can't complain," said Kip as the four slid into the booth. "The place is packed. It must be good."

"It is, even if you don't like *kimchi*." Eleni looked at the yellowish bruises on Kip's face. "What happened?"

He told her about the accident and the mounting evidence that connected Rico Niu with the problems at Shanghai Shores.

Eleni said, "Well, then, my timing today is perfect."

Kip said, "I'm all ears."

"Let's order first. By the way, I'm hearing a buzz around town that Milt Avery has been hassling you."

"You know about that?"

"Everyone does. The day he gets reassigned to a post somewhere else in the world, we'll celebrate."

Kip said, "Just make sure I'm invited."

"It's a deal. I've also overheard women attending our real estate meetings talking about the new general manager at Shores."

"And?"

She said, "He's supposed to look like a movie star."

Kip blushed. "Get out of here!"

Looking over at Angie and Heather, she rolled her eyes. "Is he always this modest?"

They both nodded and smiled without saying anything.

Kip said, "By the way, we have something to celebrate today."

"What's that?"

Kip turned to Heather, "Go ahead and tell Eleni how we did last month."

Smiling brightly, Heather said, "I signed up three new tenants. We now have thirty-eight. Even though it's no big deal, I'm thrilled because it's the first time our occupancy has gone up rather than down since early 2002."

Eleni raised her water glass. "Congratulations! That *is* great news."

The waitress stepped up to their table. Eleni said, "If you'd like, I'll go ahead and order for us since I've eaten here several times and know the menu."

"Please do," said Kip as he snapped his menu shut and handed it to the waitress.

While they were waiting for the food to arrive, Eleni said, "Okay, I said I had some news about Niu. Do you have a female manager at Shores named Mao?"

"Yes, Priscilla Mao. She's our administrator," said Kip.

Eleni leaned forward and lowered her voice. "My sources told me that Niu has offered to make her general manager of Shores if she helps him take over the place. Based on what I've heard in the past, he won't honor his promise. Nevertheless, I'm told that she is eagerly helping him. I strongly suspect that he may have had listening devices planted around the development."

Kip said, "Thanks for the information. We've already confirmed that there are bugs, and we suspected that Priscilla had to be involved somehow with Niu. Until now, we had nothing substantial to link them together. Now we do." Kip turned to Angie. "What's your take on this?"

"Well, I remember you have a saying in the states, 'follow the money.' That's what most of this is about. Everyone wants more of it including employees and government officials. Niu is trading his money to gain more power. But, the man has a problem he's not yet aware of. He comes from Anhui Province."

Eleni knowingly smiled. "Of course."

Heather said, "What?"

"Well, he's not Shanghainese."

Eleni said, "Exactly!"

Angie went on, "In this city, people who are not Shanghainese are at a disadvantage, a fact that we can exploit."

Kip shook his head slowly. "I'm not going to pretend to understand."

Eleni said, "You don't need to, Kip. Angie is absolutely right in pointing out that Niu is a *xiao hu ning*."

Kip said, "Let's see. Does that refer to a person from out of town?"

"You're close," said Eleni. "Kip, you haven't been in China long enough to know how these things work and it's way too difficult to explain."

He said, "I figured so."

They talked about Rico Niu over lunch. Between the tabletop barbecue and the wide assortment of condiments, the meal was thoroughly enjoyed by all. None of them noticed the two Chinese men sitting several tables away, paying more attention to them than to their meals.

Chapter 37

On the drive back to Shanghai Shores, Kip, Angie and Heather were talking in the back seat about what Eleni had revealed to them. Kip thought the offer Rico made to Priscilla was preposterous, yet it had to be true. Talking to no one in particular, he said, "Do you really think that she bought what Rico said?"

"You mean Priscilla?" asked Angie.

"Sure. She had to have known it was a bunch of BS."

"I don't think she did," said Heather.

With Angie sitting in the middle, Kip leaned forward to ask Heather, "How do you figure?" While it was only a flicker of a glance, Kip couldn't help but notice that Angie's knee-length skirt had ridden half way up her thighs.

A barely perceptible smile crept across Angie's face as she pushed her skirt back down.

Heather said, "Well, think about it. She's done everything possible to wrestle control of the company away from Ingram Capital. She's so delusional about running the operation that I think she'd believe anything Rico promises her."

Angie nodded her agreement.

Kip sat back thinking about Heather's comment while the Buick was making its way through Chaoyeng. He pointed. "Angie, tell Mr. Zeng to pull over near those three women up ahead."

Using bamboo poles, the white-haired women were swatting a futon hanging over a clothesline. It was attached to an ancient looking house, clad with grey stucco and mottled with black mold. The gable roof was classic Chinese with moss covered clay tiles and a dragon figure mounted at the ridge. The women looked up as the Buick crunched to a stop on the gravel shoulder.

Heather said, "What's this all about?"

Kip opened the door to the hot humid air outside. "Come on. I want to introduce you to some friends of mine."

With perspiration glistening on their weathered faces, the three women smiled seeing *da laoban*, the big boss. While they were smoothing down the front of their blouses with gnarled hands, Angie and Heather walked up behind Kip. He extended his arms between Angie and the women. "These are the sweet village women I told you about."

"So I finally get to meet them," said Angie. She exchanged cordial greetings in Shanghainese with the women and said that the boss speaks of them with respect.

They beamed with pride. The youngest looking one frowned, then reached up and gently touched the side of Kip's discolored cheek. She turned and said something to Angie.

Angie said, "She wants to know how you're feeling after the car accident."

"Tell them that I'm okay. Please ask which one of them helped me out of the van."

After asking, Angie held out her hand to the shortest and oldest of the three. Despite the deep wrinkles on her face, she had a vibrant sparkle in her eyes and rosy cheeks from the workout with the futon. She wore a colorful blouse, black pants and scuffed shoes. Angie said, "She said to thank you for your nice note and for returning the blanket."

Kip said, "*Buqui xi.*" It was nothing.

Heather sighed, "They're so sweet." At five-foot-nine, she towered over all three. Speaking Mandarin, she said how nice it was to meet them. They, in turn, just looked at each other.

"They only speak Shanghainese," said Angie. She translated for Heather.

In the meantime, about twenty villagers had gathered around them with more on their way. Kip said, "Angie, why are we attracting so much attention?"

She chuckled. "Chinese people are very curious, that's all. When we see something out of the ordinary, we want to know what's happening. You and Heather have movie star looks—something never seen in Chaoyeng before. By the way, I can overhear some of the villagers behind us saying that you're the tall man who gave the gifts to the three old women."

Kip smiled.

Angie said, "The women just told me that the homes around here are at least one hundred and fifty years old. They're sad because the government recently announced that the frontage road is to be widened sometime next year. Every house in sight will be demolished. The locals will be forced to move into government subsidized housing elsewhere."

Heather said, "That's so sad."

"It is," said Angie. "But this is happening all over China. People are uprooted from their ancestral homes to make room for new modern developments and are moved into high-rise apartment buildings."

"Don't the new apartments provide them with a higher standard of living?" asked Kip.

"Absolutely," replied Angie. "But most Chinese don't care. They just want to stay where they are."

She motioned with her hand. "Just look at these villagers crowded around us. Most were born and raised right here. They've never lived anywhere else and everyone in Chaoyeng knows each other. Then all of a sudden their homes are bulldozed down into a pile of bricks while they're forced to move into block apartment houses that have no character or familiarity. You see, they'd rather continue to live and die in their old houses."

Kip said, "Angie, I'm interested to know how the women are related."

After an animated discussion, she turned back to him and said, "Okay, this is really interesting. They are sisters."

"I thought so," said Kip."

"All three were born right here in this house." Then motioning to each of the three in turn, she said, "She's eight-six and the baby of the family. The next is eighty-eight, and the oldest just turned ninety-two a few weeks ago." As Angie was pointing, the women beamed without being self-conscious about showing their missing teeth.

Angie continued, "Except for a period of time during the Cultural Revolution, they've lived in this village."

"Would it be proper to ask if they've ever been married?" asked Kip.

"Sure." Angie conferred with the women for several more minutes and turned back with an uncomfortable look. "The youngest said that all three of them married men from the village but they've passed on." Motioning to the youngest, Angie said, "Her husband died of lung cancer about ten years ago. The other two husbands died as young men in their early twenties. They joined Chiang Kai-shek's army in 1937 during the Japanese invasion of China and ended up fighting them in Nanking, the capital city of Nationalist China at that time. They never returned home. So, the three sisters are very close, having been through hard times together."

Heather shook her head. "God, that's such a sad story." She then spontaneously went over and hugged each of the old women in turn.

By then, at least fifty villagers had gathered around, craning their necks to find out what the excitement was about.

Kip said to Angie, "Thank them for sharing their stories, and tell them that we will stop by once in a while to say hello. Also tell the people around us how much I appreciate those who came to help after the car accident."

Angie addressed the crowd and repeated Kip's message. Everyone beamed with pride and spontaneously applauded.

Kip looked at his watch. "It's time to get to work."

After the goodbyes were said, they got back into the Buick. As they pulled away, the villagers walked out in the middle of the road, blocking traffic, and waved enthusiastically.

Kip said, "Okay, now that you've met my three girlfriends, what do you think?"

Heather replied, "Kip, they are the cutest little things in the world. Don't you agree, Angie?"

"Of course." She patted Kip on the knee. "I'm so happy to see that at least someone loves the boss."

But Kip wasn't listening. "We've got to think about what Eleni said. Let's get together this afternoon to talk more about it."

Angie looked at Heather and rolled her eyes.

Chapter 38

That afternoon, Angie and Heather ran into Kip's office. Both were smiling.

Kip looked up from his desk. "What's up?"

Heather held up a sheaf of paper and said, "I just signed up another tenant!"

Kip stood up with a frown on his face. "Good. I've got something to show you." He walked out of the room. Angie and Heather followed him down the hallway.

As soon as the door closed behind them in the spare office, Angie let out a sigh. "I know, I know. I shouldn't have brought Heather into your office to talk about the leases."

Kip said, "Forget about it. I'm really pleased to hear about the contract. Are you sure you can't stick around here longer than next March? Besides, you seem to enjoy your bike rides around the nearby villages."

"I do. The thing is I've accepted a position to join one of the most prestigious law firms on the west coast. They're in Palo Alto and have recently announced plans to expand to China."

Kip said, "What firm? I probably know them."

"Sorry. I've signed a non-disclosure agreement and can't reveal anything about them until they say it's okay."

"Yeah, I know the drill. I also suspect the name of the firm includes the last names of its four founders, two of whom are Italian."

"No comment," said Heather smiling.

Kip scanned the lease contract, signed it and handed it back to Heather. "This is good. One by one, we'll slay the beast."

Heather said, "It's made such a difference to have good looking units to show."

"Are we prepared for the Saudi group tomorrow?" asked Kip while walking over to the window.

Angie said, "Yes, I've alerted Paul and told him that they do not drink alcohol. It probably won't come up anyway but I just wanted to make sure that we don't create an awkward situation."

"Good thinking."

Angie looked over at Kip. "I think we're expecting to have nice weather tomorrow"

"Perfect," he said. "It's kind of nice watching the cargo ships passing by the clubhouse. " He then turned back. "What's the chance that the restaurant's being bugged?"

Angie said, "I wouldn't worry. With a vaulted ceiling, the restaurant would have terrible acoustics. They'd have to have a pretty sophisticated system to filter through people talking, music playing, and dishes clanging. I think that we'll be okay there."

Kip said, "Let's do it then."

That evening, Kip made himself a stiff tequila tonic and walked out onto the patio. After settling down in the lounge chair, he lifted the glass to his nose to savor the familiar woody essence of tequila and the oily citrus aroma of crushed lime that was floating between the ice cubes. He took a satisfying drink, set his glass down, and punched in Sal's number on his cell phone. "*Que pasa, hombre?*"

"*Oye, baboso!*" exclaimed Sal. "How's your ribs?"

"Better. The main reason I'm calling is to alert you that I think my office and home may have been bugged."

"Holy fuck, what's next?"

"Well, I think we're ahead of it, but we can talk more about it tomorrow. Can you come over before the Saudis get here?"

"No problem, *amigo*."

After Kip flipped his phone shut, he took another sip of his drink and savored it. He sat in darkness, content to gaze out at the navigation lights of the passing ships and let his mind wander. He raked his hand through his hair. *Marci, I think I'm in way over my head.*

Chapter 39

By nine-thirty it was dark in Shanghai. The sweltering July heat was replaced by a cool onshore breeze, a good time of the day for Heather to jog around the compound for exercise. While pounding along the boardwalk twenty minutes later she noticed a figure on Kip's dimly lit patio. "Is that you?"

Kip snapped out of his musing and answered, "Yep, it's me."

Leaning on the railing of his deck fence to catch her breath, she was wearing shorts and a 49ers T-shirt with her hair tied back into a ponytail. She pulled the earbuds of her iPod off and flashed a smile. "Well, aren't you the Lord and master back here looking over your kingdom?"

"With this view and the drink I just had, why not? Care to join me and take a load off?

"Sure, thanks!" She unlatched the gate and strode across the expansive patio.

He pulled himself up from the chaise lounge. "Must have been a good jog."

Her cheeks were blotchy pink and a few strands of blond hair stuck to the sweat on her face. "Yeah. It's nice to feel those endorphins. Too much sitting lately."

"Jeez, I hear you. If my ribs weren't killing me, I'd be out there too." He motioned to the chair. "Go ahead and take my seat. I'll grab another. What can I get you?"

"Orange juice would be perfect."

He unfolded another patio chair and slid it next to Heather. "Coming right up."

A few minutes later, Kip returned with their drinks and set them down on the patio table between the two chairs. While he was in the house, he'd slipped into a sweatshirt and pulled a pair of sweatpants over his shorts. He handed her a lap blanket.

She smiled. "How did you know?"

"With this light breeze, I figured you'd get chilled being so sweaty."

"Thanks." She tucked it around her bare legs and sipped her drink. "Okay, now I'm comfy."

Kip was enjoying her unexpected visit. This was the first time he'd spent time with Heather away from work. While she chattered away about the excitement of getting new tenants, he kept glancing her way. In the soft glow lighting the patio, he was awed by her physical resemblance to Marci—even her joyful laugh reminded him of her. Contrary to Heather's focused demeanor in the office, she exuded warmth that he'd never seen in her before.

Sitting side-by-side, the two were relaxed enough with each other to periodically lapse into saying nothing. They quietly watched the running lights of cargo ships passing by as one-foot waves rhythmically splashed up against the nearby seawall. Gentle winds washed the patio in salty air.

Eventually, they began asking idle questions about their respective lives. Their banter was interrupted by the mournful call of a foghorn somewhere far offshore. Kip said, "Here it comes."

Heather lifted her head. "I'm sorry. What's coming?"

"The fog."

Like bullfrogs in a pond, the first blast of sound was answered by a second, then a third. Within a few minutes, the resonating sounds were echoing back-and-forth at regular intervals. As the leading edge of the fog bank crept ominously closer to shore, the running lights of ships gradually changed from twinkling clear to hazy halos of light.

Feeling dampness setting in, Kip said, "Let's duck inside. I'll fix you a nice cup of coffee."

Straddling the foot rest of the chair, she stood up. "Perfect. I could use one."

He said, "Just remember, the house is probably bugged."

She chuckled. "God, isn't living in China fun?"

"Yeah, tell me about it."

Heather settled on the sofa while Kip headed for the kitchen. "Cream? Sugar?"

"Both. Thanks."

Several minutes later, he returned with steaming cups of coffee and set them down on the coffee table. It was then that he noticed that she'd kicked her shoes off and curled her feet under her. Sitting next to her, he said, "Other than Reggie, I know very little about your family."

She put an arm on the sofa back and faced him. "Well, I have an older sister. She found the love of her life and lives a charmed life as a housewife in Palo Alto. My brother's attending Oxford, just as father did. My mum flies back and forth to London, the only place in the world where she's really happy. She feels that everywhere else is rather uncivilized, especially Shanghai."

"I can sure relate to that." He squeezed the bridge of his nose between his thumb and forefinger. "I haven't done many things right over here."

Heather blew steam away from the surface of her coffee and took a sip. "Well, I don't agree. Maybe you're expecting too much of yourself too soon. Besides, Angie seems to be doing a great job protecting your backside."

"*That* she does." He paused. "I have a question for you."

She looked at him expectantly.

He cleared his throat. "I was wondering why you didn't help out at Shores before now? Ever since you started, you've done such a damn good job bringing in new leases."

"Ah, a good question. You see, I'd been interning in the Shanghai office for only a month before you arrived. My dad knew that he had a problem with Ralph Maddox and was working out a plan to put Shores back on track. Actually, there wasn't any consideration for me to work here at all until Sal told my dad that you were looking for someone to get the sales going. From then on, everything seemed to fall into place."

"Do you have someone special waiting for you back home?"

She set her coffee cup down and chuckled. "God forbid, *no*. I've watched several of my girlfriends get married too young, have children, and end up trapped in relationships that *always* fall short of their dreams. After practicing law for at least a couple of years, I'll be open to meeting the right guy and start a family. Before then, my career comes first."

She arched an eyebrow. "What about you and Angie?"

Kip frowned. "What about us?"

"Come on, Kip. I can see the electricity flowing between you two. Yet, you both act like you're at a junior high school dance, too shy to make the first move."

"It's not like that at all."

Heather said nothing.

He turned back to face her. "Okay, I'll admit that I really think the world of her. After what happened to Marci, it's much too early for me to think about being with another woman. You know, it's only been ten months since Marci died."

"I understand."

"Right now, I'm just trying to focus all of my energies into turning Shores around. Besides, I don't think that I'm ready to let Marci go."

Heather bobbed her head in a knowing way. Then she cautiously asked Kip about her death.

Mellowed from the drinks, he was relaxed enough to let it out. He told her about their life together in San Francisco living in his penthouse apartment. Taking a deep breath, he recounted what he could remember about the wrenching experience of the car accident. "It seemed like I had to wait for hours before the doctor finally came out of the emergency room to report on Marci's condition. In reality, the wait may have been only ten minutes. But they were the most agonizing minutes of my life."

Chapter 40

As Kip was talking to Heather, his mind drifted deeply into what had happened ten months earlier. He saw himself sitting in the waiting room and standing up when he saw the doctor approach. He wore a green surgical outfit and rumpled mask hanging down from his neck. Kip even remembered the doctor having a deeply tanned complexion and silver tufts of hair sticking out from under a green cap. The doctor said, "Mr. Duchene?"

With a nervous voice, he said, "Yes. How's my wife?"

"Please sit down."

The doctor sat across from him. "I'm Doctor Farber. I'm afraid your wife has suffered massive head injuries."

Kip moaned, "Oh God, no."

"We've been able to stabilize her in the ER. Right now she's being wheeled into the operating room to relieve pressure on her brain."

Barely able to speak, Kip said, "Is she going to make it?"

The doctor looked away and then back at him. "I'm sorry, Mr. Duchene. She's got a rough road ahead of her. But, you know, I've seen some surprising recoveries that defy the odds, so let's remain hopeful."

"When can I see her?" stumbled out of his mouth.

"Someone will come down here to escort you to the recovery room when she's out of surgery. In the meantime, can we bring you anything?"

Kip slowly shook his head.

Dr. Farber placed a hand on Kip's shoulder and gave him a reassuring squeeze. He then stood up and walked briskly back through the swinging ER doors. Shortly thereafter, the receptionist called Kip back up to the counter and asked him to provide insurance information and sign some release forms.

Not knowing what else to do, he pulled out his cell phone to notify Marci's parents. That was the most difficult telephone call he'd made in his life. But the next call proved to be even more difficult—he dialed Sal's home number.

Sal answered, "Hello?"

No response.

With an edge, Sal said louder, "Who's there?"

Kip couldn't get any words out other than a sob.

"Kip? Is that you? . . . What the fuck's the matter?"

Stammering his words, Kip managed to say, "Marci's-been-in-an-accident." His vocal cords loosened enough to tell Sal what hospital he was in.

Sal said, "I'll be right over," and hung up.

Time slowed down almost to a standstill. Kip thought—*This can't be happening!* To pass the time, he started to count the dots in the acoustical ceiling. *Maybe they made a mistake in identifying the injured woman and she's not actually Marci.* When he could no longer focus on the dots, he tried to find imaginary figures hidden within the design of the mottled linoleum floor. He looked at his watch. *Christ! What's taking so long? She's been in surgery for over an hour now.*

"*Tuchi?*"

Snapping out of his trancelike state, Kip looked up and saw Sal walking up to him. As soon as Kip stood, both men embraced tightly. The comforting gesture from his best friend caused Kip to break down and openly cry. "*Yani*, I'm so scared. Marci's still up in surgery."

"What happened?" Sal guided Kip back down into his chair.

"We were coming back from one of Marci's fund raising events for the American Cancer Society. I remember driving down Geary, but then everything went blank." Kip brought his hand up to his face to wipe the tears away. "I woke up confused. I was in pain. I could hear sirens blaring and people yelling. I saw flashing red lights all around me. When I looked over at Marci, my God, she was slumped over unconscious and had blood covering her face."

Sal said, "Ah, no."

With a high-pitched warbled voice, Kip continued, "Just as I reached over to try and help her, the medics pried the passenger door open and took over. Before I knew it, they lifted her onto a gurney and into an ambulance. Then she was gone. A patrolman from SFPD gave me a ride here after the EMT guys checked me out and—"

He started to sob again.

Sal wrapped his arms around him—tears now streaming down his own cheeks.

When Kip looked up, his expression turned to fright. "Oh, no."

Dr. Farber was walking toward them with a serious look on his face. He pulled up a chair opposite the two men and took a deep breath. "Mr. Duchene, I'm so sorry—we lost her."

Kip heard someone crying, but it wasn't Sal. He opened his eyes to see Heather sobbing next to him on the sofa. She reached over and placed a hand on his. "You were telling me what happened when Marci had her accident. I think you might have gone into some kind of trance or something."

"Yeah, something weird happened." He wiped his hand across his face and glanced at his watch. "Jeez, it's past midnight already."

She looked at him with puffy eyes. "It's also way past my bedtime." She stood up. "Kip, thank you for sharing this with me."

Kip forced a smile and barely nodded. "Let me walk you home. The fog's gotten really thick"

"It's okay. I can make my way back."

He stood up and held out his hand. "Come on, I'll walk you home anyway."

As soon as Kip returned home, he headed directly to the bar and poured himself a three-finger drink. *I wonder what in the hell happened with me tonight?*

Feeling exhausted from the ordeal and the alcohol coursing through his body, he padded down the hallway and went straight to bed. The moment he started to slip off to sleep, the scene in the hospital waiting room jumped back into his mind. His subconscious mind told him he was actually there. The next thing he heard was Doctor Farber's calm, measured voice. "I'm so sorry for your loss. Mr. Duchene, we've placed your wife's body in a private room. Would you like to spend time with her?"

Kip nodded. "Yes, thank you."

Sal stood. "*Tuchi*, do you want me to go in there with you?"

Kip turned in his direction and softly pressed his palm against Sal's cheek while shaking his head. He half-smiled at Sal before following Doctor Farber out of the waiting room and disappeared through double doors.

Kip could hardly breathe when he first saw Marci's body in the darkened room. She was draped with a bright-white sheet and laid motionless on a stretcher. Except for the Ace bandages wrapped around her head, she looked to Kip like she was just taking a nap. He reached under the sheet and held her hand in his, occasionally squeezing it as if it would arouse her. "Marci?"

Silence.

For the next thirty minutes, he talked to her as if she were alive, declaring his everlasting love for her. Overwhelmed with grief, he became engulfed in waves of wracking sobs. As he spoke, he believed that she was listening from somewhere. Had to be. After telling her how deeply he loved her and would never forget their cherished times together, he leaned down over her lifeless body and kissed her on the lips. "Good night, princess."

He had no idea how much time he'd spent with her by the time he walked out of the room. Her parents were sitting in chairs just outside in the hallway. Seeing Kip emerge, they stood up. Marci's mom walked over to put her arms around him, letting out a moan that sounded as though it came from deep in her chest. Releasing him, she paused for a moment before pushing through the treatment room door. With red-rimmed eyes, Mr. Cunningham stiffly followed.

Kip turned down the labyrinth of hallways and somehow managed to find the waiting room where Sal was seated. Kip mumbled, "I should wait here until Marci's parents come out."

Seeing Kip's unfocused gaze and ashen face, Sal put an arm around his shoulders. "Let's just get you home."

Kip was only partially aware that his dear friend was guiding him out of the hospital and through the fog-shrouded parking lot. Somewhere in the distance, he distinctly heard the moan of a foghorn.

Chapter 41

Kip woke up thinking about Heather. *That was some visit last night. Jesus, she even had me talking about Marci.* He slid out of bed and peeked through the window blinds. The dense fog had receded offshore, leaving Shanghai Shores bathed in bright morning sunlight and vast blue skies.

That afternoon Kip meandered through the restaurant and was pleased to see that everything looked well prepared for the Saudis visit. Paul had set up a table to accommodate eight people. It was located next to the twenty-foot high windowed wall which afforded a commanding view of the ocean. Other tables were moved away so the group would have privacy.

When Kip stepped into his third-floor office, Sal was waiting on the couch. "*Oye, Tuchi*, I wanted to get here a little early to learn more about what you started to tell me yesterday."

Kip put a finger to his lips and motioned for Sal to follow him. The two men walked down two flights of stairs and out onto the boardwalk. Kip said, "We're okay to talk out here."

"It must be a bitch having to watch what you say in there."

"Yeah, it is. After we set that little trap for Priscilla last week, Eleni confirmed that we were probably being bugged. I was surprised when she said that eavesdropping in China is so pervasive."

Sal looked over at Kip. "Shhiiiit, everyone knows that."

"Well, thanks for getting around to telling me."

"Don't mention it." Sal flashed his best Mexican bandito smile.

Kip shook his head. "Okay, here's the big news." He looked around. "Eleni learned that Niu had offered Priscilla the next general manager's position at Shores after he takes it over."

Sal chuckled. "Fat fuckin' chance."

"Yeah, we think the same thing."

Sal looked back at the clubhouse. "On the bugging thing, I think Reggie knows someone in the business. He's a security expert who can sweep the property for all kinds of bugs and shit like that."

"That'd be great. Save me from trying to find someone. I don't intend to have any of the bugs removed after they're discovered."

"Why in the hell not?"

"Think about it, *Yani*. We don't tip Rico off that he's been had. Moreover, we can use the bugs in our favor, saying things that we want the man to hear."

"Smart. I'll go ahead and tell Reggie to make contact with the guy."

While they were walking back, Kip reminded Sal about his offer to take the kids so he and Maria could get away for a romantic weekend.

Sal said, "I'm on it, *amigo*."

In the clubhouse lobby, they saw Reggie and the Saudis making their way up to the front entrance. Kip pushed open the door and greeted them.

"You have a nice looking development here," said Mohammed while he swept his hand through the air behind him.

"Thanks," said Kip with a tone of pride to his voice. "The property will look even better in the months ahead."

"From what Reggie told me about your previous work, I'm sure it will."

"Hello, Kip, old boy," said Reggie. "I see that you've dialed in some bloody good weather for us."

"I'm not sure I have that much talent. Maybe it was Heather's doing?"

"Rubbish!"

On their way through the lobby, Kip asked the receptionist to alert Angie and Heather that their guests had arrived. Shortly after the group was seated, the two beautiful ladies walked up to the table. The men stood for introductions.

After the refreshments were served, Reggie turned to Kip. "I've got some bloody good news for you."

"Great. I could use whatever I can get."

Reggie chomped on his pipe. "Quite right. Well, I spent the whole of yesterday with my honorable Saudi friends here exploring how we might team up in Shanghai. I dare say that we've decided to form a joint venture to study the feasibility of an offshore island for residential development."

Kip arched his eyebrows. "Impressive. That's no small project. Do you have any particular site in mind?"

Reggie beamed and his cheeks brought on a deeper shade of red. "It would seem the ocean topography off Shanghai Shores strikes the right balance." He looked at the Saudis. "Don't you think, gentlemen?"

Kip flashed a look at Sal, wondering why he didn't alert him to this startling news.

Mohammed answered. "Yes. Based on our experience with the Palm Island project in Dubai, all the required geophysical parameters look good so far." He went on to explain that their group had already made significant investments in Japan, United States, and Europe, but not China. Recent improvements in China's economy had encouraged them to look for investment opportunities in that country, starting with Shanghai. Because of their longstanding relationship with Reggie, they'd decided to proceed by partnering with Ingram Capital Corporation.

Kip said to Reggie, "Well I'm certainly impressed. That's huge."

The subject then turned back to Shanghai Shores. The Saudi group expressed interest in participating as investors in its secondary offering once the Shanghai government gives them the go ahead.

After the business part of the meeting concluded, Kip led the group down to the boardwalk and over to his home. They meandered through the rooms and ended up relaxing on the deck with refreshments. Twenty minutes later, Mohammed said "Kip, we understand that you have four unoccupied estate homes along the shoreline."

"We do."

"Is it possible for us to take a look at them?"

"That would be our pleasure." Kip turned to Heather. "Could you show them the homes?"

"I'd love to." She reached into her purse and pulled out a set of keys.

The Saudis ended up taking a full hour sauntering through the homes, speaking non-stop in a Gulf Arabic dialect with each other, occasionally switching to English to ask Heather a question.

By five-thirty, Reggie and his three guests were in the parking lot saying their goodbyes to Kip, Sal, Heather and Angie. The Saudis were eloquent in expressing their gratitude for the hospitality extended to them. Mohammed said to Heather, "Thank you for all your patience in showing us through those beautiful estates."

She said, "You're very welcome."

As the Mercedes sedan pulled away, Kip looked at his watch and suggested, "How about if I treat the three of you to a nice dinner in the clubhouse?" Everyone nodded.

On the way in, Kip tugged on Sal's jacket. "What's up with not telling me about the offshore development?"

"Oh that. Reggie asked that I keep it to myself until he personally made the announcement. You understand the drill."

Kip let out a, "Humph," slowly shaking his head.

All through their meal, light banter swirled around the table with everyone expressing excitement about the news of the offshore island and the Saudis interest to invest in

Shores. During the evening, Angie caught Heather casually placing her hand on Kip's sleeve several times.

After they finished, Sal offered to take Angie home. After the two left, Kip said to Heather, "I'll walk you home."

Before Heather let herself into the townhouse, she turned around to face Kip. "Thanks for sharing your thoughts with me last night about Marci. It must have been difficult."

Kip shrugged his shoulders. "It was probably good for me to talk about it. I'm just now coming to terms about losing her." He started to say something else, but stopped himself short. Instead he smiled and waved. "See you tomorrow."

Kip glanced down at his watch. It was eight forty-five. On his way past the clubhouse, Kip saw Manny pushing out through the lobby doors. Kip called up to him, "Hey, Manny, can I buy you a drink?"

Manny's face lit up with his classic wide smile. "That sounds good to me, boss."

No sooner had they walked into the lounge than Hans stood up on the other side and waved them over. He was sitting with three other tenants. Kip motioned for Manny to take a seat at a table next to the window. "Hold on. I'll be right back."

Walking over to Hans, Kip shook everyone's hands around the table. He smiled at Hans. "Say, that was quite a party after the tenants meeting, wasn't it?"

"Vat party?" Hans bellowed with twinkling eyes and face erupting into a big smile.

"Where's Trudy?" asked Kip.

Hans cupped a hand to the side of his mouth, leaned towards Kip, and whispered, "I think she's mad. She said you guys had a hell of a time getting me home."

Kip patted him on the shoulder. "Not to worry."

Hans said, "Why don't you and Manny join us?"

"Can't. We have some business to discuss."

Hans insisted on at least buying them a drink. Kip agreed and headed back to join Manny. Since coming to Shores, Kip's hectic schedule had kept him from spending much time with him. Manny was adored and respected by all of the residents and staff. His immediate reaction to most situations would be to flash a captivating smile, showing a full set of pearly-white teeth. But Kip recognized an underlying sadness with Manny, catching glimpses of him staring off in space at times with a far-away look. Kip guessed it may have come from his days in Uganda.

Holding up his glass, Kip said, "Cheers!"

"Boss, I'm so happy to have drink with you."

"Hey, the pleasure's mine. I'm just sorry that we haven't had much of an opportunity to do so before now."

Still smiling, Manny said, "Sometime when free, I like to take you to a neighborhood restaurant near my apartment. It not fancy but I think you enjoy real Chinese meal."

"I'd like that, Manny. Just suggest a time."

After several drinks, the conversation gravitated to Uganda. "You know, boss, I love my country and want it to become a safe place to live. I'll go back someday."

"What was it like when you were a boy?"

"When I was a boy? Well . . . not so good. Do you know about our leader, Idi Amin?"

"Yes."

Manny took another sip of his drink and said, "Then you know that he was an evil man who slaughtered many people"

"Yeah, I know."

"Maybe now, we have something even worse—AIDS. There too many children in Uganda without any parents. They die of AIDS. I believe best way to solve problems of Uganda is for people to get out and get educated in other countries."

"Like you did in China?"

"Yes, boss. Then they come back and help give new life to our motherland."

Kip smiled. "Sounds nice. What are *your* plans?"

"The same, boss. I want to get Masters in Engineering in Australia. Then, I go back and help my people."

Kip was thoroughly captivated listening to Manny and learning about a side of him that he'd never heard before. He thought that Shores was very fortunate to have the services of this fine man.

Before calling it a night, they agreed to have dinner on Friday evening at the restaurant Manny mentioned. His village was called Heqing. Manny pronounced it, "Her ching."

The last thing Kip remembered before falling to sleep was the horrific stories Manny told about Uganda. Yet, the man still found a reason to smile. In the darkness of his room, he compared Manny's outlook in life with how he was handling Marci's death. Kip felt ashamed.

Chapter 42

As planned, Manny pulled his pickup truck in front of Kip's house at eight o'clock sharp. This was the day Manny had invited Kip for dinner in *Heqing*, the small town where he was living. On their way out of the main gate, one of the guards gave them a second look. Kip noticed. Curious, he leaned forward to look through the side-view mirror as the truck headed down the village road. The guard continued to eye the truck while bringing his walkie-talkie up his mouth. Kip thought—*I wonder what the hell that's all about?*

Several minutes later Manny was zigzagging the truck along narrow roads through quaint villages and farms. Crops were planted on every square foot of land.

"You like the nice scenery out here, boss?"

Kip looked over at Manny, "Yeah, this is all so fascinating to me."

Manny chuckled. "To me, *this* is real China." He motioned with his hand in a sweeping matter. "And right up ahead is Heqing."

Manny drove into the center of his village, a town so small it didn't even merit a traffic signal. The streets were dimly lit, dusty and lined with shops that looked like they sold just about everything. The streets and sidewalks teemed with people, either walking or riding bicycles. Children ran up and down the street, squealing with delight with their little friends.

As Manny was pulling to the curb, the front-right side of the truck dropped down with a loud thud and brought it to a jarring stop. Kip's hands flew up to brace himself against the dashboard. Manny just chuckled.

Kip said, "What the hell?"

"Oh, it's nothing, boss. People steal metal grates from street drains, is all. They then sell to scrap metal dealers. It too dark for me to see grate was missing so our tire sank into an uncovered drain hole."

As they got out, Kip looked down and saw that the front right tire had wedged six inches into the hole. Manny said, "Boss, forget about it now. After dinner, we get pulled out."

"Whatever you say." Kip shrugged his shoulders unconvinced.

Taking a look at the restaurant from the street, Kip wondered if he'd made a mistake to accept Manny's invitation. The large plate glass window in front had a crack running diagonally across the pane. Someone had tried to repair it with 4" transparent tape, now yellowed with age and curled along the edges. Overall, the restaurant looked shabby with a dented sheet-metal sign mounted across the width of the building between the first and second levels. Inside, the floor was wet. The four tables in the cramped dining area were all occupied by Chinese families. Fish tanks were stacked on sturdy shelves against the wall on the other side of the dining room. A reception counter stood at the back of the room. *What in the hell did I get myself into?*

A man wearing a soiled apron came around from behind the counter to greet Manny with a smile and enthusiastic handshake. He and Manny chatted for a while in Chinese before Manny turned to Kip. "Let me introduce you to Mr. Sun, the owner." Manny then translated Kip's greeting. The regular patrons sitting at nearby tables stopped eating and stared at the tall Caucasian man talking with Mr. Sun and their neighbor, Manny.

The owner escorted the two men up a narrow stairway to the second floor. It opened to a room only fourteen-foot square. He then motioned for them to be seated at the only vacant table. It was wooden and covered by a clear plastic table cover. Thumbtacks held it in place around its edges.

Manny smiled at Kip. "I call ahead and got reservations."

Kip chuckled.

There was a thick wad of napkins wedged beneath one of the legs to stabilize it from rocking. As soon as the two men sat down, a waitress dutifully brought over two sweaty bottles of Budweiser and snapped off the tops.

Kip said, "They must know you."

"Yes, boss. I come here a lot. If you want, I order dinner."

Kip flipped his menu closed and set it down. "Great."

The variety of food was plentiful, delicious, yet totally unfamiliar to Kip. Occasionally, Kip would ask, "Manny, what's this dish?"

Each time, Manny would smile and say, "No ask, boss."

During dinner, they went through several large bottles of cold beer. At Kip's urging, Manny talked more about his life as a boy in Uganda. The gruesome stories of what it was like to live in Uganda caused Kip to reflect more on his own personal loss. Manny was fast becoming a trusted friend and enjoyable companion.

As Manny finished telling Kip about one of his experiences in Uganda, he paused and became serious. "I think you keep eye on Heather."

"Whataya mean?" asked Kip, surprised by Manny's abrupt change in their conversation.

"I just hear things, boss. You need make sure she protected."

"Manny, I'm lost. Do you have anything specific to tell me?"

"No. In China, stories get around funny pieces. I don't have all pieces yet."

"Well, thanks for the forewarning." *I'll never figure this place out.*

"No to mention it, boss."

When Kip waved the waitress over, Manny put his hand on his and said, "Boss, someone paid already the bill."

"Who?"

Manny broke out in laughter.

They then navigated back down the uneven stairs. When they reached the bottom, Kip said, "Manny, what about the truck?"

Manny chuckled. "No worry, boss."

At the counter, Manny spoke to Mr. Sun who immediately laughed while craning his neck to see Manny's tilted truck parked in front. He disappeared into the kitchen and reemerged with five other employees. As they headed out the front door and walked over to the curb, Manny climbed into the truck and started the engine. The six men surrounded the front right side of the truck and bent down, grabbing whatever handhold they could find. In unison, they called out, "Yi-er-san, yi-er-san, YI-ER-SAN!"

With the third chant, the truck was lifted out of the rut while Manny pulled it away from the curb. He leaned across to the open window. "Hop in, boss."

As the pickup rounded the next corner, Kip thought about what just happened. "Won't another car drop into that hole?"

Manny smiled and said, "Yes, many time. Government replace it maybe next week, maybe not."

Kip said, "Amazing."

At the main gate, Kip noticed the same guard as before speaking into his walkie-talkie. He said, "Manny, I have a funny feeling about that guard's behavior tonight. He's been paying too much attention to our coming and going."

"I think nothing, boss. Maybe just spy for Priscilla."

"Maybe."

When Manny pulled up to the curb, Kip reached over and shook his hand. "Hey, Manny, thanks for the great dinner. I really liked it."

Manny smiled broadly. "Let me know when want to know what you ate."

From the sidewalk, Kip waved. "Never."

After unlocking the front door and stepping in, he sensed that someone had broken in. The air smelled of rotten fish, like someone's bad breath. With beads of perspiration forming on his forehead, he slowly turned the knob of the coat closet and felt for the baseball bat leaning in the corner. Grasping it with both hands, he tiptoed down the hallway.

Chapter 43

With each step, Kip's vision and hearing senses increased. He held the tip of the bat high in the air, ready to bludgeon any intruder. As he inched his way down the carpeted hallway, the rotten breath odor got stronger. He flicked on the lights in the bedrooms, peeked under beds, and opened closet doors. Nothing. But when he looked down at the end of the hallway to his master suite, he was surprised to see the double doors were closed. *Shit, I never close them. Okay, this is it.*

He slowly turned the doorknob and nudged the door open with his foot. No sound. He reached in and flipped on the light switch. There was no movement in the brightly lit room. As he started to tip-toe toward the bathroom, there was a flash of movement to his far left. He spun in that direction ready to swing the bat. The door leading to the veranda was wide open and the ocean breeze had sucked the curtain outside. Kip bolted out the door in pursuit, but saw no sign of anyone running away.

Back in the house he inspected the rest of the house. Since becoming suspicious about listening devices, he'd made it a habit to leave the TV on with the volume turned up before taking off for the evening. He figured that leaving the TV volume turned up would interfere with an intruder hearing him returning home. As he rounded the corner into the family room, the large-screen TV stood before him, completely black and without sound. The guard at the front gate must have alerted whoever had been here that he was on his way home. That gave the intruder just enough time to run out the veranda door but not enough time to turn the TV back on.

Convinced that the intruder was long gone, Kip set the bat on the countertop and grabbed a can of Budweiser out of the refrigerator. Draining it, he flipped opened his phone and called Sal.

After hearing the story, Sal said, "*Tuchi*, it's probably good that you didn't catch the fucker."

"Why?"

"For starters, you would have probably killed him with your handy Louisville Slugger. The corrupt Shanghai Court would have loved to hear that and throw your ass into a Chinese prison to rot away."

"I don't think so," said Kip without much conviction.

"Shit, you know I'm right. Then Reggie would have to pay a fortune to get your sorry ass out."

"The fact is that I didn't even catch the guy."

Sal said, "Well, he was a stupid enough fuck."

"And how's that?"

"He didn't even have the two brain cells needed to talk to each other and tell him to turn the TV back on."

Kip couldn't stop himself from chuckling.

Sal said with an innocent tone, "What?"

"Nothing. I'm glad I called you."

"Me too. Say, if you're free tomorrow, let's plan to have lunch together at Shanghai Center."

"Yeah, that'd be nice."

"Great. In the meantime, remember to watch your back."

"At least it's getting interesting over here."

With a serious tone to his voice, Sal said, "Be careful, *amigo*."

Kip woke up the next morning thinking about the break-in, but also how nice a time he had with Manny. In truth, he was getting lonely and was in need of companionship. Maybe that also explained why he was starting to feel close to Angie. Despite her dishing out regular doses of irreverent comments his way, he enjoyed her mere presence. He was also drawn to her intelligence and insight into Chinese ways. *But we come from entirely different worlds. Being Chinese, she's perhaps much too complicated for me to ever understand. I think she's also attracted to me—I'm not sure. Her response to my hug after the sleep-over was something. It felt good for me. Could that mean that that I'm ready to love someone again?*

Then Kip thought of Heather. She certainly reminded him of Marci, offering him the comfort of familiarity. She was beautiful, uncomplicated, intelligent, and dedicated to a career in law. *What in the hell am I doing for Christ's sake? This is just too much to think about right now.*

When Kip called the receptionist to arrange for Mr. Zeng to pick him up at eleven, she let him know that Benjamin had recovered enough from his injuries to return to work. So Mr. Zeng was not needed.

Before leaving, Kip went through the routine of hiding his laptop computer in the bottom of his dirty clothes hamper and turning up the volume on his TV. Thirty minutes later, Benjamin knocked on the front door. He had several butterfly bandages across his forehead. "Hi, boss!"

Kip felt a quick surge of anger at the sight of the man who had betrayed him, but he managed to choke it down. He pointed toward Benjamin's wound. "How are you feeling?"

"No problem, boss. I confuse when wake up in hospital and headache. But better okay now."

Sliding into the car, Kip said, "That's good to hear."

Chapter 44

Kip had made the trip back and forth along Longdong Avenue so many times now that he was familiar with most of the landmarks on both sides of the street. As Benjamin pulled the car into the porte-cochere entry of the Shanghai Center, Kip wasn't surprised to see Sal standing in front.

They decided to eat at Element Fresh. As they were being seated, Kip looked around the area and smiled to himself, recalling his first few days in Shanghai. Then, the people, the smells, and the sights were all strange to him. Not any longer.

"Hello, Mr. Kip, may I bring you two some coffee?" asked a waitress as she walked up to the table.

"Hi Jenny. Yes, that'd be great."

A few minutes later she set two steaming coffees in front of them and took their orders. After she left, Sal motioned with his head, "See that guy over there?"

Looking to the other side of the patio, Kip said, "Yeah. What about him?"

"It's amazing how a forty-year-old, fat expat could hook up with a drop-dead gorgeous Chinese woman who is probably half his age."

Kip said, "I noticed the couple when we were being seated. Though it's not my style, I can't judge whether it will end up to be a problem or not."

Sal looked back at Kip. "I just worry about you, *hermano*. It could be easy for a single guy to be tempted over here."

"Relax, *Yani*—I'm not the least bit interested in one-night stands."

Peering over his coffee cup, Sal said, "What about Angie?"

"Christ, *now* I understand!"

"What?"

Kip leaned forward and said, "You've been making innuendos about me and Angie since I got here. What's up?"

Sal smiled. "Keep going."

"Well, instead of trying to be the savior for Angie as I first assumed, maybe you're actually trying to protect *me* from falling for her or another beautiful Chinese woman like *her*." Kip nodded toward the couple at the other table. "Am I close?"

"Close, but no banana," said Sal laughing. "Before I say anything more, you've got to promise not to tell anyone."

"I promise—shoot."

"Okay then. You know that Maria and I have a solid marriage. Well, I'm also Mexican so I flirt a little."

"That's for damn sure."

"But I've never cheated on my wife. When I first saw Angie, she blew me away with her beauty."

Kip looked at Sal worried what he was about to say next.

Sal held up his hands. "I know—I was stupid. I met her at a Chinese-American job fair sponsored by UC Berkeley in 1998. Just before she got her MBA, she attended the fair and was hoping to find a job with an American company based in Shanghai. So, she naturally sought me out since I was there representing Ingram Capital. In the process of interviewing her, I was mesmerized by how fucking beautiful she looked."

"What happened?" asked Kip nervously. He was surprised to find himself irritated by Sal's admission. *Shit, am I feeling jealousy?*

"Nothing! Angie might have guessed that I was intrigued with her, but she never knew for sure because I never gave her any obvious signals. Reggie ended up hiring her just before the Moscone meeting and you know the rest."

"Bullshit, *hermano*! In the six weeks since I've been here you're way too curious about what's happening between Angie and me. What's up with that?"

"Think about it. Wherever she goes, men can't keep their eyes off of her. *Tuchi*, I know that your heart's been ripped apart and you might be susceptible to falling for Angie since you work so closely together. With everything else on your plate at Shores, an affair with Angie could fuck everything up. Buddy or not, I have to think of the best interests of Ingram Capital." Sal brought his hands in front of him and turned his palm up. "That's all."

Jenny, the waitress walked back to their table and set their plates down. "Warm ups on your coffee?"

Both men nodded. After she poured the coffee and walked off, Kip said, "You know, if I believe you and Eleni, I should be afraid of all Chinese women over here."

Sal said, "Okay, here's how it gets complicated. You're damn sure not ready to get emotionally involved in another woman, but I have to admit that you and Angie really do look good together. Despite that, I still think it would be a conflict at Shores."

"You mean you're actually finished trying to be my personal advisor?"

Sal smiled. "Yeah . . . just enjoy your fuckin' lunch."

"Okay, it's really nice to see you too, *Yani*. We haven't had a lot of time together lately. How's everything going?"

Sal told Kip how much he'd been out of town recently, flying around China, Hong Kong and Thailand to visit Ingram portfolio companies. He admitted that Maria was upset about his being gone so much, but that his travel schedule should taper off by the start of the Chinese New Year.

"Sal, remind me when the Chinese New Year starts."

"January twenty-ninth."

"Talking about New Years, Bev Shen has warned me that we may have problems from some of our creditors in advance of the New Year."

"Why's that?"

"As I understand, it's traditional in China for creditors to try and collect what's owed to them before the New Year so they can have a little more money for the Spring Festival. It's the most important time in the year for Chinese people because many return to their birthplaces to renew family bonds."

Sal said, "So, what did Bev say the creditors may do?"

"She said that in the past creditors have organized demonstrations in front of the main gates complete with loud shouts and signs demanding that they get paid. Others may try to block the main gates or even worse."

"Like what?"

"*Yani*, we can't rule out violence breaking out."

"I assume that you have a handle on this."

Kip said, "I think I do. I just wanted you to know what might lie ahead."

"Okay, thanks for telling me. By the way, I talked to Reggie about your request for contingency funds. He said that the original fund to capitalize Shores was fully expended and that no other funds could be made available until we're ready to go ahead with the second round of capitalization. Of course in an emergency, he's not going to leave you high and dry. He'll just have to be a little unorthodox, like digging into his own deep pockets."

"That's disappointing, but I understand."

"Yeah, it is. Despite this, please let me know how I can help. We'll come up with something, maybe a bridge loan from the bank."

Kip said, "Well, if Heather continues to bring in more new leases, we may just squeak by on the increased cash flow."

"That'd be great. So how are you and Angie really getting along—I mean work-wise?"

"Just fine. She's incredibly bright and an asset to have on our side. Underneath all that beauty is one savvy woman. That's a necessity when stepping through the minefield of doing business in China and staying in one piece. Without question, she's helped me rethink how we can neutralize Rico Niu and the Gang of Three."

"The gang of what?"

"I assumed you knew."

"I don't know shit about a gang."

"Well, we have a problem with Priscilla Mao, Naomi Chen, and Shelly Tang. They work together as one, for their own interest and not the company's. So Angie, Heather, and I have formed our own little gang. We quietly meet at a place where we're sure no listening devices are planted."

"It's that much of a problem, huh?"

"It's impossible to know for sure. By the way, have you found someone who can sweep suspected areas for bugs?"

"I have. It's taken me longer than anticipated because I did not want to use any of the local security companies. They would be tempted to get money under the table from Niu for revealing what we're up to. It's the fact of life over here. Anyway, he's a private investigator from Hong Kong who does a lot of work for embassies and other foreign government offices. Reggie knows him personally and says he's trustworthy. I'll make sure the man gives you a call."

"Thanks. I want to at least know how much of a problem we really have."

Sal said, "How's everything else going out there?"

"Other than the break-in, being run off the road, the suspected bugging, and learning that my driver is a spy, everything is going better than expected."

They laughed and reached across the table to give each other a high-five hand slap. Neither man had any idea that every gesture between them was caught by a digital camera with a 500mm telephoto lens taken from the eighth floor of the JC Mandarin Hotel across the street.

Rico Niu was in a particularly foul mood that day and didn't care who knew it. On the telephone, he said, "The next time there's a fuckup, someone's going to pay. And if Benjamin ever asks for more money again, go ahead and pay him. Yes, stupid, with a bullet in the back of his head. Now listen to me carefully unless you want Mr. Tao to make an unscheduled trip up there and give you that bullet for yourself. Tomorrow, I want you to go ahead with the plans for Ingram's daughter. She won't be daddy's pretty little girl much longer."

After hanging up, he broke out in uncontrolled laughter.

Chapter 45

Benjamin drove through the main gates of Shanghai Shores an hour after Kip and Sal had their Saturday lunch. As soon as Kip walked into his house, he began his routine check for an intruder. He started by inspecting the door jambs. Before he had left that morning, he had stuck straight pins in some of the door casings so they would fall to the floor if any door was opened. Even if an intruder were to discover a pin on the floor, he'd have no idea where it came from. Kip was pleased to see that they were all still in place.

That evening, he called Philip Starr, the Hong Kong investigator, to arrange for him to come to Shanghai Shores to sweep for listening devices. Starr said that he could do the job on Thursday afternoon.

After finishing off his breakfast the next day, Kip stretched out on the recliner and tried to figure out what was nagging him. He had a feeling that it was related to Manny's warning about Ricc coming after Heather. Images of the kidnapped American girls flashed in his mind. *Why hell, I don't think Heather's that exposed. She's either safely inside the gates of Shanghai Shores or with other people when she ventures out. I don't think she's ever alone, unless . . . OH, SHIT!*

Kip snatched up the phone, hoping to catch Heather before she left for her Sunday bicycle ride. After the third ring, beads of sweat formed on his forehead. He said, "Come on, pick up the damn phone!"

He listened intently to the fourth ring. On the fifth ring, Heather answered, "Hello?"

Audibly exhaling, Kip said, "Hi, Heather."

"Hi, Kip. You sound out of breath?"

"Nah. It's nothing."

"I was just heading out the front door. What's up?"

"I was just wondering if I could join you today?"

"You have a bike?"

"Yeah. When I first moved into the house, Jessie had a practically new one dropped off at my place. A tenant had left it behind."

"Great. When can you get here?"

"Give me ten minutes."

He packed a knapsack with bottled water, a camera, and binoculars.

Before heading out, he set the straight pins in the door jambs and turned the volume up on the TV. As he bicycled around the corner to Heather's place, he saw her pushing her bike out of the garage.

Kip said, "Do you have your phone with you?"

Smiling, she held her cell phone up for Kip to see.

He said, "Good. Just in case we get separated along the way, I wanted to make sure we can communicate."

Flashing a gorgeous smile, she said, "Let's go, old man! I hope you can keep up."

In a flash, she jumped on her bike and sped off toward the main gates. Caught off guard, Kip cranked the pedals and barely caught up to her by the time she was passing through. Heather looked over at Kip and said, "Don't look so smug, Mr. Duchene. I deliberately eased up so you could catch me."

"Like I believe you, girl. Where to?"

"Just follow me."

They rode side by side heading south down a potholed lane. It was a brisk, sunny morning with just a trace of the usual haze.

"I'm glad you thought of joining me," said Heather. "The company's nice."

They rode through small farming communities where crops were growing in family gardens. For every plot of land, there was a plain two-story cement house with tiled roof and few windows. Clothes were hung out to dry on long poles that protruded from second-floor balconies. Occasionally the two would ride past a fenced-in pond full of white-feathered ducks paddling around in endless circles. Chickens ran freely between the homes.

Along the way, villagers looked up from whatever they were doing to stare at the foreign couple riding by. Heather, with her long flaxen hair blowing in the wind, got most of the attention. Further down the road, a group of children ran behind them, calling out, "Hello? Hello? Hello?"

Smiling, Kip and Heather said in unison, "Hello!"

Finally running out of breath, the children fell behind, giggling with delight.

A few miles south of Shanghai Shores, they rode into a larger village with vendors selling vegetables and fruit along each side of a busy road. They seemed to be doing a brisk business with villagers clustered around each one of them. The frenzied activity suggested that serious bargaining was part of each sale.

Heather said, "Let's stop for a minute." She pointed. "I want to ask that man standing over there something."

The man looked surprised by the two Caucasians approaching him. When Heather began to speak, he shrugged his shoulders as if to indicate he couldn't understand. After a few more exchanges between the two, the man's eyebrows lifted and he broke out in a smile. "*Ahhh . . . wa je da!*" I understand!

They chatted for another minute before Heather remounted the bike and said to the villager, "*Xièxie.*"

She then turned to Kip and said, "Okay. Let's go."

Kip said, "What was that all about?"

Heather chuckled. "Well, this happens to me a lot in China. Sometimes when I talk with people on the street, they cannot understand me, even though I'm speaking fluent Mandarin. The reason for this is that they're trying to figure out what English words I'm saying, not thinking that a blonde foreign woman would speak their own language. Once they catch on, everything's okay."

Picking up speed, Kip said, "Fascinating."

Edging her bike in front of Kip, Heather said, "Anyway, the man said that this is an old village called *Bai Long Gang*. It means white dragon port. He said that there's a golf course for rich people down that way." She pointed at the main road that passed through the village.

"That must be the Shanghai Links Golf and Country Club," said Kip. "Since we're just wandering around, let's ride past there. I've been curious about it."

"I'm game."

They took a road that headed due east. "Say, I have a stupid question for you," said Kip.

"What's that?"

"Well, I see these bundled-up toddlers in the villages being led around by their mothers. Then, out of the blue, a kid squats in the curb or between buildings and goes to the bathroom right then and there. How does that work?"

Laughing at the innocence of Kip's question, Heather said, "All clothes made for kids in China have slits sewn into the crotch. When a child squats, the slit automatically opens enough for business to occur. Do you want to know more?"

He chuckled. "I don't think so. I was just curious, that's all."

The further they rode away from the village proper the more Kip thought that the man gave Heather the wrong directions. The area they were riding through looked run down and littered with debris. There was an abandoned housing development on the right where the windows in the two-story homes were all broken out and the grounds were overgrown with tall weeds. Just as Kip was about to suggest that they turn around and head back to the village, the road made a sharp right-hand turn. On the far side of the road, the wrought-iron ornate front gates of the golf course were revealed.

Kip said, "Wow, there it is. I thought we were lost for a minute."

They stayed on the perimeter road bordering the golf course and enjoyed watching groups of golfers walking across the fairways or putting on the greens. Further down the road, they rode into a small fishing village. The air was permeated with the pungent smell of fish. Weathered-looking fishermen sat alongside of the road selling their morning's catch or repairing nets. Seagulls circled overhead in an attempt to swoop down and snatch a discarded morsel of fish. Beyond the fishing village, more rural farming areas came into view. Road traffic thinned down to only a few cars. In a nearby field a tractor was belching out black clouds of exhaust.

Kip said, "This is nice without a lot of cars on the road."

"It sure is."

"One of the first things I noticed in China," said Kip, "was how terrible people drive. Most of them don't seem to pay much attention to anything, including bicyclists."

"Amen, brother Duchene," said Heather smiling.

They continued south on a rural, two-lane rutted road. There was a seawall on the left where the East China Sea gently lapped against its banks. Greenhouses, like transparent Quonset huts, stretched along the fields on the right for a far as they could see. Bicycling carefree alongside of Heather, Kip felt more relaxed than he had in a long time.

The serenity of the moment was broken by the high-pitch sound of a fast-approaching car. Kip whirled around to look behind him and was shocked to see a dark-colored Toyota barreling down on them.

Chapter 46

"Follow me!" Kip stood up on the pedals. He yanked his bicycle hard right and sped off to a narrow pathway between the nearest greenhouses. With a look of sheer terror, Heather followed closely behind.

The Toyota's driver slammed on the brakes, causing the black sedan to fishtail into a screeching halt.

Hearing the car skidding, Kip stole a quick glance back to see if Heather was keeping up. She was. A hundred yards away from the road he stopped to take a breather. Heather pulled up right behind. They instinctively ducked their heads below the line of sight from the road.

Out of breath with flushed cheeks, Kip asked, "You okay?"

Between gasps, she said, "Yeah . . . What the hell's happening?"

"Not sure. That's the same damn car that ran Benjamin and me off the road."

"God, that's all we need!" She reached down to her water bottle and took a gulp. "Shouldn't we call the cops?" She handed the water bottle to Kip.

"Thanks." He took a drink and peeked above the greenhouse. The Toyota was idling in the same place. "No, the cops are useless. Besides, Rico is probably paying them off." While flipping open his phone, he said, "I'm calling Manny to pick us up. Since those goons can't drive out here without plowing through the greenhouses, I think we're okay for now."

He pressed the phone to his ear and heard, "*Wei?*"

"Are you home?" asked Kip with a sense of urgency to his voice.

"Yes, boss. What's the matter?"

"Heather and I are taking a bike ride and nearly got run down by the same Toyota that crashed into the Buick."

"Where are you?"

"In a field of greenhouses south of the fishing village."

"Oh, too many fishing villages, boss. Tell me more."

"We rode past Shanghai Links Golf Course just before going through a little fishing village. We're only two or three miles south of there. "

Heather nudged Kip's arm and pointed to the Toyota. It was slowly pulling away from the side of the road and creeping further south away from them.

Manny said he'd find them. Kip ended the call by urging, "Please hurry."

He took a few deep breaths and looked around. The greenhouses stretched out in perfectly aligned rows for miles in every direction. Narrow tractor-rutted roads cut through the greenhouse plantation in a haphazard pattern— *Shit, this isn't good. How will Manny ever find us out here in this maze?*

Turning to Heather, he said, "He's on his way."

"Shouldn't you try to call Sal?"

"He's in Hong Kong."

"Oh."

Kip watched the Toyota pull off the main road a quarter mile away onto one of the dirt corridors that traversed through the farm. "I think we should ride a little further away. Crouch close to the handlebars so we're below the tops of the greenhouse roofs."

"Okay. I hope Manny gets here soon."

"Count on it."

Before they had a chance to take off, Kip's phone rang. He pressed it to his ear and listened to someone speaking rapidly in Chinese. He handed the phone to Heather, "I can't understand—a Chinese man."

Her shaky voice greeted the caller in Mandarin. Listening, she flashed a look at Kip, said, "*Xièxie,*" and flipped the phone shut. "That was our sweet Mr. Zeng. Manny called him and told him what was happening. Since Zeng lives in Chuansha, right over there," she pointed west, "Manny thought that he could help locate us faster. He'll pick him up on the way over here."

"Shit!" said Kip.

She looked in the direction of the slow moving Toyota. "I'm really scared, Kip. I keep thinking of those kidnapped girls who had their left legs amputated."

He reached over and patted her arm. "We'll be okay. Let's keep moving."

The two remounted their bikes and slowly zigzagged through the labyrinth of greenhouses. Kip paid careful attention to the drone of the Toyota's engine in the distance as it changed course from one dirt road to another. A jumbo jet screamed overhead, making its final approach to the nearby Pudong International Airport. He couldn't hear much of anything until it passed by.

Several minutes later, Kip pulled his bike to a stop and motioned for Heather to do the same. With his binoculars, he scanned the area near the Toyota. Adjusting the glasses into sharper focus, he saw two men slowly creeping between the greenhouses. Both were holding something in their hands. Steadying his shaky grip, he thought—*Ah, shit. They have Billy clubs. Time to change plans. Clubs or no clubs, I'm going to give those fuckers something to think about.*

"Heather, it's time to change plans. Two of those guys are coming on foot. Switch your ringer to vibrate. I don't want anyone to call us at the wrong time. I'm going to circle around to them."

Heather pleaded, "Don't do that. We shouldn't mess around with those thugs. Besides, I don't want to be left alone."

"You'll be okay. When they see me, they'll be preoccupied with me and away from you."

"I'm not so sure about that."

"Just trust me." Saying those words, Kip got a painful flashback of the night Marci died in the car accident. He remembered saying those exact words to her when she asked if he'd had too much to drink and drive.

Looking at him with a frown, she said, "What's the matter?"

"Nothing. I'm okay." He wiped the sweat off of his face. "I just want to keep you safe."

She nodded.

He pointed to a water tower on the horizon to the north. "I want you to head off in that direction, but don't go beyond the greenhouses. You'll get to the road we came in on. Stay hidden until you see Manny's truck. Wave him down. We can stay in contact by phone."

"What about you?"

"It's time for those assholes to get a dose of their own medicine."

"Ah, Kip . . . please don't." The tears rimming her eyes spilled down her face.

He reached over and brushed the back of his fingers across her cheek. "I'll be okay. Just watch your back." He swung onto the bicycle and pedaled off.

Heather went in the opposite direction, periodically looking back until Kip was out of sight.

After riding for about a mile, Kip was close enough to hear one of the goons talking in a low voice. He thought— *Okay, it's show time. First, I want to get a few snapshots of the car.*

He slipped off his bike and approached the idling car without being seen by the two men on foot. Once in place, he took a few quick shots of the Toyota. The driver didn't appear to notice. Just as Kip was slipping the camera back into his knapsack, the two men raced out between nearby greenhouses and jumped back into the car. When it roared past spewing out a cloud of dust, one of the men in the back seat looked directly at Kip and smiled. Kip thought—*What the hell? That doesn't make any sense, unless . . . oh my God, I've been set up.*

He pulled out his phone to warn Heather.

Crouched behind a greenhouse waiting for Manny, Heather felt the phone vibrate in her pocket and thought— *Good, it's Manny.* But, when she put the phone to her ear, no one was there. She glanced down at the phone and was mortified to see that the battery level-indicator registered low.

She wondered if Kip was trying to call her and looked around the edge of the greenhouse where she was hiding. In the distance, she could just barely make him out. He looked as though he was racing in her direction at a high speed. *Good, Manny must be almost here.*

Just then, she heard his truck coming down the road. Excited, she bounded out from behind her hiding place and waved her arms. Just as suddenly, her eyes flashed wide in shock when she saw that it wasn't Manny's truck she'd heard.

The black Toyota sped toward her and screeched to a stop only a few feet in front of her. She stood paralyzed, just staring at the driver smiling at her. A second later, she snapped out of her trance and bolted in the opposite direction.

She was frightfully aware that someone was chasing after her. She could hear the pounding footfalls behind her getting closer. Her lungs felt as if they were on fire and about to burst. A moment later, hands slammed hard against her shoulders. Her head snapped back and she went down, somersaulting over herself in the dirt. Disoriented, she felt the weight of a man straddled on top of her. He lifted a Billy club and began to bludgeon her face.

The terrified screams that followed were heard above the dissipating whine of an overhead jumbo jet. Then silence.

Chapter 47

Within seconds, Heather's face was transformed from utter beauty into ugly splotches of red swollen tissue. Blood oozed from out of both nostrils. By the fourth blow, she lapsed into unconsciousness. As her assailant reached down to lift up her inert body, a blur of movement came from his side. Before he had time to react, a spray of blood erupted from his head. The force of a powerful blow propelled his body several feet away from Heather. Mr. Zeng stood over him with a bloodied Billy club ready to smash it down on the man's head again in case it was needed. It wasn't.

At the same time, Manny was in pursuit of the other man on foot. Just before he caught up with him, the man reached the Toyota and dove through the lowered rear window. With tires churning up gravel and dust, the car sped off down the road, allowing the driver and the man in the back seat to escape.

Kip skidded to a stop in front of Heather and threw his bike aside. Seeing her face, a wave of nausea brought a surge of bile into his throat. Swallowing it, he dropped to his knees and cradled her limp body into his arms—*My God, what did they do to you?*

Just then, Manny rounded the corner of a greenhouse and pulled up just short of the scene, panting to catch his breath. His eyes darted back and forth between Kip attending to Heather and Zeng standing over the assailant.

Kip pointed to his bike and called out, "Quick . . . water!"

Manny slipped the water bottle out from its holder, snapped it open, and handed it to Kip. Pouring the cool liquid onto his handkerchief, Kip gently dabbed it across Heather's face. Her eyes fluttered open.

He said, "How ya doing, kiddo?"

She cried, "Oh, Kip, I'm really hurt." She brought her hands to her swollen face and gently probed her fingers along her forehead, nose and eyes, and down across her cheeks and mouth.

"Well, you should see the other guy." He winced. *Christ, what a stupid thing to say.*

She managed a weak smile and looked over at her assailant lying beside her. Blood pooled outward from underneath his head. "Please help him."

Kip pointed to the man. "Manny, tie some cloth tight around his head to stop the bleeding, then get him into the truck." While Kip was comforting Heather, Manny and Zeng hog-tied their unconscious captive and threw him into the truck bed along with the bikes.

Still holding Heather, Kip murmured, "Do you think you can stand?"

"I'll try."

He helped her to her feet and slowly led her to the truck while holding his handkerchief against her upper lip. Her nosebleed wasn't letting up. After guiding her into the back seat of the king cab, he ran around and got in beside her. "I think we should take you to a hospital."

"I don't want to." Heather pressed her palms against her cheeks. "Just take me home. I'll be all right"

In the meantime, the driver of the black Toyota got up the nerve to pull out his cell phone to call Rico Niu and report that they failed to capture Heather.

An hour later, Heather's place was a beehive of activity. Propped up in bed, she had bags of frozen peas pressed against her face and small wads of Kleenex stuffed up her nostrils. The swollen areas on her face were turning from pink to a light shade of purple. As a result of trying to fend off her attacker, she had blotchy bruises on both forearms.

Angie arrived first. Shortly after, Bev, Patti and Jessie showed up. Kip brought chairs into the bedroom so he and the women could sit and keep Heather company.

Heather looked around the room and tried to smile. "You guys are too much."

Patti perked up. "Talking about *too much*, I'd like to spend five minutes alone with the creep who beat up our little princess here."

Understanding what Patti meant, Kip chuckled.

Patti reached over to Heather's dresser and grabbed a pair of scissors. She held her free hand upright as if she was holding a cluster of grapes. Above it, she opened and snapped the scissors closed. With an exaggerated smile, she said, "I'm even willing to go to jail to give the man a little tuck and trim."

Heather moaned, "Oh, Patti, please don't."

Patti shrugged, "Okay, just give me three minutes with him."

"No. What I meant was please don't make me laugh. It hurts my face all over."

Patti arched her eyebrows. "Oh, now I understand! Then only one minute."

Everyone in the room started to laugh, including Heather who moaned, "Oh, God, stop! It hurts, it hurts, it hurts!"

Their revelry was interrupted when a Caucasian man knocked on the bedroom door and walked in. He wore tan slacks, a short-sleeve white shirt and a stethoscope looped around his neck. He also carried a small black satchel in one hand.

Heather looked at Kip with one eyebrow raised.

Kip shrugged his shoulder. "There's no way we're going to take a chance, so I arranged for Doctor Flynn to make a house call." Kip turned to the doctor shook his hand. "Thanks for coming over from the clinic so soon."

The doctor smiled. "You did the right thing to call me." He looked around the room and said, "How about if I ask everyone to clear out of the room for a minute so I can check Heather's condition?"

After Doctor Flynn examined Heather, he said that she checked out okay and wouldn't need to be admitted. He added that someone should stay the night with her in the unlikely event she experienced a complication from her head trauma. Bev insisted that she would.

Since Heather joined the staff, she and Bev had quietly forged a close friendship. Both were attorneys, well educated, and came from affluent households. With Bev staying behind, Kip speculated that Angie and Heather must have had a falling out.

By 5:00 p.m., everyone but Kip and Bev had left.

Heather asked, "Kip, how's the man doing who attacked me?"

He shook his head. "Why in the world do you care how he's doing?"

"I don't know. I just do."

"Manny told me that he regained consciousness soon after they dropped him off at the police station."

"Why didn't they take him directly to the hospital?"

Kip shrugged his shoulders. "Beats me."

"Probably because this was such a serious crime," said Bev, "especially since it was a botched kidnapping of an American girl."

"I thought the local police chief was on Rico's payroll," said Kip. "Christ, I wouldn't be surprised if he let the thug go free."

"Won't happen," asserted Bev. "Being the daughter of someone as prominent as Reggie, Heather is big news around here. The Shanghai media will sensationalize the story."

"Well, shit, it *is* sensational!" exclaimed Kip.

Bev raised her hands. "Hear me out. Without question, the news of her assault has already reached the mayor's office. The Shanghai government will do anything to save face. You can count on them to come down hard on the assailant to show that they're tough on crime. The local police chief won't say a word."

Kip sat back in the chair and clasped his hands on top of his head. "I hope you're right. You know, as I think about what happened, everything points to them not wanting to just rough Heather up."

Heather lifted her head from the pillow. "Like what?"

"Well, I think they planned to kidnap you."

"God, I was afraid of that when they were chasing me. I was so scared. Kip, do you have any reason to think that other than a hunch?"

"Yeah." He held up one finger. "First of all, I rode up just when Zeng smacked the guy on the head. I saw that he was trying to lift you up but never got that far." He then held up two fingers. "Second, while the doctor was examining you, I called Manny to find out what was happening at the police station. He said that they found a roll of duct tape fastened to the man's belt."

Tears gathered in Heather's eyes. Bev said, "I'm going to head back downstairs. How does soup sound?"

Heather smiled. "That would be nice. Thanks."

Alone with Kip, Heather said, "Do you realize what might have happened if you hadn't been riding with me?"

"Thank Manny, not me."

"What do you mean?"

"He alerted me last night to keep a better eye on you. He'd heard a rumor about a threat against you and didn't want to take any chances by ignoring it."

"I'm sure glad he said something. Actually, I intend to do something special for both Manny and Mr. Zeng." Then smiling, she added, "You were also my savior. What can I do for you?"

Kip blushed. "I'd better head home."

"God, I didn't mean *that*."

"I know," Kip said with a chuckle. "Is there anything you need from me right now?"

"No. Thanks so much, Kip, for taking such good care of me. I appreciate it." She reached out and squeezed his hand.

"It was nothing. Should I give Reggie a call?"

"Please don't. He's in San Francisco and powerless to do anything right now. He'll just worry. I'll do it in the morning."

"Okay." Kip cleared his throat and said, "Heather, I'm so sorry about what happened. Believe me, those bastards will be sorry for what they did to you—the goddamn cowards."

While walking home, Kip thought about what would have happened if Manny and Zeng hadn't come on the scene when they did. He thought about the two kidnapped American girls with amputated legs.

Once inside, he grabbed a can of beer and placed two telephone calls from his back patio. Despite what Heather had said, he slipped Reggie's business card out of his wallet and dialed his private number. Then he called Sal. Within twenty minutes, he'd given each man a detailed report of what had happened and answered their questions. As expected, both men were shocked at the news. Reggie said that he would catch the next flight to Shanghai but agreed not to call his daughter tonight.

Later that evening, Kip wasn't surprised that he couldn't sleep. Lying in bed, he replayed the day's events and realized that Rico Niu had escalated the game. The man had stepped over the line when he decided to add Heather to his list of victims. He promised himself that Niu would regret that the events of this day ever happened.

Chapter 48

After getting in a few hours of sleep, Kip woke up feeling groggy. Over and over again he wondered what would have happened if Heather had been kidnapped. He shuddered at the terrifying images that filled his head.

Come on! Focus on protecting the company and taking out Rico Niu.

He slipped out of bed and headed for the shower.

After breakfast, he called over to Heather's place. "How's she doing, Bev?"

"Hi, Kip. The swelling's gone down in her face. I guess she's doing better. The bruising doesn't look so good though."

"How about if I stop by?"

"She'd like that."

Bev was right about Heather's appearance. She sported two black eyes and had several purple bruises rimmed with a yellowish tint. He quipped, "No makeup this morning?"

Heather smiled and pointed to her face. "There's not enough makeup in China to cover all this."

"What about a burka?"

"Cute."

Kip held up his hands. "Okay, bad idea. Can I bring you anything?"

"Nah, I'm comfy. The pain meds Dr. Flynn gave me really helped."

"Good." He placed a hand on her shoulder and gave it a reassuring squeeze. "If you don't mind, I've assigned one of the housekeeping girls to hang out downstairs. I understand she's a good cook and can bring up whatever you need."

"That'll be nice. Thanks."

"Not a problem." Kip started to head for the door when he turned back round. "Just so you know I've also assigned a guard to watch your house."

Heather sighed, "My hero."

"Good morning, boss," said Angie when Kip walked into her office. "How's Heather?"

Kip pointed down the hallway. Without needing to say anything further, they walked to the spare office. Inside, he said "Well, she looks like hell, but the doctor doesn't think she's incurred any permanent damage."

"That's a relief. When I walked into her bedroom yesterday, I didn't even recognize her. I feel so badly that she was hurt like that."

"Yeah, I know."

"What are you going to do about Rico?"

"I'm thinking about it." Kip looked down at his notes and changed the subject. "I talked to Sal over the weekend about the bugging problems. He's recommended a private investigator from Hong Kong, Philip Starr. He's flying in to do a sweep for bugs on Thursday."

"It'll be interesting to see what he finds." Angie then opened her notebook and briefed Kip on the week's activities. When she finished, she looked up. "Avery called from the U.S. Consulate's office."

"And?"

"He wants to see you today. He's concerned about what happened to Heather and thinks the accident was your fault."

"Why am I not surprised? Just delay the jerk for as long as you can."

"Will do."

Kip said, "One more thing. Let me know when you've got a plan to deal with the power company. Priscilla hinted at the managers' meeting that they were seriously considering shutting off our electricity. I don't want to think about what will happen if they pull the plug on us"

The next few days were a blur for Kip. Reggie flew in on Tuesday afternoon and came directly to meet with him to get the latest on Heather's condition and hear what he had in mind for Rico. The Chairman told him to do whatever he thought would rid them of the problem. He'd supply whatever funds were needed.

Kip had never seen the steely look of resolve in Reggie's eyes before. In the next moment, he reverted to his normal demeanor as a proper Englishman. "Spot on then. I think I shall pop over to see my daughter and cheer her up."

After Reggie walked out, Kip slowly shook his head and smiled—*Hey, Marci, I think things are about to really heat up.*

At 2:00 p.m. on Thursday, Angie poked her head around the door and said, "Your appointment's here."

"Good. I'll meet with him in the usual place."

A minute later, Angie escorted the visitor into the spare office. He was carrying an oversized attaché case.

Kip stood up and extended his hand, "Mr. Starr, it's a pleasure to meet you."

"Please call me Phil." He took a quick look at the furniture stacked along the far wall of the unused office.

"Excuse our meeting place. It's safer for us to talk in here."

Starr said nothing. He reached into his case and pulled out something that looked like a TV remote control device. He pushed a thumb lever and turned a dial several clicks. "No bugs here."

Kip thought Philip Starr looked more like an accountant than a private investigator. He wore outdated plastic-rim glasses, had a pale complexion, and wore a plain dark suit. His blank facial expression seemed to be stuck on deadpan. He hadn't even given a cursory smile of greeting.

After Angie poured tea for the three of them, Kip said, "Phil, we appreciate you coming here on such short notice."

"May I ask why you suspect you're being bugged?" asked Starr.

"We have reason to believe that members of the Pudong government are being bribed by a man who wants to take over Shanghai Shores. This individual is also suspected of recruiting our own employees. Too many of our moves are being thwarted as if someone knows what we're planning in advance. Everything points to us being bugged."

Starr said, "The man's name?"

"Rico Niu."

"I assume you're talking about Rico Niu from Haikou?"

"The same," said Kip. "Anyway, we've been told that Niu is working behind the scenes to gain control of Shores and is doing everything possible to make that happen. Without question, he knows that Ingram had belatedly booted out the former general manager and brought me in to turn the place around. That's exactly what Niu didn't want to see happen. Since coming to Shanghai, I've been tailed, run off the road, and have even had my house broken into. Since nothing was actually stolen or vandalized, I assumed that someone might have broken in to plant listening devices."

Starr said, "No question. Many Chinese companies and government officials are enamored with bugging people. If I detect some devices, do you want them disabled or removed?"

"Actually neither," said Kip. "It wouldn't be in our interest to alert whoever is involved by revealing we've discovered the bugs. So they should be left undisturbed."

"Very well," said Starr. "Where do you suspect the bugs have been placed?"

"Well . . . we're not sure. Certainly my office and home would be likely places. I would think they would also consider Angie's office and Heather's townhouse."

"Heather?"

"She's Reggie Ingram's daughter and is temporarily working here."

"The one roughed up over the weekend?"

Kip nodded.

"Did you have a computer in your house when it was broken into?"

"Just my laptop."

While Starr was writing something down on his notepad, he said, "It's most likely bugged also."

Kip raked his fingers through his head. "Never even thought about my computer. Okay then. How do you want to proceed?"

"To begin with, introduce me to your staff as an architect who's providing some design consultation. Trust none of your Chinese staff." He flicked his eyes at Angie and back.

Kip reached over and playfully shook Angie's shoulder. "This is one Chinese we can trust."

Angie rolled her eyes.

Starr didn't respond. "I carry a measuring tape as part of my equipment, a good prop for an architect. I'll have a good idea where to check and can probably do an initial sweep in just a few hours. I hope by then to pinpoint the bugs and let you know the kinds of devices used. I assume you have a company car?"

"I use a minivan and a Buick sedan."

"They on site?"

"Yes."

"Good. I'll sweep them also."

Reaching into his case, Starr said, "Well, let's start on this floor."

As soon as they stepped into Kip's office, Starr slipped on a set of headphones connected to a device the size of a laptop. It had blinking LED lights and a series of dials. Waving around a baton-like rod, he walked around the entire room. He then picked up the telephone on Kip's desk and connected a series of wires to it. After disconnecting everything, he pulled a clipboard out, made a sketch of the room and placed various symbols on it. He repeated the process throughout the offices on the third floor. When they were going through the offices on the second floor, Kip asked employees to step out of their rooms for a minute, explaining that Starr was an architect who needed to make some quick measurements.

The three went through Kip's house and Heather's townhouse unit. Three hours later, they headed back to the spare office to hear Starr's findings.

Starr spread out his notes and said, "You were certainly justified in wanting the place swept. I discovered fourteen listening devices. Fortunately, the bugs are not very sophisticated, all using older technology. That made my job easier. Let's start with Heather's home. By the way, I saw that she looked quite banged up. Is she okay?"

Kip said, "Her doctor thinks so."

"Good. I found only two bugs there: one in the family room and the other in the den. Both were hidden in ceiling light fixtures and were connected to a radio transmitter. When we drove around the compound, I was able to pinpoint the listening post that receives the signals; it's located in the green building on the north side of the main gate."

Kip said, "The Green Latrine."

"The what?" asked Starr.

"It's not important."

"Kip, your house was riddled with bugs. I found six of them hidden in the living room, dining room, family room, sunroom, kitchen and den. Your bedrooms and patio area were clean. The only offices bugged in the clubhouse were yours and Angie's. In these, they hid hook switch bypasses in your telephones. They'll pick up conversations in the room and transmit them through telephone wires to the remote listening post."

Kip said, "What happens when the handset is hung up?"

"Makes no difference. It continues to transmit. Bugs were planted in the overhead lights in the conference room.

Nothing in the common areas of the clubhouse, such as the lobby or restaurant."

"That's good to know," said Kip.

"Even though I didn't find any listening devices in the van or the Buick, someone planted Bumper Beepers under the rear left fenders of both vehicles. With these in place, someone can tail either vehicle with ease." Reviewing his notes, Starr looked up and closed the binder. "That's it. I'll send you a copy of my sketches pinpointing the location of each bug."

Kip thanked him and asked that he send the written reports and bill for his services to the Ingram Capital office in Shanghai. "I don't want this going through our books here," he explained.

Kip and Angie escorted Starr to the parking lot where a taxi was waiting. As it pulled away, Angie said, "Did you hear about the two men they pulled from the Huangpu River last night?"

"No. What about them?"

"According to the news, they were murdered by professionals. Both were shot in the back of the head and dumped into the river."

"And?"

"They fit the description of the driver of the black Toyota and the man Manny chased."

Chapter 49

"Rico must be getting desperate to murder his own men," said Kip.

Angie shrugged her shoulders. "They were witnesses. The guy in jail will probably be next."

Kip shook his head. "Rico's insane."

Angie said nothing.

Kip continued, "Getting back to what Starr found, give Heather a call and see if she's feeling well enough to come over."

Heather knocked on the door of the spare office a few minutes later. Kip looked up and was pleased to see that the blotchy bruises on her face were beginning to fade. He said, "How ya doing?"

"Much better, thanks. Other than the headaches and soreness, I'll survive."

"I'm glad you're feeling better." He then told her about Starr's discoveries.

Heather said, "Sounds like your instincts were right."

He smiled and turned the palms of his hands up. "We'll have an advantage over Niu and the Gang of Three if we keep all this to ourselves. So let's be careful."

Angie raised her eyebrows and smiled. "At least Niu wasn't interested in what happens in your bedrooms."

Kip said, "They'd get bored listening to anything coming from mine."

The three of them laughed.

Since Benjamin had returned to work after being in the hospital, he resumed feeding information about what he heard and saw to Shelly. The day after Philip Starr's visit,

Benjamin and Shelly met in her office late in the afternoon. Unnoticed by them, Patti was working overtime in an adjoining room, preoccupied with installing software on a computer. But the moment Benjamin and Shelly began to talk, Patti knew she was hearing a conversation not meant for her ears.

She heard Benjamin say, "Shelly, I'm getting worried. Kip went through a change after what happened to Heather."

"What do you mean?"

"Not sure. He's got a different look in his eyes I haven't seen before. It's been obvious from the day he started that he is intelligent, but he's made a lot of mistakes because he's not Chinese. Now, I don't know . . . maybe we've underestimated him."

Patti quietly backed into a clothes closet and hid as far back she could. From her hiding place, she could still hear most of what was being said in the next room. As each second passed, she became increasingly more frightened.

Shelly said, "In a way, I don't blame Kip. Mr. Niu made a mistake in trying to have Heather kidnapped. I don't think he even told Priscilla about what he was going to do. Rather than forcing Reggie to give up Shores, I think that Mr. Niu's actions made Reggie and Kip mad enough to be a real threat to us. Besides, I've heard that American men tend to be overly protective of their women."

Benjamin said, "If they'd actually kidnapped Heather, would Rico really have had her leg amputated?"

She looked down and murmured, "I don't know."

Patti couldn't hear Shelly's answer. The adrenaline flooding her body caused her heart to pound and her ears to ring. Sweat soaked her clothes and her bladder cramped in pain. She curled up on the floor farther back in the dark closet and squeezed her legs together.

"Well, I don't like it," said Benjamin. "Kip has always been kind to me. When we first started to share information with Mr. Niu, I thought the whole thing was kind of an adventure. Besides, I needed the extra money. But now, this is way over my head."

To Patti's horror, she heard chairs being scooted back and footsteps walking into the room.

Shelly said, "Don't tell anyone, but I'm starting to have the same doubts."

Patti heard a set of heels walk directly up to the closet door and stop. When Shelly opened the door, light flooded over Patti's prone body on the floor. She froze. The scraping sound of a coat hanger was right above her. Then the closet door clicked shut, shrouding her in darkness again.

Shelly and Benjamin continued their conversation, clicking off lights as they exited the building.

Realizing that she was still holding her breath, Patti gasped for air and pushed the closet doors open with her feet. She dashed off to the bathroom and went into a stall weeping hysterically. Once she was able to calm herself, she pulled her cell phone out of her purse. Still sitting on a toilet, she placed a call. "Hi, Angie. This is Patti. I just heard something you need to know."

Benjamin sensed that something was amiss as soon as he got to work on Monday morning. Kip and Angie looked at him differently, but he couldn't discern exactly what had changed.

During the lunch hour he slipped a letter of resignation onto Angie's desk. Five minutes later, he walked out the front gate of Shanghai Shores on foot, knowing that he'd never return.

In the vacant office that afternoon, Kip asked, "Angie, what do you think happened to make Benjamin quit like that?"

"Chinese tend to be really good at knowing things without being told. He must have sensed that we suspected what he was doing. We'll probably never find out for sure."

"Why?" asked Kip.

"Well, I heard that he's planning to head off to Australia to live with his cousin in Brisbane."

"What would he do there?"

"I think the cousin has a job waiting for him in a poultry processing plant."

"On the negative side, we can no longer feed Benjamin with information we want leaked to Niu. On the positive side, we get Mr. Zeng back."

"Mr. Zeng is a good man." said Angie.

Heather's assault had rekindled nightmares of Marci's accident. Kip believed they were a dire warning about what Niu was capable of doing next. To maintain his own sanity, he was determined not to let Heather or anyone else at Shores gets hurt. He picked up the phone and asked her to come over to his place.

"Sounds good," she said. "I'm starting to get cabin fever anyway. See you in ten minutes."

Right on time, Heather knocked on Kip's door. Opening it, he said, "How ya feeling?"

"Look for yourself," she said, motioning to her face.

He winked. "Why shucks, you're mighty pretty again."

She smiled.

Kip got her settled in the family room and put on some music. He put together a plate of cheese, crackers and sliced vegetables and set it down on the coffee table between them.

"Aren't you the perfect host?"

"I try. What would you like to drink?"

"A glass of Perrier would be nice."

Kip sat down across from her while they chatted about the incident and her condition. After about twenty minutes, he said, "Heather, you're the last person I would want to see leave Shores, but now there's good enough reason for you to consider doing just that."

"Kip, you're too cute." She giggled.

"I'm serious. Have you thought what could have happened if things had gone wrong on Sunday?"

"They didn't, did they? My father and I have already had a long talk about my leaving and he's agreed to support me in staying. Besides, Mr. Duchene, you really need me here right now."

"Yeah, I do. But not if you're in harm's way. I don't want to spend all my time worrying about you."

"Believe me, I'll be extra careful."

He smiled.

After walking her home, he gave her a warm embrace at the door.

"You want to come in?" she asked.

Kip took a step onto her porch, paused and then stepped back. He chuckled. "Better not."

Chapter 50

A month had passed since Benjamin left for Australia. Mr. Zeng was proving to be a reliable driver for Kip, proud that he'd learned how to say simple greetings in English like, "Hello, boss."

Kip viewed Milt Avery as going from a bothersome irritant to a serious liability—one that Kip couldn't afford. The fact that Rico Niu hadn't caused any more disturbances since the assault on Heather didn't give him any comfort. He also had a foreboding premonition that something more ominous was coming from Niu—and soon.

By mid-September, the oppressive summer heat and humidity in Shanghai had begun to ease. In the aftermath of the assault on Heather, Kip was experiencing anxiety attacks with greater frequency. As soon as he felt one coming on, he would make an excuse to be alone. Symptoms included feeling light-headed and on the verge of passing out, difficulty breathing, and sweating profusely. During the more severe episodes, he would see flashes of Heather screaming for help while her attacker plummeled her head. By the time Kip reached her, it was too late. She was dead, just like Marci. He'd failed once again.

One Sunday morning, Kip tried to quell his anxieties by walking along the seawall. Buffeted by the stinging spray of an onshore wind, he felt slightly better. Later in the day he questioned the idea of staying home on Monday, knowing that he needed to stay focused. But when morning rolled around he decided to tough it out. He was sitting at his desk by 7:00 a.m.

Two hours later, he and Angie met in the spare office to go over the weekly schedule. Without warning, he was hit by a mountainous wave of angst.

"Kip, what's happening!" yelled Angie.

He was gripping the edges of his desk and staring straight ahead. Sweat cascaded from his face and soaked the top of his shirt. He motioned with one hand as if to say it was okay. At the same time, he was thinking—*Christ, this is a bad one!*

He muttered, "Give me a minute."

"I'm staying."

He pointed to the door. "Pleaseeeee."

She rushed out of the room and hit an automatic dial button on her cell phone. As soon as she heard a click on the other end, she blurted, "Sal, something's happening to Kip! I think he's having a heart attack or something."

"I thought this would happen. Don't do anything. Just make sure he doesn't leave. I'll be right there."

An hour passed and Kip still hadn't come out of the spare office. She rolled her office chair down the hall and parked herself outside the door. The stillness of the third floor was broken by the sound of footsteps bounding up the stairs. Sal rounded the corner and saw Angie. He walked up to her and whispered. "Anything change?"

She shook her head.

"Thank you," he said and walked into the room.

Within a minute, he reemerged with a ghost-white Kip following right behind. They walked past Angie and into the elevator. Sal punched the ground floor button, bypassing the lobby on the second level. When the elevator came to a smooth stop, the two men stepped out and headed for the exit. Outside, Kip mumbled, "*Yani*, I don't know what happened."

"Well, I do." He led Kip for the short walk to his house.

In the family room, Sal fixed them both a stuff drink and said, "I don't know fuckin' A about psychological shit, but I do know this. For most people who lost a loved one, the first year anniversary after their death is a bitch to get through."

Kip nodded. He didn't need Sal to tell him that. He'd been looking at the calendar almost every hour for the past several days, his mind flooding with memories of exactly what he and Marci were doing the year before. "I didn't know it would affect me this way, *Yani*."

"Shit, *cabrón*, it's normal. Look, things seem to be quiet around here these days. There's no fuckin' reason that you can't take some time off and just hang out here for a day or two. Angie can take care of everything."

Kip nodded.

"Do you want me to stick around for a while?"

"Nah. I'll be okay now. Thanks for understanding."

Before heading back to his office, Sal ran up to see Angie for a minute.

Kip woke up the next morning with a sinking feeling— *Marci died exactly one year ago.* He couldn't seem to shake off the gruesome images of the accident. *Her death was my fault.* He started to hyper-salivate and bolted out of bed and made it to the toilet just in time to vomit. He sat on the floor resting his head on the rim of cold porcelain. A few minutes later, the second wave of nausea overtook him. Once his stomach settled down, he took a shower then slipped back to bed and drifted into a deep but troubled sleep.

Two hours later he woke up ravenous. While making coffee, he picked up the phone. "Hey, *Yani*, I just wanted to hear a familiar voice."

"Do you want me to come over?"

"Nah. I just wanted to thank you for rescuing me yesterday."

"No problem. Listen, Angie's been calling me and wanting to go over there and watch after you. I suggested that she didn't."

"Thanks. I know she's worried, but she can't do anything to make me feel better."

"Oh, yes she can," Sal chuckled with a lecherous tone in his voice.

"You're disgusting, *Yani*."

"Look, I'm just a phone call away. If you want to be left alone, I understand. If you want me to come over, I can get there within an hour. I could even bring over the bottle of Gran Patron; that'd help smooth out the pain."

"I'm okay. Thanks for the offer."

An hour later, Kip jumped up when he heard a knock at the front door. Outside, a deliveryman stood with a bored look on his face as he handed Kip a flower arrangement. It was wrapped in a clear plastic sleeve with colorful ribbons dangling down from its base. The man said something in Chinese before he walked back to his van and drove away. Curious about who could be sending him flowers, Kip brought them into the family room and set the vase on the fireplace mantel. A card was wedged between the stems.

> Dear Kip,
> I admire your courage in mourning the loss of your wife. I could never imagine the pain you must be feeling.
> Angie

Contrary to Angie's normally flippant style, her simple gesture of warmth triggered an outpouring of pent-up emotion in him. He brought his hands to his face and began to cry.

At seven-thirty the following morning, Kip's phone rang. "Are ju still alive, *amigo?*" asked Sal.

Smiling, Kip said, "Yes, I'm still here. Say, did you say anything to Angie about Marci yesterday?"

"I did, *hermano*. Under the circumstances, I thought that she should know. Shit, man, I can't be there watching your fuckin' ass all the time. I need Angie to cover for me."

"No problem. Talk to you later."

"Okay, *Tuchi*, see you."

Kip put a couple drops of Visine in his eyes to try to clear the redness. A quick glance in the mirror assured him that his appearance was passable so he headed for the office. He looked forward to hearing the comforting sounds of Angie banging around her office when she first gets in. A few minutes after nine, he heard her. "Angie?"

"Yes?" she said from her room.

"Thank you."

"You're welcome, boss."

No one else could have guessed what they were talking about.

Chapter 51

October brought a welcomed relief from the high humidity and scorching heat of the summer months. Along with the improved weather, Shanghai Shores seemed to be responding favorably to the changes Kip had put in place. Now, there was a clear chain of command. Employees liked the idea of answering to only one boss instead of the two or three they'd had before. Priscilla still wielded too much power in the company even after Kip had slowly whittled down her influence to a more manageable level. Cash flow was improving due to tighter financial controls. Heather showed no physical or emotional signs that she'd been attacked six weeks earlier. Thankfully, Rico Niu hadn't made any further moves against them. Milt Avery was the exception to the good news. His unannounced visits to Shanghai Shores were becoming increasingly difficult for Kip to manage.

On a Monday afternoon, Kip was surprised to receive a rare call from Reggie. "Listen, old boy, Sal sent me an update on your September figures. Bloody well done!"

Kip said, "Thanks."

"I'm wondering if you've gone through any other wretched encounters with that bloke from Hainan?"

"Reggie, please hold on for a minute." With his cell phone in hand, Kip dashed down the hallway and into the vacant office. "Okay, sorry about that—the walls have ears."

"Indeed they do."

"In answer to your question, no, it's been quiet since Heather was attacked. However, my gut instincts tell me that something big is brewing behind the scenes. We're being very careful."

"Good show! I also wanted to tell you that our Saudi friends will be in town in early November. They'd like to make a return visit to Shores."

"They're most welcome here. As a matter of fact, we could even put them up in one of the renovated homes."

"Well, carry on then, I'll put your offer to them."

Kip said, "Sounds good."

Reggie added, "Ah . . . Kip . . . how's Heather doing?"

"She's fully recovered and as determined as ever to fill this place."

"Good show!"

After Reggie hung up, Kip called Sal and said, "*Oye, que pasa?*"

"I'm doing well, *Tuchi*. What's happening on your end?"

"Since the Heather thing, there's nothing earthshaking to report. I just wanted to say hello—it's been a while."

"I hear you. My schedule is taking me out of town a lot. Maria has been really patient about it, but I'm starting to tread on thin ice with her."

"Just take care of yourself."

Sal said, "I will. Say, I talked to Reggie earlier today. It's been a long time since I've heard him get excited about Shores."

"I know what you're saying. He just called me a few minutes ago to say how pleased he was."

"Great. That also makes me look fuckin' good."

"When will your schedule ease enough for us to get together?"

Sal said, "I think soon. Do you need anything from me?"

"Show me the money!"

"*Adios, Tuchi.*"

Kip flipped his phone shut and walked back to his office.

The next day, Kip asked Angie if she'd like to join him for dinner that night.

"You're asking me out on a date?" she said in a surprised voice.

"Well . . . not really. Manny and I are planning to have dinner in his favorite little restaurant in Heqing. I think that you'd enjoy the occasion. Besides, I'd like your company."

With a smile, she said, "Sure. It sounds like fun."

"Good. How about if we took off around six?"

"Great. That'll give me time to get caught up here on some of my work."

Just before Kip and Angie were planning to leave, Kip walked into her office and sat on the edge of her desk. "Has Manny ever talked to you about Uganda?"

Looking up, she said, "No, why?"

"Well, he's started to share with me some of his boyhood experiences over there. You know, he's very private about his years in Uganda and is pretty much closed-mouth about that part of his life."

"I don't understand. Why would he say anything to you then?"

"I don't think he intended to. We had a few beers together last week. I'm not sure why, but I asked about Uganda. With some hesitation, he came out with some pretty startling stuff—some humorous, but mostly terrifying. I'm absolutely fascinated with his stories and might ask him more questions tonight. After listening to his stories, I realize that I know nothing about Uganda except for the AIDS problem over there. It's been on the news lately."

"Come to think about it, I've never heard him say anything about his past. He's such a kind soul. I guess that no one really thinks to ask. "

At 6:10 p.m., Mr. Zeng drove the couple out through the front gate of the compound and headed towards Heqing. In the back seat, Kip said to Angie, "Please warn Mr. Zeng that there's a grate missing from a street drain right in front of the restaurant. He'll need to steer clear of it."

She leaned forward to pass the message on to him. Mr. Zeng chuckled without comment.

Manny was talking with the owner of restaurant when they walked in. Seeing them, Manny smiled.

The owner showed them upstairs to Manny's regular table by the window. A young waitress automatically placed a bottle of beer in front of Manny and one in front of Kip. Manny slid his over to Angie and told the waitress to bring over another bottle. Once it arrived, Manny held up his bottle and said, "*Ganbei!*"

Twenty minutes later, steaming plates of Suzhou-style fish, stir-fried vegetables with hot peppers, dumplings, baked tofu, and fried rice with shrimp were set on their table. Having finished off six bottles of beer, the three of them were feeling mellow and ready to eat.

Kip said, "Jesus, Manny, this smells fantastic. I'm famished."

Angie pointed to the vegetables laced with red peppers and said to Kip, "Just be careful of these. You take a big mouthful and the top of your head will blow off and cause a mess."

Manny chuckled and held his bottle of beer up for another toast, "Thanks you come to my little restaurant."

"The pleasure's ours." Kip smiled and took a satisfying pull of his beer.

Even though Angie stopped drinking after the second bottle, Kip and Manny continued to enjoy their beers and accompanying toasts. Angie was amused watching the two men relax. She thought it was good for Kip to forget about work for a few hours.

As the three were digesting their meal and chatting about a myriad of things, Kip asked, "Manny, you've said that you grew up in Uganda. Exactly where was that?"

"It's in northwest Uganda."

Angie said, "Did you live in a town?"

Turning to Angie, he said, "No. My family live very hard life in bush country about fifteen miles away from dusty little town called Arua."

Kip asked, "What were the people like?"

"People of my country are very nice. But government officials were evil and corrupt. When Arua district get some aid money from other countries to build medical clinics and schools, officials take the money for their pockets. So poor people suffer even more."

While Manny stopped to take a drink of beer, his eyes glistened with tears. Without looking up, he said, "We caught between soldiers from south and LRA in north."

Kip said, "I'm sorry. I'm not familiar with LRA."

"They Lord's Resistance Army. Oh, boss, they very terrible. In middle of night, they kidnapped little children and forced them to take up arms to fight for them. The kids who escaped being captured were called night commuters."

Angie said, "Why?"

"Well, as sun would go down, they walk out of their villages in mass to a northern town called Gulu. Safe there. In mornings, they walk back home. Soldiers from both sides raid villages and chop down the houses, making the area like ghost town and people even get poorer. They had so little from start." Manny slowly shook his head thinking about the past.

Kip said, "Manny, please tell us about what your home was like."

Perking up, he said, "We live on coffee plantation. Our mud house had thatched roof of spear grass."

"What's spear grass?" asked Angie.

"It savannah grass that looks like spear." Manny chuckled.

"What was your childhood like living at home?" she asked.

Manny smiled. "When I was little boy, I did not know we were poor. I was a happy. I play with my brother or make roads and houses in red soil. Sometimes, I bring bucket of water up from river and make mud. Because I did not have toys, I'd make my own." He looked across the table at Kip and Angie and laughed.

"I sit with just me in shade of banana tree. I am content to just shape clay into cars, stick men, or animals. When I good enough, people in village come down to take look at face masks I made."

Kip said, "Did you make the dragonfly sculpture you gave me when you were in Uganda."

"Yes, boss. I brought with me for good luck. Now you have it."

"Well, I'm truly grateful. It seems to be working so far."

Angie said, "What about when you got to be an older boy."

"Oh, that different. I was afraid of nothing when I was six years, even the venomous snakes. I learn about life trying things and touching. So I touch everything. I remember time when I was eight. I jump on daddy's bicycle to think I could ride like a horse. But it fall down on top of me and I cried. It was good no one saw me cry." He laughed again and clicked his bottle of beer against Kip's.

After taking a pull, he continued but with a serious expression on his face, "Then bad memories start and I learn how to be afraid because of soldiers. My daddy smart though. When everyone go to their huts for night, he sneak out of camp to special place and dig secret hiding place underground. He dug little more every night until done. Then next night, he took mother, brother and me to try it. It hidden in middle of thick bushes. He made trap door out of sunbaked clay and leaves and twigs on top. We slipped down into small cavern about five feet down. It just wide enough for four of us. It had reed mats on floor. When word spread that soldiers were to raid area, my daddy took us to our secret underground hideaway."

With a far off look in his eyes, Manny said almost at a whisper, "I have nightmares about what I hear coming from above. I curl up in ball and cover my ears."

"I think I know what that's like, Manny," said Kip.

"I think you do, boss."

Wanting to change the subject, Kip asked, "What about girls?"

"What you mean?" asked Manny while taking a quick glance at Angie.

Angie piped in looking in Kip's direction, "Yeah, what do you mean?"

"You know, did you have any girlfriends in Uganda?"

"Well I remember my parents telling me that when I was only three, my hair was very nice. It was black and stood tall. The little girls in the village wanted to touch my hair and that made them want to play with me." Breaking out in a smile, he added, "I wish I had that chance now."

Kip and Angie laughed, totally enchanted with Manny's way of telling stories.

"That's it?" Kip asked.

"I guess so. My parents sent me away to boarding school for all boys when I was fourteen. So I didn't get chance to know about girls."

"Was it a hard life?" asked Angie.

"Yes, but mostly for my parents. They work very hard for long hours in fields. To protect coffee plants from hot sun, they plant banana trees for shade. Before I go to school, I helped my daddy cut down leaves for firewood. Harvest time was hardest though. All the schools close for two weeks so students go to villages to help parents collect coffee beans."

Looking out the window, Manny said, "Young girls experience most terrible things. If they do not hide quickly when soldiers came through, they get raped and sometimes beat. Some even die."

Angie gasped, "Oh, those poor children."

"I hope those men rot in hell," said Kip. "I could never understand what would cause a man to rape a woman, let alone a girl. How terrible for you, Manny, to have witnessed that."

Manny looked at Angie for a second and turned to Kip, "Yeah, memories won't wash away with mud."

"Was there a low point for you over there?" asked Kip.

"Yes. It was later. I qualify to attend college in capital. I was so poor I do not get enough to eat and had no relatives around to help support. It very difficult and lonely for me in college."

Kip asked, "How in the world did you get to China?"

"Well, I got very good grades and qualify for scholarship program that offer by Chinese government. After hear I was picked and go to Hong Kong, I need to get Ugandan passport. But it very difficult for poor people to do. I work hard sell vegetables and finally save money to bribe official to get passport. In Uganda, we have old saying, 'One frog can dirty a whole pool of water'."

"Yeah, we have the same saying," said Kip. "One rotten apple can spoil the barrel."

"Same thing," laughed Manny. "Before takeoff to Hong Kong, I go back home to say goodbye to parents. Before I go, my mama cry and my daddy shake my hand. I return to the capital where Chinese sponsors take group to the airport. Everyone else from rich families and have nanny, except me. All other students had money in pocket for long journey, except me. I have 300 Ugandan shillings, enough to buy bottle of soda. In the airport waiting room, the officials give advice to students, except me. I was happy to sit with me in corner and give me my own advice and enjoy the nice bottle of soda."

Kip held up his bottle and said, "Manny, here's to you. Thanks for sharing a part of your incredible life with us – *Ganbei!*"

Manny smiled and said, *"Ganbei!* Now you know, boss."

Kip said, "Know what?"

"If you need someone by you to defend you, just turn to your Ugandan friend. I already see everything."

"Manny, thank you. I'll remember that."

That night, Kip thought a lot about Manny's stories of Uganda compared to what he was up against at Shanghai Shores. He fell asleep thinking that he was fortunate.

Chapter 52

Returning from the Monday managers' meeting, Kip walked into his office and heard the phone ringing. He picked it up. "This is Kip."

"Hi, Kip. It's Eleni. Am I calling at a bad time?"

"Not at all. It's always nice to hear from you."

"Good. Since we haven't talked in a while, I called to check up on how you're doing?"

"Thanks. I think we're doing well. Heather closed ten or eleven new leases, cash flow is improving, the tenants are happy, and the infamous Rico Niu hasn't been seen in a while."

"How wonderful! I had a feeling that you'd pull it off. Just don't get too complacent about Niu. I doubt that he's finished with his dastardly deeds. I'd guess that he's planning his next move, probably something worse than what they did to Heather."

"I hope not."

"Listen, the real reason I'm calling is to let you know that I had brunch with Daleep Gupta yesterday and put in a good word for you."

"Thanks. Did he give you any clues about what he's thinking?"

"Not a lot. From what little he said, you may have an uphill climb convincing him to lease your homes. I was disappointed to hear his skepticism. He doesn't give you much of a chance to fix the problems by the December deadline."

Kip's shoulders slumped. "What a bummer. I was hoping that he'd be more open to the idea."

"Me too. I guess all you can do is to keep plowing ahead. Even though Gupta is not convinced, I think you're doing great."

"Thanks, Eleni. Let me know if you hear anything more from him."

"Will do. Bye."

Sal called later in the day. "*Oye*, I've been given marching orders. Maria told me that you're expected at our place for Thanksgiving. Can you make it?"

"*Yani*, I'd love to. Do you have any of that righteous Gran Patron tequila around?"

"As a matter of fact, I do." He added, "Ah . . . why don't you bring Angie along."

Kip said nothing.

Sal said, "You there, *Tuchi*?"

"Yeah, I'm here. Just whose idea was that, yours or Maria's?"

"Maria's. So what?"

"Nothing. I'll think about it, okay?"

"Good. Let me know when you decide."

"Will do. Before you hang up, I have a question for you. I assume that you're going to be celebrating Tony's birthday on Thanksgiving as usual?

"Yeah."

"Good. I'd like to buy him a Cub Scouts Swiss Army pocket knife but wanted to clear it with you first."

"Shit, it's fine with me, but I know Maria will worry that he's too young. My dad gave him a compass last year and the little shit carries it around in his pocket everywhere, always checking which direction we're heading. By now, he probably knows his way around Shanghai better than many expats."

"What about the knife idea?"

"Just go ahead and get it. I know he'll love it. While you're at it, don't forget to call me back about Angie."

"Talk to you soon."

After hanging up, Kip thought about taking Angie. He was comfortable with her. He still couldn't shake the feeling he got when she responded to his hug the morning after the tenants meeting. Despite his weak denial that he was growing more attracted to her, the idea of taking her to Sal's felt good to him. He called out from his desk, "Angie, can you come in for a minute?"

She peeked her head around the door. "What's up?"

"Sal just called and invited me over to their place for Thanksgiving dinner."

"That's nice."

"He also suggested that I bring a guest."

"And?" Her face became flushed.

"Well . . . would you like to go with me?"

She ducked back into her office and smiled. From the other room, she said, "Yes."

In the middle of the weekly managers' meeting the following Monday, the lights in the conference room unexpectedly went out. Rory and Manny bolted from their chairs and rushed out of the room while pulling their cell phones out of their pockets.

A minute later, Rory poked his head back into the room and said, "Kip, we've got a problem."

"What's wrong?"

"Some guys with the Shanghai Power Bureau are down at our power plant and have shut off our electricity. Manny and I will run down there to see what the hell's going on. I'll call you from there."

"Okay." After he hung up, he thought – *Christ, I was worried that this would happen.* He turned to Priscilla and said, "Do you know anything about the power being shut off?"

Shelly translated Kip's message. After Priscilla answered, Shelly said, "She said no."

Bev stood and said, "Kip, I think that I should go down there too."

"Good idea."

Bev gathered her purse and hurried out of the room.

Heather blurted out, "God, this is not good at all!"

Everyone sitting around the conference room table swiveled around to look at her.

Kip said, "What?"

"Mr. Gupta is scheduled to meet with us tomorrow morning. If the power is off, it could ruin the deal."

Kip said, "Just cancel the meeting until we can figure this out."

Angie cleared her throat. "Kip, that's not a good idea. Cancelling appointments in China is considered very rude."

"Gupta's not Chinese."

"It doesn't matter. He's been here for five years and knows the rules."

"Okay." He looked at the rest of the managers and said, "Since there's nothing more we can do about this now, go ahead and take off early. Be careful going down the stairs. It may be a little dark. Angie, you and Heather stay behind."

As people were filing out of the room, Kip's cell phone chimed.

Out of breath, Rory said, "Kip, we have three complete assholes down here. They have a document authorizing them to shut off the power. I ended up getting into a wee bit of a shoving match with one of them."

"What happened?" asked Kip.

"Nothing much. But I swear to God, I could easily have taken on all three of these little fuckers."

Envisioning the scene, Kip couldn't help chucking.

Rory said, "By the way, I overheard one of these guys saying that Priscilla was informed in advance about the shutoff."

Chapter 53

Kip gripped his phone tighter and said to Rory. "Okay. Please keep that to yourself."

"Got it. I'm looking at these guys right now and they're attaching a Power Bureau tag seal around the clasp of the main power switch and are about to leave."

"Okay. I want you and Manny to meet me in the restaurant right away so we can figure this out. Is Bev there yet?"

"Yeah, she just walked in."

"Rory, ask her to talk with the senior guy before they get a chance to leave, but don't stick around there yourself. Also tell Bev to meet us in the restaurant after she's through."

After Kip hung up, Angie and Heather followed him down to the restaurant where he began to lay out a plan of action to manage the power outage. Before Kip had a chance to finish, Rory and Manny walked in to join them.

As they got closer, Manny covered his mouth with his hands and his shoulders were jerking up and down.

Kip noticed. "What in the hell has gotten you so tickled?"

Manny burst into uncontrolled laughter. After taking a moment to calm down and wipe tears from his eyes, he said, "Sorry, boss. I not hold it together any longer. When we first walk into substation, one Power Bureau man got to our faces and start to yell. The little man do not know that *no one* yell at Rory. But he quickly find out what happens."

Kip turned his palms up. "And?"

"Rory grab him by his jacket and slam him up against wall. His feet dangle below. The man so shock, he piss his pants."

Everyone at the table laughed along with Manny.

Rory said, "I could have done more to the wee bugger."

"I'll bet you could," said Kip, still chuckling.

Bev walked in and reported to Kip. "They said the electricity was turned off because we haven't paid our delinquent bill."

Kip's face reddened with anger. "Christ, I thought that they gave us a four-month warning notice to pay?"

Bev said, "They did."

"Then why are they here now? According to my calculations, we have until November 18th to pay up."

"Kip, they can do whatever they want. They're the government. I know it sounds crazy." Bev's serious expression then softened into a smile. Blushing, she said, "I think that the senior official from the Power Bureau had a little problem."

Despite feeling frustrated, Kip couldn't help smiling. "Yeah, we already heard."

Out of breath, Jessie walked up to the table. "Twelve tenants have already called, complaining about the loss of electricity. More will be calling soon."

Kip said, "Okay, Jessie, I want you to get together with your staff right now and start calling every tenant to let them know that we've experienced some technical problems."

Just then, the lights in the restaurant flickered on.

Kip said, "Hey. That was fast!"

Rory said, "Kip, the problem isn't fixed. We're on an emergency generator here. It must have just kicked in."

Kip said, "Jessie, go ahead and take off. Get as many people as you need to start calling tenants—the sooner the better. Once you've got that done, come back here right away."

"Okay." Jessie ran out of the room.

"Bev, please call the Power Bureau and schedule an emergency meeting for today." Kip turned to Rory. "What's the negative impact of the loss of electricity on our water and sewer treatment plants?"

"While we were down there, I checked and confirmed that they've both successfully switched over to the backup generators."

"Good. Manny, what about the houses?"

"Well, we have no power to houses. There is problem with spoil food in refrigerators and no hot water for shower."

Bev came back in. "Kip, they've agreed to meet with us tomorrow morning at ten."

"Christ, that's unacceptable!" Kip blurted. "Call them back and tell them that we either have a meeting today, or I'll have Reggie call the Mayor of Shanghai to let him know that we have forty-one families and their children without electricity out here."

Bev had her cell phone out and up to her ear while walking back out of the room.

Kip called Paul over to the table. "Do you have extra space in your walk-in refrigerator and freezer?"

"Yes, boss. No problem."

Jessie bounded back in the room out of breath. "The staff was able to call all of the tenants. They seemed satisfied with our explanations—at least for now."

"Jessie, make sure that the tenants know that they can drop off perishable and frozen foods at the restaurant, but everything should be clearly marked with their unit number."

"Okay."

Bev came back with a smile on her face, "Four o'clock today."

"Excellent!" exclaimed Kip.

Heather said, "Kip, even though you're able to meet with the Power Bureau people today I know how slow government officials move over here. I'm really worried that we'll still have no power tomorrow when Mr. Gupta shows up. That'll be a disaster."

Kip took a deep breath, determined to look calm and in control. "I understand. For now, let's just get through today and deal with tomorrow as best as we can."

"If you say so."

While Kip and Angie were walking back to their offices, Kip said nothing, but he was weighing how to best resolve the crisis. Before Angie sat at her desk, she looked over at Kip and said, "You okay?"

Kip sighed. "Why do you ask?"

"For starters, I see that your face is flushed. On top of that, you haven't said a word since we left the restaurant. Neither of those two things is like you—that's all."

"I'm okay."

Kip then closed the door separating their two offices—something he'd never done before. In the privacy of his room, he began to pace back and forth. Rather than calming himself down, he worked himself into frenzy thinking about the Power Bureau breaking their promise. *What in the hell do those assholes think they're doing!*

In frustration, he threw his notebook down on his desk and punched the nearest wall. The drywall exploded inward, leaving Kip surprised that his fist had pushed all the way through. He heard Angie scream in the next room.

Just as he yanked his arm back out of the ragged hole with broken pieces of gypsum falling to the floor, Angie ran in. "What happened?"

Rubbing his knuckles, he said, "Sorry about that. I'm just pissed."

"Wow! That's a side of you I haven't seen before. Maybe it'd be good if you showed more of that."

"Maybe."

Angie smiled and slowly shook her head as she retreated into her office.

Kip looked down at his reddened knuckles—*how about that?*

Chapter 54

Kip picked up his notebook and headed down to the spare office. Once inside, he flipped open his cell phone to call PriceWaterhouse. "This is Kip Duchene at Shanghai Shores. Is Mr. Liu available?"

A moment later, there was a click on the phone. "Good morning, Kip. What can I do for you?"

"Thanks for taking my call. David, I've got a problem here and was hoping that you could help."

"Sure, anything."

Kip went on to tell Liu about the power being turned off and that he was scheduled to meet with the Power Bureau authorities that afternoon. "While I realize that you're still in the middle of auditing our books, I was hoping that you've discovered something I could possibly use to our advantage with the power people."

Mr. Liu cleared his throat. "In that case, I might have exactly what you need."

"Please go ahead."

"Well, we've discovered that Naomi has been cleverly diverting company funds that were intended to pay the Power Bureau."

"How do you know the funds were connected to the Power Bureau?"

"The disbursements perfectly matched the corresponding monthly bills from them."

"Where did the money go?"

"This is where it gets really interesting. We traced the money to investments in stocks. The fund is owned by none other than Naomi Chen and Priscilla Mao."

"No kidding!"

"No."

"Can you get those documents over to me before three o'clock today?"

"Consider it done."

Kip left his notebook in the spare office and walked to Angie's office. "Ask Bev to come up." He then pointed down the hall towards the spare office without explanation.

Angie nodded.

Five minutes later, Angie and Bev joined Kip in the spare office. Bev looked around at the piled-up furniture in the room and asked, "Why are we meeting in here?"

Kip motioned with his hand. "Please take a seat. I'll explain later."

After they sat down, he continued. "I was at a loss on what to do with the power company and needed some help. What I'm about to reveal is confidential. It stays in this room—is that understood?"

Both women nodded.

"Okay. As you know, our accounting firm is still in the process of conducting an audit of our books. On a hunch, I gave Mr. Liu a call several minutes ago and asked him if they had uncovered any irregularities yet. They had, and it's a whopper." Kip then revealed what he'd learned about how Naomi and Priscilla funneled money out of the company.

Angie and Bev both looked astonished.

Kip glanced down at his notes. "Liu also said that according to Chinese law both Naomi and Priscilla could be prosecuted and jailed for embezzlement. So the question is this: Can this information be used to convince the Power Bureau to restore our power?"

Bev was the first to speak. "No."

Kip frowned. "No?"

"That's correct. While I agree that we can use this new information to our advantage, it's not enough. But there may be a better way."

"I'm listening."

"Is Mr. Ingram in town?"

"Yes, I believe he is. Why do you ask?"

"I suggest that you give him a call, and ask him to use his *guangxi* with the Power Bureau."

Kip said, "What's *guangxi*?"

"The simple translation is getting things done through people connections. In China it's a little more complicated than that, but you can get the idea," explained Bev.

Kip said, "Got it. Then what exactly would Reggie ask for from the Power Bureau?"

"He needs to arrange for us to meet only with the director of the bureau, not the subordinates you previously saw."

"What do you think that'll accomplish?"

"You'll have a much better chance of getting them to restore power if you talk directly with the head man. In state-owned companies, lower level employees are always afraid to make a decision. They protect themselves by getting approval from their boss, who then needs approval from his boss and so on. Since we don't have the time, I think that we should go straight to the top. But *you're* not powerful enough to make that happen—Mr. Ingram is."

Angie said, "Bev, I agree. It's a great idea."

Then turning to Kip, Angie continued, "We may be able to turn this crisis into our favor. If we're able to meet with the director, you could tell him that you just learned that Naomi and Priscilla funneled money from the company that was earmarked to pay for electricity. Then let him know that you intend to fire the two women."

"Keep going."

"Well, I don't think that Naomi and Priscilla could have pulled this off without working with people inside the Power Bureau and bribing them. The director would also make the same conclusion while you're talking and would not want the Shores problem to end up becoming his."

Kip said, "I see. In regard to the idea of firing Naomi and Priscilla, I thought that it was almost impossible to do that."

Bev said, "Kip, it's all about how we use leverage in our culture. Before this incident happened, the leverage belonged to Naomi and Priscilla. They had the time to manipulate enough inside information against the company to have the ability to create major trouble for us. Now that we know that they've embezzled funds, the leverage they had over us no longer exists. I can assure you that if you confronted them with the threat of going to prison, both Naomi and Priscilla would quietly leave without saying a word."

A wide smile crept across Kip's face. "Jesus, that'd be sweet."

After the two women left the room, Kip pulled out his cell phone and dialed. "Reggie, this is Kip. Have I caught you at a bad time?"

On their ride to the Power Bureau, Kip filled Angie and Bev in on his conversation with Reggie. He said, "Reggie actually chuckled when I told him about the meeting. He told me not to worry and that everything would turn out *peachy*, if you can believe that."

Angie said, "Well, you'll just have to trust what Bev said about *guangxi*."

"I hope you're right. I damn sure can't figure it out."

At the Power Bureau, the three of them were shown up to the same conference room as before and again served tea in flimsy plastic cups. After they were seated, Kip said, "I hope that Reggie was able do his magic. I wouldn't want to face the same group we saw before."

Just as he said the words, his worst fears were realized. The four officials they met before walked into the room with exaggerated smiles. He became even more uncomfortable when he looked over at Angie and Bev and saw their nervousness.

After the group took their seats, one of the officials greeted them. Angie translated for Kip. "He said that he was pleased to meet with you again and hoped that the present crisis could be solved with harmony. He then asked if you were prepared to pay in full today."

Kip clenched his teeth in frustration, but made every effort to stay calm. Before he had an opportunity to respond, the door to the conference room flew open and a professional looking woman nervously rattled off something to the group in Chinese. The four officials in the room looked at each other in confusion.

While Angie and Bev were getting up from their chairs, Angie tugged on Kip's sleeve and said, "We're being asked to move to another room."

The three of them followed the woman down the hall and up another flight of stairs. They were shown into a well-appointed office and were served tea in porcelain cups. The woman said something and left.

"What in the hell's happening?" asked Kip.

Angie said, "I'm not sure. The woman said for us to enjoy our tea. Someone will be right with us."

"Jesus, I was about to lose it downstairs," said Kip.

"Like I couldn't tell."

Before Kip could reply, a well-dressed man in his fifties walked into the office. The three guests stood as the man went directly to Kip with his hand extended and a pleasant smile on his face.

Angie translated, "This is Director Zhou Wei Dong, the head official of the power bureau."

He exchanged business cards with Kip, then with Angie and Bev in turn.

Angie said, "Director Zhou said he was very sorry about the mix-up downstairs and asks that we sit down and make ourselves comfortable."

As the group sat down, Kip took a better look at the director. The man presented himself as a distinguished executive who had obviously kept himself in good physical shape. He looked like he could have walked off a page from GQ magazine. His pinstriped suit was smartly tailored to fit his slim body, and his shoes were polished like mirrors.

When Director Zhou began speaking, Angie simultaneously translated. "The Director said that he looked over the records and saw that Shores has been delinquent for quite a while. He asked for you to explain this. He also said that if you have new information that is not yet in the report, you should give it to him now."

"That's not quite what I said, Miss Li" exclaimed Director Zhou in perfect English to the surprise of everyone in the room. Angie looked down in embarrassment.

Kip said, "I'm not used to hearing a senior government official speak English so fluently."

Director Zhou smiled and said, "UCLA. Graduating class of 1974. Mr. Duchene, what I said was that I would be most interested to hear any new information you *may* have, not a demand for you to just give it to me—a subtle, but important distinction."

Kip explained the circumstances of their payment dilemma without fanfare. He laid out the facts exactly as he knew them, and forthrightly answered Director Zhou's follow-up questions regarding their ability to repay their debt. Kip also informed him about his plans to fire Naomi and Priscilla and the reasons behind that action.

Considering the information that Kip just shared, Director Zhou smiled and began to talk about his time at UCLA. "It was very rare for a young Chinese student to have the opportunity to attend college in the United States in those early days. I was one of the fortunate few who received a scholarship from a philanthropic organization."

As Director Zhou talked, Kip was at a loss in trying to figure out why the man was reminiscing about his days at UCLA rather than the subject at hand. *I wonder where in the hell this is going?*

The director then stood and motioned with his hand toward the door. The three guests automatically followed him. While he was shaking Kip's hand in the hallway, he added, "You see, just before graduation I had an opportunity to personally meet the man who funded my scholarship at UCLA. You know him well. His name is Reginald Ingram."

Chapter 55

As soon as the three got back in the car, Kip said, "I'm totally confused. What in the hell just happened back there?"

Angie smiled and placed a reassuring hand on Kip's arm. "The problem's solved."

"How can you say that? He didn't give any indication that he'd help us."

Angie looked over at Bev and rolled her eyes. To Kip, she said, "It's the Chinese way."

Kip wasn't convinced. He dreaded what would happen the next morning if the power wasn't restored.

Before Angie had time to slip out of her coat the next morning, Kip stepped into her office and gave her a "follow-me" sign with his finger.

In the hallway, he said, "Okay how do we get out of this pickle?"

She said, "Sorry?"

"You know. Daleep Gupta is due here in a few minutes and we still have no power. I don't know what the hell's going on."

"I still think everything will be okay."

"Ask Heather to come up. We need to talk."

A few minutes later, Kip shared his ideas about Gupta with the two women in the spare office. "First of all, we do have power here in the clubhouse. Since we're meeting with Mr. Gupta here, there should be no questions concerning our power outage. However, if anything comes up that brings his attention to the problem, then we forthrightly tell him what has happened without making excuses. He either accepts it or he doesn't."

Angie's cell phone chimed. She listened for a moment and said, "*Xièxie.*"

She flipped her phone shut and said, "That was the receptionist. Mr. Gupta is waiting in the lobby."

The group met in the restaurant where Heather made a brief presentation to Gupta on their housing renovation project. She provided convincing information on how they'd improved in tenant satisfaction. When she nodded at Kip, he took over the presentation by sharing what's he'd done to reorganize the management structure and plans to bring Shores back to life.

After the meeting ended, Kip walked Gupta down to his chauffeured car waiting at curbside. Gupta turned to Kip and shook his hand. "Kip, I have to admit that I didn't expect this much progress so soon. You're to be commended."

"I appreciate hearing that."

Before Gupta slipped into the car, he looked back and smiled. "By the way, I hope you're able to get your power restored before too long. It can be frustrating."

"How did you know?"

Mr. Gupta laughed for the first time and placed his hand on Kip's shoulder. "I deal with the Power Bureau all the time. Their eagerness to shut off the power for the flimsiest reasons can be annoying. Anytime I hear a generator humming in the background, I know the power's been shut off."

Kip chuckled with relief. "Daleep, you're an observant man."

When Kip returned to the conference room, he gave Angie and Heather a high-five greeting.

Angie said, "Wow, that was great! We got through that without Mr. Gupta ever knowing that our power was off."

Kip said, "I hate to pop your bubble, but he knew the whole time."

At the same time, Angie and Heather said, "What?"

"He told me that they had the same problem at the academy in the past. You see, he heard our generator running."

Heather said, "What a relief." She stood up. "I've got a prospective client waiting for me downstairs so I'd better run."

After Heather left the room, Kip said to Angie, "I want you to call Priscilla and Naomi and ask them to meet with us up here at 4:30 p.m. Also tell Bev to be here."

"Okay. What's up?"

"It's time to send them on their way."

"Are you serious?"

"Yes."

"Oh, this is going to be exciting."

Kip said, "In the meantime, I want to meet with you, Bev, Jessie, Rory, and Manny down in the restaurant right away."

"I'll call them."

Fifteen minutes later, Kip walked into the restaurant and was pleased that everyone was already sitting around the table. He knew by the animated chatter that they were curious about why he'd call them together with such short notice. As soon as he sat down he said, "I wanted you to know what a great team you are. I also need to inform you that I'll be firing Priscilla and Naomi before the end of the day."

The group looked at each other in total shock. Rory blurted out "Good show—about freecking time!"

Kip continued, "I need to know right now what problems may arise out of this."

Bev said, "Kip, I think that someone needs to go over to the finance department and make sure that Naomi removes only her personal things after you've notified her. You should also have her sign a notice that she no longer has any signing authority regarding banking and other financial transactions."

Kip said, "Good. Bev, please draw up a formal memorandum to that effect for her to sign. What else?"

"Priscilla's reign over the security guards may be our biggest problem," said Rory. "Kip, you need to do something very dramatic in order to make sure that you are able to take control of the guards."

Bev said, "My uncle supervises a private security force that's made up of former military officers. Their company is for hire for this kind of situation. I could call him and ask if they could send a few men out here as observers."

Kip said, "Good idea. Okay, which one of you knows the security guards the best?"

"I guess I do," said Jessie.

"Jessie, as soon as I call Priscilla and Naomi into the meeting, find the head of security and ask him to wait in my office. Stay with him and make him comfortable. Are you okay with that?" asked Kip.

"No problem."

"Good. Rory, I want you to temporarily take over managing the guards until we figure out how to insure control over them. I don't think that anyone will mess with you. I plan to either fire the head guard or put him on a leave of absence."

Rory said, "No worries, mate."

"Bev, would you mind following Naomi over to her office after I terminate her and make sure she removes only her personal items?"

"No problem."

"Good. You can call your uncle and see if he's available. As a matter of fact, go ahead and excuse yourself right now to make that call."

She said, "Okay," and left.

Angie said, "I think that we should also do the same for Priscilla."

Looking at Angie, Kip said, "Can you handle that?"

"It'll be my pleasure."

"Manny, I want you to be available to back up anyone who needs it, okay?"

"Can do, boss."

"Jessie, as soon as I finish the meeting with Naomi and Priscilla, I will come to my office to talk with the head guard. You'll need to translate for me."

"I understand."

"One more thing," said Kip. "We recently had a security expert comb the development for bugs after we suspected that Niu had listening devices planted around the place." He then pushed a folder across to Rory. "Rory, I want you to be in charge of yanking every one of them out from their hiding places. You'll find detailed schematics inside pinpointing they're located. There are honing devices planted in the Buick and minivan. Yank them also."

Angie said, "What about Shelly?"

"Let's not worry about her for now. Without Priscilla and Naomi around, she'll have no power."

"Okay then, I want everyone back here after Naomi and Priscilla have left the premises. We'll need to make telephone calls to those employees who report to either Naomi or Priscilla right away. We'll probably end up back here around six o'clock. Thanks, everyone."

Needing to get a breath of fresh air, Kip walked out on the restaurant balcony and placed a call to Sal. He briefed him on the events of the day. After hanging up, he left a voice mail for Reggie to thank him for his help with Director Zhou at the Power Bureau.

"Rico, your accountant should have never turned over those financial statements to Duchene. That was a big mistake," said the Director of Construction of Shanghai.

The other three government officials in the room nodded their agreement.

"Don't worry." Rico held up a glass of Motai and smiled. "Believe me, what I've planned next for Shores will have that old Englishman begging me to take over the project."

Everyone laughed and held up their glasses. *"Ganbei!"*

Chapter 56

At five o'clock sharp, Kip was looking across the conference room table at Naomi and Priscilla. With blank expressions on their faces, neither said a word. Angie and Bev were sitting on each side of Kip. He started by saying, "In the United States, every American would recognize the words, 'Houston, we have a problem.' Well, I'm telling you both that you two also have a problem."

As Angie translated, both women looked at each other frowning.

When Priscilla started to speak, Kip put his hand out with his palm facing her. She stopped. He said, "As of this moment, you're both fired for insubordination, fraud, and embezzlement of company funds."

As soon as Angie translated, Priscilla immediately bolted to her feet and yelled something in Shanghainese. Angie turned back to Kip. "She said you couldn't fire them and had no proof whatsoever that they were guilty of anything."

Kip calmly opened a file folder in front of him and pointed to it. "This is a preliminary report from our accounting firm. It proves that you two have funneled money into your own pockets. The investigation is still in the early stages, but there is enough information to have you two thrown in jail for a very long time."

As Angie was translating, both women went pale.

Kip continued, "Now if you want to continue to resist the inevitable, we'll place a call to the main office of Public

Security and file formal criminal charges against you. Or, you can just keep your mouths shut and immediately clear out your personal possessions and leave the premises. You are to never be seen around here again. Do I make myself clear?"

When Angie finished translating Naomi and Priscilla nodded without saying a word.

"Naomi, Bev will escort you to your office and make sure that you only take your personal property. You are to turn over any keys and other items belonging to the company. Bev also has a release form that you are to sign. Priscilla, Angie will do the same for you. Any questions?"

Naomi said, "What about our vacation and severance pay?"

Kip slapped his hand down on the table with a loud report. Both women jerked in shock. He said, "You have none. In my ten years of being in business, I've met some pretty unsavory people along the way. None can compare with you. Heather could have been murdered, but you did nothing to stop it. If I hear that either one of you try to cause any more trouble for Shanghai Shores after you leave, I guarantee that you end up rotting in some Godforsaken prison."

Kip then took a deep breath and pointed to the door. "Get out of my sight."

Kip walked into his office and saw Jessie and the head guard sitting on the couch. He said, "Jessie, please ask him if he knows anything about Rico Niu."

She translated and listened to his answer. She said, "He said he's never heard of him."

Kip said, "Tell him he's fired as of this moment. If he wants to argue, tell him that he'll be arrested within the hour."

Hearing the translation, the red-faced guard hung his head and walked out of the office with Jessie in tow. Kip then gave Rory a call and told him what happened.

Rory said, "Got it, mate. I'll take care of everything on this end."

Just as Kip was feeling that they had the situation under control, Angie called him with a high pitched voice. "Kip, I'm still with Priscilla in her office. She's got a knife pressed against her wrist and is threatening to slash it if we don't pay her something."

"Christ! Do you think she's serious?"

"After seeing a few drops of blood run down her arm, I do."

"I'll be right over."

Kip called Bev and met her in Priscilla's office. By the time they walked in, there was a pool of blood under Priscilla's arm. She looked frenzied with her eyes darting around the room. She was yelling something Kip couldn't understand. Kip deferred to Angie and Bev to try to find a way to appease the woman. Kip watched as the three of them talked back and forth, sometimes in soft voices, sometimes not. After an hour had passed, Bev turned to Kip and said, "Priscilla said she'd stop this if we agree to pay her 6,000 RMB a month for the next twelve months."

Kip quickly did the math in his head and said, "I agree."

Bev translated. Priscilla looked up at Kip and slowly released the knife from her arm and set it down on the desk. Her wound was oozing blood.

Kip said to Angie, "Get something to dress her arm."

Priscilla rested her head on her arms and started to cry.

Kip thought—*Well, at least this particular round is over.*

The next morning, Angie told Kip, "I came in earlier this morning to walk through the compound and check to see how everything's going. I ran into Inspector Jiang wandering around the place without talking to anyone."

Kip said, "Is he the one who's close to Priscilla?"

"Yes. Priscilla's staff was quiet and somewhat in shock. When I walked through the finance department I could tell that they were nervous. Maybe they wondered who was going to get fired next."

"Good. They should."

"I also talked with Rory. He said that the military men supplied by Bev's uncle were very effective in maintaining control. He said that most of our guards seemed to be positive about the change. Others were scared."

Kip said, "Okay, we seemed to have stabilized the situation. I want you to appoint Mr. Zeng as manager of the transportation department. I'll give Mr. Liu a call and brief him on what's happened. He can probably suggest some good candidates to replace Naomi."

Just before the end of the day, Angie called out from her office and said, "Kip?"

"Yes."

"You've been really different these last few days."

"Like what?"

"A stronger leader—maybe not so nice anymore."

"Are you complaining?"

"No. I actually like it. Where did all that come from?"

"It's always been there, my dear."

Chapter 57

It was a crisp, sunny Thanksgiving Day in Shanghai. On the drive to pick up Angie, Kip thought about his father and wondered if he would be spending the day with one of his women friends. He hoped he wasn't feeling lonely and getting loaded.

Angie was waiting for Kip in the lobby of her apartment building when he arrived. She wore a black pant suit and minimal jewelry, a simple gold chain necklace and gold earrings. Kip said, "You look quite lovely, Miss Li."

"So do you, Mr. Duchene."

"Lovely?"

She laughed and gave him a jab in the shoulder. "Come on, let's go."

Mr. Zeng pulled the Buick up to the guard station at the front gate of Sal's housing development. While Zeng was talking to the guard, Kip said to Angie, "I'm glad Heather decided to take some well-deserved time off to fly home for the holiday."

Angie, said, "So am I. Besides, I think she has a thing for you."

Kip arched his eyebrows. "What?"

"You heard me."

"Why don't we just enjoy the evening, Miss Li?"

Sal's three children ran out of the house to meet them as soon as the car pulled up in front. Mr. Zeng quickly ran around the Buick to open the door for Kip and Angie. As Angie stepped out, the kids stared at her. With his mouth open, Tony said, "Wow!"

Kip said, "This is Angie Li."

Almost in unison, they sang out, "Hi, Angie!"

Kip said, "Angie, this is Lara, Tony, and Carla."

"You're *all* so beautiful!" she said.

Tony said, "I'm supposed to be *handsome*."

"Oh, that's what I meant to say." Looking from one to the other, she said, "How old are you?"

Lara said, "I'm twelve, Tony's eleven, and Carla is eight."

On the way to the front door Kip held hands with Lara on one side and Carla on the other. Angie grabbed Tony's hand. Despite looking embarrassed, he smiled and kept looking up at her as they headed for the house.

Sal came to the door drying his hands on a dish towel. He looked at Tony and said, "*Hijo*, why is your face so red?"

Tony dropped Angie's hand and ran ahead into the house.

Sal shrugged. "What'd I do?"

Kip said, "I think Tony's in love?"

"Hey, that's my boy!"

Just then, Maria came up from behind Sal, swatting him with the apron she'd just taken off. Walking past Sal, she went up to Angie on the front porch and said, "Hi, Angie, I'm Maria. I'm so happy that you could join us." With that, she gave Angie a warm embrace.

Knowing that Chinese don't tend to hug, Kip saw that Angie had a smile on her face.

Maria then turned to Kip and hugged him. "How're you doing, sweetie?"

"Good."

Inside, Angie followed Maria into the kitchen while the two men headed for the den. While Sal was pouring their drinks, Kip listened to the two women chatting away in the next room as if they were old friends. Convinced Maria was preoccupied with Angie, he called out, "Hey, Tony, can you come in here for a minute?"

Running into the room, Tony said, "Sure!"

Kip handed him a wrapped gift. "Happy Birthday."

"Thanks!" Tony tore off the paper and immediately saw the words on the box, *Cub Scout Swiss Army Knife*. "Gee whiz, Uncle Kip! How did you know I wanted this?"

Kip said, "Well, I wanted one when I was your age, so I guessed you did too. Go ahead and hand me the knife. I'll show you how to use it."

Kip demonstrated how to safely pull out the two blades and fold them back into the knife. He said to Tony, "You're eleven now and will be a man before you know it. You can never mess around with it in front of your sisters or friends. It's really sharp and could hurt someone. Do you understand?"

Tony flashed a look at his dad, then back to Kip and said, "Yes, Uncle Kip."

"Okay, then. Follow your Cub Scout rules and you'll be just fine. Now your dad and I have some serious business to discuss, so scat!"

"Thanks! I love my knife." He slipped it into his pocket and ran off.

Kip turned to Sal and said, "What were we talking about?"

Sal smiled and held up his glass of Gran Patron, "*Salud*."

An hour later, Maria called out, "Dinner's served."

As everyone was taking their seats, Tony maneuvered himself so he could sit next to Angie.

Maria looked across at Angie and said, "Do you say Grace in China?"

"Not really."

"Well, it's a part of what we do in our family. We start off by linking hands around the table."

"Okay." Angie held Kip's hand on her left and Tony's on the right while Maria said the blessing.

As soon as Maria said, "Amen," all five of the Estradas started to talk simultaneously, none of them caring whether anyone else was listening. Bowls and platters of food were passed from one person to the next or across the table in no particular order. They had sliced turkey, dressing, mashed potatoes, yams, cranberry sauce, and gravy.

Kip said to Angie, "Hey, you'll miss out just sitting there watching everyone else. Let me dish some food onto your plate."

She nodded and said, "But not such big portions." After sampling the food, she looked at Maria. "This is all so delicious. You're an amazing cook."

"It's nothing. But when it comes to preparing my famous chimichangas, I do alright."

"You're too modest."

Kip said, "Maria, I didn't know all these traditional American foods were available in Shanghai."

"Sweetie, you can find everything here if you know where to look."

After dinner the kids went upstairs and Sal pulled out the bottle of Gran Patron. Curious about the taste of tequila, Angie took a sip of Kip's drink and scrunched up her face. "How could anyone drink this?" She turned to Sal. "You know, the Chinese military might be interested in using this to fuel their next generation of rockets."

Sal said smiling, "We fuel our own rockets," and gave Kip a wink.

Angie grabbed a pillow off the sofa and threw it at Sal. Everyone burst out laughing when the errant pillow hit Sal in the crotch by mistake. Angie's face turned bright red.

While Sal and Kip were getting caught up on Shores and the latest news on the San Francisco 49ers, Maria and Angie wandered into the living room and sat down. From their vantage point, the men could be heard letting loose with the kind of guttural laughter that was a sure sign of raunchy storytelling.

While the men were preoccupied in the next room, Maria said to Angie, "I have a feeling that you care deeply for Kip."

A subtle smile crept across Angie's mouth, but she said nothing. Maria went on to share a lot about Kip's past life in Santa Monica, Stanford University, and San Francisco. She held nothing back when telling Angie what happened with Kip in the aftermath of Marci's death. Both women ended up wiping tears from their eyes.

Angie, said, "You know, Maria, despite Kip's gregarious nature, he's really a shy man, isn't he?"

"You've got that right, honey."

"Well, Kip has never shared any of that with me. I care for him in ways he may never know. But I don't have a clue what he thinks of me. Now that I understand a bit of what he's gone through, I can appreciate his reluctance to get involved with another woman. It must have been very painful for him to lose a woman that he loved so much."

Maria looked up and said, "And their unborn child."

Angie brought a hand up to her mouth and gasped, "Oh my God! I didn't know."

"He's suffered beyond anything that we could ever imagine. Angie, I think you're doing the right thing to go slow with him."

"I'm trying."

"Well, like I said, just take your time and everything will come out as it should. If you two ever do get together, you'll both be very lucky to have each other."

Starting to cry again, Angie said, "Oh, thank you, Maria. I haven't been able to talk with anyone about Kip before you. It feels *so* good."

"What about your parents?"

"They're traditional Chinese. I don't think they would understand if their daughter announced that she cared for a white man. My father is quite ill, so the family is focused on him. Kip could be an unwanted distraction."

"Well, you're welcome to come over here to visit anytime."

"Thank you."

Their conversation was interrupted by raucous outbursts from the two men in the next room. When Maria motioned with her head, the women got up and walked back into the family room in time to see Kip and Sal rolling on the floor in hysterics.

Maria turned to Angie and said, "You know, when these characters start to talk Spanish, something comes over them and they regress to Neanderthals."

"No, we don't," whined Sal, wiping tears off his cheeks.

Twenty minutes later Maria yelled up to the kids that Kip and Angie were leaving. The sound of all three of them racing down the stairs at the same time was like the rumble of thunder. On the front porch, everyone traded goodbyes and hugs. Just before the pair stepped off the porch, Angie turned back and gave Tony a kiss on the cheek. She received an adoring smile in return.

Kip walked Angie up a path to her building while they were chatting about Sal's family. When they stopped in front of the lobby door, she said, "I enjoyed the evening so much, Kip. Thanks for asking me. It was nice to be included in an American tradition like Thanksgiving. And of course, Sal and his family were all so wonderful to me."

"Yeah, that was nice to see. You were certainly a hit with them, particularly Maria. I think she really enjoyed your company." He then gave her a quick hug and said, "Thank you for coming." Touching her back caused a jolt of electricity to course through his body. After fishing a set of keys out from the bottom of her purse, she said, "Thank you again. It was a fabulous evening."

Kip said, "Good night, Angie."

On his walk back to the car, he thought—*Marci, what am I supposed to do?*

On the following Saturday, Sal called Kip. "Hey, *Tuchi*, are you still up for the kids to spend a weekend over at your place?"

"Hell, yes."

"How about next weekend?"

"Sure."

"Great. I want to take Maria on a romantic getaway to Xi'an."

"Remind me where that is?"

"It's in the Shaanxi Province, west of here. It's an ancient city where the terracotta soldiers are buried."

"Oh, yeah, I've read about it. I look forward to having the kids over. Let Maria know they'll be safe with me. "

"Will do. Thanks."

After Kip told Angie about the children's upcoming visit, she volunteered to stay over at Kip's to help referee. "Lara, and Carla and I should commandeer your master suite with you and Tony taking one of the guest bedrooms."

Kip said, "Great. This'll be quite a weekend."

In Haikou, Rico Niu was about to conclude his conversation with Tao. "And do understand. I hold you personally responsible if there are any mistakes this time. You know what that means, don't you?"

"Yes, boss."

"Okay then. Once I hear from you that you've successfully carried out my plan, I'll contact Mr. Estrada and demand that Ingram Capital agree to abandon Shanghai Shores. I'll give them only 24 hours to decide. If they don't agree by the deadline, then go ahead and tell the doctor to proceed with all three of them."

"All three?"

"Yes, all three." Rico Niu looked up from his desk with a crazed look in his red-rimmed eyes.

Chapter 58

On their way to the Pudong International Airport on Friday afternoon, Sal and Maria dropped the kids off at Kip's house. While the driver was unloading backpacks from the trunk, Maria gave the children last minute instructions.

Tony said, "Don't worry, mom, we'll behave like sweet little angels."

Swatting him gently on the back of his head, she said, "That's what I'm afraid of, *hijo*."

When Kip and Angie walked out to greet them, Maria said, "Just call me on my cell phone if they're any problem for you. If our return flight arrives on time, we should be back to pick up the kids on Sunday around 3:00 p.m."

Kip said, "No problem."

Sal said, "Don't call me. I've already turned my phone off."

"Get out of here, you two, and don't worry about the kids," Kip said. "You'll miss your flight."

After everyone hugged and said their goodbyes, Sal and Maria were driven away by the driver.

In the house Angie told the kids what the sleeping arrangements would be.

Kip looked over at a smiling Tony and warned him, "Just no funny stuff, understand?"

Tony giggled with delight.

That night, Kip treated everyone to dinner at Cucina's Restaurant in the Jin Mao Tower. He wanted the kids to see the sunset and watch the buildings along the Bund light up.

They all took bets on who would be the first to see the lights go on. Carla won. Tony accused her of cheating.

Lara didn't care; she was too impressed with being in such an elegant place surrounded by rich people. Of course, she was secretly in love with Kip. She particularly liked watching Kip's hands, whether he was picking up a glass of beer, scratching his ear or just resting them on the table. She had also taken a point-and-shoot camera along. She asked the waiter to take a snapshot of the five of them.

Back at the house, a game of tag led to a knock-down pillow fight. Before long, Tony's pillow ripped open and feathers went flying in every direction. When it first happened, all three kids froze and looked over at Kip. He smiled and took advantage of the pause by swinging his pillow at Angie, knocking her down on the floor onto her rear end. The kids resumed the fight with unrelenting gusto. Occasionally there would be a flash from Lara's camera as she tried to catch the action.

Once the kids got tired of the pummeling, Kip told them that he had a treat for them but that they'd have to clean up all the feathers first, then go wash their hands. While he and Angie headed for the kitchen, he said, "This'll be interesting."

She said, "What?"

"How the kids will figure out how to pick up the feathers."

"It should be easy."

Kip chuckled but didn't say anything more.

Just then, Lara walked in the kitchen and asked for three bags to put the feathers in.

Kip pulled open a bottom drawer and handed her the bags.

At first, the kids had no problem scurrying around and grabbing handfuls of the feathers and releasing them into the bags. Tony was quick to announce that he'd picked up more than Lara and Carla had. Then, the task started to prove more challenging. The children had built up a lot of static electricity on their bodies grabbing for the feathers and sweeping their hands across the carpet. They were able to pick up the remaining feathers only to find out that they tenaciously clung to their fingers and clothes, but wouldn't drop down into the bags. Tony soon gave up and sat down in the hallway leaning against the wall. Carla got frustrated and started to cry. Lara figured out that if she used a damp washcloth from the bathroom she could trap the feathers on it and scrape them into the bags without them clinging to it.

Fifteen minutes later, they reappeared in the kitchen where Kip and Angie were busy preparing the treat.

Kip said, "All picked up?"

Lara said, "Tony was messing around too much, but I made sure we got them all."

"Good." Kip then lined the kids up and gave them each a blanket. He pointed to the patio and said, "Go outside and wait for us on the lounge chairs. It may be foggy out there. You can use the blankets to keep warm."

Tony was the first to get out the door.

Kip and Angie made hot fudge sundaes and took them out on a tray. After Kip and Angie got their own blankets and sat down, the five of them dug into their desserts. For the first time since the kids were dropped off, no one said a word. At that moment, Kip couldn't think of anything he'd rather do than sit out on the patio, getting chocolate syrup down the front of him, watching the kids enjoying their treats, and feeling Angie's presence in the chair next to him.

From somewhere offshore a distant fog horn marked the approach of a thick marine layer of clouds. The children decided to have a contest to see who could best mimic the eerie sound. The contest ended in pandemonium as soon as Tony suggested that they change the rules from the sound of fog horns to farts. After bringing up the idea, he snuck a quick peek over at Kip for a possible reprimand. Hearing none, the kids were delighted to proceed with their new game.

Kip and Angie quietly looked at each other and smiled.

Since Shanghai Shores was a gated community and guards patrolled the entire compound, Kip wasn't worried about the children's safety. On Saturday morning, Kip gave them permission to go exploring around the compound.

The children started by going to the basketball court where Tony challenged Lara and Carla to a game. They got tired of that within fifteen minutes and decided to check out the fitness center. From there, they walked north along the boardwalk until they reached the perimeter wall of Shores. Where the wall stopped at the sea, Tony spotted a place to walk around the wall without getting wet. He pulled out his compass and saw that the rock levee on the other side went north of the compound. Even though Kip told them to stay inside Shores, Tony motioned for the girls to follow. The three enjoyed throwing rocks into the ocean from the top of the seawall. They walked about a hundred yards before the seawall ended at a canal that flowed into the sea. Blocked from going farther, they turned around for more rock throwing until they slipped back around the perimeter wall and into Shanghai Shores.

After trudging back into the house with rosy cheeks and excitement in their voices, they told Kip and Angie about their adventures. Tony added, "We had fun throwing rocks into the water."

Kip said, "Where was that?"

Lara and Carla looked at Tony. He said, "Oh, just north of here."

They were surprised to hear Kip's unexpected anger when he said, "Don't ever promise me something and then go against it. You were wrong to go outside the development. Do you understand?"

The three children nodded. Lara became teary-eyed, crestfallen to have disappointed Kip. Tony admitted that it was his fault alone and promised never to do it again.

Looking at Angie trying to hide a smile, Kip turned back to the kids. "Who would like to eat dinner at the clubhouse tonight?"

In unison, all three kids yelled, "I would!"

Kip invited Manny to join them for dinner. Kip didn't mention to the kids that Manny was African, a rarity in China. They were already seated at the table when Manny walked through the entrance of the restaurant. Seeing the man heading towards them, the three kids stared his way. But as soon as Manny introduced himself and flashed his broad smile, their initial reaction evaporated. Impressed with Manny's solid physique, Tony asked if he could feel his muscles. Manny laughed and pulled up his shirt sleeve to flex his formidable biceps. With wide eyes, Tony said, "Wooow!"

As Kip expected, Paul put on a great spread. They were served juicy tenderloin steaks, mashed potatoes, and an assortment of Chinese stir-fried vegetables. Despite the generous portions of food, the children had no trouble eating every last morsel on their plates.

Manny watched the children, smiling the whole time at their non-stop chatter and giggles. Angie also watched with a soft smile on her face. As the group was finishing their dessert, Hans and Trudy came in. Making a beeline for their table, Hans widened his eyes and said to Kip, "Vass is dis, *you* have a wife and kids so soon?"

Playing along, Kip said, "Oh, Hans, I forgot to tell you. This is Angie, my wife, and these are our three kids: Lara, Tony, and Carla."

After Hans bowed and shook each of their hands, he turned towards Manny and said, "And who might I ask is this *black* man?" With a twinkle in his eyes and a smile on his face, he motioned for Manny to stand.

"Okay, my African friend, let's do it."

Without further ado, they joined hands held high and went into a tribal dance, modifying their steps to go with the beat of the background music. Lara grabbed her camera and took several shots. Not being able to sit still any longer, the three kids jumped up and danced with Manny and Hans. The newly-formed ensemble weaved their way through the tables, entertaining everyone in the restaurant while Kip and Angie stood up to welcome Trudy.

When the rowdy bunch trudged back to the table, Hans was out of breath and sweating profusely. "Kip, can I buy you guys a drink?"

"Maybe just one. The kids have had a long day."

They chatted with Hans and Trudy for another twenty minutes. After that, Kip turned to the kids and said, "Okay troops, it's time to head home."

While goodbyes were being said, Hans whispered to Angie, "You're getting more beautiful every day."

"Thank you."

After that, Hans and Trudy walked over to a group of residents sitting at another table. Kip heard Hans saying, "The next round's on me."

In front of the clubhouse, Manny thanked Kip for the dinner, said goodbye to everyone, and headed for the truck parked nearby. On the short walk home, the kids chattered non-stop about their dinner and dancing adventure with Hans and Manny.

In the meantime, a Chinese doctor disembarked from a domestic flight at the Pudong International Airport. While waiting for his luggage to arrive, his phone chimed. He listened to a familiar voice on the other side. "Will you have everything set up by morning?"

The doctor said, "Have I ever failed you?"

"Nor will you tomorrow." Niu snapped his phone shut. He rubbed his eyes and smiled.

Chapter 59

Despite their late night antics, the three children were dressed and ready to experience new adventures on their last day with Uncle Kip and Angie. After they ate breakfast, Tony asked Kip, "Can we go out and play for a while?"

Kip said, "What's the rule?"

"Stay in the compound."

"Don't forget."

Lara said, "We won't, Uncle Kip."

"Okay, have fun. Lunch at noon. Make sure you're back before then."

Tony said, "We will."

Angie said, "I think you kids should take your coats. It's still foggy outside and it'll be a little chilly."

The kids grabbed their jackets and made a dash for the front door. Angie followed them out to the street and watched as they headed in the direction of the clubhouse. Before getting there, they turned around and waved at her. Waving back, she smiled at the sound of their excited voices and giggles.

While the children were out exploring the development, Angie and Kip cleared the dishes and made sure that their belongings were gathered up and packed. Sal and Maria would be tired after their flight back to Shanghai.

By that time, Lara, Tony and Carla had made their way to the playground. Seeing that it was already 11:45 a.m., Lara was about to tell the other two that they should be heading back for lunch. At the same time, a Chinese man appeared on the other side of the playground fence walking a Golden Labrador puppy. Without hesitation, all three kids dashed through the enclosure gate and knelt down to pet the little dog. As they did, three men bolted from a white commercial van parked ten feet away and grabbed the kids. Within a few seconds they were hoisted into the back of the van and the doors slammed shut. Two of the men held the terrified children down while the third man wrapped duct tape tightly around their arms and legs. He then tore strips of tape off the roll and stretched each piece across their mouths. As the van approached the front gate, the smiling driver—with a puppy on his lap—leaned out the window and waved to the guards. They waved back and let him through.

Satisfied the children were immobilized, the three men crab walked from the rear of the van and took seats up front. All four of them talked with an edge of excitement in their voices.

Lara, Tony and Carla were lying motionless back in the cargo area. Behind the tape covering their mouths, the two girls were crying and moaning. Tony was dazed from a painful gash on his forehead. When he lifted his head to look over at his sisters, he felt a moist stickiness on the side of his face. There was a small pool of blood where his head had been on the floorboard. From the darkened area of the cargo area, Tony saw the four men up front, silhouetted by the bright sunlight coming in through the dirty windshield.

After traveling several blocks through Chaoyeng, the van turned right, leaving the pavement and continuing on a rural road. Gravel kicked up onto the undercarriage of the van, making loud pinging noises. Five minutes later, they turned right and immediately stopped. One of the men jumped out of the passenger's door and opened a chain-link fence gate. The truck drove through until it reached a two-story abandoned factory located twenty yards from the gate. It parked in a large ground-floor loading bay where it was hidden from view.

The rear doors of the truck whipped open and the three men hefted each kid over their shoulders while the driver peeked around the edge of the building to see if anyone had spotted them. The children were carried up a flight of cement stairs to the second floor. From the landing, the men stepped through a doorway and into a large open manufacturing space that had been stripped of machinery. The air reeked of the foul smell of damp mold and urine. Rusty bolts protruded up from the debris-strewn floor. All of the factory windows were dingy and either cracked or broken.

As the men walked across the factory floor, a rustling noise and movement caused them to abruptly stop. A large rat sprang from a pile of trash and escaped through one of the broken window panes. One of the men muttered something and headed toward the far end of the factory and into a dark littered hallway. Office doors were located on both sides. Half way down the corridor, one of the doors was ajar, revealing a treatment table draped with a white sheet and a bare IV pole. The men carried the children through the next door down the hallway and set them down on the cement floor amongst piles of rubble.

Lying there, the children got their first good look at the men who kidnapped them. The shortest of the three men drew most of their attention. His remarkably ugly face and deformed left ear scared them. Seeing their stares, Mr. Tao smiled directly at Lara, then reached down to stroke her face. She jerked away and let out a muffled scream.

The other two men yelled at him and one cuffed him hard on the back of his head. Tao yelled back and shoved the man against the wall. Just as suddenly, the three men walked out the room without saying another word. After the door hasp was padlocked, they headed down the hallway and out across the factory floor.

Inside the room, the children strained to hear every sound. Somewhere in the distance, they heard men's voices embroiled in a heated argument. Except for an occasional gust of wind rattling the window frame in their room, the factory was eerily quiet.

Feeling that it was safe to move, Tony lifted his head to take a better look at Lara and Carla. Both looked back to him with large frightened eyes. Carla's body was shivering. He motioned with his head for Lara to get closer to Carla while he scooted over to the other side of her. Between them, they sandwiched Carla between their bodies to give her warmth and comfort. Within five minutes, they could feel her body begin to relax.

Lara was terrified what the ugly man might do to her if he returned.

Lying up against Carla, Tony knew that he had to find a way for them to escape before any of the men could hurt them. He hated the way the ugly one touched Lara's face. At the age of twelve, she was budding into a beautiful Hispanic girl. He thought—*What would my daddy do?*

Back at Shanghai Shores, Kip cracked the top on this third can of beer when he glanced at his watch. "Hey, I'm starting to get worried. It's not like the kids to show up late to eat. It's past noon already."

Angie said, "Gosh, I hadn't realized."

He said, "Why don't you stick around the house and I'll go find them. If they show up, just give me a call." He walked over to the clubhouse and asked the receptionist if she had seen the children lately. She told him that they were down in the fitness center a little earlier but had taken off. He said, "Andrea, if you happen to see them, please give me a call right away."

"Okay, I will."

Kip jogged through the development, looking up and down the streets for any sign of the kids. Along the way, he asked several tenants if they had seen them. None had. Five minutes later, a resident in front of a garden home said, "You know, Kip, I thought I saw them heading for the playground on the north end."

Relieved, Kip said, "Thanks."

He sprinted in that direction, hoping to find them preoccupied in play. But as he rounded the corner and looked in the direction of the playground, Kip felt bile rise in his throat. The children's jackets were draped haphazardly across the play equipment—none of them, however, were anywhere in sight.

"Hey, Kip, what's wrong?" said Henry Young from his backyard fence next to the playground.

"Jesus, Henry, Sal Estrada's children are staying with me for the weekend and they've disappeared."

"I'm sorry, Kip, I just walked out here to do some watering and haven't seen anyone. Is there something I can do to help you look for them?"

Henry's five year old daughter was standing by his side. She tugged on his pant leg and pointed towards the road, "Daddy, I saw men put kids in big white car."

"What's that, honey?"

"The men put the kids in a big white car. I think the kids maybe did something wrong because they didn't want to go."

Oh my God, they've been kidnapped!—screamed the words in Kip's head. He yanked out his phone and called the receptionist, "Andrea, we have an emergency! Please call the gate immediately and tell them that no one is to leave until I say otherwise. Ask the guards if any white car or truck left the development this morning. Please call me right back."

Kip called Angie and told her what was happening. She said she'd call the police. While they were talking, Kip's phone beeped. "Angie, got to go! Someone's trying to get through."

Punching the incoming call button, he said, "Yes?"

"This is Andrea. The head guard said that a white panel truck left the premises at 11:50 but only the driver and his puppy were seen in the front seat."

Kip thought—*Shit, I just missed them!* "Do they have a description of it?"

"Yes. They said that it was a white Toyota truck with a lot of rust spots on it. They also have its license plate number since they automatically write it down whenever a car comes through the gate."

"Thanks, Andrea. Please call me if you hear anything."

Kip felt like he was running in slow motion on his way back to his house. As he stepped up to his front porch, he could hear approaching sirens in the background. He bolted through the door and called out, "Angie, it was a white van and the guards have its license plate number!"

Running up to him, she said, "The police should be here any second."

"I heard the sirens just now."

Angie said, "I also called Bev. She'll call Chairman Zhang and ask for his help to get the attention of the police."

"Good. When does Sal's flight arrive?"

"Around two."

"Okay. Please make sure that the police intercept them as soon as they get off the plane. Have them tell Sal to call me immediately. I don't want Sal and Maria to hear from anyone other than myself about the kids. The police should bring them directly here as fast as possible. Also call Sal's driver and tell him to come here and not the airport."

"I'll take care of it."

Pacing back and forth, Kip moaned, "Oh, Jesus, I've let this happen to the kids. Sal and Maria will be devastated. I've got to get their children back safely before they arrive."

Chapter 60

Tony was trying to figure out how they could escape. *I have to find a way to talk to my sisters.* Then an idea came to him. He rolled over to the nearest wall and rubbed his face against its roughened surface. After several attempts, he was able to get an edge of the tape to stick to the wall. Little by little, the tape rolled away from his mouth. Breaking the silence in the room, he whispered, "I'm going to get us out of here."

Lara and Carla eyes flashed open the moment they heard their brother's voice. They moaned with excitement from behind their gags. Tony jerked his head towards the door and whispered, "Shhhh, I hear something . . . I think they're coming back!" He quickly scooted away from the wall to lie alongside Carla, and then rubbed his face against her shoulder to roll the tape back across his mouth.

The approaching footsteps became loud enough for the two girls to hear. The padlock clicked and the door swung open. Two men walked in—one of them was the ugly one with the crooked ear. They looked around the room, and then checked the kids' bindings. Mr. Tao straddled directly over Lara, then leaned down and touched her leg. She was terrified what the ugly man was going to do next and kicked her bound legs as hard as she could. Hearing the commotion, the other man slapped Tao's shoulder and gruffly said something to him. Without further ado, the two walked back out and refastened the lock.

Tony listened to their retreating footfalls until all was quiet. He rubbed his face against Carla's shoulder until the tape unrolled from his mouth. He whispered, "I'm going to try to stand up and look out the window."

He scooted over to the wall and propped his back against it in a sitting position. After making several attempts to shimmy upward, he managed to stand. The room was about ten feet square and had one window. Looking through the thick layer of dust on the window pane, he whispered, "There's a balcony running along the building just outside the window. I think there are rice paddies in the field behind the building."

While Tony was trying to figure out how they could escape, the flight from Xi'an landed at the Pudong International Airport. Having been contacted by the police an hour before, the airline had quietly arranged for Sal and Maria to disembark ahead of the other passengers. Just as they stepped off the plane, they were met by an officer in street clothes with a cell phone pressed to his ear and his identity badge held for them to see. They instantly knew something was terribly wrong. Maria started to weep. The officer pulled the phone away from his face and said, "Mr. Estrada, I'm Detective Wu Yibing of Pudong Public Security. I have Mr. Duchene on the phone for you."

As soon as Kip heard Sal's strained voice, he told him about the kidnapping without hesitation. Sal looked down at his watch and barely managed to say, "We'll be there as fast as possible."

While Sal and Maria were in route, Manny, Bev, and Jessie showed up at Kip's house, busily making calls on their cell phones to muster more manpower to search for the children. Police detectives talked to Kip, Angie, Henry Young's daughter, and the guards. Other officers worked their way through the village questioning the locals about the rusty white van. News reporters were gathering at the entry gate wanting to get inside to learn more about the three American children who had been reported kidnapped. Sal's driver and Mr. Zeng had their cars parked across the street from Kip's house in case they were needed. The two men stood on the sidewalk and shared what they knew about what had happened.

Sal and Maria were sitting in the back seat of an unmarked police car when Sal's cell phone chimed. He flipped it open, assuming it was Kip. "*Tuchi*, tell me you found them."

With a heavy Chinese accent, the caller said, "Ah, Mr. Estrada, I presume. I do not believe anyone has found your precious little children."

"Who's this?" said Sal in a high pitched voice.

Listening intently to Sal's conversation, Maria started to openly cry.

The man calmly said, "Who I am is not important, Mr. Estrada. What is important, however, is for you to understand that you have only 24 hours to submit a formal notice to the Shanghai government that Ingram Capital will abandon its ownership of Shanghai Shores."

"ARE YOU FUCKING CRAZY?"

"Ah, that's entirely possible, Mr. Estrada. You'll find out how crazy I really am if my demand is not met."

Sal yelled, "Who in the fuck is this!"

"24 hours, Mr. Estrada."

Maria was now pulling on Sal's sleeve. "What's happening?"

Pressing the phone to his ear, Sal heard a click, then a dial tone. He turned to Maria and said, "Nothing. A crank call."

The unmarked police car was forced to slow down as it approached the main gate of Shanghai Shores. The entrance was partially blocked by a large group of onlookers. As the car nosed its way through the crowd, some of them cupped their hands around their faces and pressed against the rear windows trying to see who was inside. Sal gave Maria's hand a gentle squeeze and said, "Don't pay any attention to them. We're almost there."

Typical for China, word about the kidnapping of three American children had spread throughout Shanghai with blinding speed, mostly by person-to-person cell phone calls. News reporters and some of the more curious people headed directly to Shanghai Shores to find out what happened. Conflicting reports were being widely circulated, some claiming that the children had been found with their left legs amputated. A vendor in Chaoyeng was telling people that he'd heard they were found murdered.

The police car pulled up in front of Kip's home where Kip and Angie were waiting at curbside. Four officers from Public Security stood on each side of the walkway with their arms outstretched to insure that curious neighbors and employees were kept at bay. Sal helped Maria out of the car.

Kip motioned with his head. "Let's get you and Maria inside. We can talk in my study."

Sal nodded without comment. Maria held a handkerchief up to her reddened eyes. As soon as the foursome sat down in the study, Maria let loose with a long mournful cry. Sal wrapped his arm around her and pulled her close to him. He whispered, "I promise we'll get them back."

Turning towards Kip, Sal said, "Go ahead and tell us what you know. Don't leave anything out."

Kip took a deep breath and recited the events of the kidnapping in chronological order, starting with the kids not showing up for lunch. He had to pause several times as his voice faltered with emotion. Maria quietly wept while Kip spoke. Sal sat rigidly, listening to every word. Five minutes later, Kip said, "That's everything I know . . . I'm so sorry."

Sal said, "*Tuchi*, give us a few minutes."

Kip stood up with Angie and said, "We'll be right in the next room. Can we bring you anything?"

Sal said, "Water."

A moment later, Angie walked back in the room with a pitcher of ice water and drinking glasses. Sal had his arms wrapped around Maria. Both were crying. Angie poured the water and quietly slipped back out.

When Sal emerged from the study, Kip and Angie were in the dining room organizing the managers. A long line of volunteers were being sent out in the village to search for the children in predetermined grids. Sal leaned in the doorway and motioned for Kip and Angie to join him in the hallway. Sal said, "I'm pleased to see all these people trying to help."

Kip said, "Yeah, they're a Godsend."

Sal turned to Angie. "Maria has asked for you."

As soon as Angie headed off, Sal draped his arm around Kip's shoulder and said, "I know what you're thinking."

"What do you mean?"

"That this was all your fault."

Kip said nothing.

Sal continued, "So please listen up. Those three children are relying on their daddy and uncle to help them. If you're preoccupied with feeling guilty, you won't be much good to me or to them. Does that make any sense?"

"Yes."

"Okay, then, let's put our heads together and bring my children home."

Kip nodded.

Sal said, "And another thing. Don't tell Maria, but I received a call on my cell phone from a man while we were driving here from the airport. He had a Chinese accent and spoke with broken English. He demanded that we give up Shores within 24 hours or else. Even though I've never heard his voice, I think it could have been none other than Rico Niu."

"Who else would have any reason to make the call?"

"Exactly. We've only got twenty-three more hours to find the kids. Once we get them safely in our hands, those bastards who took them are going to pay."

A short time later, Sal and Kip joined the two women. Maria looked up and said, "Has anyone demanded money?"

Kip said, "No. Maria, I'm one-hundred percent convinced that the kids will be released unharmed. No one could possibly benefit from hurting them—they'll be fine."

Buoyed by Kip's optimism, Maria give him a wan smile.

Kip said, "I think the van will be sighted in no time at all. There's at least forty police officers are actively on the case and that Mr. Zhang, the Chairman of the Political Committee in Pudong, is personally involved. He's already contacted the mayor of Shanghai and briefed him on what's happened. In the meantime, most of our managers are in the dining room. It looks as though they've already sent out more than sixty volunteers to comb through the village."

Maria turned to Sal and said, "I want to go out and join in the search."

Sal said, "I understand, sweetheart, but you'll be more help to them by staying right here and being ready for them. Kip and I are heading out in a minute."

Maria looked defeated. "Angie, please stay with me."

Angie smiled. "I'm right here."

Sal kissed Maria, and the two men walked out. In the hallway, Sal said, "We're going to kill those goddamn fuckers."

In the dining room the managers stood up when they saw Kip and Sal walk in, not sure of what to say. Sal said with a broken voice, "Thank you for all you're doing to help find my children. Maria and I are very grateful."

Chapter 61

While there was still daylight, Tony looked out through the dingy window, trying to memorize as much of the terrain below as possible. It would be getting dark soon. He could make out rice paddies. Straight ahead in the distance, he could also make out the water tower in Chaoyeng, visible through the haze. Then he strained to look to the far left. *Wait a minute! That's the coastline. Let's see, we must be somewhere north of Shanghai Shores.*

His concentration was broken by the sound of Carla weeping. He turned his back to the wall and slid down to a sitting position. "Don't worry. I'm going to get us out of here. Okay, now, listen up. I know that dad expects me to be the man in charge right now."

There was just enough light in the room for him to see Lara rolling her eyes. He said, "Come on, Lara, I'm serious!"

He then tried to explain how he thought they could escape. By the blank looks on the girls' faces, he knew they had no idea what he was talking about. He shrugged his shoulders and rolled the gag back across his mouth in case the men came back again. Still thinking about his plot to escape, he scooted over to Carla and curled up behind her, hoping his body would help keep her warm. In December, the nighttime temperature in Shanghai was dropping close to freezing. The colder Tony got, the less confident he felt about his plan. Within an hour, the three children were shivering with bone-chilling cold.

Lara and Carla finally drifted off to sleep. Tony stayed wide awake going over and over different ways he thought they could escape. *I don't like the way that ugly man touched Lara.* No sooner had the thought crossed his mind, he heard the sound of approaching footsteps. He wiggled to make sure that Lara and Carla woke up. The padlock clicked open. The beam of a flashlight swept across the children. The unseen intruder threw blankets on top of them, then stepped over to where Lara was lying and just stood there for a minute. The silence of the room was pierced when Lara let out a muffled scream. The man had slipped his hand under the blanket and started caressing her leg.

Terrified at seeing what was happening, Tony scraped off his gag and yelled as loud as he could. The man flicked the beam of the flashlight in Tony's face, leaped over Carla, and began to kick him savagely. But Tony kept screaming. Two other men burst into the room with flashlights and pulled the attacker away from Tony. In the scuffle, a beam of light swept across the man's face—it was the ugly one with the bent ear. His two companions threw him out of the room and all three walked down the hallway, leaving the door to the room ajar.

Seeing this, Tony thought—*Maybe this is our chance!* Before he could act, he heard someone coming back.

One of the men stepped back into the room and knelt down to pull the tape off of the girls' mouths. He unscrewed a large plastic water bottle and held it up so each of them could take a drink. Before the children had much of a chance to enjoy breathing through their mouths, the man tore off fresh strips of duct tape from a roll and placed them across their mouths. Without saying a word, he walked out and locked the door.

Tony felt something oozing down the side of his head and assumed that his head wound must have reopened during the scuffle. A short time later, he was pleased to see that Carla had fallen asleep. *The blankets really felt good.*

He and Lara lay awake in pitch darkness listening intently to every little sound outside of their room.

Earlier in the evening Manny and Rory walked around Chaoyeng to question the locals. They ran into other volunteers on almost every street. Rory poked Manny on his shoulder and said, "You know, mate, me thinks there's more blokes out here looking for Sal's kids than the villagers who live here."

Manny smiled without comment.

Mr. Zeng drove Kip and Sal through the maze of back alleyways looking for anything suspicious. Police cars had saturated the area. By the first light of dawn, Sal said to Kip, "Let's take a quick break and check in on Maria."

Kip said, "Yeah—good idea. I could use a little java."

As soon as they walked in the house, Maria ran up to Sal. "Have you found anything promising?" She wore no makeup and her eyes were red and puffy.

"Maybe. A night watchman at a factory on the north side of the village thought he might have seen a white van drive past, but he couldn't be sure. Other than that, we didn't find anything. So as soon as we get some coffee in us, we'll head back out and concentrate on that area."

She said, "Please hurry."

Sal said, "How ya doing?"

"I'm trying my best."

"I know you are, sweetheart." Sal looked down at his watch and thought—*Que la mádre! Only eight more hours left.*

Just as Sal and Kip were pulling their jackets back on, they heard someone pounding on the front door. Before they could open it, Rory bolted in.

"Holy shit, mates, I might know where the kids are being held! One of my wee engineers just called me. He saw the morning newscast about the kidnapping and remembered seeing a rusty white van pull into an old factory right across the road from his house."

Sal said, "Where does he live?"

Rory said, "North of the village."

Angie said, "I had better call the police and give them this information."

Sal ran over to Maria and said, "We'll bring them home."

"I'm going too!"

Placing his hands on her shoulders, Sal calmly said, "Sweetheart, you'll be more helpful if you stay right here with Angie . . . please."

She nodded.

On his way out the door, he called to Angie, "Give us a ten-minute start before you make that call."

Mr. Zeng was already waiting for them in the minivan with Manny sitting inside. There was a truckload of Rory's men waiting right behind the van. As Kip, Sal and Rory jumped in, Rory barked directions. Kip said, "Do we have any weapons?"

Rory held up a crowbar. "This is all we should need. Besides, I know Mr. Zeng always keeps a Billy club stashed under his seat."

Mr. Zeng peeled away from the curb and sped towards the front gate with the horn blaring. The pickup truck full of Rory's crew followed. Hearing the commotion coming towards them, the guards opened the gate just in time for the speeding vehicles to fly past.

After going only a few blocks into Chaoyeng, Mr. Zeng skidded the van into a sharp right-hand turn and sped off down a narrow road heading north. Kip, Sal and Rory had to lower their heads in order to keep from banging them on the ceiling when the van lifted off the ground. The two vehicles were spewing gravel along the road, leaving billowing clouds of dust in their wake.

Kip was first to see a two-story cement building on the right side of the road up ahead. *That must be it.* Realizing that Mr. Zeng was not slowing down for the chain-length fence blocking the way, Kip crouched in his seat and yelled, "Hold on—we're going through!"

The minivan slammed through the gate with a section of fence cart-wheeling off to the right. As soon as they pulled alongside the building, the doors of the minivan flew open and everyone ran into the loading zone.

The first thing they came upon was two startled men who'd been sleeping on cots. Both sat upright with confused looks on their faces. Within a few seconds, they were surrounded. The puppy tied to a support post nearby was yapping. Mr. Zeng held a Billy club above one of the men's head and yelled something at him in Shanghainese. After the wide-eyed man nervously responded, Mr. Zeng pointed to a cement staircase and yelled in Mandarin that the kids were being held in a locked room on the second floor.

With Mr. Zeng staying behind, Sal was the first to bolt towards the stairs, closely followed by Kip, Manny and Rory. The four men ran through the second floor manufacturing space toward the corridor at the far end. Along the way, Rory said to no one in particular, "Smells like a wee bit of pong, doesn't it?"

In the darkened hallway, they pushed through a rusted door and froze at the gruesome sight inside. A treatment table sat in the middle of the room with a bloodied white sheet draped on top. Blood-soaked squares of gauze were scattered on the floor beneath the table. Sal stared unbelieving at stained surgical instruments arranged haphazardly on a side table and uttered, "Mother of Jesus!"

He then bolted out of the room and ran further down the hallway to the next door. It was padlocked. Juggling on the knob, he yelled, "Daddy's here . . . daddy's here! Everything's okay!"

Rory ran up behind Sal, reaching over him to smash the padlock with the crowbar. It flew open with the impact of the first powerful blow. When Sal yanked it open, he moaned, "Oh, noooo!"

Chapter 62

The room was empty except for scattered debris, torn pieces of duct tape, and rumpled blankets on the floor. When the men walked further into the room, Sal saw that there were also several dried pools of blood on the floor. He said, "Holy Mother of God, Kip. Look at this." He pointed to the stains.

Kip said, "Sal, I think the two missing men must have snatched up the kids and drove away before we got here. We don't know how long these blood stains have been here."

"What about those on the examining table next door?"

Kip said nothing.

In the background, they could hear the approaching sound of sirens.

Sal, Manny, and Rory gathered up the crew to continue their search for the children. Kip volunteered to stay behind in the derelict factory to the answer questions by an English-speaking detective. Kip said, "Sal, I'll catch up to you later as soon as I'm finished here."

While Kip was showing the detective around the second floor, Mr. Zeng dutifully stood by the minivan down in the parking area, ready to drive his boss whenever he needed to leave. Fifteen minutes later, the detective thanked Kip for his cooperation and said that he didn't have any more questions.

Racing down the stairs to the ground floor, he grimaced when he saw Milt Avery getting out of the black Buick from the U.S. Consulate's Office. Avery followed Kip to the van and said, "Kip, this kidnapping thing is getting out of hand for us at the Consulate. I'm here to get a personal update from you."

Without slowing down, Kip jumped into the van. As it was backing up, he leaned out the window and said, "Milt, you can take your goddamn update and shove it up your ass!"

The detective was standing nearby. He took out his notepad and wrote something down.

Kip turned to Mr. Zeng and said, "*Zǒu Ba?*" Ready to go? Mr. Zeng nodded and stomped on the accelerator pedal. As they were heading down the gravel road toward the village, Kip flipped open his cell phone. "*Yani*, I'm finished and on my way. Where are you now?"

In the meantime, Maria and Angie were waiting nervously in the family room for the phone to ring. Maria paced back-and-forth, making the sign of the cross and whispering urgent prayers.

Through the corner of her eye, Angie caught movement outside on the patio. Turning in that direction, she was shocked to see the three children barreling directly towards the back door. Angie bolted upright and screamed, "THEY'RE HERE!"

The kids hit the back door at the same time, running past Angie and into their mother's arms. Caught off balance, Maria fell onto the carpet with the children flopping on top of her.

Between the crying, laughing, and everyone trying to talk at the same time, it was impossible for Angie to understand a word. She grabbed her cell phone and punched in Sal's number. As soon as she heard his voice, she said, "Sal, just a moment!"

She handed the phone to Maria. "Sal's on the line."

Maria cried, "HONEY, THE KIDS ARE SAFE! They're safe! They're right here!"

Sal stammered, "Th-th-they're what?"

"They're all on top of me right now! They're okay except for being dirty, smelly, and soaking wet! Please hurry!"

Lara called out to her mother, "Tell daddy that I love him!"

She handed the phone back to Angie and smiled at Lara. "Sorry, honey, your daddy already hung up, but he'll be here before you know it."

Angie grabbed plastic water bottles out of the refrigerator and handed them to the kids. They drank eagerly. She ran out of the room and returned carrying a stack of blankets. "Maria, I think the kids may be in shock. Carla's lips look a little blue."

After the kids were swaddled up in the blankets, they began to calm down from the warmth. Tony had blood caked on the back of his head and all three of them had patches of red skin where the duct tape covered their mouths. Despite the children's disheveled appearance, Maria had them in her clutch, kissing them all over their heads, cheeks, and mouths, murmuring, "I love you, I love you, I love you."

A few minutes later, Sal burst through the front door and made a beeline for the kids. Crying and out of breath, he said, "Is everyone okay?" He knelt down and opened his arms to them. He noticed the blood on Tony's head. "*Hijo*, what happened to your head?"

"I'm okay." Despite the bravado, Tony put his hands up to his face and started to cry.

Sal held him closer and said, "Just let it out, son—just let it all out."

By then, Kip, Rory and Manny were in the room watching the scene unfold. Rory nudged Manny, then turned to Kip and gave him a wink. "We'll be leaving now, mate."

As Rory and Manny quietly slipped out the front door, Sal turned to the children and said, "Okay, who's going to tell us what happened?"

By then, Lara and Carla were nestled on each side of Maria, and Tony stayed wrapped up in his father's arms.

Lara said, "Since I'm the oldest, I should."

She looked up at her mother and took a deep breath. "Tony was the one who saved us from those terrible men." She explained what had happened beginning with the moment they saw the man and his puppy walking in front of the playground. She explained what they had experienced, except for the parts about the ugly man trying to touch her. She described how the men bound their hands and legs and taped their mouths shut. As she was telling her story, Sal thought back to the bloody scene in the makeshift surgical room. *I'm so thankful they didn't hurt my children. I wonder what really happened in there?*

Lara was saying "—when Carla fell asleep last night, Tony and I were too afraid of the men returning. So we stayed awake, like all night long. The factory had rats. We could hear them scurrying around and even scratching against our door. It was like so scary. We were afraid that they would get in and bite us. When it finally started to get light outside, Tony scooted over to me and told me to get his Cub Scout knife out of his front pocket. He couldn't reach it with his hands tied behind him."

Maria had a funny look on her face but remained silent. Sal looked down at Tony and said, "How could you talk with your mouth gagged, *hijo?*"

"I figured out how to rub my face along the back of Carla to roll enough to talk. It stung but it really worked."

Sal gave him a squeeze as Lara continued. "After what seemed like a long time, I was able to pull the knife out of his pocket and open the blade. With my hands tied behind my back, doing that was like really hard. I held the knife straight out while Tony scooted around with his back against me. He put his hands so the blade would cut into the tape binding. Then he moved his hands back-and-forth until the blade sliced through."

Tony held up his left wrist and said, "See, only a small nick."

Lara said, "I was so scared that I would cut Tony. But, I didn't. Once he was free, he took the knife from me and cut the tape off of Carla and my hands and feet. That really felt good."

Maria said to Tony. "Where did you get the knife?"

Tony glanced nervously over at Kip.

Smiling and nodding her head, she said, "That figures." She turned back to Lara. "Go ahead, sweetheart."

"Well, Tony was able to pull the window open and we climbed out onto a second-floor balcony. He told us to be quiet. From up there, we could see the ocean in the distance. There was a stairway on the far side of the building. We tiptoed down it. Tony headed off towards the rice paddies and ran on top of one of the mounds of dirt that separated the ponds. Carla and I followed right behind him. When we got about halfway across the field, we heard someone yelling at us from the factory. We stopped and turned around. Two of the men had seen us from the balcony. They ran down the stairs and headed right towards us. We ran as fast as we could until we finally got to the seawall levee. By then, we were so out of breath. When we looked back to see where the men were, we were relieved that they'd turned around and were like running back towards the factory. Tony told us to follow him along the seawall.

About twenty minutes later, we came up to a canal that emptied into the ocean. It blocked us from going any farther. While we were trying to figure out how to get across the canal to the other side, we heard the sound of a car somewhere in the distance. We saw a cloud of dust following it along the dirt road by the canal. Then we realized that the car was heading towards us. It was the white van."

Everyone in the room was listening to Lara's account of what happened without comment.

Taking a breath, she continued, "Tony ran over to where a ladder went down the inside wall of the canal and told Carla to follow right behind him. I went last. When he reached the water, he and Carla pushed off together and swam across to the other side. Like the water was really freezing, but we swam pretty fast. There was a floating platform on the other side so it made it easy to pull ourselves up onto it. We could hear the van getting really close while we were climbing up the ladder. When we got to the top and looked back across, the truck was just sitting there idling and the two men inside were looking at us through an open window. We turned around and ran towards the wall of Shanghai Shores. After we got on the other side, we ran until we came to Uncle Kip's house."

Carla piped in, "That's right!"

Maria looked over at her son snuggled against his father and said, "Well, what do you think, my little hero?"

Tony shrugged his shoulders and said, "That sounds about right. I'm sure glad that Uncle Kip gave me my Boy Scout's knife."

Ignoring the comment about the knife, Maria said to Tony, "How did you know how to find your way back here?"

"When we were still locked in the room, I looked out the window and could see the water tower in Chaoyeng. Then I kinda knew where we were. If we were north of the village, then Shores had to be south of us. I took the girls straight across the rice field towards the ocean and then turned right—that was south."

"How did you know the seawall would lead to Shanghai Shores?"

Tony looked over at Kip. "Well . . . we took a walk along it on Saturday."

Maria said, "You did?"

"Yeah, but Uncle Kip got mad at us because we weren't supposed to leave Shores."

"Go on."

"So I already knew if we got to the ocean, I could find Shores."

Sal pulled Tony closer to him and said, "I'm so proud of you, son."

"Does this mean that I can have a root beer float?

"How about some for all three of you?"

He said, "Cool!"

Angie's phone rang. After talking for a moment, she looked up. "Would it be okay if the police came over to interview the kids?"

Maria said, "Yes, but ask them if they could wait for about an hour. The kids are still cold and filthy. They really need to have hot showers and eat something."

Angie spoke into the phone and flipped it shut. "The detective said it'll be no problem at all."

Maria said, "Good. We might as well get it over with. I'd like to get the kids home as soon as we can. They're exhausted."

While the kids were being interviewed and shown photographs of men's faces, Maria caught Kip in the hallway and gave him a hug. "Thanks for trusting my son so much that you gave him that knife. And thanks also for *not* telling me." Chuckling, she reached up and gave him a kiss.

Kip said, "I can't tell you how much I needed that."

"You're a good man, Kip."

Seeing the three children bounding down the hallway towards them, Kip said, "I guess the police interviews are over."

Maria said, "I guess so."

Lara said, "Mom, can we come back to visit Uncle Kip and Angie? We had so much fun with them."

Tony and Carla also piped in, "Yeah, can we?"

Maria smiled and said, "Of course you can."

The children jumped up and down and gave Kip and Angie big hugs. By then, Sal had their driver pack all of the children's belongings in the trunk of the car. Sal walked back through the front door and called out, "It's time to go."

Kip and Angie followed the Estrada clan to their car and stood curbside waving to them until they were out of sight. As soon as they walked back into the house and closed the door, Kip collapsed in the hallway and started to sob uncontrollably. Angie sat down on the floor beside him and cradled him in her arms without saying a word.

When Rico Niu was finally told that the kidnapping was botched, he lost control yelling incoherently and throwing whatever was in reach against the wall. After ranting for several minutes, he calmed down as a plan began to take form in his mind. *Okay, it's time to get their attention.*

Four days after the kidnapping, Milt Avery's battered body was found in a dark alleyway in Hongkou, a rundown district in Shanghai still awaiting redevelopment. The White House's reaction to the incident was immediate. How could a senior official from the U.S. Consular's office be brutally murdered on the streets of Shanghai?

The answer came the following day in a terse statement released by the Chinese government:

> Shanghai — Mr. Kip Duchene, an American citizen and General Manager of Shanghai Shores in Pudong, was arrested at 7:55 p.m. today for the premeditated murder of Mr. Milt Avery. The weapon suspected of bludgeoning Avery to death was recovered in Duchene's garage. A detective from the Bureau of Public Security witnessed Duchene threatening Mr. Avery only a few days before the murder occurred.

Chapter 63

Sal was in his family room with Maria and the kids when his cell phone chimed. It was Angie. "Sal, Kip's been arrested!"

"WHAT?"

Her voice began to break. "The po-police arrested Kip as a suspect in Avery's murder."

"That's fuckin' impossible."

Openly sobbing, she said, "You'd better turn on the TV."

"I'll call you back." While Sal reached out to grab the television controller, Maria called out, "What's wrong?"

"It was Angie. She said Kip was arrested for killing Milt Avery."

"Oh, no." She looked at the television as it flicked on.

The words "BREAKING NEWS—AMERICAN EXECUTIVE CHARGED WITH BRUTAL MURDER OF U.S. DIPLOMAT IN SHANGHAI," scrolled across the bottom of the screen. A CNN anchorwoman was saying, "—but the Shanghai government isn't releasing any further details about the arrest."

Sal turned up the volume.

"However, CNN has learned that a government official claimed to have an iron-clad case against Duchene. We have learned through a reliable source that the suspect had sent Avery threatening e-mails over the past several months. A detective of the Shanghai Public Security was reported to have seen Duchene threaten Avery only days before the murder. With Duchene's fingerprints found on the baseball bat used to murder Avery, things don't look good for the American executive."

A photo of an evidence tag tied to a baseball bat was flashed on the TV. Tony cried out, "Daddy, that looks like the bat we played with when we were at Uncle Kip's house!"

The anchorwoman was saying, "—so let's go now to Amy Chang in our Shanghai bureau, standing by at the crime scene."

While Chang was narrating, a video feed showed Kip being led away from his house in handcuffs and looking dazed in front of the bright camera lights. He turned his face away.

Sal flicked the television off, saying to Maria, "I don't want the kids watching this." He headed down the hallway while punching Reggie's number in his phone.

Clips of Kip's arrest aired on every television station in Shanghai.

At the time Avery's body was discovered, the Shanghai government was deeply embarrassed and needed to find a suspect. They pounced on information provided by an anonymous caller to the Shanghai headquarters of Public Security Bureau naming Kip as a suspect. Before Kip was arrested, the decision was made to leak the information to the press. Camera crews were already on the scene at Shanghai Shores when three black sedans screeched to a stop in front of Kip's house.

"I was expecting your call," said the Chairman to Sal. "I'll arrange to get Kip released from jail in the morning. It's a bloody shame that the exchange of money solves almost everything in China, even the bad things. But in this case, it's for the good. It's rubbish to think that Kip killed anyone."

Sal said, "Well, I've known him for the last eleven years and would stake my life on his innocence."

"Sal, old boy, I've got to go and make some calls. I'll talk to you as soon as I know something more."

Within hours of the arrest, Reggie had pulled together his legal teams from Hong Kong and Shanghai to mount an aggressive defense on Kip's behalf. A substantial bribe gave the lead attorney from the Shanghai law firm access to Kip in his holding cell. The two reviewed the government's case against him and discovered how his innocence could be proven without a doubt. At the time the government estimated that Avery died, Kip was meeting with a group of creditors at Shanghai Shores. Statements from the witnesses who attended the meeting were quickly obtained and turned over to the authorities.

At eleven forty-five the next morning, Sal was waiting in the basement garage of the Public Security Bureau to pick up Kip. An hour later, Sal saw Kip emerge from the elevator with two uniformed officers accompanying him. The officers had angry expressions on their faces as they walked up to Sal's car. Kip looked like he'd aged ten years in the last eighteen hours. Ignoring the officers, Sal jumped out of the car and gave Kip a big hug. Still in Sal's clutches, Kip said, "Let's get out of this fucking place."

Sal flashed his classic smile and said, "*Tuchi*, you give me chills when I hear you say 'fucking'."

That afternoon, Sal gave called Kip a call. "How ya doing?"

In a bland voice, Kip said, "I'll survive."

"I want you to know, *Tuchi*, both Maria and I know that you weren't responsible for the kidnapping. If the kids weren't snatched at Shores, they could have been nabbed just as easily somewhere else where the outcome could have been gruesome. We're really lucky that the kids are all okay."

Unconvinced, Kip said, "Thanks." Uncomfortable with the conversation, Kip changed the subject. "How was Xi'an anyway?"

"The trip was absolutely fantastic. I'll tell you all about it when we get together."

By Friday, activities around Shores were starting to return to normal—inwardly, Kip wasn't doing so well. In the aftermath of Marci's death, he had developed an acute sensitivity to witnessing trauma to others. One of his doctors in San Francisco had diagnosed him as having PTSD, Post Traumatic Stress Disorder.

Since the kidnapping, he was having an increasingly difficult time coping with what happened to the kids. He criticized himself for his lapse in judgment for not doing a better job watching after them. He also couldn't remember how many beers he'd drunk that morning. He'd reached bottom of the consequences of his drinking. It was time to stop.

If Rico Niu was ruthless enough to attack Heather and kidnap three innocent children, what else would he be willing to do? He was not in the least bit concerned for his own safety, but he didn't want to see others injured or worse at the hands of a madman. Kip knew that the man was willing to do anything to gain ownership of Shanghai Shoes. He thought—*Will Angie be next*? He decided that it was time for him to resign and go back to San Francisco. Picking up the telephone, he called Sal.

That evening, Sal rang Kip's doorbell while balancing a pizza in the other hand. When Kip opened the door, Sal said, "You better have some fuckin' cold beer in the fridge!"

"Come on in, *Yani*. What's the occasion?"

"What the occasion? I'm about ready to drop this fuckin' pizza on your porch if you don't let me in."

A few minutes later, they were pulling off slices of pizza from the take-home box. Sal was surprised when Kip announced his decision to stop drinking. "Are you serious?"

"Yeah, it's time, don't you think?"

"*Tuchi*, you're doing the right thing."

After finishing off the last slice, Sal looked over at his troubled friend and said, "Okay, you can tell me what's on your mind?"

"Sal, I'm sorry, but it's time for me to resign."

"You already said that on the phone. Are you're fuckin' nuts, *mi amigo*?"

"Look, you asked me to come here to straighten out the mess. From a business perspective, I have. I've weeded out the dead wood and we've ended up with an outstanding management team. We've shaped up the condition of the homes and new leases are on the rise. Cash flow is improving—"

"Whoa! Wait a fuckin' goddamn minute. I know what you've done here without hearing all of this pious bullshit of yours. I agree, the turnaround of Shores is nothing less than a miracle. I know it and Reggie knows it. What the hell happened for you to be thinking crazy like this?"

Kip said, "It was the kidnapping."

"What? Are you blaming yourself for that?"

"I would be hard for anyone in my shoes not to. But, *Yani*, that's not the only reason. I literally collapsed after you and Maria left on Monday. I was pathetic, not the kind of person you need to be managing Shores. In truth, I was probably not ready to come over here in the first place. I'm simply carrying around too much garbage."

Looking intently at Kip, Sal said, "Keep going."

"Well, that's about it. Rico Niu is not going to go away. If he is willing to kidnap three children he will not hesitate to take the next step in his crazed push drive to take over Shanghai Shores. Despite the financial loss to Ingram Capital, I think Reggie should consider giving up the development. Is its success more important than others getting hurt or even murdered?"

Sal sat back in his chair. "I agree with you."

Kip looked at Sal with a surprised look on his face. "You do?"

"Absoluta-fucking-mente! I couldn't agree with you more. No amount of business is worth someone getting killed. But I want you to see if you can follow me beyond that thought. Kip, I'm Mexican. Someone took my precious children away from me and Maria. Those kids are going to relive their terrifying night tied up in that filthy room over and over again—maybe for the rest of their lives. Someday, I suspect that they'll eventually hear about that gruesome surgical setup in the room next to theirs, and what could have happened to them. I'm their father who is bound by deeply-seeded tradition to seek revenge for what they did to my children. I will not rest until that happens. And believe me, it will."

Sal's voice started to break down with emotion. "I am your brother, *Tuchi*, and I really do understand why you've had enough. I think I understand what happened to you after Marci died better than anyone else. But I'll never really know what it did to you. No one will. Despite that, I will not quit and go back to the States with my tail between my legs. I cannot allow Niu and his fuckin' goons to beat up on Heather without paying the price. I cannot allow them to kidnap my children and go unpunished. And before I die, I will not allow that freak with the bent ear to molest Lara and get away with it without killing him first."

Kip snapped his head up. *"What?"*

"Maria made me promise not to tell you that. But fuck it! And, *Tuchi*, you can never say anything about this to anyone."

Visibly shaken, Kip said, "I won't. Christ, what happened?"

"Lara told Maria in private that the ugly one tried to fondle her on three occasions. After the kids were given blankets at night, he slipped his hands under the blanket and stroked her legs. Tony yelled so fuckin' loud the other men came up and yanked the ugly fucker away from her."

"My God, I never knew!"

"As far as anyone else is concerned, you still don't know. Anyway, I'm going to find a way to destroy Rico Niu and his thugs—it's my solemn duty to my family. You have to do what you have to do. But please know this. If I ever needed your help, it's now. Fuck Shanghai Shores—this is a personal matter—this is family."

Kip said nothing while he tried to absorb what Sal had just said. Then quietly, he said, "Okay, *Yani*, I'll at least think about it. Until you hear from me otherwise, I'm here."

"I'm grateful, *mi amigo*." Sal took a quick glance at his watch and stood. "I have to get back home. With the kidnapping, I need to stay close to Maria and the kids."

Chapter 64

Heather returned to Shanghai from her Thanksgiving break refreshed and determined as ever to close more leases. Once she unpacked, she called Angie to learn more about the kidnapping and Avery's murder. Both incidences were big news in the States. When they got together Angie suggested that Heather not bring the kidnapping up with Kip. She also gave her details of Milt Avery's murder that had been withheld from the news media.

Heather asked, "How did you know all that?"

Angie reached over and patted Heather's arm. "I'm Chinese, dear." She wrapped up by telling Heather about Kip firing Priscilla and Naomi and the removal of the listening devices.

Heather just sat there slowly shaking her head. "It looks like I missed all the fun."

Angie said, "Watching Kip handle the whole thing, I can now better understand why he was considered such a star in the U.S."

In the office, Kip received a call from Sal. "Say, I forgot to tell you the other night. My parents are coming over for the Christmas holidays. They'll arrive on December 20th."

Kip said, "That's wonderful news. I look forward to seeing them."

As soon as he hung up, his phone rang. It was Mohammed calling from Dubai. His group was flying in and interested in meeting at Shores with Kip the following day. Kip asked, "What time did you have in mind?"

"How about two o'clock?"

"That's good. See you then."

Kip was scheduled to meet with one of the more difficult creditors that afternoon. Bev told Kip that the man was in the sand and gravel business. At three o'clock, Kip, Angie and Bev walked into the conference room where three men and a woman were already seated. Kip walked directly up to the group, allowing Bev to make the introductions. The sand and gravel guy looked like he could have come from the Jersey docks. He was beefy with stubby fingers the size of sausages.

Bev said, "Kip, this is Mr. Wang."

As he reached out to shake Mr. Wang's hand, Kip had a feeling that the man was going to give him a bone-crushing grip. Sure enough, Mr. Wang tried to bear down on his grip. As Kip responded in kind, the man's eyes widened. Kip gave him his best smile, walked around to the other side of the table and sat down directly across from him. Kip thought—*Voila, round one for our side*.

Mr. Wang immediately launched into a tirade, yelling something Kip obviously couldn't understand. Once the man ran out of steam, Bev turned to Kip and translated. "Mr. Wang said that Shores had cheated him and that he was losing everything. He said that his workers were demanding back pay before Spring Festival and that if they didn't get it, they would come down to the front gate at Shores and cause trouble."

Hearing Bev's translation, Kip looked at the men on the other side of the table. The other two men looked just as rough around the edges as Mr. Wang. All three men had long fingernails on their baby fingers. Kip would have to remind himself to ask Angie what that meant. To him, it looked rather silly.

Kip addressed Wang, with Bev translating, "*You* are the only one in the world who could help yourself get paid. I'm sorry that you haven't been paid on time and for the problems it's caused your family and workers. The money to pay you can only come from the coffers of Shores, nowhere else. Since the company is starting to do much better, you can expect to start receiving payments soon."

Waiting for Bev to get caught up with the translation, Kip ended by saying, "You have an important decision to make. You can either work cooperatively with me, or not. Yelling or protesting at the front gate won't produce anything for you. However, through cooperation, I promise to help you get paid as soon as possible. If you agree to this approach, then I'll pay 100,000 Yuan right now as a token of my good faith. I also want to invite you to check in with me personally at any time."

Even though Wang looked confused by Kip's unexpected response, he reluctantly agreed to take the money and check back later.

He lumbered out of the room with his cohorts trailing behind. Bev smiled at Kip and said, "Boy, Mr. Wang has never behaved so well. You must have used magic in dealing with these kinds of bullies."

"Well, that's just it. He's a bully and bullies don't tend to pick on guys bigger than they are. I allowed him to blow off pent-up steam, acknowledged his problem, and at least provided him with a solution. After he gets back home and starts thinking about what just happened, I'll bet that he'll change his mind and boil over again. In the meantime, we've bought ourselves a little needed time—exactly what we need in order to manage our creditors."

"It was still something to see."

"Bev, go ahead and coordinate meetings with the other two problem creditors. I'd like to get them out of the way before the end of the week, okay?"

"Will do. Thanks for getting personally involved with a creditor. It's never happened before."

"My pleasure. Say, I've got a question for you."

"Sure."

"What does it mean when a Chinese man grows a long fingernail?"

Bev laughed, "One of two possible reasons: First, it's a way for a man to show that he doesn't do manual labor. You see, it's not possible to do so without breaking fingernails. I don't want to sound crude, but the other reason would be to conveniently pick his nose."

Chuckling, he said, "Well, in that case, I think I'll let my nails grow."

The next morning Kip suggested to Angie and Heather that they meet with the three Saudis in the restaurant as before. When they arrived, they were impeccably dressed and exuded gentlemanly sophistication. Mohammed said, "Our team of people is working out a feasibility plan for a Palm Island off the Shanghai coast and will wrap up the study by March 2006. Also, when we visited the last time, we liked the estate home on Lot 132 and would like to discuss leasing it."

Heather said, "Let's see, that would be the unit furthest away from the clubhouse that has a lease rate of $15,000 per month."

All three of them looked at each other and smiled. Mohammed said, "Yes, we understand the price. It's not a problem. We need to make sure that we can use the house as both an office and a residence. Would that be a problem?"

Heather said, "Would you intend to have much traffic visiting you there?"

"No, no, just to the contrary. We really do not want our clients coming out here to see us at all. We have an office in downtown Shanghai for that. But, much of our work involves being on the computer and Internet without needing the support of an office with staff. We may occasionally use our place to entertain, but I don't expect that would be any more frequent than others at Shores."

Turning to Kip, Heather asked, "Kip, what do you think?"

"We would be honored to have you as residents of Shanghai Shores. In the event we decide to proceed with a joint effort on the island project, all the better."

Mohammed said, "Thank you."

Kip went on, "Besides, there's a nice unobstructed view of the East from your place."

Mohammed looked at Kip, quietly acknowledging his meaning with a polite nod.

Later that afternoon, Heather came up to Kip's office. "Do you have a minute?"

Kip said, "Sure."

"Well, the Saudis signed a letter of intent for leasing the house and didn't even try to push for a discount. Bev and I will work on a draft contract and have it in front of you sometime tomorrow. The Saudis asked to execute the lease agreement before they fly back to Abu Dhabi on Friday."

Kip smiled and said, "Congratulations!"

Heather used the Christmas holiday lull to go back home to California for a break. She had good reason to celebrate. Besides the Saudis deal, she had brought the total number of leases from thirty-five up to forty-nine. That was a good start.

When Sal invited Kip over for a Christmas Eve dinner, he said that Maria insisted he bring Angie.

Chapter 65

Mr. Zeng helped Kip load the trunk with Christmas presents for Sal's family. On the drive over to Angie's place Kip thought about how well things were going at Shores. If only Rico Niu would go away.

Kip stepped out of the car and got goose bumps the moment he set eyes on Angie. Her glossy black hair was fixed in looping swags and fastened in back with two crossed wooden sticks. She wore a long black coat, open in front, revealing a dazzling brocade black dress. He said, "Wow, you look scrumptious!"

Smiling, she said, "Is that good or bad?"

He blushed. "It's meant to be a compliment."

"In that case, thank you."

As soon as the Buick pulled in front of Sal's house, his three children bounded out of the house and down the walkway. Kip smiled, seeing Tony stare at Angie. Lara gushed, "Oh, you look so beautiful!"

Sal walked down from the porch and joined the kids in greeting his guests. "*Hay, carumba! Que bonita!*" he said to Angie.

"Sal, you behave yourself!" called Sal's mother as she walked down from the porch. She approached Kip and said, "*Pobrecito*, your face is happy but you're still too skinny." She gave him a comforting hug and whispered, "*Hijo*, I've been worrying so much about you that I've had to say some special prayers at Saint Malachy Church."

Then she turned to Angie and said, "And who is this precious lady you brought with you?"

Kip said, "Mama Estrada, I would like to introduce you to Miss Angie Li."

Graciously extending her hand, Angie said, "Mrs. Estrada, I am so happy to meet you."

Sal's mom ignored her hand and gave her a full, embracing hug, "Oh, child, you're so beautiful but too skinny, like Kip. We'll have to do something about it."

In China, daughters are rarely embraced by their mothers. But Angie definitely enjoyed the warm hug she got from Sal's mother.

Sal piped up, "Okay, Mama, it's my turn."

She laughed. "Mind your manners, *Hijo.*"

Kip leaned towards Sal and whispered, "See, your mama said for you to behave."

"Be careful, *Tuchi*, or you won't get any of my Gran Patron."

Maria was waiting for them in the foyer and greeted Angie with another hug. She asked Angie how she was holding up to the flurry of attention.

"Gosh, I'm loving it!"

"Good. Let me introduce you to Sal's father," said Maria. "He's in the family room watching TV."

Mr. Estrada was sitting quietly in a recliner content to avoid the family commotion by watching TV by himself and sipping tequila. As soon as he saw Maria walking toward him with a beautiful Chinese woman, he smiled and slowly stood up. Even though he spoke some English, Maria chose to use Spanish, knowing it was much easier for him to understand. After Maria introduced Angie, he held his hand out to shake hers and said, "Nice to meet you, Miss *Angelita*."

"Nice to meet you, Mr. Estrada."

Angie liked the way Mr. Estrada said her name.

Walking back down the hall with Angie, Maria explained, "In Spanish, 'ita' is added to the end of a name as an expression of endearment."

While the kids cajoled Angie into coming up to see their rooms, Kip and Sal brought the presents in from the car and arranged them under the Christmas tree. "*Tuchi*, you shouldn't have done all this. The kids have plenty of presents as it is."

"Well, they're from both Angie and me."

"Thanks, *hermano*."

Angie offered to help in the kitchen but was shooed out and told to enjoy herself with Kip and Sal. Just as Angie was sitting down next to Kip on the sofa, the kids raced back down the stairs. As they walked over to the couple, Lara held out gift-wrapped package and handed it to Kip. "This is from the three of us."

Kip handed it to Angie. "You open it."

She pulled off the wrapping and saw that it was a handmade photo album. "Oh, how sweet."

Leaning over, Kip said, "Let me see."

On the front cover, there was a photo of Kip and Angie behind a cut-out heart. They were leaning on the boardwalk rail looking out to sea. Kip turned to Lara and said, "It's a wonderful photo, but I don't remember you taking it."

She said, "I took a lot of photos when you weren't looking."

Angie said, "Lara, they're darling."

The next photo was of the five of them sitting together at Cucina's Restaurant. Kip and Angie were seated in front and the girls were standing in back on each side of Tony. He was smiling giving the "V" sign with both hands, one sticking behind Kip's head and the other behind Angie. There was a flash reflection in the window behind them but the photo was still cute.

The following snapshots showed the pillow fight, the kids eating hot fudge Sundaes, and Manny and Hans dancing together in the clubhouse. After they finished flipping through all the photos, Angie said, "You kids are wonderful. Thank you for putting together such a sweet photo album. I will cherish it forever."

Lara said, "What about Uncle Kip?"

"Well, he can come over to look at it anytime he wants."

"Oh . . . okay!"

Just then, the maid appeared and said, "Miss Maria said that dinner is ready."

At the end of the evening, Kip and Angie excused themselves by saying that it was getting late. It took ten minutes for all of their hugs and goodbyes.

As the Buick pulled away, Kip said, "Did you enjoy yourself?"

"I really did. Thanks. To me, it was truly wonderful."

She then said, "You know, Mexicans are completely opposite from the Chinese in their customs. We don't touch, but they're all over each other with hugs and kisses. We keep much of our feelings to ourselves. They can't wait to find an excuse to tell you how much they love you. By the time the evening was over, everyone but Mr. Estrada had told me they loved me. And surprisingly, I think that they all meant it. We are generally quiet by nature. They're loud. We're reserved. They're passionate."

During the ride over to Angie's apartment, Kip had mixed feelings. It was his second Christmas without Marci and he left with a gnawing ache in his chest. Yet, having Angie by his side was comforting. Several times at Sal's, he found himself glancing across the room at her and hearing her joyful laughter or his whispering conspiratorially into Tony's ear.

Rounding the last corner before Angie's place, he could feel the heat of her body close to him. When he looked at her, she smiled warmly and her dark eyes glistening. She said, "Thank you again for a wonderful evening."

"Well, you were certainly a hit with the Estradas."

Kip escorted Angie to the entrance of her building. Awkwardly, he gave her a gentle hug and a kiss on the cheek. "Merry Christmas, Angie."

She said, "Merry Christmas to you, Mr. Duchene."

Kip mistakenly thought that he had to get a good night's sleep that night. But he didn't. He laid wide awake much of the night thinking about Angie. There was no question that he was torn between his growing affection for her and something that kept him from letting their relationship take its own course. *Maybe I'm feeling guilty if I give my heart to another woman. Jesus, I simply don't know.*

Early the next morning, Angie called Kip on the telephone. "Thanks again for last night."

"Well, I enjoyed it too."

"Kip, the main reason I'm calling is that I'm really getting worried about Rico Niu."

Setting his coffee down, he said, "What about?"

"I've been thinking. Chinese don't typically just walk away from something they really want. You see, they'd lose face. I don't think that Niu has decided to walk away either. I have a gut feeling that we should be prepared for him to strike again now that you've been cleared of the Avery murder. If my hunch is right, he's plotting to do something far more serious against us. I'm mostly worried about you."

"Why's that?"

"Well, you have to admit that his setting you up for killing Avery was brilliant. All the evidence seemed to point to you. You had a motive and the means to kill the man. Niu had every reason to believe that you'd be locked away in some godforsaken Chinese prison for the rest of your life. He thought of everything except the unthinkable. You had a convincing alibi."

Kip said, "I still don't know where you're going with this."

"I have a gut feeling that Niu is planning to have *you* murdered."

Chapter 66

Hans Friedrich sensed that there was a growing attraction between Kip and Angie. He'd also heard about Marci's death from others in the clubhouse lounge. After bringing up the idea with Trudy, she agreed that they invite the pair to a New Year's Eve dinner at the exclusive restaurant, *M on the Bund*. It would be a romantic setting, located on the seventh floor of one of the colonial buildings on the Bund overlooking the Huangpu River.

Kip immediately liked the idea and asked Angie if she'd like to go.

She said, "Oh, yes. That sounds wonderful."

When Kip called Hans back to confirm, he said he'd like for the company to pick up the tab. He asked if he would mind if they invited Jessie and her fiancée. Hans said, "Yes, of course! She works hard enough around Shores to keep two people busy."

Angie called Jessie up to the conference room to meet with Kip.

After tea was poured for the three of them, Kip asked, "Jessie, how do you think you're doing here?"

"What do you mean?"

"Well, how good a job do you think you're doing?"

"Okay, I think."

"Well, you're actually doing an outstanding job."

Jessie broke out with an excited smile. "Thanks."

"How would you and your fiancée like to join a small group of us for a New Year's Eve dinner at *M on the Bund* Friday night for New Year's Eve?"

"Kip, thank you but I can't," she said and glanced nervously at Angie.

Angie smiled and said to Kip, "What she's really saying is that dinner would be too expensive, but she'd love to come."

Jessie whacked Angie on the arm.

Kip said, "Okay, then it's settled. Jessie, this is a company event to thank you for all your hard work. In appreciation, the company will pay your way. It's important to me that you come. Besides, I need to check out your fiancé to see if he measures up."

Jessie giggled, "Oh, I'm so excited. I've dreamed about going to the *M on the Bund* for a long time, but knew that I could never afford it. Thank you so much, boss. I am so grateful."

"Well, you deserve it. Now get out of here."

Kip woke up on New Year's Eve morning and was surprised to see a carpet of snow blanketing the ground. He picked up the phone and dialed Angie's number, "I thought you said that it rarely snowed in Shanghai."

Angie said, "This must be one of those rare times. The last time it snowed here was about eight years ago. Experts blame the air pollution for the unexpected snowfall. Anyway, it must be a good omen. Snow makes everything look beautiful."

That evening, Hans and Trudy were already seated in the restaurant when Kip and Angie arrived. They stood up to greet them. Hans beamed, "You two look like movie stars."

Angie was wearing a full-length black sequined gown that hugged her shapely body. Kip wore an elegant black suit and designer lavender tie with a white silk scarf draped over his shoulders. After everyone hugged, they sat down.

Hans said, "What about starting off with a little Grappa?"

Kip said, "That would be fine for me—probably not for Angie."

"A glass of chardonnay would be perfect," said Angie.

Just then, a smiling Jessie walked up to their table with her fiancée following close behind. She said, "Hello, everybody, this is David Lin."

After another round of greetings, Hans said, "We're ordering drinks. What would you like?"

"Coconut juice, please."

Hans wagged his finger. "No, no, no. That's not an option tonight. I didn't ask if you wanted nourishment, but a drink."

"Well, Mr. Friedrich, we're not used to drinking alcohol," said David.

"One drink never hurt anyone. David, please join us have a little Grappa and Jessie, I think a glass of champagne would be okay for you. We need to celebrate tonight."

David and Jessie looked at each other and nodded hesitantly.

As soon as the drinks arrived, Kip held up his glass and said, "This is a toast to you, Jessie, for doing an outstanding job at Shores. We couldn't have accomplished so much without you – cheers!"

Everyone at the table clicked their glasses. Jessie was taken aback by all the attention, but she definitely enjoyed it. She couldn't be talked into having more than one glass of champagne, but David was a good sport and agreed to a second glass of Grappa. By the time he finished it off, his face was bright red.

Noticing this, Kip leaned over to Sal and whispered, "I hope David's not getting sick."

"Relax, *Tuchi*, it's a common reaction over here. Many Asians are allergic to alcohol and react to it by getting red in the face."

"Oh."

Everyone at the table seemed to be having a good time, talking and eating. Kip marveled about how ravishing Angie looked, sitting across from him and occasionally looking over at him with a smile.

It was planned for the six of them to stay until after midnight so they could watch the big New Year's fireworks display from the balcony of the restaurant. A barge on the river would fire off hundreds of rockets. By eleven-forty, they finished dessert and the bill was paid. Kip scooted back his chair and said, "Let's bundle up and head out to the balcony before it gets too crowded."

They slipped into their coats, scarves, and mittens and headed toward elegant French doors leading to the balcony. As soon as they stepped outside, they felt the chilly damp air. At least thirty people were milling around already. Hans saw space at the railing wide enough for the group and motioned for them to follow him.

The view was spectacular. Right below, they could see Zhongshan Road, a wide boulevard that ran parallel with the Huangpu River. The popular boardwalk of the Bund was packed with people waiting for the fireworks. To the left, they could see the Bund curve away with a stream of red taillights on the right and haloed headlights on the left.

Angie turned to Kip and said, "Kip, look how beautiful the old bank buildings are. They're all lit up with white flood lights on the lower floors and the roof structures are bathed in orange light."

He said, "This looks so much different from here than the 56th floor of the Jin Mao Tower."

"Kip, I can't see the tower from here, can you?" asked Angie.

"Yep, it's right over there." Reaching across her shoulder, he pointed across the river. "It's kind of hard to see through the mist."

"Okay, now I can see it. That building with the Aurora sign is so bright it's hard to see what's behind it." While they were gazing across the river, Angie pulled her coat closer to her chest. "Burr, it's colder than I thought out here."

Standing behind her, Kip unbuttoned his overcoat and pulled it around the front of her. They both immediately felt the warmth of their bodies pressed together. Angie turned her head toward him and whispered, "That feels much better."

Hans said, "Okay, you two, that isn't allowed in public."

Trudy turned and said, "You should try it, Hans, I'm cold too."

While she was still facing him, he pulled opened his coat and engulfed her before she could react. So there they were face-to-face with Hans giggling with delight. It was a sight to see since his rotund belly was jiggling the both of them.

Kip laughed. "Now *that's* what's not allowed!"

With only five minutes to go before midnight, the balcony was quickly filling with people. On the boardwalk below there was a throng of revelers waiting to bring in the New Year. Many of them had donned pointed hats with tassels on top, while others wore masks. The noise they were making gradually built to a crescendo of whistles, honks, yells and clacking sounds. Someone in the distance was beating a bongo drum. The staccato sound of firecrackers echoed between the buildings.

Looking at his watch, Hans said, "We're almost there. Just one minute to go."

Pressed up against Angie's backside, Kip felt deliriously happy in the waning moments of 2005.

A chant rippled through the balcony crowd and the street below: "Ten, nine, eight, seven, six, five, four, three, two, one . . . HAPPY NEW YEAR!" Simultaneously, rockets began to soar into the sky and explode above them with blinding flashes, immediately followed with the booming concussions of the bursting charges.

Kip turned Angie around to face him. She looked up in his tear-filled eyes and smiled. "Happy New Year, dear Kip."

"Happy New Year."

When their lips came together, an entirely different kind of fireworks went off.

In the morning, Mr. Zeng picked up Jessie and Angie to take them to Shores to sign in the teachers from the Pudong International Academy. Since it was Sunday, the drive was much quicker than normal. As soon as Angie walked into her office, she called Kip's house. "Hi, just letting you know I'm here."

"Great. I'll be right over."

When he walked into his office, Angie was already there sitting on one of the sofas with a steaming cup of coffee for him.

"How are you feeling after last night?" asked Kip.

"I'm feeling incredibly happy. I thought that Jessie was going to keel over when she saw you wrap your arms around me. With the girls gossiping all of the time, she probably suspected that something was going on anyway. But for her to see it right next to her must have been a real shock."

"Yeah, I saw that too."

"Kip, I hate to change the subject about such a wonderful night, but I think that we may have a problem."

"What's that?"

"On the way in I noticed a couple of cars full of men just outside the main gate. It's my guess that they could be employees of one of our creditors who plan to demonstrate out front. I also think that the timing is suspect, since it's occurring just before the teachers are expected to arrive."

"I'll go out there and see what's happening."

"*No*, you can't! The idea of the protest is to provoke a response. As the *da laoban*, you'll just add fuel to the fire. Besides, this smells like Rico Niu's work. It's not difficult for someone like Niu to recruit migrant workers in Chaoyeng to rough someone up, like you for instance."

Kip's phone rang and he picked up the receiver. "I understand. Yes. Please don't worry. We'll take care of it. Yes, you're welcome to call me at any time."

After hanging up, Kip looked over at Angie. "That was Mr. Gupta and he was not a happy guy. One of the teachers must have gotten here early and complained about the crowd gathering in front. I'll send Rory and Manny out there with their crews. When the demonstrators see those two charging out they'll surely go back home."

Angie said, "That's certainly better than you walking out there alone."

"Angie, are we prepared today for processing so many teachers as new tenants?"

"No problem. Jessie's handling it."

"Okay, then. I better give Rory a call."

Fifteen minutes later, Rory and Manny loaded three pickup trucks full of men which sped off towards the main gate. As soon as trucks skidded to a stop in front, the men jumped to the ground and engaged the demonstrators. Rory plowed straight into the gathering crowd, straight-arming anyone who got in his way. Those on the receiving end of Rory's wrath got knocked to the ground gasping for breath. Manny waded into the fray with a baseball bat, but never had to swing it even once. Just seeing Manny approaching, those in front of him ran in the opposite direction. In less than a minute, the bewildered demonstrators began to disburse, humiliated by the victorious employees cheering behind them.

Rory flipped open his phone. "Hi Kip. Just to let you know the wee problem is solved."

"That might have been interesting to watch."

"It was," said Rory, chuckling. "Actually, Manny was the guy to watch. He was brilliant, mate."

Kip said, "Thanks for handling it, Rory. Please thank Manny for me."

By the end of the day, all twenty-four families had been checked in and given keys to their assigned homes. Before Angie and Jessie left for the day, Kip said, "See you bright and early tomorrow. Today went really well—thank you."

Both women smiled.

As he walked back to his house, Kip was thinking that maybe the worst was over with Niu.

Chapter 67

Monday, January 2, 2006, was a bone-chilling morning in Shanghai. The Chinese were masters at layering their clothes to protect them from the frigid winter winds that swept down from Siberia. The toddlers in Chaoyeng were swaddled in brightly colored pants and jackets. Kip hadn't seen the three old ladies in a month. The blustery weather probably had kept them inside. He made a note to himself to stop by their house later in the week to drop off some gifts for the Spring Festival.

The managers' meeting went particularly well that day. *A good way to start 2006*—thought Kip. Everyone had a good laugh as Rory recounted the skirmish with the demonstrators, adding an extra touch of exaggeration for dramatic effect.

Heather had returned from her holiday break the previous night. Despite looking a little tired, she was energized and ready to get back to work. She told everyone that they were only seven leases short of reaching their goal of having eighty homes occupied. There was a spontaneous outburst of hoorays and applause from the managers. She said, "On the flight back to Shanghai, I made a commitment to myself to try to get all of them leased before Spring Festival."

Kip said, "Outstanding. Anything else?"

Smiling, she said, "No, that's it."

"Well, we missed you, too. You might want to consider taking some time off later today to get caught up on your sleep."

"Do I look that bad?"

Kip chuckled. "No, just tired."

The managers gave reports on their respective departments. With Priscilla and Naomi gone, Shelly looked somewhat lost and didn't have much to say. There was something about her subdued behavior that seemed odd to Kip.

After the meeting ended, Kip asked Heather to stay behind. He waited until everyone had filed out of the room before saying, "How was your holiday break?"

"It was wonderful, thanks. You know, Reggie is big on Christmas. He's like a little kid. We always end up eating too many traditional English dishes like steak and kidney pie, Yorkshire pudding, and mince pies, all of which are guaranteed to clog every artery in your body."

Kip laughed. "Heather, try to get some rest today."

"Can't. I promised to help Angie with the new tenants."

At two o'clock that afternoon, Kip received a disturbing call from Trudy. She'd just got in from a shopping trip and noticed carloads of men pulling up just outside the front gate. He thanked her and hung up.

"Are you out there?" he called to Angie in her office. There was no reply. He then remembered her saying that she and Heather were meeting in the restaurant to help Jessie handle the arriving tenants. Not wanting to bother Angie, he called over to Rory to ask him if he knew what was happening. His phone was busy.

He then called Bev and asked her if she knew what was happening at the front gate. She said, "I'll check and call you right back."

A minute later, she called. "I talked to a guard at the front gate. He thinks it might be Mr. Wang and his crew protesting. Remember, he was the creditor in the sand and gravel business?"

"Oh, yeah, the big guy."

"The same."

"Well, despite his bad humor, we ended up getting along okay. I think I'll run out there and see if I can calm things down."

"Ah, Kip . . . I wouldn't do that. It's too dangerous."

"Not to worry. I'll get Manny and Rory to help."

"It's still not a good idea. Kip, you might—"

"Bev, I'll be careful."

She started to say something more, but Kip had already hung up.

Kip thought about what Bev said and started to get upset. He was furious that Mr. Wang had made a deal with him and now was going back on his promise. After stewing about it for another ten minutes, he picked up the phone, "Hey, Patti, it's Kip."

"Hi, boss!"

"Are you busy right now?"

"Not for you. What can I do?"

"Patti, I think that one of our creditors is about to demonstrate at our main gate. I'd like to stop it before it gets started. Angie is tied up and I need someone to help translate for me."

"Okay."

"Meet me in the parking lot."

Mr. Zeng had the minivan waiting at the curb. Patti was already there when Kip walked up. "Okay, let's get this thing over with. Please tell Mr. Zeng what's happening and ask him to drive us to the main gate."

Patti translated what Kip had said. Mr. Zeng's response was unexpected. As he replied to Patti, he never took his eyes off Kip.

"Kip, Mr. Zeng thinks that our going out there is a very bad idea."

"Well, talking shouldn't hurt anyone. Let's go."

Mr. Zeng drove them just inside the main gate and parked the van off to the side. Kip had learned that the Chinese respected people who looked powerful. He was wearing one of his favorite combinations today—a dark blue pin-striped suit, white dress shirt and a colorful Italian silk tie.

While he and Patti were getting out of the van, Zeng reached under the driver's seat and pulled out his Billy club. Kip said to Patti, "Tell Mr. Zeng to put his club away. He won't need it. He should stay here by the van. We shouldn't take long to straighten things out."

The guards wore nervous expressions as the boss and Patti waded into the crowd of demonstrators. At the gate, Mr. Zeng picked up his cell phone and started to talk.

Kip recognized Mr. Wang. He was dressed in a black leather jacket and surrounded by five or six other men. Kip walked right up to him and held out his hand. Wang reluctantly shook it with a surprised look on his face.

"Patti, tell Mr. Wang that I'm pleased to see him again, and ask if there's anything I can do for him."

Kip noticed that Patti's voice was a little shaky during the translation. He thought—*Have I put her in harm's way?*

While Kip and Patti were talking to Mr. Wang, Angie, Heather and Jessie were in the restaurant briefing the newly arrived tenants. When Angie's cell phone rang, she looked at the LED screen and saw it displaying Shelly's name. "Hi Shelly, what's up?"

"Angie, I'm afraid I did a stupid . . ." She couldn't finish and started to cry.

"Shelly, what's wrong?" Angie pressed the phone closer to her ear.

Shelly tried to stop crying but could only get out a guttural moan.

"Shelly, please calm down and tell me what's happening!"

Sobbing, she said, "Angie, I'm so sorry. Priscilla told me that Rico Niu made arrangements to pay a lot of money to Mr. Wang to make a big scene out front and rough up our staff. I think he offered a big bonus if they hurt Kip."

Angie said, "Don't worry, Kip's okay. He's up in his office."

"No he's not! I just got a call from Mr. Zeng. He told me that Kip and Patti are out in front right now. Kip's trying to reason with Mr. Wang. I think that Mr. Zeng is very worried."

Angie gripped the phone. "Shelly, listen to me and do exactly what I say. Call the police right now and get some help out here."

After she hung, Angie called Manny and then Rory. She told them to get their crews back to the front gate as fast as possible.

Overhearing the telephone conversation, Heather said, "Angie, what's wrong?"

"Niu paid Wang and his men to hurt Kip and they're out at the front gate right now. I've got to stop them." Angie bolted toward the door. Heather and Jessie ran after her.

Mr. Wang acted confused. The boss of Shores was standing in front of him wearing fancy clothes and smiling. Rico Niu told him that Kip would be hostile, but he wasn't. With his men standing all around, Wang could not look weak and lose face so he started yelling at Kip.

Kip was surprised by Wang's sudden outburst. He looked over at Patti and saw that she was frightened. "Patti, listen carefully to me. Walk over to the gate. Once you're safely inside, call Manny or Rory and tell them I need help out here."

With tears running down her cheeks, she said, "What about—"

Pointing to the front gate, he said, "Patti, you can't help me. Get going!"

As she started to walk away, one of the thugs grabbed her arm. Filled with rage, Kip flew over to the man and cold cocked him on the side of his face and then pushed Patti toward the front gate. "RUN!"

Chapter 68

The men surrounding Kip started to shove against him. Taller and stronger, Kip was able to fend them off without any punches being exchanged. He stole a glance at the main gate and was relieved to see that Patti had made it through safely. He also saw Mr. Zeng running past her and heading directly towards him. Zeng was swinging his Billy club and screaming something in Chinese. Along the way, several men made the mistake of trying to block him but were savagely knocked to the ground with painful blows from his club. When he reached Kip, they both instinctively backed up to a parked car for protection. Down the street, local villagers were pouring out of their homes and weaving their way through the mob to help the two men.

The stand-off between Kip and Zeng and the demonstrators surrounding them was broken when one of them threw a punch at Kip. It missed his head by inches, but caused a flurry of punches to unleash from both sides. Mr. Zeng swung his Billy club with blinding accuracy. The demonstrators who inched their way too close to the two men were greeted with vicious blows. But as Kip and Mr. Zeng started to tire from the onslaught, more and more punches were getting through to them. Their faces were beginning to resemble those of boxers in the tenth round of a fight—swollen and bloody.

Patti and Angie were running in opposite directions and almost collided near the main gate. Patti yelled to Angie, "You can't go out there. Some of the men have shovels and picks!"

As Patti was pleading with Angie, four truckloads of men, along with Manny and Rory, roared past them and out through the gate. In the street, the altercation had escalated into a full-blown riot. The villagers were beginning to disburse the crowd on the far side, but had not yet reached the besieged Kip and Mr. Zeng. By then, the two men had their backs pressed up against the car and were fighting for their lives. Striking out and fueled with pure adrenalin, they'd managed to fend off the mob from overpowering them.

Out of eyesight of Kip and Mr. Zeng, two of the hired thugs climbed on top of the car from the other side. As soon as they stood up, someone handed them shovels. They nodded to each other and swung the shovels in an arc over their heads and down towards their targets. Just before impact, Mr. Zeng saw a blur from above and tried to shield Kip with his free arm.

Kip sensed that Mr. Zeng was lifting his arm. He then heard a surreal shattering sound in his head. Then he was floating downward.

The shovels made loud cracking sounds against the two men's heads. Everyone within earshot froze as Kip and Zeng collapsed.

Kip had a close-up view of the ground a few inches away from his eyes. Dazed, he was curious as to why the colors were fading into black and white. Feeling nothing, he watched as the black and white images gradually faded to total darkness.

Manny and Rory forcefully parted the crowd trying to reach Kip. Looking down at the two fallen men, Rory cried, "Oh, Christ! Manny, call the emergency number and get some ambulances out here."

While Manny called, Rory knelt down to get a better look at Kip's injuries. The sight of Kip's bloody head wounds made Rory almost pass out. He instinctively unfastened Kip's necktie and unbuttoned the top button of his dress shirt. He looked up just in time to see Angie running towards them. Rory stood and forcefully grabbed her. "You don't want to see this!"

Despite his efforts, she managed to get a glimpse of Kip and immediately vomited down the front of Rory's shirt.

He yelled to his workers, "Get her out of here!"

The men lifted Angie up off the ground while she kicked and screamed all the way back to the front gate. She cried, "He's dead, isn't he?"

At the front gate, Patti took over and guided Angie into the van beside Jessie. Heather jumped into the front seat and drove them back to the clubhouse. All four women were sobbing and in shock. In the distance, they heard the sound of sirens.

With calm thinking, Heather made the decision to set up a central meeting place in the restaurant. When they drove up to the curb of the clubhouse, eight staff members, including Bev, were there to assist. Jessie yelled, "Clear the tenants out of the restaurant!"

Angie's face was ashen and she had splotches of Kip's blood on her blouse from when Rory had pulled her away. The group made their way through the lobby and into the restaurant. Bev pulled out her phone and placed a call. "Shelly, we're in the restaurant. Kip is hurt badly. Do you have any special instructions for Kip in case of emergency?"

In the meantime, four ambulances were making their way through Chaoyeng to the scene. The troublemakers were starting to run off in different directions. The three old women had organized the village people to bring blankets and pieces of cloth to dress the wounds of those injured.

Noticing that Kip had stopped breathing, Rory knelt over him and started mouth-to-mouth resuscitation.

The first ambulance had to blast its air horn to get gawking bystanders to step out of its path. Then it drove up alongside Kip and Mr. Zeng where the attendants jumped out and took over for Rory. Within a few minutes, they'd inserted an endotracheal tube down Kip's throat, started an

IV, lifted him into the ambulance, and sped back down the road with their siren blaring and emergency lights flashing. Attendants from the second ambulance were working on Mr. Zeng.

Only then did Rory bring his hands to his face and break down crying. Not a stranger to violence from his childhood days in Uganda, Manny quietly walked over to Rory and put his arms around him. He didn't say a word or shed a tear. He just held the big man and let him cry.

Chapter 69

Shelly ran into the restaurant with a folder in her hand and offered it to Bev. "Kip gave me this on his first day. I don't understand everything but I remember him saying that if he were ever seriously hurt, he's to be flown back to the United States by air evacuation."

Focused on what to do next, Bev scanned the information quickly and picked up the phone. After talking for ten minutes, she said to the group, "The medivac company just flew a terminally-ill patient back home on Cheju Island in Korea. They were refueling the plane and scheduled to take off in just a few minutes from now. The lady said that Cheju is less than an hour's flying time to Pudong International Airport. They'll make arrangements to divert the plane and file a new flight plan for Shanghai as soon as they hear back from us."

Bev said to Shelly, "Please call the hospital and give them this information." She slid her notes over to her. "If Kip is still alive, they'll need to stabilize him enough for the flight."

Shelly ran out of the room with the information in hand.

Angie whispered, "I want to go to the hospital. I should be with Kip."

Heather said, "Sweetie, you'll be more of a help to Kip right here. There are lots of arrangements that need to be made. Kip is in good hands—you'd only be in the way."

Angie nodded without comment.

Five minutes later Shelly came back in and said, "The hospital spokesperson said that Kip is in very serious condition with a traumatic brain injury. The neurosurgeon, Dr. Liang, refuses to release him for air transport."

Heather said, "I'm surprised they even gave you that much information."

"Being manager of HR, they assumed it was appropriate."

Angie bolted upright and ran out of the restaurant and up to her office. Heather followed. Angie pulled out a file out of a cabinet and grabbed the phone. When someone answered, she said, "Dr. Duchene? This is Angie Li at Shanghai Shores. I'm sorry to call you so early in the morning but I have some very bad news."

With a catch in his voice, he asked, "What happened?"

"Your son was involved in a serious accident. He had a head injury." She could feel herself start to break down—*I have to be strong.*

"Oh my god, how bad is it?" said Dr. Duchene.

"I think it's pretty bad. When Kip first got here, he left instructions that if anything serious ever happened to him, he was to be air evacuated back to the States. We learned that an evacuation jet could be here in one hour but the hospital refuses to release him because of his brain injury."

"I understand."

"Can you do anything to help?"

"I'll take care of it. Give me their number and the name of the attending physician."

After writing down the information, he said, "Angie, what is your number so I can call you back?"

She gave it and said, "Thank you."

In the unlikely chance that the hospital agreed to release Kip, Shelly called the office of immigration to explain what happened and pre-arrange his return.

When Angie and Heather walked back into the restaurant, Shelly briefed them.

"Oh, Shelly, that's great," said Angie.

Shelly said, "Do you know where he keeps his passport? He'll need it to leave the country."

"Yes!" Angie again ran out of the room and over to Kip's house. She unlocked the front door and ran to his study. She found the desk key on the top shelf of the bookcase where he hid it and unlocked his desk drawer. She pulled out his travel wallet that held his passport and other essential papers.

Back in the restaurant, Angie handed the travel wallet to Shelly. Shelly said, "Bev, can you drive me over to the airport? If the hospital decides to release Kip, I want the immigration officials to have everything already processed so there's no delay."

Bev jumped up and said, "Let's go."

After Bev and Shelly left, Angie said to Heather, "I feel a little weak. Can we go over to Kip's place?"

Heather said, "That's a great idea. Let's just have everyone meet over there. It's more private than the restaurant."

The group gathered in the family room with Angie bundled up in a blanket on the sofa. She said, "If anyone would like to stay over, Kip has five bedrooms."

Jessie and Patti volunteered to do so. Angie said, "I think that Bev will want to as well."

Patti went into the kitchen and put on some water for tea. Manny had quietly walked in but didn't know what to do. So he sat off to the side and thought about the terrible scene he'd witnessed. He just wanted to be there in case he could help with anything.

Heather asked Angie, "How about a spot of tea?"

"Thank you. You know, I keep thinking that we're forgetting to do something."

Heather said, "Has Sal been called?"

"That's it!"

Heather said she would make the call and walked out of the room.

"THOSE FUCKING BASTARDS!" were Sal's first words. "Where is he now?"

Kent W. Sorensen

Heather calmly gave Sal the information and added, "We're trying to get Kip evacuated back to the States."

"What's the holdup?"

She explained.

"Okay, Heather, find out what needs to be done so that I can be with him on that flight. Then call me back."

"Okay," she said and hung up. Walking back into the family room, Heather said, "Has anyone called his father yet?"

"Yes, I did," said Angie. "He's going to call Dr. Liang at the hospital and try to get Kip released."

"Good."

With blood and vomit caked on his clothes, Rory went to his office where thankfully there was a full bathroom. After showering and changing into clean clothes, he headed over to Kip's house. By the time he walked in, Angie had gone into the bedroom and explained what happened and that she wouldn't be coming home that evening.

Just then Angie's phone rang. "Hello?"

"Angie, this is John Duchene. I've talked to both Dr. Liang and the medivac people. I've agreed to pay for all the costs involved to have Dr. Liang and his personal nurse fly back to the States with Kip. Otherwise, they wouldn't agree to release him. I'll arrange for an ambulance from Stanford Medical Center to pick them up at the airport in San Francisco so they can rush him to the hospital without delay. I think they'll try to take off from Shanghai by 6:00 p.m. which will put them in San Francisco around 3:00 p.m."

"Thank you so much, Dr. Duchene. There are a lot of people here who care about your son. By the way, Sal plans to accompany Kip on the trip."

"That's good to hear. Thank you, Angie. My son has mentioned you and Heather."

"Please call me anytime." *Why would Kip mention Heather?*

"You do the same," he said and hung up.

Angie said, "Heather, please call the medivac company and tell them it's a go. Then call Sal and tell him that it's okay for him to go. It's four-thirty now. He should leave right away for the airport. Tell him the flight is due to leave around six."

Rory had turned on Kip's CD player to fill the quiet void with soothing music.

Sitting together on the couch, Angie turned to Heather and said, "Would you mind filling everyone in on what's happening."

"Sure." Heather stood and called out, "I'd like to give you the latest."

People in the room stopped what they were doing and listened to Heather's announcement. When she said that Kip would be evacuated back home, everyone erupted with cheers. That brought a smile on Angie's face.

Heather's phone rang and she left the room to answer it.

It was Sal. "Heather, I'm here at the airport and just saw Kip. His head is heavily wrapped in bandages and his face looks all puffed up. Don't say anything to the others, particularly Angie, but I heard Dr. Liang say to his nurse about a depressed skull fracture. He also said something about a Glasgow Coma Scale, whatever that means. Anyway, I'll be with Kip every minute. As soon as we get to San Francisco, I'll call you."

She said, "Was he awake?"

"No. By the way, I also called Reggie, just to let you know."

"What did he say?"

"You'd be surprised."

"No, I wouldn't. Thanks again."

"Bye."

Before she had a chance to rejoin the group, the doorbell rang. She opened the door and saw Paul with one of his staff, both holding up trays of food.

"I thought you guys might be hungry."

"God, Paul, you're so sweet."

They set the trays on the kitchen island and pulled off the plastic wrap. Paul said, "We made this up as finger food so it's easier to eat."

Heather said, "Paul, it looks wonderful. Thank you. Would you like to stay?"

"No, I can't. With all of the new tenants, we're really busy over there."

"Okay, I understand."

Paul walked over to Angie and reached out to hold her hand. She smiled, understanding his special ways, and pulled his hand up to press it against her cheek. She noticed tears welling up in his eyes. He smiled awkwardly and headed back out.

Heather asked Jessie if anyone had heard how Mr. Zeng was doing. Jessie said she didn't know.

Chapter 70

Despite the number of times Sal had flown from Shanghai across the International Date Line, he was always amused that the plane landed in San Francisco four hours before it took off.

Kip survived the flight. The doctor and his assistant were awake the whole time, monitoring Kip's condition and replenishing his IV bags. An immigration officer boarded the plane soon after it had taxied to a special area on the tarmac and had shut down its engines. The officer quickly stamped everyone's passports and left. An ambulance was parked just below the stairway.

Kip's father was sitting in the waiting room at Stanford Hospital when they arrived. Sal shook his hand and reported what he knew about Kip's condition. Both men's faces were drawn.

A couple of hours later, a neurosurgeon walked over to them in the waiting room. He said, "I'm Max Renneker." Looking at the two men, he said, "You must be John Duchene, and you, Sal Estrada."

They nodded.

Renneker continued, "Kip must have been hit with great force on the top of his head with a blunt object, which fractured his skull and caused a subdural hematoma. Be assured that Dr. Liang provided Kip with outstanding care both in Shanghai and during the trip. We couldn't have done better. Kip had a CT scan and is being prepped for cranial surgery. I'm guessing that the procedure will take three or four hours."

Kip's father asked, "Dr. Renneker, can you give us a preliminary prognosis?"

"I'll have a better idea after surgery and will talk to you then." The surgeon headed back toward the elevators.

While Kip's father went to get some coffee in the cafeteria, Sal flipped open his phone to call Angie. "Hi, it's Sal."

"How's Kip?"

"We're at Stanford Hospital. They just took him up to surgery. The doctor said that he'll be under for about four hours."

"Sal—how's he *really* doing?"

"It's too early to know. I'll call you again when he's out of surgery."

"Thank you. I know this must be incredibly hard on you."

Feeling himself getting choked up, he quickly said, "Yes, it is. I'll call you when I have something more."

Sal walked back to the waiting room and reflected on his friend's life. When he first met him at Stanford just a few blocks away from where he was sitting now, he'd secretly resented him as the rich kid from Santa Monica. Sal had to work hard for everything he'd accomplished. He assumed that most affluent white guys looked down on Mexicans as being second-rate. He quickly learned that Kip wasn't one of them. Ever since they had become friends, they'd been very close ever since.

Who else in the world would have agreed to fly to the other side of the world to help him solve a business problem less than a year after losing his wife? He knew damn well that Kip's experience and skills far exceeded the job at Shores, yet he came to Shanghai anyway.

Sal then thought about Rico Niu—*I swear that I'll kill the motherfucker with my bare hands*. He'd heard that Niu offered a special reward to anyone who could rough Kip up. Remembering his days on the streets of Tehachapi, he knew he would one day teach Niu what it was like to get roughed up.

He called his mother to let her know about Kip. She told Sal not to worry. He was going to be just fine—just trust her to take care of everything. After he hung up, he knew that she would be grabbing her coat at that very moment and walking down the street to Saint Malachy Church to pray for Kip. She'd told Sal since he was a young boy that she had a direct connection with Jesus. He guessed that his dad would be quietly pouring a glass of tequila as soon as his mom had left the house. He could toast to his own gods and down the drink in one gulp.

Sal had fallen asleep in his chair by the time Dr. Renneker walked back into the waiting room. Feeling a hand on his shoulder, Sal stirred awake. The wall clock indicated that it was 10:35 p.m. Kip's dad was sitting nearby.

Dr. Renneker smiled. "So far, so good. We were mostly worried about the brain swelling and infection. Dr. Liang used a promising new technique for treating post-traumatic head injuries. He applied chilling pads to Kip's body as soon as he was admitted to the hospital in Shanghai and kept them in place until he arrived here. I have a feeling that the process of lowering Kip's body temperature down to 90 degrees had minimized the brain swelling we usually see in these cases. We were fortunate because Kip was in great physical shape and tolerated the anesthesia much better than expected. His vital signs looked good throughout the operation. At this time, I have reason to have guarded optimism about the outcome. In the next twenty-four hours we'll know more."

Sal said, "Is he awake now?"

"No. He will be in an induced coma for several days. After that, we can't rule out post traumatic amnesia. But for now, we'll have someone come down to get you in a few minutes and take you up to ICU. There won't be much to see but I know you'd like to at least stop in."

Twenty minutes later, Sal and Kip's father walked into a cubicle in ICU. Kip was hooked up to a respirator and his head was heavily swathed in gauze bandages. A nurse was bent over him taking his blood pressure.

Sal could feel his emotions quickly percolating up to his throat. He walked around to the side of the bed and took Kip's hand. He was comforted by its warmth. He gave him a momentary squeeze hoping that Kip would somehow sense his presence. After releasing his hand, he nodded to Kip's father and walked out.

In the hospital parking lot, he found the car which had been dropped off by the car rental company. Earlier in the evening, an agent had dropped off the keys and had him sign the contract. While still in the waiting room, he had also booked a room at the Stanford Terrace Inn just down the street from the hospital.

In his room, he looked at his face in the mirror and was aghast at his disheveled appearance. He had a dark, one-day growth of stubble on his face, his hair was matted unnaturally, and his eyes were red and swollen. He decided to get back to Angie. "Hi, Angie, it's Sal."

"Oh, I'm so glad to hear your voice. I'm here with Heather. We've been so nervous waiting for your call."

"Kip came through the operation okay." Sal thought he heard a sigh on the other end of the line. "The surgeon said that he had to open his skull and clean up the injured area. They located the point of bleeding and were able to seal it off. I went up to see Kip after the operation and he seemed to be stable despite looking like an imitation of Frankenstein."

Angie chuckled and then started to cry.

"The doctor said that these kinds of brain injuries are difficult to predict. He said that Kip was in great physical shape. For now, I guess it's just a waiting game."

"Sal, thanks for calling us. You're our only lifeline to knowing what's happening. Please make sure you call if anything changes."

"I will. You know, I have no idea if or when Kip will wake up. If there's any chance that you two could make the trip over here, it might be helpful to his recovery."

"We're way ahead of you and have already picked up all of the paperwork so Angie can apply for a non-immigration visa with the US Consulate."

"Sounds great. What time is it there anyway?

"About 2:00 p.m."

"Okay, I'll talk to you soon."

Next he called Maria and told her the news. She was glad that Kip was stable and that Sal was in a position to help. After he signed off with Maria, he called his mother. "Mama, your special prayers are working. Kip made it through the operation to the surprise of the entire medical staff."

"*Hijo*, I told you not to worry. Now go to sleep. Kip's going to need your strength in the days ahead."

After hanging up, Sal slipped the "Do Not Disturb" sign on the front of his door handle, undressed, and tumbled into the inviting bed. He instantly fell into a deep sleep.

Despite Angie's previous trips to the Unites States, the US Consulate summarily turned her visa application down, citing that she was a single Chinese woman trying to go to the States. In the post-911 era, it simply wasn't allowed. Besides, being disheartened at the news, she was also frustrated that Heather would be with Kip while she was stuck in Shanghai. She ignored the fact that Heather's house in Atherton was only fifteen minutes away from the hospital, making it practical for her to visit.

After spending three days floating in a warm dark abyss, Kip heard voices from somewhere on the other side, but he couldn't figure out where the other side was. In the next instant, he slipped back into nothingness.

Chapter 71

Once Dr. Renneker reduced the dosage of sedatives, Kip showed signs of coming out of the medically-induced coma. The critical period for Kip's brain to swell had ended and he was reacting to physical stimuli more readily.

He began to feel himself floating up from a dark void. Voices were coming through an invisible barrier a little louder. He could barely make out some of the words. For the first time, he started to feel parts of his body change from being suspended in space to having sensations of pressure. The more he concentrated, the clearer the voices became. He even felt someone squeeze his hand. From somewhere deep in his mind, he flashed back to holding Marci's hand. Then he saw her face. He had to struggle out of the void so he could hold her again. She didn't die after all. It must have been a bad dream.

He could hear her say, "Kip, I can feel you squeezing my hand."

He strained to squeeze her hand as hard as he could.

Earlier that morning, Heather had been nervous about how Kip would look when she saw him for the first time. When she walked into his room, she thought that the man lying unconscious in bed couldn't be Kip. His face was puffy and had two black eyes. But the longer she stared at the man, the more she began to recognize him. Feeling emotional, she pulled up a chair beside the bed and held his hand. After about fifteen minutes, she thought she felt him squeeze her hand.

"Kip, I can feel you squeezing my hand. Please come back. I can feel you. Please open your eyes!"

This time, Kip could clearly hear Marci's voice. He knew he was getting closer.

Heather was excited when she saw him move his head and heard him moan something unintelligible.

"Kip, you're almost back here. I'm just a little further. Please keep trying." She could see back-and-forth movements behind his closed eyelids.

He clearly heard Marci talking. Now he could feel the warmth of her hand in his. He concentrated all of his might and tried to open his eyes. There! He saw a slit of light.

Seeing his eyes flicker for a moment, Heather couldn't stop the tears from flowing down her cheeks. "Kip, listen to me. You're only just one more step away. I'm right here. Just one more step."

Kip could hear Marci as if she was right beside him in the void. He had to make one more push to reach her. Focusing on opening his eyes again, he mentally tried to pry his eyelids open from the slit of light to see more. Sure enough, the light was getting brighter and starting to fill in with vague shapes. His vision was flooded with beautiful light. Then he saw faint splashes of color. He saw Marci's face smiling just above him. She had a halo around her golden hair. She was wiping tears off her cheeks.

He said, "Hi, Marci."

As soon as the words were out of his mouth, he slipped back into the warm void of darkness and his eyes closed.

Heather pushed the call button. A red-headed nurse rushed into the room. "Do you need something?" Seeing Heather's tears, she added, "Is something wrong, dear?"

"I don't think so. He opened his eyes and said something."

"That's wonderful news. I'll notify Dr. Renneker."

That evening, Heather called Angie and told her the good news. She didn't see any reason to mention that Kip had called her Marci.

Hearing about Kip's progress, Angie broke down and sobbed with joy. Yet, she was uncomfortable that Heather had Kip all to herself while she was stuck in Shanghai. The two women talked back and forth for a while and ended with Heather assuring her that she would try to visit Kip for the remaining five days before returning to Shanghai.

At ten o'clock the next morning Heather walked back into the surgical ward. Looking at Kip, she saw more life in his face, even though he was asleep. She couldn't explain it to herself, but she sensed a change had occurred. She slid a chair over to his bedside and held his hand. "Kip, I'm back."

He heard her clearly and felt her holding his hand.

Opening his eyes, he looked over and said, "Marci?"

"Welcome back, Kip."

"You look different."

"Kip, it's Heather."

Kip could now look around the room and focus. The woman sitting by him was beautiful. She looked incredibly like Marci. "I'm sorry. I thought you were someone else."

"It doesn't matter. It's wonderful to see that you're awake."

"Where am I and why am I in bed?"

"You're at Stanford Medical Center."

"Oh. Where's Marci?"

Heather swallowed. "I don't know."

"Where's Sal?"

"He'll be here this afternoon."

"Why do I have a bandage around my head?"

"You'll have to ask your doctor."

Kip looked more closely at Heather. "Did we ever date?"

"Sort of."

"Did we . . . ?"

"Not really."

"Was it me?" He smiled for the first time.

Heather smiled back. "Not a chance."

Dr. Renneker walked in. "It looks like my favorite patient has decided to rejoin the human race."

"Sure have. When can I get out of here?"

Heather pulled on the doctor's sleeve and whispered, "He doesn't recognize me. I'm worried."

"Post traumatic amnesia is quite common in these kinds of cases. I don't think there's anything to worry about."

She motioned with her hand, "Thanks. I'll wait outside while you're talking with him."

Fifteen minutes later, Dr. Renneker walked out of room and said to Heather, "Please take a seat."

He sat next to her. "First of all, Kip's doing great, much better than I expected. His speech pattern is quite remarkable. I didn't recognize any slurring of words and that pleases me. Frankly, I was worried. He hasn't experienced any seizures and the pupils of his eyes are reacting evenly to light—all very good signs. His head wound is healing nicely, no apparent infection. Now that he's regaining consciousness, we can get him started with physical therapy. He's going to be stiff and sore for a while after lying in bed for the past four days.

"He's retained long-term memory but it seems as though much of the last ten years is out of his reach. Brain injuries are unpredictable. Right now, I see nothing out of the ordinary that concerns me. He knows who he is and he remembers everything up to the time he attended Stanford."

"But he confused me with his deceased wife, Marci."

"Who's Marci?" the doctor asked.

"He married Marci in 2001, eight years *after* he attended Stanford. She died in a terrible car accident a little over a year ago. It really devastated him at the time. Anyway, I understand that she looked a lot like me. When Kip was first coming out of the coma, he thought I was Marci."

"That's even more encouraging news to me. For now, the best thing is not to worry about Kip's memory. He shouldn't have to be put under the stress of knowing that he's forgotten a portion of his life. We'll just take it a day at a time and accept what comes."

"How long will he have amnesia?"

"I can't say. It could clear up in a few days or it may take weeks. It's remotely possible that his amnesia will keep him from ever remembering any more than he knows right now. You see, the brain is a very delicate organ. When it gets jarred around in the cranial cavity, brain cells inevitably die."

"Did you tell him what happened?"

"No. I think it's best that Sal talks to him about the assault."

Heather smiled. "Kip's fortunate to have such outstanding care. Thank you."

When she left the hospital, Heather worried that Kip might never regain any memory of his days in Shanghai.

Chapter 72

Later that afternoon, Heather placed a call to Angie. "Hi, sweetie, how are you doing?"

"I'm so happy that Kip isn't going to die and he's starting to wake up."

"Angie, the good news is that he looks great and sounds great. The doctors here think Kip is a miracle patient and should be able to return to a relatively normal life."

"The bad news?"

"He has post traumatic amnesia."

"What does that mean?

"Because of his head injury, he doesn't remember anything past his college days."

"Oh . . . Do you mean that he can't remember me?"

"I'm sorry. I spent a couple of hours talking with him today. He's charming and nice. But he doesn't know who I am either."

Heather could hear Angie softly weeping on the other side of the line.

Heather went on. "The doctor told me that amnesia typically eases or completely goes away for most patients who have experienced the same kind of trauma as Kip. He said that we should be patient and take each day at a time."

"I wish I could be there. Of all times, the U.S Government decides to tighten up on their immigration policies now. It's simply crazy that they take 9/11 out on China of all countries. When I go to the U.S. Shanghai Consulate for an interview, they see a young Chinese woman who is unmarried and their eyes glaze over. I know they're thinking—*No way, lady.*"

After they hung up, Angie sat there for a minute thinking that she may be losing Kip to Heather. *It should have been me at Kip's side, not her*.

Sal told Kip the details of what had happened to him in Shanghai. Kip had no recollection of the riot, of Shanghai Shores, or of ever being in China. Looking down at Kip, Sal said, "*Que estaś hacienda, cabroń?*"

Kip said, "I'm fine, *Yani*. I'm ready to rock-and-roll. It's time to get out of here. But the doctor said no."

"Hey, just rest up. You'll be out of here in no time at all."

Sal arranged to work out of the San Francisco office for a couple of weeks while Kip was recovering.

Heather continued to stop by the hospital every day while she was in town. She saw remarkable progress in Kip as each day passed. Their unique experience in the hospital room had given them a curious sense of intimacy and familiarity. On the fifth day, he shocked her by asking if she'd be interested in slipping under the sheets with him.

"God, what kind of a playboy *are* you?"

He gave her one of his killer smiles and said, "Just kidding. You know, there's something in the back of my mind about you."

"What's that?"

"I don't know. I see an image of us holding hands and looking out at an ocean."

"Keep that up, big guy. You're getting warm. By the way, I'm heading out of town tomorrow."

"For good?"

Smiling, she said, "I do have a job, you know."

She let him hold her hand, knowing that it felt good for him—and it certainly did for her. For the past week, she had leaned over and kissed him on the cheek when she left for the day. She felt strange knowing him so well while still realizing that he couldn't remember her, except for a few flashback memories. If it hadn't been for her budding legal career, she might have found it interesting to let their friendship evolve on its own. She cared for Kip far more that she was willing to admit publicly.

On her way to the airport the following day, she stopped by the hospital to say goodbye. He was sitting up in a chair and beaming from ear to ear. The doctor had removed his head dressing. He was wearing a baseball cap to cover the dressing on his incision wounds. He said, "Hi, gorgeous!"

"Hey, I like the new look."

He bowed his head and said, "Thank you very much."

God, she's sure a beautiful woman!

She smiled and said, "Listen, lover boy, I need to leave for the airport. I've got a plane to catch."

"Where are you going anyway?"

"Shanghai."

"Maybe you'll take me there sometime."

"Maybe . . . Kip, would you mind if I took some snapshots of you so I can show my friends in Shanghai?"

"Sure, why not?"

Heather pulled out her point-and-shoot camera and clicked away. She then gathered her things and gave him a goodbye kiss.

"You can come back anytime and do whatever you'd like with my body."

Stopping her in her tracks, she said, "I bet you would. I'm out of here, Mr. Duchene."

Angie looked forward to getting a firsthand account of Kip's progress when Heather got back. She said she expected to get in on January 15th. On the next morning, Angie grabbed the phone as soon as it rang.

Heather said, "Hi, Angie, it's me. I got in last night and should get to the office within the hour. Would that be a good time to get together?"

"Of course. It'll be good to see you." After she hung up, she thought—*I'm also glad you're away from Kip.*

As soon as Heather walked into the office, Angie said, "Hello, girl. You look fabulous! The break must have done you a lot of good."

"Actually, I intended to get a lot more done while I was in the Bay Area. But seeing Kip every day made that impossible."

"So, tell me how he's doing."

"His doctor thinks he's made a miracle recovery. He's alert and already making excellent progress in physical therapy. You'd be surprised at how his personality has changed."

"What do you mean?" Angie's smile faded.

"Since he can't recall Marci's death, he hasn't been suffering depression like before. That has made him more spontaneous—more devilish."

"I'm not following you."

Heather said, "He flirts."

Angie was beginning to feel a gnawing pain in her stomach. *That must mean that Kip has been flirting with her.*

Heather kept talking, giving Angie more and more information on Kip's condition. She lifted her laptop onto Angie desk and said, "I thought you might like to see some photos I took of him yesterday."

Feeling her heart racing, Angie said, "Oh, thank you."

Heather flipped open the computer and pulled up her photo album. The first one to appear on the screen was Kip lying on the bed with his tongue sticking out."

Angie said, "He looks so skinny. What's with the cap?"

"He didn't want anyone to see his bandaged head."

"How silly," said Angie.

Heather thought—*The poor thing.*

Most of the snapshots showed Kip clowning around with his 49er cap frontwards, backwards and pulled to the side. However, in the last shot, Heather had taken a close-up of him looking directly into the camera blowing it a kiss.

Angie began to cry.

Heather thought—*He doesn't know you even exist.*

Chapter 73

Three weeks after Kip was admitted to the hospital, he'd made such remarkable progress that Dr. Renneker decided to send him home. He cautioned Kip, "Do not drive, do not drink alcohol, and do not engage in any strenuous activity."

"Got it."

Sal picked Kip up from the hospital and offered to stay with him for the next three or four days. While Sal was pushing him out of hospital in a wheelchair, he said, "What a pussy needing to be rolled around in a wheelchair."

"Fuck you, *Yani*."

"Hey, when did you start to swear?"

"When did I not? By the way, have I really lost the last ten years of my life?"

"I'm afraid so, *Tuchi*."

In the car, Kip said, "Tell me about Marci again."

"Oh, man, do I have to?"

"Just one more time. I keep forgetting."

While they drove north on highway 101, Sal patiently retold how Kip and Marci met, about their marriage, and about her accident and death. He refrained from telling Kip that Marci was pregnant when she died. Even though Kip couldn't remember anything about her accident, he felt a wave of sadness sweep over him.

Sal said, "And, *Tuchi*, your ass is rich. You own a penthouse apartment in San Francisco and have a net worth in the millions."

Forty-five minutes later they walked through the front door of the penthouse. Once inside, Kip gazed around and walked through every room touching objects as he went. "Sal, so much of this looks and smells familiar to me. Before even going over to the window, I already know what's out there. I know you can see the tops of the Golden Gate Bridge towers. I know you can see the new Kezar Stadium and Golden Gate Park. Sal, I know we watched a lot of 49er games on TV in here."

"Well, that's a start anyway. Your memory won't come back all the way until it's ready."

Sal unzipped his attaché case and handled Kip a bundle of documents. "Here are the records for your bank and investment accounts. Since you don't have any cash, you should probably make a withdrawal tomorrow."

The following day, they went through Kip's personal files together and then went out to go to his bank and stock broker. During lunch, Sal introduced Kip to Roger Carrington, Kip's attorney, and was amused listening to the two men get reacquainted. Roger said, "You know, Kip, I still can't get over the fact that you don't remember me or anything about what we've done."

Kip said, "Why shit, Roger, that might be a good thing, particularly if you've been overbilling the crap out of me."

The three men burst out laughing.

That evening, Kip and Sal agreed to have Chinese food delivered up to the penthouse. After dinner, they sprawled out in the family room to relax. Sal asked, "Do you want me to tell you anything about what has happened to your life since Marci died?"

"Yes."

Sal talked non-stop for the next hour. He told Kip about his depression and the alcoholism he'd been fighting over the last year. He recounted Kip's decision to come to Shanghai as a favor to him. He told him about Shanghai Shores. He told him about Rico Niu, the assault on Heather, and the kidnapping. He then told him about Angie.

"Angie? Is she the same woman Reggie introduced at the Moscone Convention Center?"

"Yes."

"Well, at least I remember that she's gorgeous. Are you telling me that we hooked up later?"

"Listen, you were still struggling over Marci's death and stayed away from getting involved with another woman. So I don't think that you and Angie ever really got together. Just a lot of kissy face stuff."

Kip slicked his hair back. "I must have lost my Duchene charm."

"It wasn't her holding back==it was *you*."

"Shit, man, that's worse."

"Yeah, I agree. You were pathetic, *amigo*."

"Does Maria know about Angie?"

"Fucking-a-right she does. She'd just as soon adopt her as a sister. And Tony has fallen completely in love with her so watch your back."

Kip laughed. "Sal . . . I'd like to talk with her."

"When?"

"Right now."

Sal glanced at his watch and said, "Okay, *Tuchi*, but please be careful. She's deeply in love with your ass, far more than you deserve. She's hanging on by a thread. You understand?"

"Yeah, I understand."

"Let's see, it should be about nine in the morning over there. She'll be just getting into the office. Should be a good time."

He dialed her cell phone number.

She answered on the third ring. "Hi, Sal. How's Kip doing?"

Sal filled her in on what had happened during the day. When he told her that Kip remembered seeing her at the Moscone Convention Center, he could hear her draw in a breath. "I told him you were ugly, but he said he remembered you differently."

She laughed.

Sal went on. "Angie . . . ah, he wants to talk with you. Are you okay with that?"

With a giddy voice, she said, "Oh, please. Put him on."

Sal handed the phone to Kip. He said, "Angie?"

A muffled cry escaped her throat.

Kip said, "Angie, it's okay. Just listen for a moment. You know that I haven't been able to remember anything about Shanghai. It's simply not there yet, but I believe that it will come back eventually."

Very faintly, she managed to say, "Oh, I hope so."

"Angie, so do I. You know, I've only made two serious promises in my life and that was when I got married and later to this dear Mexican man sitting across from me. I'm going to make my third promise to you."

"You are?"

"Yes. No matter how much I remember or don't remember, I promise that I'll come to Shanghai as soon as the doctor gives his okay. How does that sound?"

"Heavenly."

"Good, then Sal's my witness. And Angie?"

"Yes?"

"Please don't worry. Everything will be okay."

After Kip hung up, Sal said, "*Tuchi*, that's a big fuckin' promise to a woman you can't even remember."

"Well, I owe her that."

"You're a good man." Sal then handed Kip a stack of composition binders.

"What's this?"

"I brought them over with me from Shanghai—they're yours. You made it a habit of writing daily notes in those after Marci died. They're almost like a diary. If you read them, you might start to remember some things."

When Rico Niu heard that Kip was flown back to the United States to undergo emergency brain surgery, he was ecstatic. His plan to eliminate the man was successful. Sensing that he was getting closer than ever to his prize,

Niu stepped up his campaign to influence officials in the Shanghai government. The bribe money he was forced to pay after Kip was injured was much higher than he anticipated, but it was worth it. Mr. Wang, the sand and gravel contractor, was arrested for assault and disturbing the peace. Rico Niu's name was never brought up in connection with the case.

Chapter 74

Sal returned home on Chinese New Year, January 29th. As soon as he got in the door, he was mobbed by Maria and the kids. They questioned him about Kip and when he was coming back to Shanghai.

He spent the next morning at his office tackling some of the backlog of work that had accumulated while he was gone. In the afternoon he went over to Shanghai Shores to check with Angie. He sat down and told her everything he could remember about Kip. She listened attentively.

"Sal, was he really serious when he said that he would come over here?"

"He promised, didn't he?"

"Yes."

"Kip has never broken a promise that I know of so why would he think of doing so now?"

"I don't know. I'm so excited."

"Angie, Kip has made a miraculous recovery. The most important thing is that he's alive. If it turns out that he makes no more progress in remembering things, we'll have to just accept it."

"That's easy for you to say."

Sal reached over and patted her forearm. "I know how terrible this must be for you."

She nodded.

He said, "To change the subject, where do we currently stand with the government's threat to take back Shores?"

"You know how the government works. It's really difficult to know what's happening behind the scenes.

Chairman Zhang is trying to help us, but the outcome of his efforts is uncertain. One thing is in our favor however."

"What's that?"

"The government would lose face if they kicked us out after what happened to Kip."

Sal smiled. "Have they nabbed Niu yet for setting up the riot?"

"You don't want to know."

"What?"

Angie sighed. "I just found out that they arrested the gravel contractor, Mr. Wang, for aggravated assault on Kip. All other charges were thrown out of court, and no one else was named in the incident, including Niu."

Sal unexpectedly slammed his fist down on top of Angie's desk, causing her to jump. "Sorry about that," he said. "Is there no justice in this frigging country?"

Angie said nothing.

"Angie, this is one of the reasons I didn't tell Kip all about the miraculous turnaround that you two had accomplished here despite Rico's dirty tricks. Since he can't remember anything about Shanghai Shores, he'd be lost if I tried to explain how Niu bribes government officials."

"Yeah, I agree."

Sal said, "How's Heather doing?"

"Well, she was originally planning to leave us at the beginning of March, just a month away. The good news is that she convinced the law firm to allow her wait until May to start"

"Fantastic."

Back in San Francisco, Kip was working hard on his recovery. He arranged to have someone drive him to Stanford for physical therapy twice a week. He also started seeing Dr. David Grand, a psychotherapist, to help him cope with amnesia. Dr. Renneker expressed surprise at Kip's recovery from surgery. He gave Kip permission to fly down to Santa Monica to see his father but still wouldn't approve any international travel or driving on his own. Sporting a one-inch bristle of hair and a scar on his scalp, Kip was glad to board the flight to LAX and get away for the weekend.

As soon as he returned to San Francisco, Kip started the long process of leafing through his notebooks and reading about people he couldn't remember. *Rico Niu must be a psychopathic nut case. I'm fascinated about the Gang of Three. Jesus, what in the hell is the Green Latrine. I'll look forward to meeting Manny and Rory someday. My driver was evidently a man of outstanding character. I think Sal told me that Mr. Zeng stood by my side to fight off the rioters when I got injured. I want to meet the man and thank him personally.*

Reading ahead, he began to laugh—*Oh, my God, I also had a thing for Heather! I thought I remembered something about her when she visited me at Stanford! I'll be damn. What about Angie? This is really crazy.*

When he came across his notes about her, he better understood why Sal cautioned him earlier. There was no question that he had strongly resisted his initial attraction to her. He saw notations of comments that Eleni and Sal had made about Shanghai women seeking foreign men as a ticket out of China. As he read further, Kip saw the gradual transformation of his feelings for Angie to where he'd fallen in love with her. Looking back through his notes, Kip couldn't find a place where they'd slept together. That didn't seem to fit.

The more he read about Rico Niu the more the anger boiled up inside of him. He concluded that the man must be one sick human. He must also be incredibly bright to have executed such methodical plans to take over Shores. He was unquestionably a formidable adversary, one who had to be stopped. As Kip was reading his notes about Niu, he experienced a sudden flashback of seeing Niu's photo in a newspaper from a street kiosk. *Okay, mind, it's time to start remembering Shanghai. We have to nail this goddamned creep and put him out of business for good.*

The process of reading his notes paid off. Kip slowly began to recover his lost memory of Shanghai, his life at Shanghai Shores, and Angie Li. Most of all, however, Kip felt searing pain from his recall of Rico Niu. He also remembered that Mike Lerner in Las Vegas had offered to help. He picked up the telephone. "Mike, this is Kip."

"Hey, Kipper! God, it's nice to hear your voice. For a while there, I thought you weren't going to make it. Do you remember me calling you when you were in the hospital?"

"Just barely. But I can't remember what we talked about."

"I had information about Rico Niu, but you didn't even know who he was. So I let it drop, hoping that you'd regain your memory of him later."

"Well, that time has come. What can you tell me?"

Michael Lerner shared what he had learned about Rico Niu. He then talked about his close contact in Macao, explaining that Danny Tong was a kingpin in the gaming industry there. He also said that Danny would like to see Rico Niu put out of business.

Six weeks later, Kip placed a call to Sal and said, "*Yani*, we've got to talk. When are you planning your next trip to San Francisco?"

"I'm coming in Thursday and will head back out on Saturday."

"Okay, that's perfect. Please plan to stay over at my place."

"Sure, it'd be nice to see your fuckin' ass. I should be able to get over there around 6:00 p.m."

"That's good."

"How are you doing anyway?"

"I'll tell you when you get here."

Chapter 75

Kip arranged for the neighborhood pizza place to deliver his favorite combination, made with sourdough crust. Sal arrived at 6:20 p.m. and greeted Kip with one of his trademark hugs. When he peered over Kip's shoulder at the dining room table set for two, he said, "Well, isn't this romantic."

"I just wanted to make you comfortable, *Yani*, after your long flight today."

"Stuff the bullshit, would you? I know damn well when you're trying to butter me up."

Kip smiled and shook his head. "Jesus, just take your coat off and enjoy the pizza and beer."

Sal Said, "You drinking again?"

"The beer's for you, *Yani*."

"Good."

While the two friends were digging into the pizza, Kip answered Sal's questions about his recovery. When the last wedge of pizza disappeared from the platter, Kip asked, "What's happening at Shores?"

"All things considered, the staff has been doing a great job keeping things going after your accident. I'm worried that Angie might be burning herself out. She stays at your house on site during the weekdays and puts in at least twelve-hour days. People have also told me that she frequently comes in on the weekends."

"Is there something you can do to relieve her?"

"Nothing. She won't hear of it."

"That's too bad. What's Niu been up to lately?"

"Bad news, *hermano*. There have been more sightings of him entertaining officials from the Shanghai government."

"Jesus, is this man untouchable?"

"I know. We're doing everything we can. Reggie is working closely with Chairman Zhang behind the scenes in an attempt to slow the man down."

"Is it doing any good?"

"No."

Kip grabbed another beer for Sal and said, "Let's move into the living room."

After they got settled, Sal said, "Okay, *pendejos*, what do you want to talk about?"

Kip looked directly at Sal and said, "I'm beginning to regain my memory of Shanghai."

"What fuckin' great news to hear!" Sal leaned forward and clicked his bottle against Kip's water glass.

Kip said, "My recollection of Shanghai looks more like Swiss cheese right now than a complete picture, but the holes are filling in faster and faster every day."

"What started it?"

"I remembered seeing a photo of Niu in a newspaper during my first day in Shanghai. Why that stuck, I don't know. Then I remembered the time we had dinner with Reggie at Cucina's. I remembered the bicycling incident with Heather. I remembered meeting Chairman Zhang of the Political Committee. I remembered when we found the listening devices at Shores. But, Sal, most of all—"

Kip felt emotion wash over him and his chest tighten, forcing him to stop talking until it subsided. "Most of all, I remembered that Lara, Tony and Carla were kidnapped. I recalled my feeling of complete helplessness and guilt. With excruciating clarity, I remembered the exact moment we were at the abandoned building looking for the kids, and you getting Maria's call telling you that they were safe. I'm just now starting to remember Angie—a lot to think about.

However, I have no recall at all of the day I got whacked on the head."

"That's remarkable!"

"Yeah. The important thing is that I have vivid memories of Rico Niu. I must tell you, *Yani* . . . I—feel—fucking—hatred—for—the—man!"

"Fuckin' a right!" Sal leaned across to Kip and gave him a high five.

"For the first time in my life, I understand vengeance. I can live with my head injury and the partial loss of memory. But I swear to God, I will not live with the knowledge that a man like Rico Niu can continue to walk around after what he did to Heather, Milt Avery, and mostly what he did to the kids. Sal, I'm determined to destroy the bastard."

Sal yelled, "*Hay, carumba!*" and set his glass down. He walked over to Kip and gave him a hug. "*Tuchi*, I've been waiting for more than two months to hear those words. I'm a proud Mexican father who needs to defend the honor of my wife and three children. I've been wracking my brain thinking about how to even the score with that piece of dog shit. But I knew I needed someone to help me so I wouldn't wind up in jail. Since our Stanford days, we've gone through a lot together, and we've always succeeded. I'm ready to make sure that Rico can never hurt anyone else again."

Kip cleared his throat. "I want you to really listen carefully because this is not going to be some back-slapping buddy game of taking on the world. This is about you and me walking into a very dark world, one in which we could both end up dead. Do you understand what I'm saying, *Yani*?"

Pointing to the scar that crossed from the bridge of his nose down his cheek, he said, "I've done things that I've never told you about. It's from my past life and should be left behind in Tehachapi. *Tuchi*, I already know what it's like to be face-to-face with death."

Kip stood up and walked into his study. A moment later he returned and unfurled two oversized sheets of paper. After clearing off the coffee table between them, he spread them out. "The first sheet is a map of Macao."

Sal said, "What the fuck's in Macao?"

"Just listen, *Yani*. As you can see Macao is split into three pieces of land, the peninsula connecting with Mainland China, Taipa Island and Coloane Island. The airport is on Taipa and the downtown area is on the peninsula."

Kip spread the other sheet out on the table. "This shows a close-up street map in the seedy part of the downtown area. It's not a place you'd want to accidentally wander into." Pointing to a highlighted dot on the map, Kip said, "This is *Bar da Vitoria*, an old Portuguese tavern. It's a rough place where strangers are *never* welcome. A massively-built man, Patricio, owns it and has been known to have killed people with his bare hands."

Sal said, "What the fuck does this has to do with Rico Niu."

"Christ, be patient, would you?"

"Go ahead."

"Do you remember me talking about Mike Lerner, a high school classmate of mine?"

"Yeah."

"Well, he ended up in the gaming business in Las Vegas. Since Niu is also in gaming, I thought that Mike might have some ideas about how to get to the man. I found out that Mike is very close to the second most important guy in Macao. His name is Danny Tong. After a lot of telephone calls back and forth between the three of us, we now have a plan for Niu."

"And how does the Macao bar fit in?"

"Patricio and Danny go back a very long way. They went to high school together in Macao. Danny believes that he can lure Niu into Macao by promising to introduce him to someone who could secure the Shores deal for him without delay. Danny thinks that Niu will jump at the chance. He'll arrange for a meeting at the *Bar da Vitoria*, a place where no one talks about what happens inside."

"Who will meet with Nui at the bar?"

"Us, *pendejos!* It will be a little unexpected surprise for the famous Rico Niu. Of course, we'll change our appearances. I'll be an accountant and you'll be my bodyguard."

Sal chuckled.

"No one besides you and Reggie should know that we've made a trip to Macao. Sal, not even Angie or Maria can know."

"I understand."

"We'll get help from Danny to set up the whole thing and to get back out of Macao. However, we're on our own dealing with Niu. For sure, Niu will have his own bodyguard with him, maybe more. If we get into trouble, we're fucked."

"I hope the freak with the deformed ear is with him."

"So do I," said Kip.

"So what's our plan?" asked Sal.

"I'll fill you in on the details later. But for now, I suggest that you increase your life insurance policy. You need to do that for Maria and the kids."

On the twelve-and-a-half-hour flight back to Shanghai the next day, Sal had plenty of time to think about the consequences of what he was about to do. Sweat broke out on his forehead and he pushed the call button overhead. When the flight attendant leaned down to ask what he wanted, Sal said, "I'll take a tequila please."

Chapter 76

Kip got word from Danny Tong that the day of reckoning was set for Wednesday, April 5th.

As planned, he and Sal rendezvoused in the Hong Kong International Airport the day before and took a mid-afternoon flight to Macao. Upon their arrival, the weather was breezy, warm, with blue skies and puffy white clouds. Within minutes of hailing a taxi, they were being driven across the Friendship Bridge that connected Taipa Island with the peninsula. As they were crossing the bridge, the casino area of Macao came into view on the left side. It looked like the Las Vegas strip in a sea of neon lights except for the densely populated hills in the background.

The taxi took them to an underground reception area below the Landmark Hotel, where they were escorted up to a two-bedroom suite by a handsome Chinese man in a crisp dark business suit. He wore an earpiece with a spiral cord that went beneath his suit collar. Speaking with a British accent, he said, "Gentlemen, please make yourselves comfortable. As special guests of Mr. Tong, all hotel services are provided to you as a courtesy. If you need anything, please just press five on your telephone."

Kip said, "Thank you."

The man said, "Not at all. Mr. Tong has invited you to join him in a private dining room at 6:00 p.m. You'll be escorted up there at that time. In the meantime, you are welcome to visit the Pharaoh's Palace Casino or other facilities on the property. Any questions, gentlemen?"

Kip asked, "Does Mr. Tong own the hotel?"

"No. He's just a frequent guest. And I'm not employed by the hotel—I work for Mr. Tong."

After the man left, Kip turned to Sal and said, "This is quite a place, isn't it?"

"Yeah, it's a good place to calm my nerves."

"You okay, *Yani*?"

"No problem."

Rather than exploring the hotel, Kip and Sal decided to stay in their suite and focus on reviewing their plans for the next day. At 5:55 p.m., they heard a light rap on the door. The same man who had showed them to their room earlier escorted them up to a private dining room on the sixth floor. The walls were painted a deep Chinese red and overlaid with gold-embossed serpentine dragons. The visual effect was dramatic, yet elegant.

"Mr. Tong will be with you momentarily," said as the escort left them alone.

Kip pointed to an intricately carved figurine sitting on the credenza. It looked to him like a mythical lion which had one paw resting on a ball. It was white with a light pink hue. He said, "That's jade."

"You're shitting me, *Tuchi*. It's not green."

"Your partner's right," said an Asian man who had walked into the room. Kip and Sal faced him. He wore a dark suit that was perfectly tailored to fit his trim body, a starched white dress shirt, and a silk necktie. "Most people don't realize that real jade is actually harder than steel."

"Well, I didn't know that either. I'm Kip Duchene and this is Sal Estrada."

After the men shook hands and exchanged business cards, Danny Tong motioned for them to be seated. "How about a drink to get started?"

"Any chance you have tequila?" asked Sal.

Smiling, Tong said, "We have everything."

"Gran Patron?"

"We have everything."

As drinks were served, the three men kept their conversation light as they got acquainted. Tong looked to be in his early fifties. He had chiseled facial features and was well-groomed. His shiny black hair was combed straight back and fastened into a short ponytail.

Five minutes into their exchange, Tong said, "After dinner, I have a package to give you. You'll need it tomorrow."

Kip said, "What might that be?"

"Later. For now, let's enjoy our meal."

Their Chinese dinner consisted of freshly caught pompano, a variety of stir-fried vegetables, Jasmine rice, and a scoop of mango gelato. Tong told them that the special tea they were drinking was *Da Hong Pao* grown in the legendary Wuyi Mountain of mainland China.

After the waiter had cleared the table, he poured iced Pellegrino for the three men. Tong gave the man a subtle nod, signaling that he was to leave the room. As soon as the door clicked shut, his expression turned serious. "We've never met, and this conversation never took place. Do we understand each other?"

"Of course," said Kip.

Sal nodded.

"Okay, I'm glad to help you gentlemen, but not as any favor to you. Mr. Niu has been the nemesis of the gaming business in Macao for far too long. Considerable progress has been made to clean up the industry here in Asia with a few notable exceptions, Mr. Niu being the worst of them. Rather than convert his business into a legitimate enterprise, he chooses to operate like a cheap thug, having people roughed up or murdered. If he's taken off the streets, I will benefit."

Kip said, "We understand."

"So far, gentlemen, Niu has swallowed the bait. My people convinced him that we know someone who can deliver Shanghai Shores to him on a platter. He's definitely interested. He'll be on the direct flight from Haikou to

Macao tomorrow morning and is expected to show up at the *Bar da Vitoria* around noon to negotiate a deal. He'll be bringing a leather satchel with him containing $1.0 million in U.S. dollars."

"The purpose of the money?" asked Kip.

"To pay you off. The Chinese know that nothing is free."

"I see."

Tong continued, "I know the owner. No one in the bar will ever remember seeing you or Niu."

Kip said, "Got it."

"If there was another place where I could get this thing set up, I'd prefer to go that route, but there isn't. You see, most of the locals consider the *Bar da Vitoria* to be unsafe and wouldn't dare to step inside."

"And there won't be a problem for us?" said Sal.

Smiling, Danny said, "No. Even though Patricio is feared in Macao, he'll accommodate you just fine. He's my oldest and dearest friend even though we've taken remarkably different paths since our high school days. We've always helped each other and we *never* ask questions."

"How will he know it's us when we walk in?" asked Kip.

Tong laughed. "He'll know."

Kip and Sal glanced at each other.

"Patricio has been told what you're planning to wear. No changes in that, I assume?"

Kip said, "No. I'll be wearing the same casual clothes as we discussed. Sal will definitely look the part of my bodyguard, complete with a black leather jacket and slicked-back hair."

Danny took a second look at the long scar that ran down Sal's cheek.

Sal noticed him staring and said, "Streets of Tehachapi—summer of 1985."

Danny nodded. "Clear everything out of your suite by 11:15 and be ready to be escorted down to the basement garage. You won't be coming back here. You'll be transported to the bar in a white panel truck, courtesy of our municipal power company. No one will pay any attention to the truck going into the seedy part of town or to the safe house in Taipa after you settle things with Niu . . . that is, if you survive."

Kip and Sal said nothing.

"You can clean up and change into a new set of clothes in the safe house. There'll be medical supplies there in case you need them. Anything left behind will be incinerated. From there, you'll be taken to the airport in our limousine. I've already made arrangements for you to clear airport security quickly."

Kip said, "Earlier you said that you had something to give us."

"Yes." Danny walked over to the credenza and slid open a panel. He brought back a sealed plastic bag with several pairs of rubber gloves fastened around it with a strip of cloth. He handed the package to Kip. "Please make sure that you don't touch anything inside this bag without wearing the gloves. Assuming that you're able to incapacitate Mr. Niu, use gloves when you strap the money belt around his waist. It contains cash and enough heroin to send him away for a very long time. His fingerprints are already on some of the bills inside."

"How's that possible?" asked Sal.

"You don't need to know. I want to impress upon you that you'll be on your own and whatever happens tomorrow won't be connected to me. Any questions?"

Kip said, "Yes. We do have a favor to ask of you."

"Yes?"

Kip nodded to Sal, who, in turn, handed Danny five addressed envelopes. Kip handed Danny two. "Just in case this thing goes sideways on us, these are personal notes to our families. Please have them mailed if the worst happens."

Danny stood up and held the envelopes in his hand. "It'll be my greatest pleasure to be able to toss these into the shredder instead."

Kip said, "Danny, we're grateful for all your help. Thank you."

"Good luck, gentlemen."

As Kip and Sal were on their way to the elevator, Sal said, "I knew you'd write to your dad. Who's the second letter for?"

"Angie."

Sal stopped. "Angie?"

"Yes. I forgot to tell you that almost everything came back to me. I love that woman."

Sal threw his arm around Kip's shoulder when they stepped into the elevator. "You amaze me, you fuckin' old fox!"

Later that evening, Kip walked into Sal's room and saw him kneeling beside his bed. "Bedtime prayers?"

Sal jerked his head up and said, "Fuck, no!"

Softening his voice, Kip said, "How are you doing, *hermano*?"

Sal flipped his pearl-handled stiletto into the air and snatched it on the way back down. "Believe me, I'm fuckin' ready. I'll have two friends backing me up tomorrow, you and this old guy." Sal held the knife in front of him. He then lowered his voice and added, "I'm going to call my mom in case we need for a little extra insurance."

"What are you talking about?"

"I really can't explain because I don't really understand exactly what she does. Ever since I can remember, my mother has gone down to St. Malachy's Church and prayed when someone needed help. Whatever the problem, it would mysteriously disappear after she returned." With emotion breaking in his voice, Sal said, "I'm going to ask her to pray for us."

Kip said, "You're kidding."

"Don't worry, I won't tell her what we're going to do.

Chapter 77

At eleven o'clock the next morning, Kip and Sal were dressing in their separate bathrooms and applying theater makeup to disguise their appearance.

Kip had already gone down to the hotel's beauty parlor on the second floor to have his hair dyed dark brown. An hour later he looked rather ordinary—a conservative man with simple tastes. He stood in front of the full length mirror in the suite and smiled at his new appearance. He was wearing a short-sleeve cotton shirt and tan slacks. Horn-rimmed glasses gave the final touch to disguise any resemblance he had to the manager of Shanghai Shores. Kip walked into Sal's bedroom and said, "Whataya think?"

Sal looked at him and broke up laughing. "Shit, *hermano*, you look like an ugly white dude. What happened to the fuckin' know-it-all executive?"

Kip said, "Don't be so smug, *Yani*. You don't look any better than that bent-ear gargoyle who protects Rico Niu. And, Jesus, are you really going to walk out in public with that greasy slicked back hair?"

Sal just laughed. He'd transform his facial scar from a thin pink line into a jagged, puckered disfigurement. He slipped on a black leather jacket and made the sign of the cross before grabbing his overnight bag and strutted towards the door. "Okay, *Tuchi*, let's take care of business."

The two were escorted from their suite down to the basement and into a panel truck with *Companhia de Electricidade de Macau* painted on its sides. From the hotel, the driver navigated the truck through heavy traffic toward the north end of town. The truck slowed on the

Avenida Longevidade and turned left into a narrow, grungy alley that had crisscrossing clotheslines strung overhead.

Kip and Sal were let out directly in front of the *Bar da Vitoria.* They watched the truck pull away and continue down the alley until it was out of sight. As they turned to face the doorway of the bar, Kip gave Sal a reassuring pat on the shoulder and said, "Take a deep breath, *Yani.* Your mama won't let us down."

Sal made the sign of the cross and was the first to push through the door. They only took a few steps before needing to stop. It was so dark inside they couldn't see what was in front of them. As their eyes began to adjust, they could make out the outline of a large man approaching them. With a raspy voice, the man said, "Follow me."

The place smelled of tobacco, whisky and stale urine. Even though they could see the movement of patrons, the bar was relatively quiet with hushed conversations. The big man showed them to a booth in the far corner. He said, "What are you drinking?"

Kip said, "A couple of Budweisers."

By the time the man returned with their beers, Kip and Sal could see well enough to assume the waiter must be Patricio. He was massively built with neck muscles so thick his head seemed to be mounted directly onto his torso. He had an oily, pocked-marked complexion and black wavy hair. He wore a thin gold chain around his neck with a crucifix hanging from it.

After Patricio walked back behind the bar, Sal said, "This place smells like shit!"

"Suck it up, *Yani.* Let's just focus on what we have to do."

Sal asked, "Are you really having beer?"

"No."

The two men talked about their plans for the next fifteen minutes. When the front door opened, two men walked in. They were silhouetted by the bright sunlight from outside, but Rico was easy to recognize. Sal nudged Kip. "Is that guy with Niu the one with the crooked ear?"

Kip said, "It's too dark to know for sure."

Sal whispered, "Too fuckin' bad."

As the door swung shut, the bar returned to darkness. Near the entrance, the raspy voice could be heard giving the same direction. "Follow me."

With Patricio in the lead, Niu and his companion walked with their outstretched arms to keep from running into the tables. When they got to the booth, they slid in opposite Kip and Sal. Patricio took their orders for drinks and left. Niu hefted a black attaché case and set it down between him and his beefy companion. It wasn't scarface.

Kip said, "Mr. Niu, I'm Bob Maxwell. I appreciate your willingness to meet with me."

"*Mei wenti.* It's not a problem, Mr. Maxwell. I understand you have something that might interest me."

"Yes, indeed I do." Kip smiled over at Niu. "You may have been told by Mr. Tong that I was recently fired as comptroller of Ingram Capital. Since I saw it coming, I secretly made copies of internal memos that showed how the company avoided paying PRC taxes. If this information were leaked, Reggie would be finished in China."

"How much?"

Kip said, "How much what?"

"Look, I don't have time to waste, Mr. Maxwell. How much do you want for handing the memos over to me?"

"Like I told Mr. Tong, this information should be worth at least a million U.S. dollars to you."

"Just a minute." Niu spoke to his partner in Cantonese, a southern dialect that Sal couldn't understand. After the man stood up and headed for the restroom, Niu looked back over at Kip. "Okay, Mr. Maxwell. I'm definitely interested. The only problem we have here is that your price is too high."

"Well, I'd be willing to take $800,000, assuming you have the cash with you. Otherwise, we're out of here."

While Niu was thinking about the proposal, Kip concentrated on the best way to take Niu and his companion down. Niu wasn't big enough to present any problem. The guy in the restroom, however, was compact and well built.

Niu said, "Agreed."

"When could we make the exchange?"

"As soon as I can verify that the documents you have are authentic."

The other man returned and slipped back into the booth next to Niu. He leaned over and said something to his boss.

Kip said to Niu, "Okay, then, it's a deal."

Niu said, "It's too dark in here to see anything. My friend just told me that there's an alleyway behind the bar. Any problem if we go out there?"

Kip thought—*Here we go!*

Just as they reached the back door, a man walked in the front door of the bar and followed the foursome into the alleyway. Kip and Sal positioned themselves half way across the narrow alley and faced the three men standing on the rear stoop.

Niu set his briefcase down and flashed a knowing smile. "Mr. Maxwell, I brought these men with me just in case this was a ruse. And by the way, I noticed you were wearing a Rolex watch, hardly one that a Mr. Maxwell could afford. However, Kip Duchene could though, couldn't he?"

Kip inhaled deeply and tried to calm himself for what was about to happen.

Niu's two companions stepped down and proceeded to slowly circle where Kip and Sal were standing. At the back door, Niu turned to his two goons and nodded.

Chapter 78

Kip and Sal easily sidestepped the first roundhouse punches thrown at them. For the next few minutes the alley was transformed into a blur of fists and feet. When Kip felt blood run down the side of his face, an extra surge of adrenalin was pumped into his body. With lighting speed, he slipped a crushing overhead right onto the bridge of his opponent's nose, feeling bone and cartilage give way. The man cried out and collapsed to the ground with blood gushing out of his nose.

Kip whipped around to face Niu who was no longer smiling. Kip raced over to him and grabbed him by the front of his shirt with his left hand and punched his face repeatedly with his right. Blood splattering down the front of Niu's designer shirt and he went down whimpering.

Just as Sal knocked his opponent out on the far side of the alleyway, the man with the crushed nose had recovered enough to pull out a snub-nose pistol tucked in his belt and fire it in Sal's direction. The impact of the bullet lifted Sal off his feet, somersaulting him onto the ground.

Kip's blind rage propelled him back across the alleyway before the man could swing the gun around in his direction. In one quick movement, he twisted the gun out of the man's grasp and pummeled him until he lost consciousness. Preoccupied, Kip didn't see a fourth man step through the back door. When he turned in that direction, he saw the man with the badly deformed ear.

Mr. Tao glanced down at Niu lying motionless at his feet, then looked up and saw his fallen comrades and Sal lying in the alleyway. Only Kip was standing. Tao smiled and slowly lifted a sawed-off shotgun and leveled the barrel at Kip's midsection.

Braced for the inevitable, Kip was confused when Tao's eyes opened wide in shock.

The bodyguard looked down at his chest with an expression of disbelief. A pearl handled knife was sticking out of the left side of his chest and blood was gushing from the wound. Tao dropped the shotgun and sank to his knees before rolling over on the ground on his back. His glassy eyes stared blankly at the sky.

Kip whipped his head toward Sal. "So the bulletproof vest worked, *Yani*?"

"Fuck, no, it didn't! The motherfucker really hurt me," he whined while rubbing his chest.

Ignoring the pain from his facial abrasions, Kip laughed at Sal's wonderful sense of humor. "I can't believe you."

Niu regained consciousness and began to moan.

Kip nonchalantly walked over to him and said, "Mr. Niu, Heather Ingram asked me to give you a message."

Just as Niu looked up, Kip smashed him in the mouth with his fist and felt teeth cave inward. Nui's head snapped back against the side of the building. Then he fell forward with blood pouring out of his mouth. Kip called out, "*Yani*, if you can stop feeling sorry for yourself for a minute, did you want to give this piece of shit a message from Lara?"

Still rubbing his sore chest, Sal walked over and lifted Niu off his feet. He lifted the man straight up and pulled him back down with force. At the same time, he slammed his knee into Niu's crotch. Niu immediately passed out.

Kip said, "Hand me the plastic bag, *Yani*." He slipped on the rubber gloves and knelt beside Niu to pull his bloody shirttails out from his pants. He then fastened the money belt around his waist. Satisfied, Kip said to Sal, "You ready to get the hell out of here?"

Sal leaned down over the bodyguard and pulled the stiletto out of the man's chest, wiping the handle clean with a handkerchief. After he curled Niu's fingers around the handle, Sal stood up and said, "Yeah, I'm ready."

When Kip and Sal walked back into the bar, the patrons stopped talking and stared at the blood-splattered men with reddened swollen faces. On the way to the front door, they were able to make out the outline of Patricio and nodded to him. Patricio smiled for the first time and gave them a thumbs-up sign.

The utility truck was idling just in front of the bar. Seeing the two Americans walking out, the driver lifted a cell phone to his mouth and said, "It's done."

Chapter 79

For the next twenty-four hours, there was no news reports about what had happened in Macao. Then on the second day, the Macao police department held a news briefing and revealed that Mr. Rico Niu from Hainan was involved in a drug smuggling case and was arrested for possession of illegal drugs with the intent to distribute. He was also suspected of murdering Mr. Erdong Tao. They speculated that a drug deal had gone wrong and a fight broke out leaving one man dead and three seriously injured. The three wounded were rushed to the Kiang Wu Hospital to receive emergency treatment and were listed in satisfactorily condition. The alleged incident took place behind the notorious *Bar da Vitoria*, but none of the patrons on the scene could recollect seeing anything out of the ordinary.

Two weeks later, The Pudong Government sent Ingram Capital a formal notice, stating that they were satisfied that Shanghai Shores had successfully turned the ailing development around and would accept its plan for raising a second round of funding for development of Stage Two. The notice was personally hand delivered to Sal Estrada by Chairman Zhang. Before Zhang left, he looked deliberately at Sal's bruised face and said, "It looks as though you had a little accident, Mr. Estrada." Not waiting for a reply, he smiled and walked out the door.

Jubilant with the news, Reggie reserved a ballroom at the Ritz-Carlton Hotel for a gala celebration on Sunday evening on May 7th. The party would be first class, down to the last detail.

As soon as Angie heard about Reggie's plans, she snatched up the phone. "Sal, is Kip coming to Shanghai?"

"You mean for the party?"

"Duh."

Sal chuckled. "I don't think so. His doctor in the States hasn't cleared him for the long flight."

"That's not right for Kip to miss the celebration."

"Yeah, I agree. But I *can* tell you something that'll please you."

"What?" she said with a hopeful lilt to her voice.

"Reggie's going to make a special tribute to Kip at the ceremony for saving the company."

"I'd rather see Kip."

"So would I, kitten."

Invitations for the gala event were sent to the employees, tenants, honored guests, and senior officials of the Shanghai government. Chairman Zhang of the Political Committee was assigned a seat at the VIP table next to Mayor Ji Dachao. Reggie called Danny Tong in Macao and personally invited him. A table located directly in front of the stage was reserved for Angie, Heather, Manny, Rory, Sal, Maria, and the three children. In all, about four hundred and fifty people were expected.

As soon as Angie pushed through the gilded double doors into the ballroom, Heather rushed up to her and said, "Look at you, girl! Where did you get that gorgeous outfit?"

Angie smiled while twirling around in a black-sequined dress. "Thanks. It's special. I wore it the time Kip took me to a New Year's Eve dinner. When he saw me in it, his mouth actually dropped open."

"I guess so, honey."

Both women laughed. Angie gazed around the hall and said, "Gosh, the decorations look spectacular."

"Well, you know my father. He doesn't do anything halfway."

Each of the fifty round tables was adorned with a flower centerpiece of rare lavender orchids, an array of helium-filled balloons tied down with three-foot strings and Neiman Marcus gift bags for every guest. Large format photographs of Shanghai Shores were displayed on the walls around the room. The stage was backed with a giant convex screen showing a man riding a galloping black horse. A 20-foot banner draped across the proscenium arch read:

SHANGHAI SHORES FINISHES AS THE WINNER!

A quartet was playing mellow jazz from an elevated platform on the right side of the ballroom. In the spirit of the evening, two of the players were Chinese and two were Americans, all top-tier musicians. The four bars set up around the room were surrounded with guests jockeying to get the attention of a bartender.

Heather said to Angie, "Well, that's kind of neat."

"What?"

"The service people are either Chinese wearing ancient traditional dress or Caucasians wearing the Roaring 20's costumes."

"I noticed. It's fantastic." Motioning with her hand, Angie said, "Let's go ahead and find our table."

While the two women were making their way down the center aisle toward the front of the hall, Heather said, "Sorry that Kip couldn't come. It would have been great if he had been able to attend."

"Let's not talk about it, okay?" said Angie.

By eight o'clock, the room was almost full. Young Chinese women, wearing red dresses slit up the sides, helped guests find their assigned tables. At eight-fifteen, the overhead lights flickered. People who were still standing shuffled toward their seats. A few minutes later the lights were dimmed to a mere glow; a hush of anticipation filled the darkened room.

In a flash, spotlights lit up the podium at center stage where Sal stood, smiling at the audience with the practiced confidence of a seasoned executive. Dressed in a tuxedo and impeccably groomed, he acknowledged the ovation with a thumbs-up sign. He cleared his throat and leaned closer to the microphone. "My name is Sal Estrada, and I am proud to open this celebration for Shanghai Shores on behalf of Ingram Capital Corporation." He quickly repeated his statement in Chinese.

From the front row table, little Carla yelled out, "Hi, Daddy!"

The audience broke out laughing. Sal looked at her and replied, "Hello, sweetheart."

Looking back at the audience, he said, "Six years ago, Reginald Ingram was invited to see a parcel of undeveloped oceanfront property in Shanghai. He was told that it was slated to be a housing community that would showcase Chinese/American cooperation. Captured by the international spirit of the project, Reggie decided to submit a proposal to develop the land, a proposal that was ultimately awarded to him by the Shanghai government. Many of you know that we got off to a very promising start by leasing the homes almost as fast as they were built. Then the unthinkable happened: we began to lose tenants at an alarming rate, so fast that the locals were calling the development 'The Dark Horse of Shanghai.' People believed that we'd failed." Sal motioned with his hand to the banner above him and smiled. "Well . . . I guess we didn't!"

That got a mixture of applause and laughter from the audience. Angie was thinking—*No one could ever imagine what it really took. I hope Rico Niu rots in his prison cell.*

"Well, enough of hearing from *me*." Sal took a deep breath and announced, "Let—the—party—begin!"

The ballroom immediately plunged into darkness. The audience began to chatter with excitement, some giggled.

Angie nudged Heather and whispered, "What's happening?"

"I don't know."

Just then, the high-pitched screech of a traditional Chinese lute resonated from the rear of the hall. It played only one bar of music. Then silence.

A moment later, the same tune was mimicked by the soulful cry of a tenor saxophone. The lute played two more times with the saxophone answering, bar for bar.

With the ballroom still dark, Heather said to Angie, "You ever hear of dueling banjos?"

"No."

"Well this sounds like it."

"I'm lost."

"It's not important."

The bright glare of spotlights lit up the main entrance at the rear of the ballroom. The lute and the saxophone were now playing together as the doors opened. An ancient Chinese sedan chair, being carried on poles by four men in traditional costumes, emerged and turned right along the rear wall of the room. Following right behind, a Cadillac convertible idled in the doorway and turned left. People automatically began to clap as the spectacle unfolded.

Angie whispered, "How exciting!"

Heather said, "God, my father's such a trip."

The sedan and the convertible went in opposite directions until they reached the side walls. Both turned toward the front of the ballroom at the same time, one going down the right aisle, the other going down the left. Once they met in front of the stage, the procession stopped. With his ever-present pipe clenched between his teeth, a smiling Reggie emerged from the Cadillac and waved to the audience. He wore a striped tuxedo with tails, top hat, bright red cummerbund, and spats. At the same time, Mayor Ji stepped out of the sedan, wearing the traditional garb of a 12th century Chinese emperor. The crowd roared with approval.

Both men walked up stairs on opposite sides of the stage and met in front of the podium, greeting each other with a congratulatory handshake. The two faced forward and held up their clasped hands in victory. In response, the audience gave them a standing ovation. Mayor Ji then walked behind the dais and gave a long flowery speech. After he concluded and left the stage. Reggie stepped up to the microphone. "Thank you, Mayor Ji Dachao, for your words of great wisdom and your steadfast support of Shanghai Shores."

Angie leaned toward Heather and whispered, "I think I might need a barf bag."

Heather said, "Make that two."

Angie did everything possible not to break up laughing.

Noticing Angie's red contorted face, Heather murmured, "Don't even think about it."

Reggie's speech was simultaneously translated into Chinese, transmitted to wireless headphones to Chinese speaking guests. Looking down at his notes, he asked various individuals and groups to stand in turn and be recognized for their contribution to Shores.

Ten minutes later, Reggie pointed to the large mural behind him and said, "In closing, I want to tell you about the man riding that horse. Believe me; he's quite exceptional—brilliant, I'd say. You see, he's the one who turned the dark horse of Shanghai Shores into a winner. A year ago, I told Sal that his most important mission in China was to find someone exceptional to straighten out the bloody mess at Shores. Without hesitation, Sal recommended his old Stanford buddy, Kip Duchene. Even though I wasn't keen for Sal to hire an old college chum, I ended up heeding his wishes."

Reggie looked down at Sal sitting with his family and said, "Sal, of course, you were quite right. In the end, what Kip was able to do to turn Shanghai Shores around was nothing less than a bloody miracle. You see, this man came to Shanghai with overwhelming odds against his unraveling the mystery of why Shanghai Shores was failing. The more he investigated the more problems he uncovered. He observed serious management problems. He found that corruption within the organization was rampant. Most importantly, he was able to ferret out the wretched bloke who tried to take Shanghai Shores away from us."

Reggie paused for a moment to collect his thoughts. "I spent the whole of yesterday trying to think how we could fully celebrate tonight without Kip. You see, he's still recovering in San Francisco. So I thought that the best thing would be to call him and inquire if he would address us by satellite TV. But I'm sorry to say that he declined—"

Just at that moment, there was a loud ruckus at the rear of the hall, followed by the double doors flying open.

Chapter 80

The throaty rumble of a motorcycle resonated throughout the ballroom. Everyone swiveled around in their seats, craning to see a man riding into the ballroom on a Harley Davison with his gloved hands grasping the high handlebars. He wore a business suit, long white scarf, helmet, and darkened visor. Reggie was speechless as he looked down at the spectacle from the podium. The man on the cycle revved the engine a few times as he rode straight down the middle aisle toward the stage. Once he reached the front of the ballroom, he shut the engine down, flipped the kickstand in place, and hopped up on the stage.

Sal shot up from his seat and yelled out, *"Hay carumba!"*

Reggie pulled the pipe out of his mouth and uttered, "What the bloody hell?"

When the intruder reached the podium, he bent down to pull off his helmet and goggles. Standing back upright and smoothing his hair in place, he said to a startled Reggie, "I wouldn't dare miss this party of yours for anything in the world."

While the audience was suspended in shock, Reggie smiled, "Kip, old boy, I should have known." Reggie opened his arms to give Kip an embrace while the room filled with the sound of a thunderous applause.

Still in Reggie's clutches, Kip looked down and saw Angie sitting at the front table with her hands held up to her face and her shoulders jerking. He thought—*Ah, jeez, she's crying.*

He leaned toward Reggie. "Just a minute."

He jumped down off the stage and knelt by her side. With arms around her, he whispered, "I just wanted to surprise you."

She looked up crying, "You s-sure did."

By then, all of the managers had made their way over to the table and surrounded the couple. From somewhere in the throng, Patti Bo called out, "Kip, I'm letting you go. Angie can have you."

Everyone within earshot laughed.

Kip pulled out his handkerchief and handed it to Angie then hopped back up on the stage. He said to Reggie, "Sorry about that."

"Nothing to be sorry about, old boy. It's about time you two got together." Reggie leaned toward the microphone. "Ladies and gentlemen, please welcome our surprise guest, Kip Duchene!"

The applause immediately spiked a few decibels as Kip tried in vain to address the crowd. Holding up his hands, he kept repeating, "Thank you, everyone . . . thank you . . . thank you so much."

As soon as the ovation began to ebb, Kip said, "I promise I'll make this quick. From the next room I could hear Sal share with you about the time local people were calling Shanghai Shores 'The Dark Horse of Shanghai.' Well today, the old dark horse has become the fastest growing housing development in the city with the construction of Phase Two starting next month. But, it would be a mistake for anyone to think that the success of Shanghai Shores was my doing alone. Believe me, this was a huge team effort."

Pointing to several tables in the hall, Kip said, "Would the greatest management team in the world please stand and be recognized?"

After Kip introduced each manager by name and title, his expression turned serious. He pointed to the front row table and said, "I also want to recognize a woman and her daughter sitting at that table."

People in the audience turned to look at the pair.

Seeing the apprehensive looks on their faces, Kip gave them a reassuring smile and said, "They are Mrs. Zeng and her daughter, Nancy. Many of you know that Mrs. Zeng's husband was my personal driver. Against my doctor's advice, I decided to come here tonight mostly to pay tribute to Mr. Xifan Zeng, an exceptional man of rare courage."

The entire hall went silent.

"You see, it was Mr. Zeng who helped save Heather's life when she was accosted by thugs during a bicycle outing." He looked down at Heather and smiled.

"Then in January, they attacked again. But this time, it was for their most sought after prey—me. Just before a shovel slammed into my forehead, I learned that Mr. Zeng threw an arm up to deflect the blow, leaving himself unprotected. In saving my life, he lost his."

A few gasps came from those in the audience who were hearing this news for the first time. Someone moaned, "Oh no."

"So, Nancy, I have something to give you as a gesture of my gratitude to your father. Many times he told me that the most important thing he wanted in life was for you to have a proper education. While he can't be here to see his dream come true, I have set up a trust fund to pay all costs for your college education anywhere in the world you choose to go." Struggling with his own emotions, he continued, "Your father was a distinguished man, a patriot of China, and a truly great hero."

The audience reacted with mixed emotions, many wiping tears from their eyes while others applauded the two women who sat awkwardly at their table.

Kip looked up at the ceiling and thought –*Mr. Zeng, wherever you are, I thank you and miss you very much.*

As soon as Kip left the stage, he walked up to Sal and put his arms around him. Holding him tightly, he whispered, "*Yani*, why are you crying?"

"Shit, man, why didn't you tell me?"

"Tell you what?"

"You know fucking what."

"Then it wouldn't have been a surprise, would it?"

"Well . . . I'm glad you're here."

"So am I."

Sal said, "By the way, I knew it was your ass as soon as you hopped up on the stage."

"I figured. By the way, I need to tell you something."

With tears running down his cheeks, Sal said, "What?"

"I love you, *amigo*, and I want to thank you for saving my life in Macao."

After dinner was served, Kip and Angie walked from table to table with wine glasses in their hands, saying hello to guests and making "*Ganbei*" toasts. A waitress followed them around the room to refill their glasses with grape juice, masquerading as red wine. No one else knew the difference. Between tables, Kip leaned toward Angie and said, "Today is my six month anniversary of being sober."

Angie squeezed his hand. "I'm so proud of you."

Kip chuckled. "*Xièxie*."

Just then, Kip noticed the three old ladies sitting in the back of the hall. He said to Angie, "Look who's over there." He pointed. "Let's walk over. I have something to say to them."

With effort, the three women slowly stood up to greet Kip and Angie. Kip explained to Angie that he wanted to use the $1 million dollars he'd confiscated from Niu to build homes in their village. That way, no one would have to get displaced because of the new road going in.

The old women beamed when Angie translated. The oldest one reached up with her gnarled hand and gently touched the side of Kip's face with her calloused fingertips. She simply said, "*Xièxie*."

Walking back, Angie said, "Where did the money come from?"

"Would you believe me if I said that Rico donated it?"

"Of course not."

Kip chuckled. "Say, I see someone I need to say hello to. Would you excuse me for a minute?"

"See you, big guy." Angie headed off in Reggie's direction.

Danny Tong was sitting off to one side of the hall with another man. Kip walked up to him and said, "Danny, I'm glad you could come and I will be forever grateful for what you did."

Danny and his companion stood. Danny smiled. "Why, Mr. Duchene, I have no idea what you're talking about. Permit me to introduce you to my assistant, Mr. Charles Lin."

Kip recognized the man. He was the one who had escorted them up to Danny's private dining room in Macao. Kip shook his hand. "It's a pleasure to see you again."

As the three men sat, Danny said, "You might be interested to know that Mr. Niu is cooperating fully with his interrogators."

Kip said, "Did you learn what possessed him to go to such lengths to attempt to take over Shores, and why he had those poor girls kidnapped and their legs amputated?"

Danny causally looked around to see if they were alone. Satisfied, he began, "The first one's easy. Rico Niu hated everything American, a hatred that was ignited when the U.S. bombed the Chinese Embassy in Belgrade. Then he found out about the request for proposals to develop the Shanghai Shores property. Niu learned that Ingram Capital intended to place a bid. He was already obsessed about defeating American interests whenever possible, so he jumped at the chance to compete against Ingram. He needed added assurance to get the contract, he bribed several officials in the Shanghai government. He was shocked when Ingram Capital beat him out—a huge loss of face for him. Undeterred, he promised himself he would snatch the development away from Ingram at any expense. The rest you know."

"What about the girls?"

"That question required considerably more interrogation before Mr. Niu revealed an astonishing story. There were four fatalities in the Belgrade bombing, not three that were reported. The fourth fatality was his younger sister."

"Jesus, no kidding?"

"We confirmed that she was a trainee for the Chinese Embassy and was working in the office when the bomb exploded. Evidently she survived the impact, but a ceiling beam fell on top of her, severing her left leg just below the knee. She ended up trapped under the beam and bled to death. Even though the Chinese government denied the story, we have every reason to believe it happened."

Kip said, "The poor woman. It's ironic that Niu and I now have one thing in common—we both lost someone very close to us."

Danny looked directly at Kip and quietly said, "I know."

"You do?"

"Yes. Before you go, Kip, I have one question for you."

"What's that?"

"Why did the U.S. military decide to bomb the Chinese Embassy?"

"In truth, it wasn't the U.S. military."

"Oh?"

"No. I've learned through congressional testimony given by George Tenet, our CIA director at the time that the bombing of the Chinese Embassy was planned and directed by the CIA. It was reported that a stealth B2 bomber took off from Whiteman Air Force Base in Wyoming, dropped multiple GPS-guided bombs on its target in Belgrade, and returned to base. But between you and me, I don't think we'll ever know why the CIA deliberately had the Chinese Embassy targeted."

Danny slowly shook his head and patted Kip on his shoulder. "Why am I not surprised?"

Angie was talking with Reggie on the other side of the hall by the time Kip caught up with her. He said, "Reggie, I don't know how you pulled this off so superbly, but the evening was a smashing success."

"Rubbish!" He beamed with his pipe tilting up between his teeth.

By the looks of his rosy cheeks and gleaming eyes, Kip guessed that he was on his third London Special.

Reggie turned to Angie and said, "My dear, I hope you're not angry with the old boy here for turning up without proper notice."

She wrapped her arm around Kip's waist and said, "Never."

Ten minutes later, Kip and Angie were finally alone. He whispered in her ear, "That's a beautiful dress you're wearing. I seem to remember that you wore it at a previous occasion."

Angie smiled with a flushed face. "I'm glad to see that your memory's back."

"Indeed it is. How would you like to get out of this place and out of that dress?"

"God, I thought that you'd never ask!"

They slipped out the side door, apparently unnoticed. Across the hall, Sal noticed and smiled to himself.

Epilogue

In early June, 2006, Kip recruited Jon Qian as his replacement to manage Shanghai Shores. Raised in Shanghai, Qian was an exceptionally brilliant man who had previously held a senior executive position at Goldman Sachs. He spoke several Chinese dialects and understood the Chinese ways of doing business. Within his first week on the job, Kip knew that he'd picked the right man. The staff was responding favorably to his new style of management. Kip chuckled when he heard that Patti had already fallen for him—of course Qian had no idea. *Won't he be surprised!*

Two months later, Reggie made a return appearance at the Investment Forum in San Francisco as the keynote speaker. A reserved block of seats was set aside in the front row for Kip, Sal, Angie, and Heather. During the speech, Reggie mesmerized the audience with the combination of his British wit and serious advice. Kip thought that the Chairman was in peak form—particularly for a man of seventy.

Reggie concluded his speech by saying, "Today wouldn't be complete unless I recognized a few very special people. While you've already heard me talk about the miraculous turnaround of Shanghai Shores, but you haven't met the four people who made that possible. I am proud to say that my daughter, Heather, was willing to take seven months off from her legal career to make a major contribution to the company's success." Pointing down in front, he said, "Heather, darling, would you please stand?"

Watching her, Kip could see that she looked somehow different—maybe more professional, more assured. He flashed on their harrowing bicycle ride the day she was accosted. *Feels like such a long time ago.*

Reggie went on. "As you heard today, most of Ingram's best performing projects came from our Shanghai office. I couldn't have said that last year. The difference between then and now resulted from the brilliance of our Managing Director, Mr. Sal Estrada. He's rather special, isn't he?"

After the applause died down, Reggie said, "For those of you who attended the conference in 2000, you would definitely remember the newest member of the firm, Miss Angie Li.

Just then, someone sitting on the left side of the auditorium let out with a familiar flirtatious whistle.

Reggie looked over and said, "Are *you* still here, old chap?"

The hall broke out with laughter.

Chuckling along with the audience, Reggie said, "When I sent Kip Duchene to tackle the problems at Shanghai Shores, I counted on Angie to help him understand how to do business in China. I dare say she did a splendid job. I will be forever grateful for Angie's contribution." Motioning with his hand, he said, "Permit me to reacquaint you to the remarkably beautiful and wickedly intelligent Angie Li."

Angie stood and waved to the audience.

Reggie said, "You've already heard me talk about the incredible feats of Kip Duchene in turning Shanghai Shores around and making it a success. You'll also be first to hear that Kip will be managing the most ambitious housing project ever undertaken in Far East Asia, the *Lotus Blossom Island*. In collaboration with our joint venture partners from Dubai, Ingram Capital will build a marina housing development off the coast of Shanghai, an island so large that it will be clearly visible from space. But without further ado, please help me acknowledge the incomparable, Kip Duchene."

To a standing ovation, Kip slowly stood while buttoning his suit jacket. Before stepping up to the podium, he looked at his three dearest friends who stood next to him. With an upwelling feeling of gratitude, he put his arms around them in a huddle and said something. A moment later, Kip, Sal, Angie, and Heather turned around to face the audience and held their clasped hands high in triumph.

Sitting several rows back, a Chinese man—veiled behind a pair of dark glasses—discretely held a digital voice recorder in his hand.

About The Author

Kent W. Sorensen spent eighteen years doing business in Far East Asia and Russia, where he learned that his success depended on understanding and respecting local culture. He is at home writing cultural fiction, an emerging genre in which social and cultural differences between people can end in powerful alliances or deeply destruct-  tive conflicts. Some of the books that have popularized this genre include: *The Kite Runner* (Khaled Hosseini), *Memoirs of a Geisha* (Arthur Golden), and *Snow Flower and the Secret Fan* (Lisa See).

The Dark Horse of Shanghai is the first in a series of novels that feature Kip Duchene and explore his frustrations in dealing with Chinese business practices. Sorensen is presently working on *The Jutaku Affair,* set in modern Japan in the months that followed the 1995 Kobe earthquake. Readers can also look forward to the next Kip Duchene novel, *Dragon's Head of Shanghai.*

Sorensen lives in Sonoma, California—a quaint town in the wine country located north of San Francisco.

For more information, visit: www.kentwsorensen.com

www.ingramcontent.com/pod-product-compliance
Lightning Source LLC
Chambersburg PA
CBHW071217250626
47163CB00001B/16